Grim Reflections

The Others had come, and utterly conquered, in effect, all the Younger Worlds except those of the Dorsai, Friendlies and Exotics. So these last, they had done their best to ruin. And he, Hal Mayne, who had been born the Dorsai Donal Graeme, had compounded the damage he had done as Paul Formain, by leaving the remaining populations of those Splinter Cultures helpless before the Others, while he withdrew the best that each of the three Cultures had to the defense of Old Earth. An Old Earth that was only now just beginning to appreciate what had been done for it.

And to what end? All this sacrifice had been made so that he, himself, should be free to find what no one else had ever been able to find before—a magic, hidden universe that would at once confound the Others and open a new stage of evolution for the human race. It had been a vain sacrifice. In the end, he had failed everyone else, after they had given the best of what they had, only to provide him with the chance. Worst of all . . .

The pain mounted in him.

It was the deep hurt now inside him that was the personal retribution the historic forces had brought upon him for the damage he had done; and he had not even let himself recognize it until last night, when he had taken a blow on the head no adult combat-trained Dorsai would have taken, through his own ineptitude . . .

So now he must face it.

He was no longer a Dorsai.

Gordon R. Dickson

The Childe Cycle
("The Dorsai Series")

GORDON R. DICKSON

TOR®

A TOM DOHERTY ASSOCIATES BOOK
NEW YORK

This is a work of fiction. All the characters and events portrayed in this book are either products of the author's imagination or are used fictitiously.

THE CHANTRY GUILD

Copyright © 1988 by Gordon R. Dickson

A Tor Book
Published by Tom Doherty Associates, LLC
175 Fifth Avenue
New York, NY 10010

www.tor.com

Tor® is a registered trademark of Tom Doherty Associates, LLC.

ISBN: 0-812-57559-8

First Tor edition: April 2000

Printed in the United States of America

0 9 8 7 6 5 4 3 2 1

CHAPTER 1 ■

A little before dawn, Amanda Morgan woke in the front room of the tiny apartment rented by the family which had risked giving her shelter. A young girl shared the front room floor with her; but she still slumbered, as did the rest.

Amanda had slept in the shapeless brown smock that had been all but forced on the inhabitants of this world and its sister planet of Mara by the Occupation Forces now ruling them. She rose now without putting on her ankle-high bush boots, and squatted on her heels beside her borrowed sleeping mat, and rolled it up.

Stowing it in a corner of the room and picking up the boots in one hand, she quietly let herself out into the hall. Still carrying the boots, she went along it to make use of the communal bathroom at the hall's end; then descended the narrow wooden stairs into the street.

Just inside the tenement's street door, she stopped to put on the boots. The smock had a hood, which she now pulled up over her head to hide her face. Silently, lifting the latch of the door, she slipped out into the mist-dimmed, pre-dawn light of the empty streets of Porphyry. It was a small town in the subtropical uplands of Hysperia, the northeastern continent of the Exotic planet of Kultis.

Through those streets between the graying, unpainted wood faces of the tenements, she went swiftly. Most of the local Exotics, rooted out of their countryside homes, had been brought here and required to build these dwellings for their own shelter, close under the eye of authority; and the fact that the required design and materials of the buildings made them firetraps had not been entirely unintentional on the part of the designers. For the plan behind the Occupation was for the Exotics of Mara and Kultis to die off—as much as possible by their own doing.

She thought of those sleeping within; and felt a sensation as if her heart moved under her breast at the thought of leaving them, as a mother might react at having to leave her children in the hands of brutal and antagonistic caretakers. But the word that had been sent her was the one message that could override all else; and she had no choice but to go.

After several turnings down different streets she slipped between two buildings and emerged into the open yard-space behind them. Just before her lifted the six-meter height of the wooden fence that now enclosed the town; and which those who inhabited it had also been forced to build.

At the foot of this fence she stopped and, reaching in through a slit in her robe, loosened something. As she gave her body a shake a coil of loose rope dropped about her feet. She stepped out of it and bent to pick it up by the running loop already worked into one end.

She gathered up the rest of the rope and dropped it by arm-lengths back onto the sparse grass of the untended ground at her feet, shaking it out and recoiling it up again into loose loops in her left hand, to make sure there were no kinks in it. Then, taking the last meter or so of the other end with the running loop into her right hand, she shook the loop sliding through that eye of rope to a larger circle, swung it a few times to get the feel of its weight and balance, and took a step back from the foot of the wall.

She looked up at the fence, past the flimsy, walkway that allowed it to be patrolled by those on guard, with no more than their heads showing above the pointed ends of the uprightly placed logs that made it.

Selecting one particular log-end, she swung the captive loop in her right hand in a couple of graceful circles and then let it fly upward. She had been handling a lasso since her early childhood on the distant planet of her birth, one of the few Younger Worlds where a variform of horses had flourished. The loop flew fair and true to settle over the upper end of the log she had chosen.

She pulled it tightly closed, and tried her weight on the rope. Then, with its aid, she walked up the inner face of the wall until she could pull herself onto the walkway. Loosening the loop from the log-end, she enlarged it and put it around her so that it formed a loop diagonally about her body from one shoulder and around and under her opposite hip. Doubling that loop with more of the rope, she threw the long end of it down the wall's far side, climbed over the fence and proceeded to rappel down its outside face, mountaineer fashion. Once solidly on the ground she pulled the rest of the rope around the log-end overhead and down into her hands. Recoiling it around her waist over her robe as she went, she headed for the darkness of the forest, only a short distance away.

The forest hid her and she was gone.

But she had not left unobserved. One of the early waking inhabitants of a building, looking out a back window, had seen her go. By bad luck, he was one of the few locals who tried to curry favor with the Occupation Forces—for there were good and bad Exotics, as there were people of both kinds in all cultures. His attention had been caught by a glimpse of a figure moving outside while the curfew of the night just passed was still in effect. Now he lost no time in dressing and hurrying himself to Military Headquarters.

Consequently, she was almost to her destination when she became aware of being followed by green-uniformed, booted figures, with the glint of metal in their hands that could only come from power rifles or needle guns. She went on, not hurrying her pace. They were already close enough to kill her easily with their weapons, if that was what they wanted. They would be waiting to see if she would lead them to others; and in any case their preference would be to take her alive; to question her and otherwise amuse themselves with her before killing her. However, if she could only gain a few minutes more, a small distance farther. . .

She walked on unhurriedly, her resolve hardening as she went. Even if they tried to take her now before she reached her intended destination, still all might not be lost. She was Dorsai, of the Dorsai; a native of that cold, hard, meagerly blessed planet whose only wealth of natural resources lay in its planet-wide ocean and the scanty areas of arable and pasture land on its stark islands, upthrust from the waves like the tops of the underseas mountains.

For generations, the Dorsai had seen their sons and daughters leave home to sell their military services in the wars of the other Younger Worlds; and so earn the interstellar credits the Dorsai needed to survive. While those behind her now were the sweepings of those other worlds. Not real military; and spoiled beyond that by the fact that the Exotics they were used to dominating did not know how to fight, even if they were willing to do so to save their lives. So that those who followed her now had come to believe that merely to show a weapon to any unarmed civilian produced instant obedience.

So, at close quarters, if those behind did not first cripple her with their power or needle guns, she could handle up to half a dozen of them. In any case, it would be strange if in the process she could not get her hands on at least one of their weapons. If she did that, she would have no trouble dealing with even a full platoon group.

But she was almost to the place toward which she had been headed; and they were still some meters behind her. It became more and more obvious they were merely following, unsuspecting that she might know they were there, and hoping she would lead them to others they could capture as well. She had been working here as an undercover agent from Old Earth for three years now; helping the local populace endure, and wherever possible, resist these followers of Others—the new overlords of the Younger Worlds. These soldiers would at least have heard rumors of her. Undoubtedly it was inconceivable to them that she could be alone and elude them that long—that she must have some organization helping her.

She smiled a little, to herself.

Actually, her most active work in those three years had amounted to occasionally rescuing a prisoner of these same jack-booted imitation soldiers, when this could be done without giving away her true identity. Mostly, her job had been to provide reassurance to the local Kultans. So that they, like the other dominated peoples of the Younger Worlds, would know they had not been entirely forgotten by those still holding out behind the phase-shield of Old Earth. Holding yet, against the combined strength of the Younger Worlds and the self-named, multitalented Others who ruled them.

But now, her hopes lifted. Those following had delayed almost too long. She had at last reached the little hillock of flourishing undergrowth and young trees, which she had transplanted here three years before with great care and labor. She stopped; and, almost casually, began to tear up a strip of turf between two of the trees.

That, she thought, should intrigue them enough to keep them from rushing upon her too swiftly. The turf came free, as it had been designed to do; being artificial, rather than real, like the rest of the vegetation in the hillock. Below it was the metal face and handle of a ship's entry port.

At last, she moved swiftly, now. A second later the door was open and she was inside, closing it behind her. As she turned the handle to locking position, the blast from a power rifle rang ineffectively against its outer side. She took two strides, seated herself in the chair before the command panel and laid hands on the controls.

A Dorsai courier vessel did not need time to warm its atmosphere drive before responding, even after three years of idleness. Almost in the same moment as she gripped the control rod, the ship burst from the hillock, sending an explosion of earth, grass and trees in all directions. On ordinary atmosphere drive she lifted and hedgehopped over the nearest ridge. As soon as she knew she was out of her pursuers' sight, she phase-shifted the craft clear of the planet in one jump. Her next shift was almost immediate, to two light-years beyond the sun just now rising, which was the star called Beta Procyon by those on Old Earth.

Out at last in interstellar space, she was beyond pursuit and discovery by any ship of the Younger Worlds. Here in deep space, she was as unfindable as a minnow in a world-wide ocean.

She glanced around the unkempt interior of the vessel. It was hardly in condition for a formal visit to Old Earth, let alone to the Final Encyclopedia. But that was beside the point. What mattered was that she had got away safely past whatever ships had been on guard patrol around the Worlds under Beta Procyon. Ahead of her still lay the greater task, the matter of reaching Old Earth itself; which would mean running the gauntlet of the Younger Worlds' fleet besieging that world. Somehow she must slip safely through a thick cordon of much better armed and ready battleships, to which her own small vessel would indeed be a minnow by comparison.

But that was a problem to be dealt with when she came to it.

CHAPTER 2 ■

Through the library window, the cold mountain rain of early winter in the north temperate zone of Old Earth could be seen slanting down on the leafless oaks and the pines around the little lake before the estate building that was the earliest home he could remember, as Hal Mayne. Over-head, obscuring the peaks of the surrounding mountains, the sky was an unbroken, heavy, gray ceiling of clouds; and the gusts from time to time slanted the rain at a greater angle, and made the treetops bow momentarily. The darkness of the day and the lowering clouds made the window slightly reflective; so that he saw what was barely recognizable as an image of his face, looking back at him like the face of a ghost.

An unusually early winter had commenced upon the Rocky Mountains of the North American continent. An early winter, in fact, was upon the whole northern hemisphere of the planet. Outside, the day was chill and dismal, sending forest creatures to their dens and holes. Within the library a fire burned brightly in the fireplace, with the good smell of birch wood, started by the automatic machinery of the house on a signal from a satellite overhead. The ceiling lighting was bright on the spines of the antique books that solidly filled the shelves of the bookcases covering all the walls of the room.

This was the home where the orphan Hal had been raised by his tutors, the three old men he had loved—and the place where he had watched those three killed when he had been sixteen, eleven years ago. It was an empty house now, as it had been ever since; but usually he could find comfort here.

They're not dead, he reminded himself. *No one you love ever dies—for you. They go on in you as long as you live.* But the thought did not help.

On this cold, dark day he felt the emptiness of the house inescapably around him. His mind reached out for consolation, as it had on so many such occasions, to remembered poetry. But the only lines of verse that came to him now did not comfort. They were no more than an echo of the dying year outside. They were the lines of a poem he had himself once written, here in this house, on just such a day of oncoming winter, when he had just turned thirteen.

> *Now, autumn's birch, white-armed, disrobed for sorrow,*
> *In wounded days, as that weak sun slips down*
> *From failing year and sodden forest mold,*
> *Pray for old memories like tarnished bronze;*

And when night sky and mist, like sisters, creeping.
Bring on the horned owl, hooting at no moon—
Mourn like a lute beneath the wolfskin winds,
That on the hollow log sound hollow horn.

—A chime rang its silvery note on his ear. A woman's voice spoke.

"Hal," said the voice of Ajela, "conference in twenty minutes."

"I'll be there," he said.

He sighed.

"Clear!" he added, to the invisible technological magic that surrounded him. The library, the estate and the rain winked out. He was back in his quarters at the Final Encyclopedia, in orbit far above the surface of the world he had just been experiencing. The rain and the wind and the library, all as they would actually be at the estate in this moment, were left now far below him.

He was surrounded by silence—silence, four paneled walls and three doors; one door leading to the corridor outside, one to his bedroom, and one to the carrel that was his ordinary workroom. About him in the main room where he stood were the usual padded armchair floats and a desk, above a soft red carpeting.

He was once again where he had spent most of the past three years, in that technological marvel that was an artificial satellite of the planet Earth, the Final Encyclopedia. Permanently in orbit about Earth. Earth, which in this twenty-fourth century its emigrated children now called *Old* Earth, to distinguish it from the world of New Earth, away off under the star of Sirius and settled three hundred years since.

Around him again was only the silence—of his room, and of the satellite itself. The Final Encyclopedia floated far above the surface of Earth and just below the misty white phase-shield that englobed and protected both world and Encyclopedia. Too far off to be heard, even if there had been atmosphere outside to carry the sound, were the warships which patrolled beneath that shield, guarding both the satellite and Earth against any intrusion by the warships of ten of the thirteen Younger Worlds, beyond the shield.

Hal stood for a moment longer. He had twenty minutes, he reminded himself. So, for one last time, he sank into a cross-legged, seated position on the carpeting and let his mind relax into that state that was a form of concentration; although its physical and mental mechanisms were not the usual ones for that mental state.

They were, in fact, a combination of the techniques taught him as a boy by Walter the InTeacher—one of those three who had died eleven years ago—and his own self-evolved creative methods for writing the poetry he had used to make. He had developed the synthesis while he was still young; and Walter the InTeacher, the Exotic among his tutors, had still been alive. Hal remembered how deeply and childishly disappointed he had been then, when he had not been able to show off the picture his mind had just generated, of the birch tree in the wet autumn wood. The raw image of the poem he had just written.

But Walter, usually so mild and comforting in all things, had told him sternly then that instead of being unhappy he should feel lucky that he had been able to do it at all. The ability, Walter had said, was not unknown, but rare, and few people had ever been able to conceptualize on that level. He had explained that the difference between what most could manage and what Hal had evidently been able to do was the difference in the creation of what Walter gave the name of *"vision,"* as opposed to an *"image"*—quoting an ancient artist of the twentieth century who also had the capability.

"Most people can, with concentration, evoke an *image*," Walter had told him, "and, having evoked it, they can draw it, paint it, or build it. But an *image* is never the complete thing, imagined. Parts of it are missing because the person evoking it takes for granted that they're there. While a *vision* is complete enough to be the thing, itself; if it only had solidity or life. The difference is like that between a historic episode, thoroughly researched and in the mind of a historian, ready to be written down; and the same episode in the memory of one who lived through it. Now, is it an actual *vision* you're talking about?"

"Yes. Yes!" Hal had said eagerly. "It's all there—so much you can almost touch it, as if it was solid. You could even get up and walk around it and see it from the back! Why can't you try harder and see it?"

"Because I'm not you," Walter had answered.

So, now, under the pressure of his concentration, but for the last time, there seemed to take shape in the air before Hal a reproduction of the core image of the Final Encyclopedia's stored knowledge.

Its shape resembled a very thick section of cable made of red-hot, glowing wires—but a cable in which the strands had loosened, so that now its thickness was double that it might have had originally—it appeared about a meter in cross section and perhaps three meters in length.

In this mass, each individual strand was there to be seen. Not only that; but each strand, if anyone looked closely enough, was visibly and constantly in movement, stretching or turning to touch the strands about it, sometimes only briefly, sometimes apparently welding itself to another strand in what seemed a permanent connection.

Originally it had appeared before him like this thanks to the same technological magic of the Encyclopedia that had seemed to place him in his old home, below. With the broadcast image he had formed this continually updated vision in his room so that he could study it. But over the years, as he had come to learn each strand of it, he had begun to be able to *envision* it by concentration alone.

He had begun this study after seeing Tam Olyn, then Director of the Encyclopedia, standing in the data control room and examining the same image perpetually broadcast there. For all Hal knew, at the moment that room and image could be next door to him now. There was no permanent location within the Encyclopedia to any of its parts, because it moved them around at the convenience of its occupants.

Tam Olyn had been Director of the Encyclopedia for nearly a hundred years. Before that he had been an interstellar newsman, who had tried for his own personal revenge to turn the hatred of all the occupied worlds upon the peoples of Harmony and Association, the two self-named Friendly Worlds colonized by the Splinter Culture of both true faith-holders and religious fanatics.

Tam had blamed them, then, for the death of his younger sister's husband—to avoid facing his own guilt for that death. When he had failed to make the Friendlies anathema to the rest of the human race, he had at last seen himself for what he had become. Then he had come back here, to the Encyclopedia, at which he had once shown a rare talent. Here, he had risen to the Directorship; and he alone had learned to identify the knowledge behind each apparently glowing strand, merely by gazing at it, without the help of the instruments used by the technicians who were always on duty in the core room.

So it had been Tam's example that fired the imagination of Hal. For a moment even the vision before Hal now dimmed, overlaid in his mind by the gray shadow of the old man. Tam would be sitting alone, now, in those quarters of his; that had been transformed by the Encyclopedia into an illusion of a woodland glade with a stream running through it, its day and night always as the surface of Earth directly below him saw the sun or not.

Tam would be alone now because Ajela, the Assistant Director, had left him to hold the conference. Alone, and waiting for death, as someone weary at the end of too long a day might wait for sleep. Waiting, but holding death, like sleep, at bay; because he still hoped for a word from Hal. A word of success Hal had not been able to bring him.

Three years before, Hal had had no doubt he would bring that word, eventually. Now, after those slow years with no progress, the time had come when he must face the fact he never would. He must announce it at the conference of which Ajela had reminded him. He could not be late, after his unusual offer to attend, when for so long he had avoided such administrative discussions between Ajela and Rukh Tamani, the faith-holder and kindler of Old Earth's awakening.

Now, Hal tried once more to concentrate on his vision of the knowledge store. He had gone beyond Tam in the reading of it. Like Tam he could know from a particular part of a glowing wire which specific bit of knowledge it represented. But, more than Tam, he had been able to reach through to that knowledge directly; though he had failed at becoming able to read it.

It would not have been a conscious reading in any case. What the knowledge was, would have simply, suddenly been available there in the back of his memory. A dead and buried bit of memory; but one which, with an effort, he would have been able to bring alive to his conscious mind. It was not that he lacked mental space to hold so much information. He had tried, and found that that same back of the human mind—though not the consciousness up front— could contain all the knowledge the Encyclopedia itself held; which was all the knowledge remembered and known on the world below.

But so far it was still, to him, an untouchable knowledge. To bring it back to life required its being put to use consciously; and this final step his conscious mind had proved incapable of. The human conscious could only tap stored wisdom along the straight-line, simple route of concrete thought—one piece at a time.

For the last year and a half he had struggled to find ways to put to conscious use the whole of the stored knowledge. But he had found none, and in consequence the doorway to the Creative Universe he believed in had remained closed to him. Yet he knew it was there. All the art and inventions of recorded history attested to that fact; each piece of art and each invention was an existing proof that a purely Creative Universe, where anything was possible, could be reached and used. He had made use of it himself to create poems—good or bad, made no difference, as long as they had had no existence in the known universe until he made them. And they had not. But still they came only from his unconscious.

So, the doorway was there. But he could not *enter* it. What he wanted was to physically put himself inside it, as he might put himself inside another physical universe. The bitter part was to know it could be entered, but not know how. Since he had been born as Donal Graeme, the Dorsai, he had several times entered it; but always without knowing how he did so. Once, had been his return to consciousness among the historically fixed events of the twenty-first century. In that instance he had made use of a dead man's body to move about, had heard a carved stone lion roar like the living animal; and he had come back from that past time to a moment eighty years later than he had left, physically changed from an adult man to a two-year-old boy.

The doorway had been there for him to pass through then, seemingly simply because he had believed then he could do it. Why could he not find that belief again, now? Unless he could; and unless he could enter it at will, knowing how he had done it, all he had accomplished and experienced in three different personas had been wasted.

He told himself grimly, now, that the goal he had set himself a hundred years in the past as Donal Graeme could only have been a false one. All he had achieved had been to prod the historic forces of humanity into giving birth to the Others, and the eventual certainty of Old Earth's conquest and destruction.

He could not go on this way, possibly only making matters worse. But, even thinking this, he had weakened. Now, even with Ajela and Rukh waiting, he was going to try to find the doorway one more time before giving up forever. He sat, filling his mind with the storehouse of knowledge represented by the image before him, until it was all within him.

He tried, once more, to use it, to enter the place where he could use it.

And . . .

Nothing.

He sat unchanged, unenlightened. The knowledge lay like a dead thing within him, useless as books forgotten as soon as they had been read, cloaked in an eternal darkness.

"Hal," said the voice of Ajela, "Rukh and I are already here in my office. Are you coming?"

"Coming," he answered; and put the image of the knowledge core, together with all the hopes of his lifetime, away for good.

CHAPTER 3 ■

"Sorry I'm late," Hal said. He came in and sat down in the empty float remaining of the three that were pulled up to Ajela's large desk, now awash with paper. That had never been the case up until the last year. Now, with Tam almost helpless physically—not because his body had been damaged, or lost any of its natural strength, but because the living will in him to move it was fading—Ajela begrudged every moment she could not be by his side.

"You weren't tempted to change your mind about coming?" Ajela asked. Her blue eyes were sharp upon him.

"No," said Hal.

As usual, the controls of the Final Encyclopedia had aligned his quarters with the corridor that led for a short distance past the Director's office, which Ajela had used since Tam had quitted it permanently, two years before, naming Hal to succeed him as Director. Hal had had to walk only a few meters to get here.

"No excuse. No delays. I just forgot the time."

Rukh Tamani, he saw, was also looking at him penetratingly. The two women had been talking as he came in—

something about Earth, of which Ajela had, somewhat unwillingly, become, *de facto* chief executive. This, because simply as a practical matter, with Hal leaving everything to her in order to search for a way into the Creative Universe, she controlled the Final Encyclopedia. More importantly she had *de facto* control of the Encyclopedia's contract for the services of the Dorsai.

For the Dorsai, when they had come to the defense of Earth at Hal's urging, had been too wise from over two hundred years of experience not to insist that they would refuse to give their lives without the usual contract for their military use.

Knowing history, and the minds of those on worlds that had employed them, they had made their contract with the Encyclopedia; ignoring all the frequently quarreling local governments of Earth, itself. That had meant that, in theory, at least, the defense of Earth took its orders from this desk of Ajela's.

Hal knew, and the two women at the table knew, that the Dorsai would have come to put their lives and skills at the service of the Mother World, in any case. The contract they had signed called for compensation for two million trained men and women, warships and equipment, which represented a fully prepared space force only a full world with the resources of Earth could afford to pay for; and even that, over an extended period of time. But whether the Dorsai would ever actually collect their final pay or not made little difference. They all knew that, barring a miracle, the odds were there would be few of them left to collect when the time came.

Without the breakthrough that Hal had been unable to make, these three now in this room, at least, were aware that the Others, with all the war resources of the Younger Worlds available, must, in the end, prevail. Driven by the remarkable intelligence and destructive intentions of their leader, Bleys Ahrens, eventually that fleet outside the shield would grow large enough to break through; and, dying in droves if they must, overwhelm the more skillfully crewed, but less numerous, ships that could be put up in opposition by the Dorsai alone.

Thirty-one hundred and sixty-two fighting ships, operated around the clock by a scant two million people divided into four shifts—three of them working and one rotating in reserve at all times—were few enough to patrol the inner surface of a globe large enough to enclose, not only the Earth itself, but the orbit of the Final Encyclopedia. The day had to come when the Younger Worlds' fleet would phase-shift through the shield in incredible numbers; and the end be sealed.

The fact that the Dorsai would be dead before the forces of the Others owned the skies over a helpless Earth would be little consolation to Earth's people when that day came.

"To catch you up on what I've just been talking over with Rukh," said Ajela, "we've got unexpected good news from below in the shape of the latest statistics."

The concept of "good news" jarred on Hal in the face of what he knew and had come here to say. But, surprisingly, he saw that Rukh was clearly in agreement with Ajela's assessment. Both women were looking at him with what seemed to be lifted spirits—and the difference was particularly noticeable on Rukh's part. She had been pushing her frail physical strength to the limit by adding much of Ajela's office work to her already excessive speaking engagements down on the surface, so as to free the other woman, Ajela, to have as much time as possible with Tam in his last days.

The least Hal could do for them, he told himself now, was to listen first to what they had to tell him before delivering the bad news of his own hard decision.

"Tell me," he said.

Ajela picked up a paper from the desk before her.

"These are statistics from Earth as a whole, compiled from all the areas," she said; and began to read: " ' . . . *food production as a whole up eight percent*—' (in spite of all those wild complaints we've had that the phase-shield cuts down on needed sunlight over growing areas—) *'metals production up eleven percent. Metals directly required in spaceship production up eighteen percent. Production of warships, fully fitted, armed, and test-flown, now up to an average of one every three and a half days. Enlistment in the training camps for spaceship crews by Earth-born applicants, up'*—listen to this, Hal—*'sixty-three percent! Graduation of fully trained but inexperienced crew people up eleven percent . . .'* "

She continued to read. Rukh was also watching her now, Hal saw. He sat listening to Ajela and watching them both. Rukh's dark-olive face seemed to glow with an invisible but palpable inner light from under her black crown of neat, short hair.

That light had always been there, since he had met her in the camp of the guerrillas she had led on Harmony. But it seemed to stand out more now, because she had never really recovered physically from her weeks of torture at the hands of Amyth Barbage—then an officer of the Harmony Militia, and now, ironically, her most dedicated disciple and protector.

It was an index of the power of her faith that, simply by being what she was, she had been able to turn that lean and fearless fanatic from what he had been to what he was now. Strangely, also, her unbelievable beauty had been heightened rather than lessened by that ordeal in the prison. She seemed in some ways to Hal—and he knew that those who flocked in their thousands to hear her felt it even more strongly—more spirit than flesh.

Underneath the wine-colored shift she wore, with its long sleeves and collarless neck, Hal knew she now weighed only slightly more than ten pounds over the weight she had been reduced to when he had carried her, more dead than alive, out of the Militia prison on Harmony. The skin was still stretched taut over her meager flesh and bones. And at that moment there was a glint from the narrow column of her neck, as the highly polished lines of a cross incised in a gray-white disk of Harmony granite, hung from a steel chain—the only thing resembling an ornament he had ever seen her wear—caught the overhead lighting of the room. It flashed momentarily with a light not unlike the light behind her dark eyes.

There were no circles under those eyes, no tightening of the skin over her cheekbones—if that were possible—to show the exhaustion that must be within her. But Hal knew she was tired, self-driven to the point of near-collapse; for she would not refuse the hosts of people down on all parts of the Earth who begged to see her in person. And she would not step back from the work she had taken to herself up here, too.

Nor could he blame Ajela for allowing her to take over the work at this desk. Ajela had not asked to be the ultimate authority over a clamoring, bickering Old Earth that was only now beginning to wake from its illusions. At last, now that it was possibly too late, Earth was beginning to realize that, if not for those who had come to its aid unasked, it would have been as vulnerable—or more—than any other of the human-inhabited planets.

Like Rukh, Ajela showed no obvious physical signs of the strain she was under; but the responsibility of her position, plus the gradual, inevitable slide toward death of the old man she loved more than anyone else on all the inhabited worlds, was gradually conquering her. In short, both of the people on which the Encyclopedia depended for control, were closer to reaching their limit, in Hal's opinion, than they realized—or were ready to admit.

It showed particularly in Ajela's case, in these last few months, that what she chose to wear had been different from the commonsensical clothes she had always worn and programmed the Final Encyclopedia to have ready for her at the beginning of each workday. Strangely, for someone Exotic-born, these last few months she had begun to dress flamboyantly—sexily, to be blunt about it—although Tam was almost the only person who saw her much.

His thoughts were wandering. He tried to pull them back to the statistics she was reciting, but they insisted on straying again . . . certainly as she was costumed now, no one could appear in greater contrast to Rukh than Ajela, unless it might be Amanda. Hal hastily thrust the thought of Amanda from his mind.

Ajela still looked almost as young as the day he had first met her here in the Encyclopedia, when he had been running from the killing of his tutors, on his estate, eleven years ago. Her skin was still as fair, and her hair around her bright face as literally golden and long—in fact, perhaps lately she had worn it even longer. She wore a brown brocade tunic over silky gold blouse and pantaloons that all but hid the cinnamon-colored slippers on her feet. There was no necklace around her neck, but earrings of a honey-colored amber, and on the middle finger of her right hand shone a ring with a large, irregular chunk of the same color of amber, containing tiny seeds encased there, looking alive and ready to sprout, even after the hundreds of years since the amber had been gathered.

Her face was round, her skin fresh. But in her he thought he saw the tightness around the eyes that was not visible in Rukh. No single sign, but her whole self, to him who knew her so well, betrayed an inward-held but growing desperation; growing, he knew, from her inability to keep Tam from death.

She had come originally to the Encyclopedia from Mara, one of the two Exotic worlds, where part of the philosophy had been the hope that an evolved human race would outgrow any need of death except by choice. Thoughts of those same two Exotic worlds brought Kultis and Amanda to his mind again . . . almost savagely, he pushed her out of his thoughts.

—Ajela had come here as a young girl of twelve, with her parents' permission; in love with the idea of the Encyclopedia, which Exotic funds had largely financed. She had stayed to rise to the position of Assistant Director, under Tam Olyn; and to also fall in love with Tam, himself, although already by that time he was old enough to be her great-grandfather.

Now she and Rukh sat together at this desk with its load

of paper piled over all its surface except the small rectangles of the viewing screens inset there before each of the three of them. All these screens right now showed a view of space directly above and about the Encyclopedia.

The white opacity of the shield wall was directly overhead; and it thinned off in every direction, as the screens' angle of vision began to slant, revealing both the inner and outer walls of the shield, until finally there were only the lights of the stars against the black of airless space. The sun, Hal thought inconsequentially, must be directly overhead, to be hidden by the greatest thickness of the mistwall. It could not be they were nightside now, for it had been afternoon at the estate, almost directly below them—

He woke suddenly to the fact that Ajela had stopped talking and both Rukh and Ajela were looking at him. Like an echo half heard lingering on his ear, he realized that Ajela had laid down her paper and asked him something.

"I'm sorry," he said, and his voice came out more harshly than he had intended, under the gaze of those waiting eyes, "I didn't catch the question."

The faint indentation of a frown line, if that was what it was and not an expression of puzzlement, appeared between Ajela's hazel eyes, followed immediately by an expression of concern.

"Hal," she said, "tell me—do you feel all right?"

Concern was showing on Rukh's face as well. Their reactions doubled the sense of guilt in him.

"I'm fine," he said. "I just wasn't listening as I should have—that's all. What was it you asked me, just now?"

"I said," said Ajela, "that we'd thought of checking with one of the Dorsai Sector Commanders. But since you said you were coming today, we thought we'd rather ask the question in-house. You just heard that remarkable list of how the Earth is finally realizing it has to help defend itself, and beginning to build some muscle. Do you think there's a chance, now, if we keep on improving this way, building ships and training crews for them, that we can put up a fleet as big as anything the Younger Worlds can throw at us? And, if so, how long would it take? Can we match them before they're ready to try a mass breakthrough of the shield?"

"I can only guess," he said.

Ajela looked disappointed. Not so much, Rukh.

"We thought . . . ," Ajela said, "because you told us how you were really Donal Graeme to begin with . . ."

"I'm sorry," Hal shook his head. "You two are the only people outside of Amanda who know about my past and my being first Donal, in the last century, then Paul Formain, two hundred years before that. But now Donal's only an old part of me and deeply buried. Much of what he was I've worked to get away from. But even Donal could only have guessed."

"What would he have guessed, then?" asked Rukh.

Her voice came at him so unexpectedly, for some reason, that Hal almost started. He looked at her.

"He'd guess—pretty strongly I'm afraid," he answered slowly, "—that it wouldn't matter what the answer to your questions would be, because it wouldn't make any difference, even if you were able to match the Younger Worlds' ship power."

He hesitated. It was hard to dash their hopes this way, too, when he had come to dash them as well in another.

"Go on," said Ajela.

"It wouldn't matter," Hal said, "because Bleys Ahrens doesn't want victory. He wants destruction. He's as determined to destroy the Younger Worlds as he is to reduce Earth's population to just those who'll follow him. In the case of the Younger Worlds, he plans to depopulate and impoverish them; so humanity will eventually die off there. Or be reduced at last to a handful of people who, lacking communication with other civilized worlds, will degenerate into savagery and eventually die. Die, because they'll be moving backward from, not forward toward, civilization. At the same time he and his mere handful of Others can move in and take control of a depopulated Earth."

"He's said that, I know," said Ajela, "but he's not insane. He can't really mean—"

"He does," said Hal. "He means exactly what he says. That's why he doesn't care how he bleeds the Younger Worlds to conquer Earth. All that matters is the conquest. So he'll throw his ships through the shield at you eventually; no matter what defensive position you're in. I think you'll find your Dorsai knew this and faced it from the start."

"Thou art saying," said Rukh—and her rare use of the canting speech of her religious sect was evidence enough that she was deeply moved, "—that there's no way Earth can win."

Hal took a deep breath.

"That's right. There isn't, in any ordinary way."

"I can never accept that," said Rukh—and with her words Hal again remembered her as he had first seen her, on Harmony, in all the physical strength and purpose of her earlier years. The power pistol she had worn strapped to her hip, then, had not been as strong as the sense of will and purpose that drew followers to her. "For Bleys to win he must extinguish God; and that he or no one else can ever do."

"Think, Hal," said Ajela. "Earth's got as great a population still as all the Younger Worlds combined. It still has as massive resources of metal and other materials as all the Younger Worlds, combined. If we can match their strength, or even come close to it, why can't we fight them off even if they jump through in mass attack?"

"Because it'll be a suicide attack," said Hal. "That's the measure of Bleys' control over the crews of the ships he'll be sending in. Each one will be a weapon of destruction, aimed at any target it can reach. The greatest number of them will only take out one of our ships. But some are going to reach the surface of the Earth. Only a few, maybe, but enough to kill off billions of Earth's people in the phase-explosions of their impacts."

Rukh was looking hard at him.

"Hal," she said, "you're talking very strangely. You're not telling us to give up?"

"No," he said. "That is, not you. But I'm afraid I came here today—I've got something rather hard to tell you both."

"What?" said Ajela. The single word came at him like a command.

"I'm trying to say . . . ," he began.

The words sounded suddenly clumsy in his mouth, and he felt heavily the effort of continuing.

". . . that maybe it's out of our hands to a certain extent. The phase-shield, the Dorsai coming, the contributions of wealth and knowledge from the Exotics, all the true faith-holders from Rukh's two worlds—in the end they all came here only to buy time while I found an answer to Bleys' plan." They were both staring at him. He went on.

"That's been the only possible plan, ever since, as Donal, I found out that in welding the Younger Worlds into a political unit—and playing with the laws of history, as Paul Formain—I'd produced an unexpected side effect—the emergence of the Others, the most able of the crossbreeds between the Splinter Cultures."

He looked at them. He had expected some response—at least a protest that it had not been him alone that they had all been depending upon. But neither of the other two said anything; only sat, watching and listening.

"A group like the Others," he said, "has always been outside our control. Something neither the commercial skill of the Exotics, the Faith of the Friendlies, nor the fighting abilities of the Dorsai were equipped to stop. Because the Others attack the instinct of the human race to grow and progress in a new way. A way no one had fore-seen." He stopped, but neither of them said anything. He went on.

"We dreamed of superpeople and, God help us, we got them," he said, "only too soon and with a few things like empathy and a sense of responsibility to the race, missing. But they've been unstoppable from the first because their

powers are powers of persuasion, which work on a majority of humanity. You know all this! Otherwise, why would
the only immune ones be the true Exotics, the true faith-
holders among the Friendlies, the Dorsai, and that majority of full-spectrum humans on Earth who've got that
in-born cantankerous individualism that's always rejected
any persuasion?"

He paused a moment, then went on. "So it's been necessary from the first that a new answer be found for this new
threat. And it's been up to me to find it. I thought I could
lay the devils I'd raised. Well, I was wrong. That's what
I've come here to tell you today. I've faced it now. I've
failed."

There was a moment's utter silence. Ajela was the first
to react.

"You!" said Ajela. "You, of all people, Hal—you're not
going to sit there and tell us there's no such answer!"

"And if you tell us so," said Rukh, "I will not believe
thee; for it cannot be."

She spoke in a voice that was completely serene. As
serene as a mountain, barring a pathway.

CHAPTER 4 ■

Hal gazed at Rukh, almost helplessly.

"No," he said. "No, of course not. It's not that the Others
can't be stopped; it's just that I can't stop them, in the way
I hoped to. The rest of you haven't failed. I've failed."

"Thou art alive," said Rukh. The mountain was as
impenetrable as collapsed metal. "Thou canst not therefore
use the word *failed*—yet."

"I could go on trying indefinitely," said Hal, "but it'll be best for everyone under the phase-shield if we face facts and I stop trying. Now."

"But *why* should you stop?" said Ajela.

"Because for a year now, I've tried to take the final step, and I can't do it. Ajela, you understand how the memory of the Final Encyclopedia works. But Rukh—" He turned to the other woman. "—how much do you understand?"

"Call it nothing," said Rukh, calmly. "Some scraps of understanding I've picked up in my time here. But essentially I know nothing."

"Well, I want you to understand as well as Ajela," Hal said, "because it's not easy to explain. Rukh, briefly, the Encyclopedia's memory is, for all practical purposes, bottomless. It already holds all the available knowledge of the human race. Theoretically, it could hold no one knows how many times that much more, added to what's there already. You see, like the phase-shift we use to travel between the stars in our ships, and the phase-shield that protects Earth, now—to say nothing of the earlier one that's guarded this Encyclopedia for twenty years—it's a product of phase mechanics."

"I know nothing of phase mechanics," Rukh said.

"No one else fully understands it, not even our own Jeamus Walters, here," said Hal. "You know him?"

"The Head of Technical Research at the Encyclopedia," answered Rukh.

"And you've seen the representation of that stored knowledge in the Operations Section down below us?" Hal said.

"I've seen it, yes," said Rukh, "like a mass of iron wires, red hot. And the people working with it made some attempt to explain it to me; but I still understood almost nothing."

"Basically," said Hal, "what it represents isn't the knowledge itself, but the so-called tags that identify each piece of information stored in the Encyclopedia. The information itself can be as extensive as a book-set of encyclopedias, or larger, but the tags are each represented by only a tiny section of the knowledge-chains that look like wires in the display."

"Yes," said Rukh, "I remember them telling me that much at least."

"And you know Tam was unusual in that, by just looking at the image, he could to a certain extent read it?"

"Yes." Rukh frowned. "Wasn't there something about his finding evidence that at least two of the visiting scholars from Earth had been spies for Bleys? Back at a time when the Encyclopedia was always open to qualified scholars from all the Worlds?"

Hal nodded.

"That's right," he said. "But you have to understand something. The addition of any new information always causes a slight movement in one of the chains—the apparent wires. There were tiny differences of position that gave away to Tam that the knowledge store had been systematically searched across wide fields of knowledge, in a way no one scholar would have needed to do. But if you'd been there and asked him, he wouldn't have been able to tell you *what* the knowledge was they'd examined. He could read the display, but not what it represented, not the actual information itself; and in spite of three years of trying, neither can I."

He stared hard at her.

"Do you follow me? The difference is the way it would be between having an encyclopedia in a set of books but with each book locked closed, so that you couldn't get at the information in it."

"Ah," said Rukh. She looked back at him appraisingly. "So Tam could see, but not read? And you—?"

"I was only able to go a little further," said Hal. "I spent two years at it; and I got to the point where I could hold the whole display in my mind, as I had last looked at it. But the information's still locked away from me, too."

"Now *I* don't follow you," said Ajela, leaning forward

across the table toward him. "Why do you need to do more than that? Or even that much?"

He turned to her.

"Because two things are needed to create anything— say, a great painting. The concept, which is the art of it, and the skill with colors and brush that's the craft behind its making. To have a great dream is one thing. To execute it in real elements calls for a skill with all the elements involved; and that requires knowledge."

Ajela was frowning, he thought doubtfully.

"Look," he said, "you could tell yourself *'I'd like a castle.'* But to create that castle in the real universe, you'd have to know many things; the architecture of its structure, all the crafts of building with different materials, even knowledge about the ground that would have to support its weight. To physically *enter* a creative universe you have to first create at least some kind of physical place to support your presence there. To do that, you need to know every- thing about the surface below your feet, the atmosphere around and above you, what kind of sun you want in the sky overhead . . . and a long, long list of other things."

"I see, then," said Rukh. "So that was why you wanted to be able to read from the knowledge of the core image directly?"

"I'd have to be able to," said Hal. "It's impossible other- wise."

"In effect," Ajela said, her voice sharper than usual, "you were hoping to enter the Creative Universe and use there any or all of the information stored in the Final Ency- clopedia—by making some use of phase mechanics, using your mind, alone?"

Hal nodded, slowly.

"Very well. I now understand the size of the problem. But why give up now?" demanded Rukh. "Why, at this particular point?"

"Because I believe the sooner I'm gone, the sooner my quitting is likely to improve the odds for all the rest of you."

"What makes you say that?" Ajela's voice was even more sharp.

He was a little slow answering. He had been carried away by the unusual emotion behind his own last few words.

"I'm hoping that with me gone, the pressure I've exerted, balancing the pressure of Bleys in the historical forces, will be removed; and the sudden vacuum will cause the forces to react against his side of the argument, rather than ours. It might even . . . be the cause of our winning, after all, by some different route."

"What would you do, then?" Rukh's voice was abruptly soft.

Hal smiled grimly.

"Take a new name for the last time, perhaps," he said. "Go down to the surface and enlist with the real Earthborns who're signing up for training by the Dorsai. Anything, so that as a major force I'd be permanently out of the picture. I could probably be useful on one of those new warships they're turning out so fast."

"Thou wouldst go looking for death," said Rukh, "which is a sin in the Name of God. And how would doing anything like that be best for the rest of us?"

"I think it might rectify a mistake I made, attempting to influence the historic forces," Hal answered.

"That's no answer," said Ajela with an absolutely non-Exotic near-approach to exasperation. It was, thought Hal, a sign of the exhaustion in her finally beginning to wear her to the quick. "To make an excuse out of something the workings of which apparently only you fully understand!"

"I've never claimed I fully understand the historic forces," Hal said. "I doubt if anyone in the human race will, for generations yet. There're simply too many factors operating in every case. But I thought you, at least, did— enough to understand why I'm doing this, Ajela."

"I thought I did too," she replied, "but evidently I don't. You've talked about it many times, and explained it I don't know how often. Let me see what I remember. You've said something to the effect of—*'the course of history is determined by the cumulative effect of all the decisions resulting in physical acts of the people alive in the race at any given time. It used to be thought that only a few people made decisions. We now realize that these people are influenced by the people around them, and those people by more people around them, until in effect every person may have had an influence on decisions made, and therefore on the course of history. The further back in history we go, the slower the influence of the mass of the people concerned, on any decision point.'* "

"That last bit's the crucial one," said Hal. "In earlier centuries it often took a very long time for mass decision to shape history, though it always did, in the end. The difference between then and now is communications. Present communications make it possible for the effect of mass attitudes and actions to have an effect almost immediately within the chain of human interaction. The minute I leave here permanently and this becomes known to the worlds in general, attitudes will change throughout the race and the effect of those changes be noticed very quickly. As I say, my going will leave a vacuum opposing Bleys; and the instinctive inertia of the historic forces should cause the racial momentum to react against him and for us."

"How?" said Ajela.

"You know what I've been after from my beginning as Donal," said Hal. "I've been trying to push humanity toward a greater instinctive sense of responsibility. Apparently this last effort, trying to access the Creative Universe, was too much force in one direction. The historic forces pushed back by producing something new, that none of the present human social groups could fight against. The Others, with their ability to influence any political structure from behind the scenes. They push away from responsibility, toward instinctive obedience."

He stopped, unsure about whether he had made sense to them or not.

"And?" said Rukh.

"And so you've got the present situation, with Bleys heading up the other faction, and me, until now, heading up ours."

"I'm still waiting to hear," said Ajela—but she said it patiently, this time—"what this has to do with your giving up and going off, as Rukh said, to look for death."

"It removes me as the spearhead on our side," said Hal. "That gives Bleys and the Others too much of an advantage. That means, as I said a few moments ago, he'll be the one who's pushing against the balance of forces; and they'll react against him."

"What'll happen?" said Ajela.

"I don't know," said Hal. "If you start to estimate something like that, you have to begin by estimating the influence of my leaving on people, like you, immediately around me. Then you have to figure in the impact of your reactions on the larger group of humans around you, and then on those around them, and so on and on—until you're into backlash reactions; and in the end you have to take everyone in the human race into account."

"Have you forgotten Tam?" interrupted Rukh. "All these years he's been like Simeon, in the Gospel according to Luke, in the Book of God. You know the story of Simeon?"

"Yes," said Hal, both his memory and his work with the core of the Encyclopedia bringing the passage back to his mind.

"I don't!" said Ajela. "Tell me."

Rukh turned toward her, but Hal knew that her words were still aimed at him.

" '. . . *And behold,*' " said Rukh, as steadily as if she were reading from pages open before her, " '*there was a man in Jerusalem, whose name was Simeon; and the same man was just and devout, waiting for the consolation of Israel; and the Holy Ghost was upon him.*

" '*And it was revealed unto him by the Holy Ghost that he should not see death before he had seen the Lord's Christ.*

" 'And he came by the Spirit into the temple: and when the parents brought in the child Jesus to do for him after the custom of the law,

" 'Then he took him up in his arms, and blessed God and said,

" 'Lord, now lettest thou thy servant depart in peace according to thy word,

" 'For mine eyes have seen thy salvation.' "

Rukh paused, and Ajela turned her gaze unwaveringly back to Hal.

"If you give up now, Hal," said Rukh, "what about Tam, whose whole life has been waiting for you to fulfill the promise he found in you?"

Hal felt the pain of her words as if it was a physical thing inside him.

"I know what it'll do to Tam," he said harshly. "But the race has to come first; and the only hope for the race I can see now is for me to step out of the equation. I've got to go; leaving the natural actions of the historic forces to guide us to what I couldn't reach by myself. Those forces have kept the race moving forward and upward from the beginning. It was my own good opinion of myself that led me to think I was necessary to moving it where it needed to go."

"But what about him, when he learns you've quit?" said Ajela fiercely. "What about him, I say?"

"Let him . . ." The words were painful to Hal, but he had to say them. "Let him go on thinking I'm still trying . . . to the end. It's the kindest thing; and there's no choice about my going. I have to keep repeating—unless I actually remove myself, the pressure on the historic forces won't change Rukh—"

He turned to her.

"You understand now, don't you?" he said. "All that can be done is let me go; and hope . . ."

But, surprisingly, Rukh was no longer listening to him. Instead, she was looking down at the screen inset in the desk-top before her.

"There's someone outside—a very small ship dodging

around outside the shield, trying to get inside right now," she said to Ajela, as if Hal was not only not speaking, but no longer there.

"There is?" said Ajela.

She looked down at the screen before her and her fingers began to fly on the control pad beside it, tapping out commands.

"We've talked before, you'll remember," said Hal, hoping that if he spoke on quietly, they would give up whatever had fascinated them on the screens and return to the important matter at hand, "about how the human race is, in some ways, like a single composite organism—a body made up of a number of separate and individual parts, the same way a hive of bees or an ant colony can be considered a single individual—"

But they were not listening. Looking into his own screens, Hal saw the focus there was now all on the movements of the small ship Rukh had mentioned. At Ajela's typed commands the screen were using the capabilities of the Encyclopedia to cancel out the visual blocking of a direct sight at the phase-shield, so that the ship outside it they watched was clearly visible, dodging among the enemy vessels.

Puzzled, Hal watched it, also. Its driver—no one who was familiar with spaceships used the ancient word "pilot" anymore—was phase-shifting in small jumps. His or her craft, a midge among the warships on patrol out there, was obviously trying to keep the gathering enemy from getting into formation around it. Meanwhile, it was jockeying for a position where it might be able to jump through the screen.

Just at that moment, in fact, it achieved the position it wanted, and jumped through. It was instantly englobed by two wings of defensive ships, driven by Dorsai commanders much more capable than those in the enemy ships outside—besides having had the advantage of being able to lie in wait for the small craft.

The enemy warships did not attempt to shift through in

pursuit. They probably, thought Hal, had orders not to in any case; but if they had they would have been easily destroyed by the better Dorsai-built craft and their more capable crews. The incoming vessel lay still in the midst of the defending vessels, making no effort to escape.

There was a chime on the air of the office.

"Forgive this interruption, Ajela," said a masculine voice. "I know you're not to be disturbed during conferences; but this is a ship asking to be allowed into the Encyclopedia, and you left orders—"

"It's small enough to get into one of the locks?" Ajela cut in.

"Yes," said the voice.

The vessel entrances of the Encyclopedia, Hal knew, had been designed for the shuttles that carried people up from the surface of the Earth and back down again, or out to other ships. By ordinary warship standards the lock dimensions were impossibly small. For any regular space warship, it would have been like a bear trying to get into a badger hole.

"Good. Permission to come in granted." Almost in the same breath she went on.

"Hal," she said.

He raised his head at the sound of his name.

"Hal, I want you to put this decision about giving up on hold, for a few days at least. This ship coming in is one I've been expecting. It just may have some information that could change the way you think. If you don't mind, I want to talk to the driver alone. So would you mind leaving the office, now? Rukh, wait for a minute, will you? There's something more I want to say to you."

Hal looked back, surprised. Ajela had not merely asked if he would wait a few days before making his decision—a decision he had believed he had already made—she had, in effect, ordered him to wait. Not only was that unExotic, it was totally unlike her, and to top it off, she had no authority to order him to do, or not do, anything. Technically, she was his assistant. Though in justice he knew how little he had actually run the Encyclopedia; and how fully she had.

She could probably force him to stay, for a while, at least, by refusing him transportation to the surface; but the thought of the situation coming to that pass was ridiculous.

However, of course he would wait; for as long as she wanted. Or rather, for any reasonable length of time. Anything else was unthinkable. But the way she had put it was strange. It had to be her exhaustion talking. As, come to think of it, was her excluding him from whatever business she had with the driver of this incoming ship. The driver was almost certainly one of those who had volunteered to go out as a spy on to one of the Younger Worlds; so that Earth would have some idea of how matters stood out there. Though how anything so learned could affect his present decision to leave . . . however, there was no point in worrying about it now.

"Of course," he said.

Getting up, he went out of the office, back toward his own quarters. There was, in fact, one more thing he was going to do in any case; though there was no telling if it would do any good. That was to write down and make sure it was stored in the Encyclopedia itself, all he knew or had learned, surmised or come to believe, about the Creative Universe and the possible ways into it.

He would include an account of the ways he himself had tried and failed. It might save whoever took up the work someday some time that otherwise might be wasted in duplicating efforts that had proved useless.

Behind him, neither Ajela nor Rukh even looked up from their screens as the door closed.

CHAPTER 5 ∎

Amanda had made it to the system of Earth's Sun in five phase-shifts, where any non-Dorsai would have taken ten and she herself would have broken it into at least seven, under more leisurely conditions. The last shift brought her back into specific location deep enough in the gravitic shadow of Jupiter to hide her vessel from the instruments of the ships besieging Earth. From there, she paused to examine the situation.

There were more enemy craft on patrol about the whitely gleaming sphere of the phase-shield than there had been when she had last had a report on the situation of the Home World.

It was to be expected. But Amanda chilled as she watched. It was that strange part of her which occasionally saw, or felt—neither word was quite right—what would or might be. In this case, it was the sight of the ever-growing military power of ten worlds massing for invasion about the single planet that was their Mother World, Old Earth; and she envisioned what was coming not as clear pictures in her mind, but as massive shapes half seen, moving in a clammy mist which obscured all things.

In this instance, what she sensed was something like a huge tidal wave, growing, growing, ready to smash down on sleepy small homes and other buildings, which would be wiped clean from the surface of the land, as if a giant's hand had passed. And it would come, as soon as the wave was large enough, ordered to its hammer-strike by that small but all-powerful group of highly intelligent but self-indulgent men and women who, under Bleys Ahrens, controlled all the Younger Worlds.

But there was some little time before that, yet. For now, the enemy ships blocked entrance by any others to the sphere whose surface they dared not touch; and their coverage was good. She studied them in her viewer screen. They were divided into Wings of six ships each, and each Wing patrolled a curved, rectangular sector of the globe that was the phase-shield.

Theoretically, that gave them complete coverage. But Amanda noticed that they cut inside the corners of their rectangles when a Wing's patrol route took them past one. There was a way of making a sharp corner with a spaceship in such a situation, but it required a minuscule space shift each time.

It was not that there was any difficulty involved in calculating or making such a tiny shift. But each time, the ship making it took a one in a million chance of being lost in mid-shift. Phase-shift technology was based on the Uncertainty Principle of Werner Karl Heisenberg, which said essentially that either the position or velocity of a particle could be known at any time, but not both.

The early twenty-first century, becoming informed on anti-matter and a number of such things that had only been speculated about earlier, discovered that a particle's change of position involved it passing through a phase of positionlessness—in theory, it was spread over the whole universe for a moment of no-time, before it came into being again at its specific new position.

From this understanding had developed a way around the limits of the speed of light, which until then had seemed to make travel between stars so slow as to be almost impractical. Humanity had once more gone around a problem, instead of through it. Spaceships did not actually *move* by phase-shifting. Rather, they simply abandoned one defined position, became undefined, and then redefined at a new position.

The only drawback was that once in a countless number

of such movements, they failed for some reason to redefine at their destination; and stayed instead, undefined. In effect, they had been disintegrated.

So, said the history books, Donal Graeme had met his end.

Attempting to move in any way except by phase-shift through a phase-shield made such a result certain. Otherwise the odds of reaching the desired destination were very good—but not perfect.

Once in a million times was not bad odds; but to risk them a large number of times a day, every day, was enough to make more than a few spaceship commanders and crew uneasy. There was, consequently, sometimes a reluctance to move closely into the corner of a patrolled rectangle and have to make that extra shift.

The patrols could of course have covered those corners on normal drive. But, at the velocities with which they must move to patrol their area, an abrupt, large change of direction would make jelly of anything as insubstantial as human bodies inside the turning ship. It was better to curve a little inside the corner.

Accordingly, the corners of the rectangles Amanda studied were weak areas. She sat at her calculations for a while, then put her craft into the series of shifts she had precalculated.

Her first shift was to a space just a thousand kilometers outside the shield above the south polar regions of Earth. This was far enough so uncertainty of the besieging ships as to exactly where she would be after her next shift would lessen her vulnerability. She quickly followed this shift, accordingly, with another precalculated shift to above the north polar regions.

She paused there for the seconds required to choose which, of several destinations she had picked as possible for her next move. She chose, reappearing suddenly above the Equator in an unprotected corner area, keyed in her precalculated shift through the phase-shield and appeared just inside the open corner.

As soon as she was inside, she brought her ship to a halt, and dropped its defenses. It was well she was as swift as she was in doing it; for eight great, slim shapes of the battle cruisers which made up a Dorsai fighting Wing were suddenly completely surrounding her.

Her ship-to-ship talk light was already blinking on the panel before her. She thumbed the stud that opened it from her end, and the tank of her vision screen came alight with the face of a Dorsai she did not know, a woman verging on middle age with an oriental face and high-arched eyebrows.

"Amanda Morgan," said the other. "We were told to expect you. Hold still for a retina check . . . Good. You can proceed. I'm Li Danzhun. You've never met me, but I know you from pictures and your reputation."

"I'm honored you'd recognize me from that little after these years here," said Amanda.

Li Danzhun smiled at her.

"It may be none of us will ever see our homes again," she said, "but we're still Dorsai. And you're still one of the Grey Captains."

"Nonetheless," said Amanda, "thank you."

"Now I'm honored—" The other glanced off-screen for a second. "We just got the release signal from Escort Leader. Go with all luck, Amanda Morgan."

"And you," said Amanda.

As suddenly as they had surrounded her, the cruisers were gone. She turned and drove northeasterly across the skies of the Home World until a mist-enshrouded sphere, looking like a miniature of the phase-shielded Earth, as seen from space, appeared on her screen, seeming to grow as she approached it. She was close now, and the mist was evaporating over a metallic port which itself was dilating to let her ship inside.

Her vessel was tiny by the standards of interstellar craft, but not so by the standards of the opening before her. Even for her small ship there was little room to spare at the entrance. Her ship could be brought in, but even with all her ship-handling experience it was going to be a tight fit.

But she made it. The vessel settled with a clang into its landing cradle. Amanda sat back in her control chair, relaxing for the first time in some days. A voice spoke on the interior atmosphere of the vessel.

"This is Ajela," it said. "Come as soon as you can. Just follow the corridor beyond the door to the interior of the Encyclopedia. It's being aligned with my office right now and you'll find the entrance at its end will let you directly in here. Just walk in. Rukh's with me. We're alone."

Amanda nodded to herself.

She had already changed clothes before shifting close to the star that lighted Old Earth, wearing the bush jacket and skirt she thought of as her "shore-going" wardrobe. She got to her feet, opened the ship's lock and stepped out into the clangor and bright lights of the port chamber. The ramp that led to the interior of the Final Encyclopedia was almost beside her ship. She had never been here before, but as an educated person she knew about the Encyclopedia's design and peculiarities.

The ramp led into a suddenly quiet, narrow, blue-carpeted corridor that looked exceedingly short—but, she had learned, distances would be not only variable but sometimes illusory within the Final Encyclopedia. There was a door at the far end, some twenty meters from her. She went to it, opened it without bothering to give her name to the annunciator above it, and stepped inside.

"Hello," she said, smiling at the two women sitting at the desk at the far end of the room. "It's about time we met. I'm Amanda Morgan."

CHAPTER 6 ■

"Take a float at the desk, here," Ajela answered, looking at the tall, remarkably young-looking woman, whose hair was so light blond it was almost white. "There's one waiting for you."

As Amanda came from the door, which had provided some measure of her size, her height became less apparent. The length of her arms, legs and body, and her breadth of shoulder, so well matched her size that only by some kind of contrast was it noticeable. She was, thought Ajela, like Hal in that. You did not realize how large he was, either, until someone you knew to be of ordinary size stood close to him. She was wearing serviceable, neutral-colored clothing that somehow did nothing to detract from her presence.

What Ajela found herself noticing in particular was the lightness with which Amanda moved. She had the body balance of a dancer; and that trait was curiously in harmony with the otherwise difficult to believe youthfulness she seemed to project. She could pass, thought Ajela, for a girl in her teens—and yet Ajela knew her to be certainly older than Hal; and possibly older as well than either Rukh or herself—not that either she or Rukh were out of their twenties.

The appearance of youth in the newcomer was so unbelievable it could be appreciated only when you were actually looking at her. After she had gone, memory would be doubted. That, taken together with the classical quality of her beauty—even her shoulder-length fair hair and the turquoise eyes somehow fitted—seemed to set her a little apart from everyone else. And yet, even the sum of all these different elements failed to explain the strongest effect she made on a viewer. There was a power in her.

It was a quality which words failed as memory would. But it was like something Ajela had never felt before in anyone. It was curiously comparable to, though not the same as she felt there to be in Hal when close to him. In his actual presence she had always been able to feel a concern in him for those around him that was like the warmth radiated by a lighted fireplace.

With Amanda it was something different. The closest Ajela could come to expressing it, was that in the other woman there was something which strongly reminded Ajela of the strength and clean white lines of an Ionic pillar, in a temple of classical Greece.

To Amanda, on the other hand, as she approached the desk, Rukh and Ajela were both much as she had pictured them from Hal's descriptions. She had wanted to see them for herself, for a long time. Not only because of what they were, but obviously because of what they each in their separate ways meant to Hal; and because it was also obvious that Hal's affection for each was deep and strong-running.

It was not that she feared competition for his love of her. She was the Third Amanda in eight generations of Morgans; and she had been hand-picked by the Second Amanda as a baby, in the other's old age. Hand-picked, and with her natural abilities trained until she was set apart from the mass of people around her, like a queen.

In this there was more to it than the fact there had been only three Amandas in eight generations of the Morgans of Foralie, on the Dorsai. In a very real sense, there had only been three Amandas since the human race began; and it had fallen to her to be the last and strongest. With or without Hal, she would be that. But she loved him.

However, now that she saw them in person, she knew that she would like them; and they would end up liking her—though Ajela would be the slower of the two to come to it. They were both strong women; and life had also made each of them the equivalent of royalty, in her own right. Moreover, Ajela had now had experience in the possession and exercise of great authority.

She was dressed in what seemed more like leisure than working clothes. She wore a sleeveless tunic of medium brown, ornamented with gold brocade over a blouse of filmier material with balloon-shaped sleeves, above darker brown pantaloons. Amber bracelets were on her wrists and amber earrings in her ear. Still, the way she sat and the level gaze of her hazel eyes made these garments and even her jewelry seem to fit her like a uniform of authority.

Rukh, on the other hand, had been born, as Amanda knew, with unusual strength of spirit in her, but plainly counted it as nothing in her own scale of values. Far outranking any personal power of her own, the quality that was in her of what she called Faith shone through the dark lantern of her body, even through the long, high-collared, wine-red dress she was now wearing, like the light of a candle through the horn windows of some ancient lantern, illuminating everyone around her. Also, Rukh was older than Ajela in her experience of life and death; and, like Amanda, had been a warrior. In fact she was still a warrior, for all that she lived and preached peace. She always would be. In that one element, if in no other, it was immediately recognizable to both of them as their eyes met, that they were alike.

"I came right away, as soon as the message reached me," said Amanda, taking the empty float. She looked at the others sympathetically. It would not have been easy for either of these to admit to themselves that they were helpless; and that she might do what they could not.

"Faster than we expected," said Rukh. "We didn't dare say so in the message, but it's Hal, of course. We knew you'd read that between the lines and come quickly."

Amanda smiled.

"It was clear enough, what you wanted to tell me," she said. "You'd know it would take something like that to bring me back like this. What is it with Hal?"

"He's a case of burn-out," said Ajela bluntly.

She checked herself, rubbing her fingers for a second over her eyes.

"Would you explain to her, Rukh? With Tam and all . . . I think you'll do a better job of it than I can, right now."

"He wants to go looking for death," said Rukh, "or tells himself that's what he wants, because, you know as well as I, it's not in him to do that. He's just told us he wants to give up his search for the answer we all need, the search he's been on all his life."

"What brought him to this?" said Amanda.

"Frustration—" Ajela broke off. "Sorry, Rukh. I asked you to tell it. Go ahead."

"But you're right," said Rukh. She turned her gaze back to Amanda.

"Ever since he got the necessary people back here on Old Earth and the phase-shield up, he's been expecting at any moment to find the last step to the Creative Universe he's dreamed of reaching for so long. He's been working at it without a break, all that time. In the process, he's found a way to make all the knowledge of the Final Encyclopedia available to his mind. But even with that and all else that's in him, he's made no progress at all. Now he believes he's got to find a breakthrough, give up, or go insane; and, as all of us know, he won't accept insanity as a way out. So he plans to quit. Leave Enlist with the Earth-borns under another name for Dorsai training."

"The first Dorsai that sees him will recognize who trained him—pick him out in two seconds from the rest," said Amanda.

"Would that officer force him to reveal himself as Hal Mayne?" Rukh's voice was level.

There was a moment's silence.

"No . . . of course not," said Amanda then. "Not if Hal didn't want it. That's not our way—if he had personal reasons for not being recognized or promoted, no explanation from him would be necessary. But even at that, it's only a short matter of time until Bleys would find out who and where he was and then all the worlds would know."

"Hal wants the Worlds to know," said Ajela. "He says it's a matter of the fabric of historic forces. He believes his going would leave a vacuum that'd work against Bleys."

"He could be right in that," said Amanda slowly, after a moment. "But he's wrong in giving up. Besides, he can't quit. For him, that's impossible. He must have just worked himself blind enough to make himself believe he can go hunting the dragon."

"Hunting the dragon?" echoed Rukh.

"It's a Dorsai saying," said Amanda absently. "It means roughly . . . taking on something you know you can't handle, deliberately to arrange for your own end."

She looked at them.

"Because, you realize, if he did that," she went on, "there'd be no more cause for Bleys to hold off trying to kill him."

"He'd be safe here," muttered Ajela. "You'd think common sense—"

"No place is safe, if Bleys really wanted to get him. Up until now he's shared Hal's point of view, that if either one took the simple way to a solution by killing the other, it wouldn't alter the confrontation of historic forces between the two halves of the race."

"And that's the only reason Bleys has held off, until now?" Rukh asked. "I thought there was something personal there."

"There is, in a sense." Amanda looked at her, at the slim cross cut into the circle of granite at Rukh's neck. "We, all of us, each have something. But Bleys has nothing, and never has had—except in Hal."

"How—in Hal?" Ajela leaned forward, intrigued.

"They're worst enemies," said Amanda, "which is close, in a strange way, to being best friends. Because what makes them enemies is so much larger than anything personal between them, that Bleys is free to admire Hal—and he admires no one else in the human race, alive or dead."

She became more brisk.

"However . . . tell me when this started," she went on. "When did he start giving up?"

"He didn't mention it until today—in fact, just before you got here," answered Rukh. "But in himself he must have given up some months ago, Earth time. It showed that far back—to Ajela and myself. We did what we could; and when nothing helped, finally we sent for you. You got here just in time."

"How many months?"

Ajela and Rukh exchanged glances. Ajela remained silent, so Rukh turned again to Amanda.

"My best guess would be he started giving up about half a year ago. Ajela?"

Ajela made a small, almost helpless gesture with one hand.

"I only really noticed it after you brought my attention to it, three or four months ago. I've been tied up with trying to get the Earth-born to pull all together, for the first time in their history. The trouble's been for the first couple of years, most of them couldn't actually believe THEY could really be under attack. But what with that problem . . . and Tam . . ."

She subsided.

"I'd say he started thinking he wouldn't ever be able to find what he was looking for, roughly a half year ago," Rukh went on in a level voice. "At what point he actually gave up, if he really did—internally, I mean—I don't know. I agree with you. He hasn't, really, even now. It's just that he's reached the point where he feels he has to do something, and it looks to him as if every way's blocked but back; so he's made a conscious decision to go back, by giving up. What do you think?"

Amanda looked past them.

"I think you're right," she answered. "He chose as a child to go after it—this thing he has to find. It's far too late now for him to turn away from it. He can make his body and conscious mind leave it alone; but that won't help. His instinct's to attack a problem and keep on attacking it as long as he's alive and it's still there. But my guess is his trouble may not be quite what you've believed. I don't think he could really have gotten stuck in a dead-end corridor. I think he created it."

"How?" said Rukh. "I'm not sure I follow you, Amanda Morgan."

"I'm sure," said Amanda slowly, "he *thinks* he's been trying all sorts of ways to reach through to what he wants to find and that he could go on trying forever and still not find it. But that can't be the real case."

"What is the real case then?" Ajela leaned forward.

"Perhaps, just that he's trying to prod himself to break out and find a new angle of attack," answered Amanda. "Unconsciously, I think he knows he's chased this problem until he's lost his perspective on it. He's become frustrated; and his instinct to attack's betraying him. He's gotten himself trapped into a circular path, making the same attack at the same no-answer over and over again; and telling himself it's a different route each time."

She stopped. The other two sat looking at her.

"If that's it," said Rukh at last in that same level voice, "what's to be done with him?"

"Help him to stand back and take a look at the problem from a wider angle."

"How?" asked Ajela.

Amanda looked hard at her.

"I just walked through that door a few minutes ago," she said. "Up until then I hadn't heard what was wrong with him, let alone what the symptoms are. I'll think. The two of you might be thinking also."

There was another silence, this one with a certain sharpness to it.

"You're right," said Ajela. "I'm sorry, Amanda. I've gotten a little too much in the habit of snapping out questions and orders, these last few years. I'll be frank. I don't see any answer at the moment; and I get the feeling if there is one it won't be quick or easy to find."

"Yes," said Rukh, "and I think something else. I think it's not something that's going to come calling in answer to puzzling over it. Whoever finds it is going to have to feel her way to it. And the most likely candidate to do that is you, Amanda."

"Yes," said Ajela, "you've got the advantage. He loves you, Amanda."

"You mean, I love him," said Amanda evenly.

"Yes," said Ajela, meeting her gaze squarely, "of course that's what I meant."

Rukh's voice interposed itself between them.

"Aside from any aspect of feelings," she said calmly, "we've seen him every day—well, almost. Ajela and I may be too close to this part of the problem, ourselves. You're going to be looking at him for the first time in some time."

"Over three years," said Amanda.

Rukh looked at her shrewdly.

"You're not saying you're out of touch—"

"No, he and I have never been out of touch," answered Amanda. "Don't you both know people you haven't seen for a long time; and still, when you do get back together again, you pick up just where you left off? That . . . only stronger. He can have changed. I can have changed. But there won't be any new difference that we can't make up, in one step and one moment. No, the fact we've been separated's not going to be a problem. The problem will be getting him to accept a solution to his situation besides the one he's come to himself. The Graemes are a hardheaded lot; and Donal has never been turned aside from his decisions by any other human being."

"You think there's that much of Donal Graeme left in Hal?" said Ajela.

"Of course there is, Ajela," said Rukh gently to her. "Nobody can ever escape what they've been. Have you forgotten how much of you is still Exotic? And you left Mara for the Encyclopedia when you were twelve years old, didn't you?"

Ajela smiled a little wanly.

■ *Gordon R. Dickson*

"Perhaps too often, I forget," she said. "No, you're right, Rukh. It's just that I've always just known him as Hal; and being and Exotic, I probably don't understand what all the rest of you know about violence—sorry, Amanda. I know that's the wrong word."

"No, it's not," said Amanda. "Is it, Rukh Tamani?"

"No," said Rukh. "Whoso thinketh violence, knoweth violence. It was in God's name, but I knew violence."

"But to get back to what we're talking about," said Amanda, "Rukh's right. I'll have to feel my way to answer. That doesn't say I'll find it. Either one of you may be the one to find it."

She smiled at them.

"So you'll both keep after it, too?"

"You know we will, Amanda," Rukh said.

It was the first time she had used Amanda's given name only. Amanda smiled in acknowledgement and appreciation and got a smile back that took account of the bond of experience between them.

"Of course," Amanda said. "I shouldn't have even asked. Well, then, if you've told me all you want to say for the moment, can I go to Hal now?"

"I'll call to say you're coming—"

Ajela's hand, which had been reaching out to the control studs on her desk, checked as Amanda interrupted.

"If you don't mind, I'd rather simply appear," she said. "Can you just direct me to wherever he is at the moment?"

"Of course," said Ajela. "That's a good idea, in fact. You may well learn more from him, suddenly appearing without warning. He's in his rooms. I'll align this corridor outside with them. First door to your right, then, as you go out."

"Thanks," said Amanda, getting up from her float. "We'll talk again shortly?"

"As soon as you want. It may be a quarter or a half an hour, usually, before I can get loose, if I'm tied up talking to someone, or in some kind of conference with the people down on the surface; but just as soon as I can, I'll be available. Tell Rukh whenever you want us three to meet again."

"You can reach me anytime using the internal communication system of the Encyclopedia," put in Rukh.

Amanda was already on her way to the door. She stopped and turned back for a moment.

"Good, I'll do that," she said, and smiled once more at them. "It's been very good meeting you both, at last. Don't worry. I trust in Hal—the inner Hal. You should, too."

Ajela, unlike Rukh, did not return the smile.

"We always have," said Ajela emptily, "but if after all this time he gives up and leaves us, what hope is there for Earth, for the race? For everyone?"

Rukh turned and looked across the desk at her.

"There is hope in God," she said strongly, "who never leaves us."

Neither Amanda nor Ajela spoke. There was silence in the room. Then Amanda turned once more, and went, decisively, toward the door.

"I'll talk to you both shortly," she said, and went out.

As the door clicked softly shut behind her, Amanda thought that it might not be all as simple as she had made it sound when she was inside talking about Hal. One of the other two—it might have been either or both—might have been putting pressure on him, all these months, without realizing it. Well, she would deal with that if she came across it. Ajela in particular might have been guilty of pressuring without knowing it. She turned right, as Ajela had directed. Ten meters down a somewhat longer corridor than the one she remembered walking in on the way to Ajela's office, she found the door the other woman had mentioned. Without announcing herself, she touched its latch button and stepped inside as it slid open before her. Hal was sitting at his desk and he looked up to stare at her sudden appearance.

She stopped just inside the door, which slid closed again, and stood smiling at his startled face some five meters away from her.

"So, you've forgotten what I look like already," she said.

The humor and her lightness of tone were a cover for the moment; for in that second she had seen him for the first time in three years. What she saw was a big man—for when he had chosen to regrow from babyhood as Hal Mayne, he had come back not in the bone and flesh of the man he had been as Donal Graeme, but like one of his towering twin uncles Kensie and Ian. The Dorsai were not by any means all big—though statistically they averaged more in height and weight than those of the other Younger Worlds and Old Earth. But there were some families, like the Graemes and the ap Morgans, who tended to run large compared to that average; and some among these were larger yet. Even grown, Donal had felt like a dwarf among his own family. Therefore the imitation of Ian.

It was a small vanity. Amanda, who had known Ian in his old age, had teased Hal gently about it. But she did not feel like teasing him now. The man before her no more showed obvious physical signs of stress than Ajela or Rukh had; but Amanda, who knew him so and could look into his soul better than anyone else alive, saw him there, as gaunt and sharpened by his inner struggles as a hermit.

But nearly all of that was hidden within him. Outwardly, he showed only the familiar strong-boned face, with clear green eyes under thick black eyebrows and straight, coarse black hair, his large and sinewy hands dwarfing the control keys beside the screen inset in the top of the desk, on which he was composing some piece of writing.

But the look of startlement lasted only a second. An almost imperceptible tap of his finger erased whatever he had been working on and he was up and around the desk, coming toward her. They met in the middle of the room.

"I had a report to make— " she began; but his arms were already around her and his mouth on hers was cutting off the rest of the words, with a fierce hunger she had never felt in him before. She responded for a long moment; then pulled her head back forcibly and laughed up at him.

"You won't even give me a chance to tell you how I happen to be here?" she said.

"It doesn't matter," he answered.

He kissed her hungrily again, drowning himself in her. He had wanted her here for three years, as someone lost in a desert would want a drink of water, but there was now also something else. Something new in him this last year, that had feared her coming. For he knew now that he had been refusing to face the consequences as far as they two were concerned, of the decision he had just announced to Ajela and Rukh, his decision to give up.

There was no other way it could be. His leaving the battle while she was still in it, must part them for good; whether either of them might want it that way or not.

CHAPTER 7 ■

Hal woke without opening his eyes, without moving. He felt the weight of Amanda's upper body and head come down again on the bed beside him. He would see her if he opened his eyes. This was no pressure field they slept upon, but, at his own choice, an antique form of spring and mattress such as was still used on most of the poorer Younger Worlds—which included the Dorsai. In a pressure bed he would not have been able to feel her movements a millimeter distant.

So—she had just now again lifted up to look at him as he slept, in the starlight and the light of the new moon shining through the illusion of a skylight in the room's ceiling. She had done that often, these last three nights. She was skillful enough to raise herself without waking him, but the return to a prone position was impossible without doing so. He wondered what she had seen in those dark moments, how much discovered?

For three days and nights he had avoided talking to her about what he knew he must talk to her about, eventually. It had been cowardice to have held off from it this long, the first deliberately cowardly act in all his lives. But the thought of making it final, by putting it into words that they must go away from each other—seemed to close off his throat and make him speechless every time he tried to make himself speak of it.

Or had she read it all in his face as he lay sleeping? He did not underestimate her. She was capable of reading deeper into other humans, including him, than anyone else he had ever known.

"Yes." He rolled over on his back and stared up at the stars in their true positions as seen from here, artificial illusion though the skylight was. "We should talk."

She rose on her elbow again and the darkness of her head and shoulder occulted part of the skylight. In the dimmer illumination of her own shadow, her features were just barely visible. Her hair, unloosed, fell over her shoulder and brushed with faint fingers at the left side of his face. For a moment she looked down at him. Then she lowered her head and kissed him gently on the lips. Then raised again and stayed looking down at him.

"I should have told you the moment you got here," he said. "But . . ."

"It's all right, dear?" she said. "I know. Rukk and Ajela told me. You think you have to stop searching for an answer."

Of course. They would have told her as soon as she got here, when he had just before that announced it to them.

"Yes," he answered. "I've been here for three years, Amanda; and in all that time—not one step forward."

Her dark head nodded slowly against the stars.

"I see." Her voice was thoughtful.

"Up until a year ago," he said, "I still didn't doubt. I was still sure I'd find a way into the Creative Universe. I know it's there. I know if I could have found a way in, the advantages would have been overwhelming and obvious to anyone—to everyone on Old Earth, to begin with. If nothing else, it'd be a place to which the people could escape, if the force of the Younger Worlds does finally break through the phase shield."

"And at best?"

"Why, at best—but haven't I told you all this before?"

"You've told me very little. A bit about what you hoped to reach," said Amanda's voice softly. "A good deal about what made you start reaching, a lot about the past, but little about the future."

"I guess—yes," said Hal. "You're right. I never did tell you much of what I hoped for. But that was because I didn't want to promise anything I couldn't . . ."

He ran out of words. He was fumbling for the words he wanted. An unusual thing for him, and an unusual feeling.

"You didn't want even me to get my expectations up, in case you weren't able to do it," Amanda said.

"I suppose so. Yes," he answered, "you're right. That was why. Even you."

"Didn't it ever cross your mind you didn't have to prove yourself to me by success?"

"I don't know." He hesitated. "Maybe I was afraid of just what's happened. I mean—not afraid that I wouldn't be successful; but that I'd have to decide to stop trying while there was still life in me to try with."

He waited for some response. But she said nothing to help him. He turned again to face her dark shape.

"You know this is different," he said. "No matter what you feel, and I feel, you know we have to go different ways; if I turn away, take myself out of the equation while you're still in it. And you know you'll stay in it. You're what you are. The Third Amanda could never turn her back on worlds full of people needing her, simply to follow me into nothingness, for my own sake. What you were born to be and all you were trained to be won't let you. Isn't that so?"

"It would be so," she said slowly, "if you did turn away yourself. Yes."

It was almost a relief to hear her say it, and know that it was at last stated, out in the open, final.

"That's why I've delayed like this, telling you," he went on. "Oh, Amanda . . . Amanda . . ."

His throat closed up on him. He could not say any more.

Her hand reached out and stroked his forehead, gently, soothingly, as if he was a child with a fever.

"You're not gone yet," she murmured.

"But that's just it," he said, able to talk again, although talking was painful. "I've already delayed too long. There's more to it. It's not just me stepping away from an insoluble situation before it drives me insane. If it were that alone, I'd keep trying until they had to carry me off. But every day I wait, I hold back the time when Bleys finds out I'm gone. One day longer to the change that has to come when the historic forces move into the vacuum where I was."

"Are you sure when they do move, that'll be for the good of what we've all worked for? What if it's for the worse?"

"I don't know what'll happen, of course," he said. "There's only one thing I know. My quitting's going to leave an imbalance. One that the forces—which are the result of the reactions of all the people on all the worlds— won't be able to tolerate. By going I leave Bleys unopposed, too strong. I explained that to Rukh and Ajela. The imbalance has *got* to react against Bleys, where up until now the forces of history were working for him and the Others."

"You're sure of that?" she said.

"How can it be or have been any other way?" He stared through the darkness at her, wanting to see the expression of her face more clearly. "In all our history, no one person, one side, ever held the race to its own will for any length of time. Sometimes inside a generation—or less—all that a great conqueror took, or builder erected, was gone. Something else had come to replace it. You can say the civilizations of Egypt, the Dynasties of China, the Roman Empire, lasted for hundreds of years. But steadily, even while the names lasted, what they stood for changed. Always. Even the great religions grew splintered, altered—until from one generation to another, even a hundred years later, they'd all have seemed very, very different to someone used to their earlier forms."

Amanda said nothing. She continued to stroke his forehead.

"You know this is true!" he said. "When the balance leans too far one way, it automatically swings back. If I go, Bleys can never have what he's fought for—a single, unchanging Old Earth, where all the humans alive are permanently under the control of him and his kind. The historic forces will make an adjustment—hopefully for the better. It *must* happen, just as a child grows into an adult and an adult grows into old age and death—inexorably. Without the constant change that brings adaptation, the race can't survive."

Still she said nothing. Her hand continued to stroke him, that was all. It seemed she was ready to listen eternally.

"I never hoped to stop that ceaseless back-and-forth, that oscillation," he said. "My only hope was to take advantage of its momentum to break through to some kind of permanent improvement in people; a growth, not in anything put together by men and women as a society, but already waiting in the very hearts and souls and natures of each one of them, individually. So that on the next swing each living human would have more, be more, and choose more wisely. And this improvement would have to have come inevitably, as the value of the learning and self-discipline acquired by each individual, as the price of being able to use the Creative Universe. If only I could have found the way into it for them, that pass through the mountains!"

He stopped talking, out of words. They stayed as they were a little while, Amanda's hand still gently soothing his forehead. At last, however, she ceased; and took her hand away.

"You've thought of what your leaving is going to mean to Tam, of course?" she said.

"Of course," he answered, his voice thick with self-anger and disgust. "He had faith in me, in my finding a solution. I've been holding off telling him just as I held off telling you. But perhaps it's better to, now. But it'll be hard on him, after struggling to live all these years until an answer could be found. I know it. But I can't delay leaving any longer. Bleys is driving the Younger Worlds to produce ships and man them, to the point where it'll kill them. Of course, he wants them to die. And that makes it only a matter of time before he has what he needs for a massive breakthrough. As the time before that event shortens, the time in which my quitting can begin to cause a change in the balance of forces gets smaller and smaller. I have to tell Tam now, and go—now."

He hesitated.

"I'd rather do anything than face him with that news. Anything, but not face him with it."

"You think it means only disappointment to him?"

"What else?" he said. "He counted on me to find it. He counted on me to take over the Encyclopedia. I can't do either. If I stayed here, there'd be no true vacuum of power created, and affairs would haul me back into position again."

"But only disappointment, that's all you think it'll mean to Tam?"

He stared through the darkness at her, at the face he could not read.

"What else would there be? What do you mean?" he demanded.

She said nothing for a second. Then, when she spoke, her voice was a little different, almost detached.

"Do you know the children's story of the Great Dark Place?" she asked.

His mind drew a blank, made an automatic half-effort to call up the knowledge center of the Encyclopedia to find it; but he was too sick and weary inside for the effort.

Besides, he knew Amanda must have some reason for wanting to retell it herself, or she would not have mentioned it so.

"No," he said.

"The sun, the rain and the wind happened to meet one day," she said softly. "And the rain was upset—so upset that he was almost turning into sleet.

" 'It's terrible,' he told the sun and the wind, 'I've come from seeing something. I wouldn't have believed if anyone had told me about it. A Great Dark Place. I never seen a place so dark and terrible. I got away just as fast as I could. It scared me to death.'

"The wind laughed.

" 'Come on, now,' the wind said, 'no place can be that frightening. In fact, I don't believe it even exists. You're making it up. Isn't he, sun?'

" 'Certainly can't imagine any such place,' said the sun.

" 'You go see for yourself then,' said the rain. 'Anyway, I know it's there and I'm not going anywhere near it, ever again. The very thought of it chills me clear through—look how my drops are freezing at the thought of it!"

" 'Poo!' said the wind. 'Where's it supposed to be—back the way you just came? I'll go see for myself, right now!' and off he went.

"The sun went on his regular way, because it was important that a day always have the right number of minutes in it for the day it was; and he'd almost forgotten about the rain's fright and story, when the wind came up to him. And the wind was so shaken he was blowing in irregular gusts.

" 'Calm down, now,' said the sun. 'What's wrong?'

" 'What's wrong?' said the wind. 'I'll tell you what's wrong! I went to look for that Great Dark. Place the rain talked about—*and it was there!* Just as rain said! The greatest darkest place you ever—well, there's just no describing how terribly great and dark it was, I'll never get over the fright it gave me—never!"

" 'Come, come,' said the sun, for he was a very large and comforting person, by nature, 'it just isn't possible for any place to be that frightening. How about this? I'll go have a look for myself, right now. There may have to be a few extra minutes in this day, but we can't go having the rain and wind all upset like that. The weather will turn crazy, if it's sleeting in the middle of summer and you're blowing a gusty gale when you ought to be cooling everybody's brow with gentle breezes. I'll be right back.'

"Off he went. But he didn't come right back. In fact, he didn't come back for quite a while indeed; and when he did, he was exhausted. While the wind had been waiting the rain had come up to join him and they both watched the sun approaching.

" 'Well?' called the rain, as the sun got close enough to hear. 'Now, you see? Isn't it the most terrible and greatest Dark Place you ever saw?'

" 'It certainly is not!' replied the sun as he reached them. He was hot and more than a little cross, for now the day would have at least an extra hour in it it never should have had—unless moon could be talked into shortening the night by that much. 'In fact I don't believe there ever was any such place. The two of you made it up to send me on a wild goose chase. I looked high and low. I looked into everything and under everything—and there's no dark place at all, anywhere! If there was, I couldn't have missed finding it. I don't think it ever existed in the first place, and that's the last time time I go looking for something like that!' "

Hal had been lulled almost into drowsiness by the soft, regular voice of Amanda as she told the story. Besides being natural singers, the Morgans of Fal Morgan were gifted storytellers, and Amanda had all the family skills in that area. Now, the sudden stopping of her voice woke him suddenly, to the night and what he had himself been talking of before.

"And this Dark Place," he said to her, "it has some particular application to me?"

"You know why the sun couldn't find it, of course," said Amanda. "The Dark Place was there, but the sun saw only his own light when he looked. Tam has a dark place, even after all these years, but when you look at it, you see it so fully lighted by your own vision, you don't or won't see it as a dark place, because it echoes a dark place very like it, in you. The memory of your responsibility for how your brother Mor died."

Hal closed his eyes reflexively—because Amanda's last words had slapped him like a physical blow. Yet again his mind brought him the sight of William, the finally defeated and now fully insane Prince of the great planet Ceta, as he pressed the button that opened double doors to reveal the tortured body of what had once been Mor—the image was as fresh as if it had been yesterday, instead of a century past.

He made himself open his eyes again.

"Tell me what you mean," he said.

"No one you ever knew dies—for you," said Amanda, and the eerie near-echoing of what he had told himself, standing surrounded by the image of the library on the estate back down on Earth in the mountain rains, just a few days before, was part of what she always seemed able to do.

"Similarly, for Tam, your uncle Kensie and Jamethon Black, and even David Hall his brother-in-law—will never have died. Tam's lived with his part in those deaths longer than you've lived with Mor's death. He's carried his guilt about them more than a century; and the only hope he's had was that your finding what you've been after would prove that there were other causes—that it was one of the necessary happenings that made possible your discovery of a way into the Creative Universe for all people."

She paused.

"So, that's what you're going to be taking from him, when you tell him you're giving up his last hope of some forgiveness from the darkness, before he dies. For Ajela, for the Encyclopedia, even for you in your own right, he's fought to live that long. But mostly for hope of pardon for what happened to David and Kensie and Jamethon. Nearly a hundred years of service here hasn't won that pardon for him. But you might have. This one thing of all things you couldn't see—because his darkness echoes yours too closely. When you got close to seeing it, it woke your own guilt over Mor, and so you didn't want to look deeply into him where his trouble lay."

Hal lay stiffly still in the bed.

"You make leaving harder, only," he said. "No, I didn't realize that about Tam; but knowing it now makes no difference. What can I do that I haven't done already?"

"Did it ever strike you," said Amanda softly, "that you've been going at the problem of entry to the Creative Universe in what amounts to a head-on attack—like an attempt by pure force on a fabric or situation, to break through it. Maybe you could back off for a moment, and try to find a way of approaching the problem obliquely, in a way that wouldn't provoke so much resistance."

He propped himself up on one elbow to stare at her.

"By God!" he said. "Even in this you see more than anyone else can—" He broke off and slumped back. "But there is no other way. I've tried them all."

"You've been too close to the problem even to see them all," she said.

"You think so?" He was silent for a long moment. "No," he said, "I can't believe that. It's too easy an answer."

She let him think in silence for a while.

"If you don't mind a suggestion . . ." she said at last.

"I might have known!" He smiled grimly at her, aware that the moonlight showed his face to her clearly. "No—of course I want a suggestion!"

"Then suppose I tell you that on Kultis, where I've been working underground, the people have found their own way of resisting the armed forces Bleys sent to occupy the Exotic worlds? A way that doesn't mean giving up their commitment to nonviolence? Would it make a difference if I could show you a small corner on that world where a new kind of Exotic is coming into being?"

He stared through the darkness at her, letting her words

resound and re-echo in his mind, the implications of what she had just said flying out like sound waves from each stroke of a clapper against the metal side of some heavy bell.

"New?" he said. "You mean a development—upward?"

"Yes. Possibly upward. But new—I'm sure. Totally new, unmistakably different."

"And better?"

"I think so," said Amanda, "there's a group who've revived the old name of Chantry Guild for themselves; the name of the organization back in the twenty-first century, that you were once concerned with as Paul Formain. The organization from which the whole Exotic culture sprang; changed as it was from its beginnings."

"It would mean. . . ." He rolled over once more on to his back, talking to the ceiling as much as to her, again. "It would mean one more sure indication the race as a whole is on the brink of a step forward. But the Exotics were a Splinter Culture, like the Friendlies and the Dorsai. More than the Friendlies and Dorsai, they were deliberately trying to improve all people. But to make that improvement now, under these conditions, when everything they have has been given away, or taken from them . . . It's incredible."

He shook his head.

"And even if you're right, would it work here? These are Old Earth people, the laggards of the laggards . . ."

He fell silent, his own mind answering him with the memory of how for this last year or so Ajela had been pointing out evidence that on the world below its peoples, too, had been changing, giving up more and more of their millennia-old sectionalism. Ajela had talked of how for the first time they were beginning to think and act as a unit. Rukh had insisted, not once but many times repeating what was said by those who had come from Harmony and Association to help her speak out against the nihilism of those who preached support of Bleys' and the Others' attitudes. These Friendlies had said that, even among those who did not flock by the hundreds of thousands to see Rukh herself in person, some still showed an openness, a willingness to see that it was not really the Younger Worlds, like some horde of enemies, that threatened them; but a destructive attitude on the part of Bleys and the Others that was the core and heart of their opposition.

He had thought that by saying these things Rukh and Ajela were merely trying to lift his own dulled spirits. But perhaps they had been honestly reporting. Perhaps, even here on Old Earth, there was a new wind of thought, bringing together the established, self-centered, divided and often opposed-to-each-other peoples of a world which for some hundreds of years had trailed behind the rest of the race in its thinking.

If that was true . . . then it could suddenly be important what was happening on Kultis. If the Exotics were indeed, even in one small spot, anywhere near breaking through to a new and better form of their particular Splinter-culture type of social human. If that was the case, he badly wanted to see such a thing for himself. The problem was, however, he reminded himself, that even if this was true and meaningful, he could see no way now that it could help him, personally, with the problem that had stopped him dead in his tracks these last three years.

His spark of momentary excitement had gone out. And into that void Amanda once more spoke as if she had been thinking his thoughts with him.

"Suppose," she said, "you put off telling Tam—say, for the two months it would take you to go to Kultis, see for yourself what I'm talking about—and return?"

"Yes," he said slowly, as he thought about her suggestion. Even though his excitement had cooled, he found he could cling to the thought that, in any case it was two more months for Tam, Ajela and the rest to hope in. Even Amanda might hope. She had not asked for herself, but then she would not; although she and he were so close that he could not avoid knowing how it would cost her to lose him, just as it would cost him to be parted from her.

"I'd like you to go with me," he said to her.

"I'd planned on it," she said. "I'd have to guide you to the people I've been talking about, anyway. They're hidden as well as they can be from the Others' occupying military. Once there, though, I'd have to leave you with them and just drop back at intervals. It's my district and I've got responsibilities there. Also, in this case, I better not carry you to Kultis by myself. We'll need a driver."

"So long as you get someone who can keep a secret."

"About the fact you're gone from the Encyclopedia?" she said. "Did you think I wouldn't? Leave all that to me; and we'll get under way as soon as possible."

"All right then," he said, "but two months only, including travel time."

"Including travel time. Yes," she said.

He nodded and smiled—for her sake. But it was no use, said the inner part of him. It was a false hope, only delaying the inevitable, while shortening vitally necessary time. Desperately, he wished he could find some way of estimating when the Younger Worlds would have enough properly crewed ships outside the phase-shield to try a breakthrough to Earth.

But it was no use hoping for that. Even Bleys could not know. It would depend on how much flesh and blood could stand on the Younger Worlds; how fast the people there could be driven to produce what the Others needed.

CHAPTER 8 ■

"You're leaving immediately?" said Ajela the next morning. "Hal—it's bad enough you're going. Don't tell me you're planning to leave in the next minute!"

"We'd better, I'm afraid," said Hal. "I said two months, which may make time short enough as it is, at the Kultis end. I don't want to waste any more going and coming than I have to."

He turned to Amanda.

"You've got gear on board for me, Amanda?" he asked.

"All you'll need," said Amanda. "Simon's been taking care of that, haven't you, Simon?"

She was speaking to Simon Graeme, the great-grandson of Ian, who had been Donal Graeme's uncle. It was a small double miracle that Amanda had been able to find him to be their driver. There had been none in her being able to find him on such short notice, even after three years of her being away from her own people. The Dorsai forces' location system, if greatly less sophisticated, was almost as swift as the system in the Final Encyclopedia.

But the first of the small miracles came from the fact that he had not gone out like Amanda to an undercover job on one of the Other-controlled worlds. Like her, he had had considerable contact with off-Dorsai people, which ideally suited him for such work.

The second had been the fact that the patrol duty slot he was in, here at Old Earth, was one he was willing and able to leave.

"They've got a robe Exotics are required to wear," Simon told Hal, "something like a civilian uniform, all but required by the forces occupying them—you'll see. I duplicated the one Amanda's been wearing in a somewhat larger style, thanks to the Final Encyclopedia here. Footwear's the real problem; but a lot of the Exotics moved back and forth to other worlds, including Old Earth, and some of the earlier stuff's still worn, since everything's hard to get for the native population these days."

His voice was a slightly deeper bass than Hal's. Otherwise, considering the distance in time and relationship between them, they were remarkably alike.

Simon, of course, could have no way of knowing that Hal had once been Donal. As far as ordinary information went, the Dorsai could only know what all the worlds knew: that Hal had been rescued as a baby from an antique courier-size spacecraft that had drifted into the near-vicinity of Old Earth; and that after being rescued, Hal had been raised on that world by tutors from the three Splinter Cultures. But Ian had lived long enough that Simon had been ten years old when Ian died. Simon could not fail to see Ian's likeness in Hal.

If nothing else. Simon must almost necessarily guess they had some kind of relationship. It was possible he took Hal for a descendant of a child on another world whom Ian had never acknowledged fathering. But Hal suspected that his somewhat distant and generations-younger cousin had actually guessed at something more than that.

But in any case, he had never said anything of what he might have concluded. In person, there were obvious differences between them. Simon was shorter than Hal, stockier, with a more wedge-shaped face and dark brown rather than black hair.

But for all that, the feeling of family was strong between them, as always among the Graemes of Foralie; and from their first moment of meeting three years earlier, Simon had shown that he felt it, as did Hal. As far as appearances went they might have been—not brothers perhaps, but cousins—though their similarity was most visible, oddly enough, when either or both were in motion. Simon's body movements were more fluid and balanced, as suited someone who had been born on the Dorsai and never out of training. Hal's were in some sense innate; and had—strange as the word might sound—something almost spiritual about them. But when the two men moved side by side, the attention of anyone watching was somehow drawn to the same heavy-boned leanness, and cragginess of feature, in them both.

Amanda had located Simon in two hours, Encyclopedia time; and he had been delivered to them within three hours after that. In the single hours since, he had got Amanda's ship ready to take them to Kultis.

"Thanks, Simon," Hal said now. A thought struck him.

"Would you answer a question for me, come to think of it. You've had three years here. What do you think of the Old Earth people? I mean, the ones you've had to deal with since you've been here?"

Simon frowned.

"They're different from any of the people on the Younger Worlds I've met," he said, "and than I'd imagined them. It's hard to put my finger exactly on how."

He still frowned.

"It's as if they're all very aware of the ornamental things of life; I mean, the things you've got time for after you've won the daily struggle for existence. Certainly, they've rebuilt Earth itself in the past hundred years into a green and pleasant world. But, particularly this last year or so, I get a feeling from them of a hunger, of sorts. As if they were lacking something but didn't know exactly what. Rich but unsatisfied, says it maybe. Perhaps that's why, in spite of belonging to a million different sects, groups and so forth, they all flock so to listen when Rukh, or one of her people, lectures them on faith and purpose. I don't know."

"I'd have said myself that they were in an evangelically ready state," said Ajela. "There's no doubt about the hunger behind their coming to listen to us. But Simon Graeme is right. They don't really know what it is they're hungry for."

"Yes," said Hal. "You've noticed changes, too, then. All right. Another reason to take a look at Kultis. Also, come to think of it, another reason why we need to get moving as soon as possible."

He reached out to hug Ajela, who was closest; but the golden-haired woman pulled back from him.

"You will not—I tell you flatly," said Ajela, "you will not leave without seeing Tam before you go."

Her tone was angry, but there was something more than anger in what she said.

"I hadn't intended to, of course," said Hal softly. "I wouldn't leave the Encyclopedia without seeing him. Can I talk to him now, or is he resting?"

"I'll see," said Ajela, still with an edge in her voice. She got up and went out of the room by another door than that by which the rest had all entered—a door behind her desk.

She was back within the minute.

"It's all right," she said. "You can see him now, Hal. Amanda, do you mind if I just take Hal in by himself? Tam tries to respond to everyone who comes to see him; and he hasn't got the strength for more than one person at a time, really."

"Of course not," said Amanda—and smiled. "Not that I imagine you'd let me in, even if I did."

"Of course not. But, I'm sorry—you may have another chance later to meet him and he's not strong . . . these days."

"Take Hal in and don't worry about my being upset over missing a chance to meet him," said Amanda. "Common sense first."

"Thank you for understanding," said Ajela. She turned and went to the door she had just come through, and Hal followed her. The door opened, and shut behind them.

Within, suddenly, Hal found himself in a dimness. No, not actually a dimness, he realized, but a dulling of the light after the level of illumination of Ajela's office and the corridors. For a moment it baffled him—as if a thin mist had sprung up to obscure all that was around him.

Then he remembered that these quarters of Tam's were kept always on a lighting cycle matched to the day and night of the Earth directly below the Encyclopedia; as Hal's illusion of his estate had been under the same rain and wind as the actual place itself would have been at that time.

On the Earth's surface, directly under them now, it would now therefore be the ending of the day; a time of long shadows, or of no shadows at all if the approaching evening was closing in behind a sky obscured by clouds, as it must be. The light was going from the surface underneath them, and from this room alike.

Aside from that, the room itself was as he had always

remembered Tam keeping it—half office, half forest glade, with a small stream of water flowing through it. Beside that stream were the old-fashioned overstuffed armchairs, and Tam in one of them; though that particular chair had become elongated and more slantwise of back, so that it was almost as much bed as chair. In this Tam sat, or lay, dressed as he had been every time Hal had seen him, in shirt, slacks and jacket. Only this time a cloth of red and white, its colors garish in the lesser light, lay across his knees.

As his eyes rested on it, he saw Tam's index finger make a sideways movement; and Ajela came hastily around Hal and went swiftly forward to take up the cloth and carry it away out of sight beyond the trees. It was only then that Hal recognized it as the Interplanetary Newsman's cloak Tam had been qualified to wear before he came back to the Encyclopedia for good. The cloak was still set on the colors of red and white Tam had programmed it for over a century ago, before the death of David Hall, his young brother-in-law, for whom Tam had considered himself responsible, and for whose death at the hands of a Friendly fanatic Tam had never forgiven himself.

Hal looked into the old man's eyes, and for the first time saw the stillness there. A stillness that echoed like a sound, like some massive blow in a tall, dark, many-chambered structure—so that the echoes came back, and came back again; bringing Hal strangely, in sudden, powerful emotion, a vision of the weary King Arthur Pendragon, at the end of Alfred Tennyson's poetic *Idylls of the King*. Without warning the room was overlaid in Hal's mind with even darker shadows from the vision built by the poet's lines about that last battle by the seashore.

> . . . . *but when the dolorous day*
> *Grew drearier toward twilight falling, came*
> *A bitter wind, clear from the north, and blew*
> *The mist aside, and with that wind the tide*
> *Rose, and the pale King glanced across the field*

Of battle. But no man was moving there;
Nor any cry of Christian heard thereon,
Nor yet of heathen; only the wan wave
Brake in among dead faces, to and fro
Swaying the helpless hands, and up and down
Tumbling the hollow helmets of the fallen,
*   And shiver'd brands that once had fought with Rome,*
And rolling far along the gloomy shores
The voice of days of old and days to be. . . .

For a long second Hal could not think what had brought these lines and Tam together in his mind. Then he realized that, like Arthur then, Tam now looked out and saw no one but the dead. They were all dead, all those he had known as a child, as a young man, as a man of middle age. He had left them all behind, in the closed pages of history, long since.

Hal chilled. For in the same way those he had known as Donal were now gone, all dead. Including Kensie, his uncle, who was one of the deaths Tam carried on his conscience. And as he looked at Tam now, a whisper came and went in Hal's mind, a question—*will I, too, come to this*?

He shook himself out of the vision, went forward and took one of Tam's hands, where it lay in the Tam's lap. It had been an old hand when Hal had first touched it, years ago; and it was hardly older looking now. Except that perhaps the skin had sunk a little more between the tendons, and made the veins stand out more on the back of it. Tam looked up at Hal.

"Here you are," he said. His voice had been hoarsened by years, long since. Now it was faint in volume as well. "Is she with you?"

"I'm here," said Ajela.

"Not you," said Tam, faintly still, but with a hint of his old asperity. "The other one—damn my memory—the Dorsai!"

"You mean Amanda?" said Hal. "She just got here, but

she's leaving right away, again. I'm going with her for two months to Kultis—if you can wait for me that long. She thinks she's found Exotics there who are evolving—that's what I came to tell you."

"Bring her in here," said Tam.

"Tam, too many people— " Ajela began.

"It's my life still," whispered Tam. "I have to see her. I want to talk to her."

Ajela went off. Tam's eyes sought Hal's.

"You should go with her, yes," he said, his voice strengthening, so that almost, as Hal stood holding the ancient hand still in his, there now seemed almost no change at all between this moment and that when Hal had first taken it, those long years past when he had come here in flight. He had been running then away from Bleys and the murder of his tutors, and toward a maturity that would begin with more than three years working in the mines of metal-rich Coby. Only now, the full weight of the hand he held hung strengthlessly against the palm of his own larger one.

"I knew she was here. I knew you'd be going off for a while. Got to talk to her," said Tam; and for the moment— for just the moment now—his eyes were looking no longer on the dead but on the living.

"She'll be right here," said Hal; and in fact at that moment Ajela brought Amanda through the door behind him up to the chair.

"Tam," said Ajela, "here she is. Amanda Morgan."

Tam's hand pulled away and slid out of Hal's grasp. It reached for Amanda and she took it in her own.

"Lean close," Tam said to her. "Bastard doctors! They're so proud of giving me eyes like a twenty-year-old in perfect health, and I still can't see what I want unless I have people close. There, I see you now."

Their two faces, the dark, aged mask of Tam and the taut-skinned, perfect features of Amanda, were now only inches apart as she leaned down to him.

"Yes," said Tam, looking into her eyes, "you'll do. I knew you were here. You see things, don't you?"

"Yes," said Amanda softly.

"So do I," said Tam, with a hoarse, tiny bark of a laugh, "but that's because I'm halfway through the door to death. Do you believe me, Amanda Morgan?"

"I believe you," she said.

"Then believe in your seeing, always. Yes, I know you do that now; but I want to tell you to believe always, too; except for one time. You love him, of course."

"Yes," said Amanda.

"The time's going to come . . . one time, when what you'll see will be what is to be; but that one time you'll have to remember not to believe it. You'll know the time I'm talking about when you come to it. But, do you hear me? One time, only. You'll see him then, and your seeing will be right; but if you believe what you see, you'll be wrong. So, don't believe, that one time. Have faith. Believe in what you believe, instead."

Amanda's face was very still.

"What are you telling me?" she whispered.

"When the time comes, and you see him in something that must not be, don't believe it. Promise me. At the hardest moment, the worst time, even though what you see is true, don't believe. Because he'll need to know you won't believe, then."

"Not believe . . . " she echoed.

"Promise me."

"Yes," she said, and her hand tightened on his. "I don't understand, but I'll be ready. If it comes to that, I'll have faith beyond any seeing."

"Good," said Tam on the exhale of one weary sigh. His hand slipped out of her grasp as it had slipped from Hal's, to lie again in his lap. He spoke without looking away from her. "Did you hear her, Hal?"

"Yes," said Hal. "But I don't understand you, either."

"For you, it doesn't matter." Tam turned his head away.

"You've got to go," said Ajela, moving forward. "He's worn out. He's got to rest now."

They turned away from the old man, who was no longer looking at them, as if he had already forgotten their presence; and Ajela herded them out of the room.

CHAPTER 9 ■

Amanda's ship, with Simon at the controls, hung in orbit above the night side of Kultis.

Only one of the planet's moons was in the sky with them. Once, when the Exotics had been the richest of the Younger Worlds, this, like its sister world of Mara, had owned a space-approach warning system that would have signaled the appearance of any craft within a hundred thousand kilometers of its surface. Now the men and women who had manned that system were dead or gone, and the very system itself had been cannibalized of its parts or left to grow dusty in uselessness.

Below, the planetary night side was a round shape of darkness occulting the stars and the smaller of the two moons beyond; but the instruments aboard the ship cut through the darkness and the cloud cover separating them from the surface and showed it as bright as if daylit. The screen showing that surface was already on close magnification that gave them a view of northern tropical uplands mounting to the foothills of successive ranges of sharply rising mountains, tall enough to have their peaks snow-capped even in this climate and season. As they continued their descent the viewer showed a road running upcountry past what had been homes and estates, scattered Exotic-fashion with plenty of land around them; through a small city and on into the mountains. Amanda was instructing Hal and Simon; particularly, at the moment, Simon.

"We'll be following the route of that road, approximately," she was saying to him. "The Chantry Guild is in the Zipaca Mountains, that range to our left there. The more lofty range to the right are the Grandfathers of Dawn, and the flat valley-floor in between them that widens as it comes toward us is the Mayahuel Valley. There's a more direct route to where we're going; but I want Hal to get the context for it all, first—I want him to see some of the rest of Kultis as it is now. So we'll make a couple days' walk out of it. You set us down, here . . ."

Her words were precise and clean-edged on Hal's ear, so that they stood out as if in italics. She had changed, he thought, listening, since that moment with Tam just before they left. She was more authoritative, more intense.

Without any specific alteration in her tone or her manner, her voice now seemed to carry the burden of a purpose that took precedence over everything else. As if she was now driven by something she had committed herself to carry through at any and all cost.

The difference in her had become apparent to him almost immediately they had left Tam's quarters for the ship. His first awareness of a difference in her had been when they were almost to the ship; when she had fallen back from walking at this side, turning and stopping Ajela and Rukh who were following them, so that his next few steps carried him beyond the point where he could hear what she said to them, briefly and in a low voice, before turning to catch up with him once more.

He had felt an unreasonable, but for a moment very real, flash of irritation. What was it she had to say to them that he could not be trusted to hear as well? As they had boarded the ship and all the way to where they were now above Kultis, he had waited for her to give him some explanation of what she had stopped to tell the others. But she had said nothing. In fact, she had acted as if that moment had never taken place; but since then he had noticed this driven quality in her, this difference.

It must, he thought, have something to do with Tam's vision about which he had warned her. Had some sort of private spark leaped between the two of them in that moment, without his seeing it? He told himself it was nothing; it was none of his business, in any case. But the memory and the difference in her now gnawed at him regardless.

She was reaching out now to touch the screen and a blue circle came to outline the place she had indicated; and then another, smaller screen suddenly showed a magnified view of the place she had touched. In that screen they saw things as if they hung only four or five meters above the ground, over a small patch of bushes just off the road, whose ruts were black, the higher surfaces between them palely contrasted in the cloud-filtered moonlight. The road was only some ten meters away from their point of view.

"You see this?" Amanda said to Simon, holding up a white rag of a cloth, grayed from many launderings and slightly longer than it was wide, with ragged edges forming a roughly rectangular shape. "I've made a micrograph of this, so your viewer can identify even an edge of it, if that's all that's visible. You know our general route. Search along it each night, in the area of where a day's walk should have taken us. I'll try to display this somewhere every day or night we stop. I'll put it where the viewer can sight it—tangled in the branches or laid on top of one of those bushes down there, for example. One corner should always be folded under, and that corner will point in the direction we're headed, in case we have to vary from the original route. You should be able to find it displayed every night, except if we're overnighting in the city. It's too likely to be suspected as a signal there, so in the city I may not display it. If you can't find it for one night, don't worry. After three nights in a row without seeing it or any sign of us you can investigate—if you think it's reasonably safe for you to do so. Otherwise, don't try."

"No otherwise," said Simon.

"Simon," said Amanda. "You're our driver on this. You take orders."

"Not where it comes to any chance that doing nothing might cost us Hal," said Simon. He held up a hand before she could speak. "It's what he means to our side, not just the personal connection between us—or the business of never leaving one of your own behind when you don't know what happened to them."

Slowly, she nodded. Hal felt he should say something to refute such an opinion but there was no easy short way of doing it. In any case, it was too late. Amanda was already answering.

"All right," she was saying, "I wouldn't be around to stop you, anyway, if it comes to that. Now, if you're satisfied you've got everything you want to know before we take off, you can start setting us down—" She tapped the screen where the closer view now revealed in one corner the fire-blackened wall of some ruined homestead, rather than the living villa they had seemed to view from a higher point of inspection.

"Right away, ma'am," said Simon, sitting down to the controls.

"Hal," said Amanda. "Come on back and get dressed."

"Redressed, you mean, don't you?" said Hal, following her into the stateroom. "I've already got clothes on."

"Redressed by all means, if that's the phrase you prefer," said Amanda, handing him a brown sackcloth penitential robe, similar to the one in which she had left Kultis. She started to slip out of her coveralls and back into a robe of her own.

"How about you?" she went on. "Are you satisfied you know everything you need to know? You aren't rusty on your short-language and signals after three years at a desk?"

She was referring to what was basically a secret language built up and passed down from one generation of children under twelve years of age to the next. It gained and lost words from generation to generation, and was different from family to family. But the children of neighbors as close to each other as the Graemes and Morgans of Foralie had practically a language in common. The reference to *signals* was to the silent body language, varying from minute to large physical movements, which the Dorsai as a Splinter Culture had refined into a second tongue they could use to converse, unnoticed, even as bound prisoners under the noses of captors.

"Not in the least," said Hal.

"Be sure then to pay attention if I shout '*court*,' whatever else you do. The people manning the garrisons that the Others put in here live for reprisals."

She was specifically alluding to the effective, short, one-syllable descendant of the ancient cry of "quarter"; which the Dorsai professional soldiers had early put to use to advise each other in the midst of combat that they should disable only, and if possible avoid killing, those with which they happened to be fighting at the moment.

"I'll be listening," said Hal. "Don't worry."

"I never worry," said Amanda; and he was sensible enough not to argue the point with her.

Dressed in their unflattering garments, and carrying bags with drawstring tops that held all their other possessions, they stepped out of the ship twenty minutes later into the spicily soft and warm night atmosphere of Kultis.

Amanda had picked their landing spot well—not that Simon would have done badly if the decision had been left up to him. A tall stand of trees shielded them from the road and they had landed in the darkness of one roofless room of the burned villa they had seen in the vision screen. Its walls lifted above the spacecraft and hid it further in shadow..

"Good luck," said the voice of Simon from the darkened port. The outer lock door of the port closed and the ship fell silently upward, out of sight.

Amanda's fingers caught hold of the sleeve of Hal's robe, held and towed him out of the shadow into the relative illumination of the cloud-dimmed moonlight; and from there, on through a ruined doorway into further shadow again—

And suddenly they were under attack.

The sounds of feet rushing across grimed flooring, the rustle of clothing, were adequate warning; along with the stink of breath and uncleaned bodies. The outburst of yells that came as their attackers closed around Hal and Amanda was clearly intended to be one of triumph; and in fact Hal found himself caught by at least three people at once, two aiming at his upper body and one at his legs. At the same time, high-pitched to carry over the other voices and noise, came the sound of Amanda's voice.

"Court!"

Hardly fair, thought Hal, more than a little irritated, as he spun away from those trying to hold him, breaking the finger of one who would not loosen his hold and throwing a second into a tangle with the third, leg-level attacker. Here he was, in almost total darkness, barely hours after the three years at the desk Amanda had talked about, set upon by an unknown but certainly large number of attackers; and within moments of landing, she was telling him not to hurt these people too seriously. Those who were now earnestly trying to grab and hold them did not smell like garrison soldiers who might be eager for an excuse to indulge in acts of reprisal—

His first feeling of annoyance was wiped out without warning in a sudden upsurge of something like joy within him. Joy at having something real and physical to come to grips with after the past years of fighting imponderables and unknowns. His reflexes from his training under Malachi Nasuno, the Dorsai who had been one of his tutors as the boy Hal Mayne; and his far greater training as the young Donal, growing up and working as a professional soldier—these all but forgotten memories took him over. He began to whirl among his foes, tangling them up with one another and putting them down with throws wherever possible.

An excruciating and sudden bang on the right side of his skull changed things abruptly. The lightless room seemed to spark for a moment within his own head and then gray out around him, abruptly changing his feelings to a simple, instinctive yearning for survival. The only thought that stirred in his suddenly dulled brain was that he should have sensed coming the blow that had hit him, and avoided it. Reflexively, he had already dropped to the floor, gathering himself into a ball as he did so and rolling sideways. He came up against something and hastily spun away. The Exotics, he knew from experience, had liked homes with large rooms in them; and the houses he had seen in the screen of the ship from above had been empty shells. Therefore, there should be nothing much between the walls to impede him unless it was some other human being. Moreover, it only made sense that those who attacked him and Amanda would have let them get into the center of a room, so as to come at them from all sides at once.

He did not think all this out consciously as he was spinning away from whoever or whatever he had touched. Rather, it was a conclusion reached just above the level of instinct. He needed time for his head to clear.

It did; and with his return to clarity came the beginnings of a burning anger at himself, as well as a return of the unhappiness that had been growing in him this last year and more. The fact he had been given no more than part-time instruction by a Dorsai as a growing boy on Old Earth; and that it had been a hundred years since, as Donal, he had been personally in action, did not excuse him. His lacks were clear.

He was no longer a Dorsai in the sense of the fighting potential of that name. Any adult, properly schooled Dorsai would have been moving with his ears open, would have built and carried in his head as he fought a lightless mental picture of what his opponents were doing; and been ready for that blow. He did know that it had been no thrown fist that had hit him; but something used as a weapon—a length of wood, perhaps.

He listened for a second longer, translating the sounds around him into that mental picture he now remembered being taught to form. Amanda had cleared away all who had come close to her and was now nearly at the farther door out of the room. The ones not still engaged in trying to reach her were feeling around, trying to find him— evidently under the assumption that whoever hit him had knocked him unconscious.

Then he was on his feet again, a portion of his attention continually updating the picture from the sounds he heard and looking for a pattern in the actions of his attackers. There was always a pattern, made up in separate parts by those who were ready and willing to come to grips; followed by those who would become willing once the combat began, and those who only wanted to hang around the edges safely until the prey had been secured by the strongest of their group and it was safe to pile on, shouting as if they had been in the action from the beginning.

Now he was ready to move through them to join Amanda. This time, he met what he had expected. About thirty seconds of contact were enough to satisfy him now that the group which had jumped them was no more than a dozen adults, of which only four or five were daring enough to offer real threats.

Almost as soon as the deduction was completed in the back of his head, the three full-effort fighters he had encountered on his way to the door were either all put aside or bypassed. Amanda, his ears told him, had already gone through the farther exit. He followed her; and his ears told him those they had left behind did not follow.

Amanda's soft whistle asked if he was all right.

He whistled back, went toward the sound she had made, and they came together.

"No problem," messaged Amanda's fingers, tapping

his cheek. "We can go on with no more trouble now. Follow me."

She led him farther through the darkness and they emerged after a bit into an area of no shadows at all, just as the clouds thinned slightly overhead; and he was able to see that they were now outside the walls of the ruined villa.

"Some illegal farmers, I think. A family or families who came out to work their field at night," said Amanda in a normal voice. "They didn't have the slightest idea who we might be, except that in these clothes we obviously weren't garrison soldiers and there might be something in our sacks that could be used by them."

"So those were some of the native Exotics—after only two years?" Hal demanded. A sudden suspicion stirred in him. "Did you know they were there, when you led me into that place?"

"No," she said, "but it was likely we'd run into some like that along the way."

She did not elaborate; and his unspoken question was answered. There had been a reason she had wanted him to experience that particular type of "new" Exotic; so different from what she had promised to show him, back at the Encyclopedia. He tucked the fact away. Her reasons would become apparent soon enough.

"Now," she said, as they emerged from the shell of the building into the moonlight. Across a ruined level area that must once have been either a lawn or garden, the surrounding trees made a semicircle of darkness, with a gap and the hint of what might have been a road or path curving off to the left to be lost in them. "We go this way."

She led into the woods to the right of the path.

"A driveway, once," she said. "It'll connect with the road a few dozen meters over. But we'd better stay off the road proper. We'll just travel alongside it; and we ought to be within an easy day's walk of the city you saw on the screen—Porphyry's its name. We won't make it before sun-up. When daylight comes we'll have to be careful in our travel and avoid reaching the town at the wrong time of day."

It was a not unpleasant walk by moonlight, for the cloud cover soon thinned to nothingness, and disappeared completely shortly after that; they moved easily under Sofia, the more brilliant of Kultis's moons.

The moonlight revealed, but also hid things. Almost it was possible for Hal to imagine that there had been no changes since he had been there last; and this illusion persisted except when they would come upon the shell of some sad-looking, wrecked and burned-out habitation. In the bright but colorless light, these remains of what had once been homes seemed almost magically capable of summoning up in Hal a memory of the lightness and beauty that the Exotics had put into their habitations. As if they wrapped around themselves now the ghosts of the beauty with which the Exotics had always seemed to try to make up for the abstractness of the philosophy that was their obsession as one of the three largest and most successful of the Younger Worlds' Splinter Cultures.

There were the noises of night birds, and some insects, and other stirrings, but no sounds of large creatures. The Exotics had not imported the genetic starter material for variform animals of any size, beyond what was necessary for the ecology, except for some domestic animals. Their philosophy looked askance at the keeping of pets; and most of the things they couldn't do themselves, they were wealthy enough to buy machinery to do, or to hire off-planet workers—animals were not needed except for the stock of the dairy farms or sheep ranches.

The total effect of the night, the different darktime sounds and the soft, scented air, gave Hal a feeling of dreamy unreality which was still underlaid with his return to unhappiness, and only partially affected by the growing headache from the blow to the side of his head. He had been lucky, at that, he thought, even as he automatically began to exert some of the physical self-discipline he had been taught in both his childhoods. His efforts were not as much to get rid of the pain, as to put it off to one side, mentally, so that it could be ignored by the normal workings of his body and mind. A little farther forward and it would have come against his temple, where that much of a blow, even from a length of tree limb, could—

He woke suddenly to the potential of what he was feeling and stopped walking suddenly. Amanda checked herself in mid-stride beside him.

"What is it?" she asked.

"I took a hit on the head, back there," he said. "Something more than someone's fist. Maybe a staff or a club of wood. I didn't think too much of it until just now—"

"Sit down," said Amanda. "Let me take a look."

He dropped into a sitting position, cross-legged on the earth below him; and was rewarded by a new shock of pain in his head at his body's impact with the ground.

"Right side of my head," he said.

Amanda's fingers went among his hair, parting it as she bent over him.

"This moonlight's bright enough so I ought to be able to see . . ."

She found something by his sudden feel of her touch—a cut, at least.

"No noticeable swelling about the scalp," she said, "but it's the swelling inside the skull we've got to worry about. Did it feel as if it might be enough to cause a concussion? What can you tell about it from the inside? How hard were you hit?"

"I couldn't tell you—it dazed me a bit," he said, "for maybe a dozen seconds, no more. It didn't knock me off my feet. I remember dropping deliberately and rolling away from the action. Now . . ."

He probed his own sensations for information. It was ironic, here on this world, that the techniques he was using were as much Exotic as Dorsai. The two Splinter Cultures had been on a parallel track in these matters; and when they realized it, information had been freely passed back and forth between them. Basically, there was much the body could tell the mind that drove it, if the mind could discipline itself to listen along ancient pathways of nerve and instinct.

He sat motionless, inwardly listening in this fashion. Amanda sat beside him. After a bit, he spoke.

"No," he said, "I don't think fluid's going to accumulate in the brain, at least to any point where pressure on the brain by the skull is going to cause real trouble. But I think I'd better stop; and not try to travel any more for the rest of the night."

"Absolutely," said Amanda. She looked around. "We're out of sight of the road. Lie back. I'll make you a bed of twigs and large leaves; and you can shift to that when it's ready."

He lay back, suddenly very grateful to be able to do so; resting his head on a half-buried root emerging from some large native plant, a sort of tree-sized bush. He closed his eyes and concentrated his attention, not merely on isolating the pain, but on holding back the natural responses of his body that wanted to pour fluid into the bruised area beneath the unyielding bone of his skull.

Awareness of his body, of its pressure against the naked ground, the moonlight on his eyelids, and all his other feelings, began to dwindle into nonexistence. He was relaxing. The pain was dwindling too. The forest around him ceased to be and time began to lose its meaning. He was only automatically and distantly aware of Amanda helping him to shift over a half meter or so to his right, on to a soft and springy bed a little above the surface on which he had been lying.

All things moved away from him into nothingness and he slept.

Out of that same nothingness he came into the place he had dreamed of twice before. He was aware that he dreamed now, but it changed nothing; because the dream was reality and reality was the dream.

He was once more on the rubbled plain, the small

stones underfoot long since grown to giant boulders. Far back, on his last visit here, he had passed the vine-covered gate of metal bars through which he had seen Bleys, who was unable to pass through and be on the same side as he was . . . of what? A made wall of stone? Some natural barrier of rock? He could not remember, and it did not matter now.

What mattered was that he was at last coming close to the tower. Always, it had seemed to recede from him as he worked his way toward it; but now it was undeniably close—although how close that closeness was, there was no telling. A kilometer? Half or a quarter that distance? Double or more that distance?

But it was close. Undeniably, no longer distant. It loomed over him, with its black, narrow apertures that were windows. He should be able at last, now, to reach it with just a little more effort.

But that was the problem. He was close to weeping with frustration. He lay on the lip of a steep but short drop to the bottom of a trench perhaps twenty meters wide; with as steep an upward sweep on its far side. It was perhaps four times his height in depth; but its sides were not absolutely vertical. He could slide down this side and go up the other on his hands and knees.

Only, he could not. A terrible weakness had come on him, gradually, over the long distance he had traveled. That was why he lay on the rocks now like a man half dead. Now he lacked the strength even to rise to his feet. The trench was nothing, easily passable ordinarily to anyone with even half his normal strength; but that was just what he did not have. A lack of strength like that of the dying Tam Olyn held him where he was.

He concentrated, trying to drive his body with everything that he had been taught as Donal, and as the boy Hal Mayne, by all of his tutors. Sheer fury alone should have been enough to move this dead carcass that was his body, at least down the slope before him.

But it would not.

He realized slowly that the enemy this time was within him. He could fight what lay outside; but it was himself who kept him from crossing the trench; though every fiber of his being and all his life was concentrated and dedicated to the effort of getting through and beyond it to the tower.

He struggled to isolate that inner enemy, to bring it to grips; but it was everywhere and nowhere in him. Desperate, still fighting, he slipped at last back into the grayness of slumber and slept until daylight woke him to the reality that was Kultis.

CHAPTER 10 ∎

When he woke, the sun was already well above the horizon. It was unlike him to sleep so heavily and long, out in the open. On the other hand, his headache was greatly reduced. As he came to he had not been conscious of it at all; but then it began to make itself felt, growing in intensity; and he had expected it to mount to the sharpness he had felt the night before. Clearly, though, the blow on his head had done no real harm.

However, the headache had stopped growing at a level that required hardly any concentration to put it aside from his attention. Still, since he wanted the whole of his mind free to concentrate on whatever they might run into, he made the mental effort to shift it out, off to the fringes of his consciousness. There it perched like a bird in a tree, at roost—still with him, but easily ignored except when a deliberate attempt was made to check on it.

Amanda had evidently been out gathering some of the wild fruit and vegetable products of the forest for their breakfast. She had them piled on a large lime-green leaf, others of which she had used to make a covering over the

twigs which had provided the springs for Hal's forest bed.
He recognized some variform bananas, custard apples, and
ugli fruit among the eatables she had gathered; but most
were probably variforms, or hybrid varieties, of the native
flora, adapted to be usable by the human digestive system.

Among these were a number of thick roots of various
shapes and sizes, and what seemed to be several varieties
of fruit with thick skins bristling with spines. They had all
the unfriendly appearance of the Old Earth cactus pear.
And there was something that was neither fruit nor root,
but looked like the white pith stripped from inside the
stems of some plant.

Cautiously, Hal sat up, prepared for his headache to
explode in protest at the motion. But it did not. He moved
forward and sat cross-legged at the edge of the leaf.
Amanda was already seated, cross-legged herself, on its
other side.

"Breakfast," she said, waving at the scattering on the
leaf. "I've been waiting for you. How are you?"

"Much better," said Hal. "In fact, for practical purposes,
I couldn't be much better."

"Good!" she said. She pointed to the produce on the leaf
before her.

"Tuck in," she said.

Hal looked at the food Amanda spread out.

"With all this why do they need to come out at night to
plant fields?"

"Because they want and need a more balanced diet," she
answered. "Also they want to store supplies for those days
when the Occupation authorities won't let them get out
into the woods to gather. Those allowed days have been set
up so that if the local people depended on gathering alone
they'd starve to death. Their passes simply aren't validated
for enough so-called 'travel' days—days they're allowed
outside the walls of the town."

"I see," said Hal.

"Also, out here there're only a few variform rabbits and
other small wild animals they can catch and kill to supple-

ment the protein of which they don't get enough—they need garden vegetables to make that loss up. Plus they need the root vegetables that are best raised in quantity in a plot. Those people who attacked us last night probably thought we were either there to rob their plot, or we were hunters who might have meat with us they could legitimately take—since legally we're on their ground. It'd have to be one or the other, since there's nothing left to scavenge out here."

"You *knew* they were there," said Hal. "That's why you called *'court.'* "

"I know of that family," she said, "and when they jumped us I guessed it was one of the nights they stayed out. They leave town and simply don't go back until the evening of the next day; and either bribe one of the curfew patrol to report them in, or take their chances on being found out."

"I forgot," said Hal, "this is your work district, isn't it?"

"Right up to the Zipaca Mountains," she answered. "So that's why I had Simon set us down where he did. I wanted you to see something. That while they still believe in non-violence and try to practice it, there's some things some of them'll fight for now; and one of those is survival. I don't mean all of them'll fight, even for that; but more than you'd think. It's one of the changes you needed to see first-hand, for yourself."

"Hardly a change for the better," said Hal, "from their point of view, I'd think."

"Wait until you've had time to see some more of them before you make up your mind about that," she said. "For now, it's enough that you've seen that much change. You'd better get some food into you."

Some small, sudden alteration in the tone of her voice made him look more closely at her. He thought he detected something nearly mischievous hiding in the corners of her eyes and mouth, at odds with the usual matter-of-factness of her appearance.

A suspicion stirred in him. The Morgans and the

Graemes, growing up as close as cousins, had never been above playing small tricks on each other. It was strange, but somehow mind-clearing, to leave the puzzle of changes in the Exotics and his own frustrated search to think of himself for once in that youthful, long-ago context.

"You shouldn't have waited," Hal said, calmly enough. He waved at the food spread between them. "Here, you go ahead."

She raised her eyebrows slightly, but reached out, picked up one of the strings of what looked like pith just before him and began eating. Evidently, it was more chewy than it looked. Otherwise her face told him nothing about its spiciness, bitterness, or any other aspect of its flavor.

"By the way," he said, as he reached for some himself, and bit cautiously into the whitish cordlike length, "what kind of taste—"

His mouth puckered instinctively, as if he had bitten into a lemon.

"Quite pleasant, actually, if a little bland," she replied cheerfully. "Of course, you have to be careful to eat it only when it has those pale yellow streaks like that—oh, that's too bad, you must have hit one that wasn't quite ripe yet, by mistake. Here, spit it out. There's no point trying to eat it at that stage. Try one of the others with the faint yellow streaks. I'm sorry!"

He got rid of what was in his mouth.

"I'm sure you are!" he said—but she was smiling and then suddenly they were both laughing. "So much for the sensitivity and kindness of an Amanda! Playing tricks like that on someone who might have had a concussion."

"You didn't give me a chance to warn you," she said.

"Oh? And it was pure chance nearly all the ones without yellow streaks are on this side of the leaf?"

"Well, what do you know!" she answered with a perfectly straight face. "Those on your side are, at that!"

Hal carefully took one of the strips with pale yellow streaks—which were, in fact, almost invisible—and bit cautiously into it. The pith from the ripe plant was as bland-tasting as Amanda had said, with a flavor like bread and a decided texture. It was, indeed, more like chewing a crusty home-baked loaf than anything else he could think of.

"From now on," he told her. "I expect you to warn me as I go, if something's going to be flame-hot or anything else."

"I will," she said. Her voice was suddenly serious. "I'm sorry, Hal. You should have known me when I was young—but I forget, you couldn't have. Anyway, I didn't have all that much time to play, even then. There was always too much to learn. You're sure your head's going to be all right?"

"Positive," he said. An unusual softness and gentleness made itself felt in him suddenly. "I'll bet you didn't have much time to play, at that, when you were small."

"You didn't either," she said, almost fiercely.

He opened his mouth to disagree, then realized that she was right. From the time word had come of his uncle James's death, little of his time had gone into recreation, compared to that of the boys and girls his own age around Foralie.

"That was different," he said. "I deliberately chose my life."

"Do you think I didn't choose mine?" she said. "The Second Amanda may have picked me to follow her when I was too young to have any say in the matter. But she picked me because of what I was when I was born. I was too young to know what I wanted to drive myself toward; but the driving was already in me, and working. But she saw it, even then, and gave it a goal, that was all. After that, I worked the way I did for her because it was what I wanted to do not because it was something I *had* to do. I'd have been the third Amanda among the Morgans, no matter what my name or my training!"

"Well," he said, still gently, "we are what we are now, in any case."

They finished eating and took up their traveling again.

The day warned as the sun rose, but it did not become so

much warmer as to be actively uncomfortable. Still, with Procyon now a white point too bright to be looked anywhere close to, in the greenish-blue sky overhead, Hal found himself grateful for the fact they could walk in the shade of the vegetation alongside the road.

That vegetation was thick, but not tangled. It was undeniably tropical or perhaps it could be called subtropical, but if the latter, barely so. For one thing they were at a considerable altitude above sea level; for another, the angle of the planet to its orbit was something just over ten degrees less than that Old Earth made to its orbit, so that the tropical zone here was wider. Down in the steamy lowlands near sea level, the wild vegetation could honestly be called impenetrable jungle. Here, in spite of the fact it supported tropical fruits and warm-country plants, it had more of the openness of a forest. It would be possible to move through it at good speed without cutting one's way, as they would have had to do in the coastal jungle. There were even small, open, natural glades, as well as those areas that had been cleared for homes and their surrounding grounds.

But the roadside trees were tall enough—both the natives and those variforms which had been imported and found a home here—that the shade was pleasantly thick. The brilliant sky above was cloudless; and both before and behind them were the two ranges of mountains—what had Amanda called them? Oh, yes, the Zipaca and the Grandfathers of Dawn. It was the Zipaca that held the new Chantry Guild, and lay before them. The Grandfathers were behind.

Both were sharp-peaked. Geologically young ranges, clearly by their appearance. They seemed to diverge to the far left; though this could not be established certainly, for in that direction the land became lost in distance and a blue haze. By the same token they seemed to angle together at the right, though this could also be an illusion of the distance. Ahead of Hal and Amanda, the land lifted gradually upward toward the Zipacas. But only gradually. In the main, between the ranges it was tableland; flat, with only an occasional swell or depression.

"Where's the river?" Hal asked.

Amanda turned to smile at him.

"So," she said, "you've been figuring out the terrain."

"We're all but surrounded by watersheds in the shape of those ranges," Hal said.. "And the general landslope is against us. There should be a fair number of smaller streams off the mountain slopes—particularly that of the Zipacas, ahead, to a large river running downward and back past where we landed."

"Right you are," said Amanda, "there is. It's called the Cold River, and we landed just about half a kilometer this side of it, so we've been angling away from it. We'll also be crossing a few small streams today, but that's all. The place I'm taking you to is short of the next large stream off the mountains that feeds into the main river."

Hal nodded.

"From what I've seen so far," he said, "this valley land ought to be overlaying older, sedimentary rock, younger than the ranges."

"Right. The ranges are young and still growing," answered Amanda, "and you're right, the rock under us here is sedimentary. In fact, you'll see the lower reaches of the mountains, when we come to them, are mainly limestone and sandstone, sheathing the granites and other igneous rocks that pushed up inside it. That's the reason the mountains seem to rise so suddenly from the valley floor. What you'll be looking at are slabs of the valley rock broken off and upended by the mountain rock lifting beneath it. The Exotics liked the contrast of building the peaceful sort of homes they made, in a geologically dramatic area like this one."

"Little good it's done them," said Hal, looking at the road alongside them. "They've ended up getting drama with a vengeance."

Into the tar-black, melted-earth surface of the road, deep ruts had been gouged.

"The garrison people drove heavy machinery along these roads deliberately to break them down," Amanda said. "It's part of their organized plan of destruction. Bleys isn't waiting for the normal effects of time, and the war with Earth, to manage his 'withering away' process for Kultis and Mara. The Exotics produce nothing he needs; and the Occupation troops he sent have all but explicit orders to keep trying to squeeze the local people until the last one's dead."

"Squeeze them?"

"Well, you see the road," said Amanda. "In addition to that kind of destruction, they've burned down all the country homes they didn't have a use for themselves; and made the people who had lived in them move into the nearest town or city. There, they've made them live in row house apartments they forced them to build for themselves, quickly and out of flimsy materials. Also, the town or city populace is under all sorts of rationing and restrictions. Every day the people there have to stand in line for hours for their chance to buy the barest necessities. I mean they're *deliberately* forced to stand in line for not enough of anything to go around, available from stores that can only be open too few hours a day to supply everyone who needs things. Then, there's a curfew at night and strict laws even about how and where you can move about in the towns during the day—that's why we're timing this little walk to get to the gates of Porphyry just a little before they close for the day, at sixteen hundred hours—not much more than midafternoon, here."

"We're catching up with someone," Hal said, pointing ahead.

"That's right," said Amanda. "You'll see more and more traffic as we get close to town. All the former off planet workers here—they were mainly from Ste. Marie"—Ste. Marie was a somewhat smaller agricultural world a little farther out from Procyon than the two planets of the Exotics—"were shipped home; and most of the large farming areas they operated on both Mara and Kultis are deserted now, with no Exotics allowed to try and run them. The locals here can only get permits to go out of their town for about three hours a day, on certain days, to farm family plots of land that're too small, or too useless otherwise, to do them much good anyway. That's why we ran into that bunch last night, who were undoubtedly staying out overnight, breaking curfew so they could get some real work done on an illegal extra field, by moonlight. They just hope a surprise housecheck doesn't turn them up missing, meantime. It's part of the game to quarter the soldiers on the civilian populace, to the advantage of the soldiers and a better surveillance of the populace."

They had almost caught up now with the traveler ahead of them, who was a thin, balding man in middle age, pushing a handcart. He nodded in answer to their greeting as they passed but said nothing, evidently saving his breath for the job of maneuvering the wheels of the handcart amongst the ruts on the road—the cart being too wide for the more shady edge on which Hal and Amanda were traveling. There was nothing more than a scattering of sweet potatoes in the bottom of the cart; but the cart itself was obviously homemade, and clumsy as well as heavy. The man was streaming with sweat from pushing it in the sun.

"He's taking the potatoes home to eat, or to sell?" Hal asked, once they were far enough past to be out of hearing.

"Either that, or to barter with a neighbor," said Amanda.

"He'd do better to put a bunch that small into a sack."

"Against the law," said Amanda. "All produce, to be legal inside the city, must be brought in by cart, theoretically to let the gate guards inspect it for amount, which is limited, per trip; and possible plant diseases, of which there aren't any."

They went on their way, and traffic, as Amanda had predicted, increased. All were people headed into the city, rather than away from it. A fair share of those were men or women with handcarts, like the man they had seen. Others simply carried sacks which, Hal assumed, contained something of value that was not produce. More than a few had the word DESTRUCT! marked in large letters with black paint on the front or back of their robes.

"A lot of town-to-town travelers," said Hal.

"No, they're local, too. Anything personal has to be brought in by the sack that's forbidden for produce—another law. The ones carrying those are townspeople who're taking advantage of the regulation that lets them use their free hours outside the city to scavenge the ruins of their old country property for anything useful inside town—not that anything really valuable will get by the gate guards. If there was, it'd be taken 'for inspection' to ensure there's nothing contraband hidden inside it. Scavengers are what we're supposed to be, you and I. I've got a fake address to give the gate guards. Theoretically, you and I have been out hunting through what's left of our old homestead."

"I see," said Hal. They went on.

A sadness that seemed always to lurk inside him lately was beginning to grow once more to uncomfortable strength, as it had when he had stood in his quarters at the Encyclopedia, surrounded by the image of the estate as it had been at that moment down on Old Earth.

Now, sister birch, white-armed . . .

Essentially, the ruined buildings, the destroyed and harassed people she pointed out to him, were his doing. Doubly his doing, for it was his going back in spirit to animate the body of Paul Formain in the twentieth century that had helped lead to this. If he had not done that, there would not have been the splitting apart of the investigative animal instinct in every human, one part to adventure and grow, one to hold back, to stay safe and unchanged. He had set humanity free, for this.

He had done it only so that the inner conflict could become an outer one. So that the two conflicting urges could choose up adherents of individual humans and resolve the eons-old argument in an open conflict—from which would come what he had then been sure would be an inevitable victory for the part of humanity that wanted to grow.

But he had underestimated, even then, the complexity and strength in the balance of historic forces; the interweaving of every interaction between every human. That interweaving sought stability; and to get that stability, it had responded to his efforts by giving birth to those maverick, talented individuals who called themselves the Others; and whom none of the three great Splinter Cultures could conquer or control. Not the Exotics who had grown from the original Chantry Guild of Formain's time: nor the Friendlies, who had grown from the purely sectarian fanaticisms of Old Earth into the populations of two worlds which had produced true faith-holders like Rukh; nor yet the Dorsai, who had evolved from brutal soldiers-for-hire to a people who placed independence, honor and duty above all other things.

The Others had come; and utterly conquered, in effect, all the Younger Worlds except those of the Dorsai, Friendlies and Exotics. So these last, they had done their best to ruin. And he, Hal Mayne, who had been born the Dorsai Donal Graeme, had compounded the damage he had done as Paul Formain, by leaving the remaining populations of those Splinter Cultures helpless before the Others, while he withdrew the best that each of the three Cultures had to the defense of Old Earth. An Old Earth that was only now just beginning to appreciate what had been done for it.

And to what end? All this sacrifice had been made so that he, himself, should be free to find what no one else had ever been able to find before—a magic, hidden universe that would at once confound the Others and open a new stage of evolution for the human race. It had been a vain sacrifice. In the end, he had failed everyone else, after they had given the best of what they had, only to provide him with the chance. Worst of all . . .

The pain mounted in him.

It was the deep hurt now inside him that was the per-

sonal retribution the historic forces had brought upon him
for the damage he had done; and he had not even let himself recognize it until last night, when he had taken a blow
on the head no adult combat-trained Dorsai would have
taken, through his own ineptitude. . . .

So now he must face it.

He was no longer a Dorsai.

He realized now that he had not been one for a long
time; but for that same long time he had refused to face the
fact. Now, it was inescapable. There were the Dorsai; and
there was Hal Mayne, who had been Donal. But Donal was
gone; and Hal Mayne had never been one of them, for all
that he had believed himself to be so. He was separated
from them as surely as Bleys had been locked away, once
in a dream of Hal's behind a gate of iron bars.

He half closed his eyes at the agony of realization. But it
mounted still inside him, until he suddenly found his
elbow caught, and the forward motion of his walking body
stopped in its tracks. He was turned, and looked down into
the face of Amanda.

"What is it?" she said.

He opened his mouth to tell her; but he could not
answer. His throat was so tight that no words were able to
force their way out.

Amanda flung her arms around him and pressed herself
against him, pressing her face into his shoulder.

"My dearest dear," she said. "What is it? Tell me?"

Instinctively, his own arms went around her. He held to
her, this one living link with humanity that he had; as if to
let go would be to lose not only that life, itself, but all eternity before and after it. His voice came, brokenly and
hoarsely, out of him.

"I've lost my people . . ."

It was all he could manage to say. But somehow she
read through them to what was in him. She led him away
from the road, out of sight of it. There, she made him sit
down with his back to a tree and fitted herself to him, as if

he was dangerously chilled and she would warm him with her body. He held her, and they lay together wordlessly.

He felt a tremendous comfort in her presence and her closeness to him. But it brought peace only to the top level of his mind. Below that was an ever-widening wound; as if he was a figure cut out of cardboard in which a hole had been made with a pinprick, which was now being enlarged and torn apart into a long rip by a pressure too great for him to resist.

But his gratitude for her comfort at this time was immeasurable. After a little while, still unable to speak, he lifted one hand and began to slowly stroke the shining curve of her hair. It seemed so wonderful to him that she should be this beautiful and this near to him; and so quickly understanding of what was breaking him apart inside.

After a long silence, she spoke.

"Now, listen to me," she said. "You've lost nothing."

Her voice was low and soft, but very certain.

"I have." His voice was ragged with tears he did not know how to shed. "First I sold my people into a death contract; then I lost them."

"You did neither," she said, in the same soft, even tones.

"Do you remember when you came to the Dorsai to talk about our folk coming—as many as could—to help defend Old Earth?"

"And I met you," he said.

"You met the Grey Captains, and I was one of them."

"You arranged for the rest to meet me," he said, "and I sold them a contract with the Encyclopedia, to die, defending Earth."

"You sold nothing," she said, her voice unhurried, unchanged. "Have you already forgotten that the chance of death was always a part of any Dorsai military contract? Of those who met with you, only two others besides myself had never actually been in the field. Do you think, even not counting those three, that the men and women you talked to had not realized, long before, that one day they would have to face the Others? It was only a question of where or how."

She paused, as if to let her words sink in.

"You showed them those things, as you had to others, when the part of you that was Donal broke through to your surface," she went on, "and made it plain to all of us; as he had always made things plain to people. Has your opinion of the Dorsai mind fallen so low that you think *they*—the Grey Captains—thought they could forever put off an eventual conflict with the Others? When it was the Others who wanted everything humanly owned, including the Dorsai itself? Our people couldn't become the assassins that the Exotics asked them to be, to kill the Others one by one; because life isn't worth certain costs, particularly if that cost is the abandonment of what you believe in. But you showed them a way to fight in the way they knew how to fight; and they took that way. How could it have been otherwise?"

He could not answer. What she said went through and through him; and, if it did not heal the great rent in him, it at least stopped its growing.

"And you've lost no one," she went on after a while, still quietly. "You've only gone on ahead of everyone else a little way; so that you've passed over a hill which blocks your view of the rest of us when you looked back. You've stared at that hill so long now, you've come to believe it's all space and time. But it's not. You've lost no one. Instead, you've joined in the whole human race, of which the Dorsai were always a part—but only a part. You've gone on from where Donal stood, alone and solitary."

They continued to sit for some while after that, neither of them speaking. Slowly, what she had just said soaked into him, as sea water slowly soaks into a floating length of timber, until at last it can hold no more; and so, water-logged, it begins to sink slowly and quietly to the far bottom.

So, in time, what she had told him brought relief. He could not believe her, much as he would have liked to do so. Because, much as she was Amanda and understood, he thought he recognized his own life, and his own failure, in a way no one else could. But the very fact that she had tried to warm the chill of despair from him like this, as she might have warmed him back from a death-chill, helped him. So that in time he came back again to her and all other things. The pain that had come from the great torn place inside him was still with him; but it had at last become bearable, as bearable as his headache from the blow had become, when he had pushed it away from the center of his attention, out to the fringes of his consciousness.

"We'd better go on," he said at last.

They got up and went back to the edge of the road, and continued along it under the pale brilliant star of Procyon toward the destination she had in mind for him.

CHAPTER 11 ■

Procyon had started to lower in the sky, but the Kultan evening was still quite distant when they came out of a belt of trees to see the edge of the village of Porphyry before them. The last half mile or so, traffic on the road had increased heavily in comparison to what it had been earlier; but those they passed, or who passed them, moved at some little distance from each other. Enough so that any of the travelers who were moving together could talk privately merely by lowering their voices.

Hall had been roused from the oppression of his own inner feelings by his interest in those sharing the road— and apparently their destination—with them. They had seen no one headed away from Porphyry. And these people were all Exotics. They showed it in many little ways— their calmness of feature and economy of movements, for instance. But Hal noticed that none of those they caught up with, or were passed by, seemed to be indulging in conversation simply for conversation's sake. In fact, none they passed seemed to feel it necessary to greet Hal, Amanda, or each other. At most they only acknowledged the presence of others with a gentle smile or nod.

But versions of these elements had been part of the Exotic character as long as Hal, or Donal, had known members of this Splinter Culture. What he noticed now, and a startling difference it seemed to him, was that there was something extraordinarily self-contained about these sharing the road with them. It was hard to say whether it was a change in the direction of growth or not. It was as if each had drawn inside himself or herself, and now lived a private life behind the drawn curtains of their calm faces. There was an individualism that was new in them; an individualism noticeably different from the communal feeling that had always appeared to be an integral part of the Exotics he had known; from Paoma the Outbond, when he had been Donal, to Walter the InTeacher, Hal Mayne's tutor. In no way did those about him seem a beaten or conquered people, in spite of their circumstances.

But at the same time, he got a feeling from them now as if part of the warmth that had always characterized the Exotics was now withdrawn. Not gone; pulled back away inside them, coiled like a spring under tension—but, somehow, not gone.

"We'll be at the gate in a few minutes," Amanda said, interrupting his thoughts; and he looked ahead to see a tall wooden wall, evidently recently built, surrounding what was plainly their destination. It reached to the side and back as far as Hal could see in either direction, and their road led to a wide gate as tall as the wall itself.

"Let me do the talking to the guards," Amanda said. "You're my idiot big brother; I mean, you're literally a little slow-witted. The cliches that work best are the old cliches. Look stupid."

Hal obediently slumped his shoulders, let his face go

slack and his mouth hang slightly open. There was a jam-up of people at the gates, of course; but those coming in gathered close together and waited with little talk, and without raising their voices when they did speak, any more than they had on the road. It was reasonable, Hal thought, that they should be so. Those he watched would have been brought up as children to never abandon a conversational tone and volume; and in spite of their present condition, that training would persist in them.

And yet, thought Hal again, watching them behind the mask of his loose jaw and expressionless face, there was something more going on here than just childhood training. There was something quietly in opposition to the uniformed men who were checking them. It was not a quietness of fear in any sense, but one of strength that the uniformed men did not have, or even understand.

It was curious.

At the same time, he was aware of something that was going on for him, personally, him alone. It had nothing to do with what he believed he had just seen in the people around him. It was totally unrelated to it—or was it?

It was a curious sensation of having been part of just such a scene as this, once before. He could not say why; but he felt an element that was medieval about the wooden walls, the wooden gates, the swarm of people in their rough and unlovely clothing, waiting their turn to be passed inside by the guards. It triggered off a conviction that somehow, somewhere, he had lived through this before. Not him, but someone very like him as he now was, had stood almost as he was now standing, seen much what he was now seeing, and waited with such a crowd in such a place as this. . . .

The guards, thought Hal, concentrating on them to get his mind back on ordinary channels—if these were typical of the garrison troops here, they were poor stuff indeed. They were neatly enough uniformed, in black, with power pistols holstered on their hip and swagger sticks at their belt or under their arms; but they were not really soldiers.

Hal Mayne had never seen actual soldiers on duty. Soldiers who were purely that; instead of half-police, like the Militia that Rukh's Command had fought against on Harmony. But Donal Graeme had been brought up to work with troops; and to anticipate that his life might depend on his ability to read their value at a glance.

It was Donal's eye, therefore, that now told Hal that the eight men he saw on duty at this gate were not only useless; but for practical purposes untrainable to be anything better than the bullies of unarmed civilians they presently were. Ian, Donal's uncle, who had trained troops for Donal after the assassination of Kensie, Ian's twin, would have stripped all eight of their uniforms on sight.

If the rest of the soldiers in garrison here were like these, it was likely that, weapons and all, they would break and run in the face of any serious riot; even a riot of Exotics, who, had they been any other people, would have risen against any such flimsy oppressors, long since.

But he and Amanda had now reached the gate, at the head of the crowd of waiting people. He concentrated on looking as harmless as possible for one of his size and appearance.

"Open up," said the uniformed man confronting them. He was obviously from one of the Friendly worlds. Hal had learned to recognize such in any guise, after his experience on Harmony—though this one's appearance on his surface was completely at odds both with the people Hal had met around Rukh, and his present uniform. He was oriental, young, round-faced and innocent-looking. Nonetheless, he went through the contents of their two sacks with reasonable efficiency.

"All right. Go on in. Home address?"

"Sixteen, thirty-six, seven, Happiness Lane," answered Amanda. "Downstairs apartment."

The gate guard repeated the address into his wrist recorder and turned away from them to the two bag-carrying women behind him. Hal and Amanda were free to go.

"What about that address?" Hal asked as soon as they

were far enough down the road within the gates that they were no longer too closely surrounded by others to speak without being overheard.

"It's the home of three brothers, none of which look at all like you," she answered.

"I mean, why did he ask for it?"

"They do an automatic check to see that people who've left for the day are back in their homes that night by curfew."

"But what'll happen when they find they don't even know of us at that address?"

"The one checking is going to figure the guard at the gate transposed a couple of numbers, or otherwise got the address wrong. Then he'll forget about it. They don't worry that much about people getting in, they worry about them getting out."

"I see," said Hal. "Where are we headed, then?"

"There're a few serious resistance people in every town," said Amanda. "We're going to one named Nier. She lives alone with her mother and a soldier who's quartered on them. He's a sub-officer who likes night duty; so he's not there after sundown, ordinarily. The result is, they've got room to put us up overnight; and, in addition, Nier's made something of a friend of the sub-officer, which gives them a few advantages, including freedom from a housecheck under normal conditions. I want you to talk to Nier."

"Does she live anywhere near Happiness Lane?" asked Hal dryly.

Amanda laughed.

"The other side of the town," she said. "Come on."

The streets within the walls had not been rutted and were in good shape. They had entered at what was evidently an older part of it, for the buildings were large and faced with white stone. Their fellow travelers went off in different directions among the streets of this section and there were few sackcloth robes to be seen after several blocks. There were, however, a number of uniformed soldiers who seemed to be off duty, either moving about the streets or going in and out of buildings that Hal thought might be either restaurants or drinking places. Amanda noticed Hal watching one clearly inebriated soldier entering one of the latter.

"Alcohol's the only intoxicant allowed—even to the troops," she said. "Probably because of the difficulty of enforcement. You can ferment almost any vegetable into a beverage with at least some alcohol in it. Adding a sugar of some kind helps, of course. So since they can't stop the making of illegal liqueurs by their own people, they let their soldiers drink the best the planet can produce. The civilians, of course are officially Exotics who don't drink; though that's changed for a few of them in the last two years."

"There was a joke among the troops on Ceta, a cousin who'd been on a contract there told the rest of us in the family once," Hal said absently, dropping back into Donal's memories. "That you could even make an alcoholic drink by fermenting dead rats. Impossible, of course, but the idea was to talk new recruits into drinking a homebrew, then tell them a story that'd made them sick. . . ."

He was completely in Donal's persona for the moment, Amanda noticed with some satisfaction. She had hoped to trigger some of those older memories by what she would show him. That part of him that was Donal had uses he had been too quick to forget.

They came finally to the new section of town, where the controlled locals lived. In less than two years it had become an obvious slum, its only redeeming feature being a cleanliness which was a result of ingrained habit in the older Exotics, which had caused the streets and building fronts to keep a relative decency of appearance. Here and there, a small bunch of flowers had been put in a window, or an attempt had been made to plant something decorative in the small strip of earth between the edge of the street and the front wall of a house.

Amanda turned in at the door of one of the innumerable

look-alike row houses and knocked. There was no response. She waited for what seemed to Hal an unusually long time, then knocked again. They waited. At last there was the sound of shoeleather on bare wooden flooring beyond the door, and the door itself swung back.

It opened just enough to show a woman in her fifties with a face the sagging flesh of which told of recently lost weight. Her gray hair was cut relatively short, pulled back and tied more in a ponytail than a bun, though its bunching at the back had something of the characteristics of both. She stared at them blankly.

"Marlo!" said Amanda. "Don't you know me? It's me, Corrin, and Kaspar, one of my brothers. Is Nier here? I'd like her to meet him."

"No. No, she's not."

The woman Amanda had called Marlo had opened the door just enough so that the width of her body blocked it. She raised her voice as if she wanted someone inside to hear her answering. "She doesn't live with me anymore. She went to work and live at the garrison—"

A man's voice shouted something unintelligible from inside.

"Nothing!" she called back over her shoulder. "Just some people asking about Nier. I told them to go find her at the barracks."

She looked back out at Hal and Amanda, and her face contorted suddenly into a grimace of desperate warning. She jerked her head minutely, as if to signal them to move on up the street.

But already there were the sounds of steps on the floor behind her. The door was pulled all the way open and a somewhat overweight man of medium height appeared as he pushed the old woman aside. He was wearing black military slacks and a white shirt, unbuttoned at the neck. His face was made up of small features—small eyes, small nose and small mouth. It showed a full twenty-six hours of stubble. He was in his late thirties or early forties and his red hair was graying. Through the stubble, freckles could still be seen on the weathered skin of his face and the backs of his small, soft-looking hands.

"Well, well," he said, in a voice that had a bullfrog-like croak to it. He was not drunk, but there was a slight thickening to his words that showed he was on his way to being so. "Look at this. An oversize bull, and an oversize cala lily. And you used to be friends of our dear, departed Nier, were you?"

"She barely knew Nier. This is her brother, who's never met Nier," said Marlo quickly.

"Well, well, what of it?" said the soldier. "I'm Corporal Iban. Where's your manners, Marlo? Invite these good friends of Nier's inside!"

He stood back from the door.

"I'm Corrin," said Amanda as they came into a small room that was at once kitchen, dining and living room. "My brother's name is Kaspar."

The kitchen sink, cooking surface and cupboards occupied the corner to the right of the door as they entered. Before them was a kitchen table with one straight chair drawn up to it, and on it was a bottle of clear glass three-quarters full of colorless liquid, standing beside a half-empty tumbler. Beyond were three more chairs like the one at the table and a porch bench with back, which had been furnished with cushions, obviously homemade.

"Well, now, you're really a cala lily, Corrin," said Iban. He ran his eyes over Amanda, grinning a little. "You don't know what a cala lily is, do you? But I do. It's an Earth flower. I've seen a picture of one; and you're a cala lily, all right. Yes, you are."

He gestured widely to the table.

"Sit down," he said, taking his own seat in the one chair that was already at the table. "Pull up chairs. Let's get to know each other."

Marlo hastened to help with the chairs.

"I didn't say you could sit down!" Iban's voice was abruptly ugly and his eyes were on Marlo.

Suddenly a small coal of anger glowed in the ashes of Hal's inner unhappiness with himself, so that for a moment the unhappiness was forgotten. Perhaps he could no longer think of himself as Dorsai; but nonetheless there was still the strength and knowledge in him to lay his hands on this soft-muscled bully; and by the very power and capability of the grip make the other aware that he could be broken like a dry stick. This much he could do—

Hal forced the unexpected reaction from him. That was not the way. He had learned it long since.

"I was just going to help . . ."

"Ah, that's all right, then. Yes, help. Help yourself to a drink, Lily; and you—whatever your name is. Get some glasses, woman!"

Marlo hurried to get two more tumblers.

"His name's Kaspar," said Amanda.

"Kaspar. You told me that. Kaspar—" Abruptly Iban laughed and drank, and laughed again. Seeing the other two tumblers were now on the table, he poured a small amount from the bottle into each one. "Drink up."

Amanda took a delicate sip from hers and put the tumbler back down again in front of her.

"It's strong," she said.

"Oh yes, it's strong," said Iban. Hal was trying to place the man's origins. He was neither Exotic, Friendly, Dorsai, nor a mix of any of those sub-cultures. Not educated enough for someone from Cassida or Newton. He might be from New Earth, where there was still a polyglot of subcultures, or Ceta, where there was even more. Iban suddenly turned on him.

"You, Kaspar!" said Iban sharply. "You drink!"

Hal picked up his tumbler and swallowed the inch or so of liquid inside it. It was a high-proof distilled liquor, a little too smooth in taste to have been made in some backyard still; unless on the Exotics nowadays they had some very good backyard stills. He thought that if the other had any idea of amusing himself by watching as the stranger got drunk on an unaccustomed (as alcohol would be to most Exotics) intoxicant, he would find himself very mistaken. Hal had not had a drink in over three years, but he had discovered in the Coby mines that it took more to get him drunk than it did most people.

"Kaspar," said Iban. He poured a somewhat larger amount into Hal's tumbler. "That's a dog's name. Good Kaspar. Lap that up, Kaspar."

Hal picked up the glass.

"I said lap it!" snapped Iban. "Not drink it, Kaspar. Lap it!"

"My tongue's too short," said Hal mildly, sticking his tongue down into the glass to show it could not reach the liquid within.

"You!" said Iban to Marlo, without turning his head. "Get a saucer!"

Marlo obeyed, putting the saucer without orders on the table in front of Hal.

"Pour it into the saucer, Kaspar," said Iban. "That's right. Now lap it up like a good dog—"

He shoved his chair back suddenly, its legs screeching on the bare floor, and got up.

"—And just in case you don't know how to lap, I'm going to teach you," he said over his shoulder, going through an inner doorway into the unlighted room beyond and around a corner out of their sight. His voice came back to them from the empty doorway. "It's a useful trick for a dog like you to have, you know?"

He came out again, carrying a power pistol, which he brought with him back to the table. He sat down, resting the thick, dark barrel of the pistol on the edge of the unvarnished tabletop, so that the large thumb-sized hole in its muzzle pointed directly at Hal.

"Now, this is how we do it," he said. "I say lap, and you bend your head down and start lapping with your tongue from the saucer until it's all gone. Ready? Now, lap!"

Hal bent down and began to lap. It was a clumsy way of getting the liquid into his mouth, but finally he got most of it swallowed.

"Now lick the plate clean. That's right. Lift your head up." Iban poured more of the liquor into the saucer. "You didn't do so good, last time, so we'll try it again. That's the way we do things in the Occupational Troops. Now—"

"Oh, don't make him drink another one!" said Amanda.

Iban turned his attention on her. So did Hal, in case the words were supposed to convey some hidden message to him.

"Our brother Court drank some of that once," said Amanda, "and it made him awfully sick!"

She might, thought Hal, have had a little more faith in his common sense. He was hardly about to take the man's gun away and break his neck, here in the very house where the other had been quartered; in spite of his unexpected earlier flare of fury. Then he realized that the message was not what he had assumed. What she wanted was for either one of them to put this man harmlessly out of action, and she was giving him a chance to do it whatever way he had in mind, first.

"Well, he should have gone right back and tried it again, Lily," said Iban. "That's the point. You've got to practice, practice, to learn things like that. Now, we don't want to make that mistake with Kaspar, here, do we?"

He stared hard at her for a long moment, then let his stubbled face relax into another grin.

"But of course, for you, Lily, if you don't want Brother here to lap any more, of course I don't want to make you feel bad. So I won't do it. How do you like that?"

"Thank you. Thank you very much," said Amanda.

"Of course. Anything to make you happy. Because I want to make you happy, you know that?" Iban leaned forward toward her and, finding the table in the way, beckoned her. "Bring your chair around here, beside me."

Amanda obeyed.

Hal permitted himself a slight scowl.

"You leave my sister alone," he said to Iban. "If you don't I'll put the bad eye on you. You'll be sorry."

"The bad eye?" echoed Iban absently, not even looking

at Hal, but into the eyes of Amanda, which were now less than a quarter of a meter from his own. Then the words seemed to penetrate. He turned his gaze on Hal. "The bad eye! What kind of stupid superstition's that?"

"If I look in your eyes you'll be sorry. My eyes'll eat you up."

"Oh, they will, will they?" Iban turned and stared directly into Hal's eyes. The eyes of the soldier were a muddy brown in color, the whites bloodshot. "All right, I'm looking in your eyes. Now, you better be able to eat me up or you're going to be sorry you said anything like that. Well, what're you waiting for? Go ahead. Eat me up!"

"The quality of mercy is not strained," said Hal in a soft voice, but one which carried clearly across the table to the other man, *"it droppeth as the gentle rain from heaven—"*

"What?"

"—upon the place beneath. That quality of mercy is strong within you, Iban. You are greater than any normal man in that which you have inside you. You are large, generous, compassionate; and you have a duty to yourself to make sure that all other people know this and bow down before it. . . ."

Hal went on talking, in the same soft, persuasive voice, until at last he stopped. When he did, Iban sat still, his eyes still fixed on Hal's. His gaze remained fixed on the place where Hal's eyes had been even when Hal leaned back in his chair and looked over toward Amanda.

"Oh, oh," said Hal. "I got Marlo, too."

Slightly off to one side, standing a couple of steps behind Iban's chair, Marlo was also motionless, with the same, unmoving gaze.

"Marlo," said Hal sharply. "No! Not you! Come out of it!"

The older woman blinked and stirred. She stared at the three of them.

"What . . . ?" she said.

"An Exotic and susceptible to a hypnotic trick like

that?" said Hal. "For shame. It was an Exotic that taught it to me, and a half-Exotic tried it on me once."

"I . . . I never learned," said Marlo. "Was that what it was?"

"Of course," said Hal. "You sit down now and relax." He turned back to Iban.

"Listen to me, Iban," he said. "Are you listening? Look at me."

"Yes, Kaspar," said Iban quietly, quitting the fixed focus of his eyes to turn their gaze on Hal.

"Listen to me now and remember this for a long time. Today, when you were having a day off—"

Hal broke off, turning to look at Marlo.

"That's what it was, today, wasn't it?" he asked her. "A day off duty for him?"

"Yes," Marlo said. "He goes back on at eight tomorrow morning. He's on day-duty, not nights, like the other . . ."

"I thought so." He turned back to Iban. "Iban, you were having this day off; and late in the day, who should come to the front door but a couple of lost children? It seems their parents were visiting here, by special permission, from another place—they were too young to tell you what their parents' names were, who the relatives were they were staying with, or anything but their names—which you've since forgotten. You were feeling generous, so after amusing yourself with making the little boy take a few drinks, you gave them permission to stay here overnight and their parents could be found tomorrow. Have you got that?"

"Oh yes, every word, Kaspar," said Iban, nodding.

"Good. Now, the children fell asleep in a corner and you forgot about them and went to sleep yourself. You slept clear through until the next day, except for a moment or two about midnight when there was a knock at the door and the parents showed up looking for the children. You gave them the children—you were too sleepy to ask them for any names or papers—and went back to bed. You went right back to sleep, and slept through until time to get up the next morning, after which everything went as usual—except for one thing."

He got up, took the bottle of liquor and poured it out in the kitchen sink. He came back to stand at the table and put the empty bottle in front of Iban.

"When you got up," he said to the other man, "you found you'd drunk the whole bottle by yourself the evening before—and you didn't even have a hangover. That'll be something to tell when you get over to the garrison. A whole bottle and not even a trace of a hangover. It really will be something to tell them, won't it?"

"It sure will," said Iban.

"Now," said Hal, "since you finished off the bottle, maybe you better get some sleep to be ready for duty tomorrow."

"Y'right," said Iban thickly. He got to his feet, got himself turned around and wavered unsteadily back toward and finally into the room from which he had brought out the power pistol. They heard him fall on the bed. Hal picked up the pistol and took it to the doorway and tossed it in to fall beside the man's bed.

"Iban!" he said. "Iban, answer me! You can still hear me, can't you?"

"Yesss," sighed the voice thickly from within.

"Remember how this shows that Marlo's good luck for you. No hangover's just a sample of the kind of good luck you've had since getting quartered here. It's all due to Marlo. You're good luck for each other. She knows that, that's why she takes such good care of you. You've got to remember to take good care of her. If you want that good luck to keep going. You'll remember that, won't you, Iban? You like Marlo; and even if you didn't, she's such good luck for you, you want to keep her well and happy, isn't that right?"

"Yesss . . ."

"All right, you can go to sleep now."

This time the answer was the first of a steady succession of snores.

Hal turned back into the room. Marlo burst into tears where she stood and Amanda moved to put her arms around the older woman.

Marlo was weeping hoarsely and deeply. Amanda led her off into the back of the house, through another door that evidently opened, from what Hal glimpsed, on another small bedroom. The door closed behind both women.

Hal went up to it.

"I think I'll take a bit of a walk," he said through the door panel.

"Fine. Get back here before twenty-two hundred hours. That's curfew," Amanda's voice answered him.

"I will."

He went out.

The streets outside were full of hurrying people in sack-cloth robes, none of whom paid any attention to him or each other. They gave the impression of racing against a deadline. Hal estimated that perhaps one in ten had the word DESTRUCT! painted on his or her robe. He wandered the streets, trying to get the feel of the community about him.

It was a strange feel. The locals had all the appearance and attitudes of a populace so downtrodden that it lived in fear and without hope or dignity. And still, there was something innately independent and stubbornly survival-istic about the controlled voices, the courtesy with which interactions went on; from the apparently welcome, if brief conversations between encountering individuals who seemed to be friends, to the chance collisions of those hurrying so that they bumped into each other before they could stop.

Much was gone, but something yet remained. The words from Alfred, Lord Tennyson's poem *Ulysses* came back to him. The question in his mind now was whether what remained was something upon which an Exotic structure could still build—or was this once-powerful Splinter Culture finished forever?

He could not tell. It was tempting to hope, but . . . he saw it was getting close to eighteen hundred hours and he was still some distance from Marlo's residence. He had automatically mapped his wanderings in the back of his head so that he knew he had about eight blocks to go to get back to it.

He turned toward it.

Amanda was sitting on the cushioned picnic bench in the front room when he got there. There was the smell of cooking in the air. She got up as he came in, shutting the front door behind him.

"Where's Marlo?" he asked.

"Asleep," said Amanda. "I waded into the supplies here and cooked food for the three of us. But I think she needs sleep more than she needs something to eat—though she needs that badly enough. I'll leave her food in dishes in her room; and she can eat it cold, or warm it if she likes, whenever she wakes during the night. She's bound to wake sometime. Meanwhile, you sit down and we'll have ours."

Hal sat. The meal Amanda dished up for them was nothing like the fare an Exotic house might have given a visitor once upon a time; but it was a solid dinner, with beans and local vegetables in a sort of curry, highly spiced, with local corn bread to go with it and water to drink.

"The water's safe enough. I suppose?" said Hal, lifting his glass.

"The water systems put in by the Exotics still take care of that," said Amanda. "Hal, they evidently caught Nier and the Groupman that was quartered here in some resistance action against the Occupation. Or at least, in something more than a breach of one of the smaller laws. They're undoubtedly both dead. All Marlo knows is that a squad of soldiers came to the house one day when the Groupman was here and took them both away. Marlo says Nier told her that the Groupman was being transferred to a job for which he'd have to live in the garrison from then on; and he'd found a good job for Nier there, too, so she wouldn't be at home anymore. Marlo knew she wasn't telling the truth—just trying to make Marlo feel better. The squad went off with them; and no one's seen either of them since."

Hal shook his head.

"So that's how it is," he said.

"Yes, that's how it is," answered Amanda. Their eyes met. "Do you think the suggestions you gave Iban about being kinder to Marlo are going to last?"

"Anything like that wears off in time," said Hal. "You know as well as I do how strong the powers of recovery are of both mind and body; and that's true even for characters like Iban. But maybe by the time it wears off, he'll have convinced himself it pays to be decent to Marlo. Or it may even have become a habit. He's going to have to excuse his better treatment of her to his fellow soldiers; and people like him tend to end up believing their own excuses, to avoid admitting they could be wrong about anything. But nothing lasts forever. He'll be moved out of this house, sooner or later; and someone else'll be quartered here."

"Yes. Well, we can hope for the best. Who was the half-Exotic you said tried to hypnotize you?"

"Bleys Ahrens," said Hal, "and he almost did. I was very young then, and he's very persuasive. But he was hypnotizing a good-sized group at the time and didn't know I was one of the people he was working on."

"I see," she said. "Well, give me a hand cleaning up—"

"I can do that by myself," said Hal. "Why don't you see if you can't find some clean sheets and blankets for that bed of Iban's? We'll need sleep ourselves if we want to be gone before he wakes up tomorrow, and there's no good reason for letting him have the bed. He can sleep on the floor, the way he is now, and never know the difference."

"Where're you going to put him?" asked Amanda.

"Out here. I think," said Hal, getting up and going back into Iban's bedroom. He lifted the slack body of the sleeping man, carried it out into the main room and dumped it on the cushioned picnic bench. Iban's body was a little large for the piece of furniture, but he did not seem in any immediate danger of rolling off.

"You've got him programmed to believe he got up and answered the door in the night," said Amanda. "Won't he wonder in the morning when he wakes up in this room instead? And if you try to carry him back to his bed before we go, by that time he may be sober enough to wake up."

"You're right, he probably- would wake up. Not that I couldn't just put him back to sleep again if he did. But we don't need to bother with putting him back in his own bed. He'll just think he didn't make it any further back than the bench before folding up." Hal corrected himself. "No, you're right. Of course, he may wonder a bit. But I'm counting on his puffed-up ego over drinking a whole bottle and not having a hangover to knock everything else but that out of his mind. If he regularly drinks his way through his day off, he'll be expecting to wake feeling like a three-day corpse. The face he doesn't ought to be enough by itself to keep him from any dangerous self-questioning. Now, for those dishes and pots."

He had already turned away, when a question occurred to him. He turned back in time to catch her before she left the room for the bedroom.

"Amanda," he said, "what's happened to them, inside, as a result of all this—the Exotics here, I mean?"

She smiled at him.

"You tell me what you think," she answered. "And then I'll let you know if that agrees with my own ideas. Remember? I brought you here to see for yourself. If it'd simply been a matter of telling it, I could have told you back at the Encyclopedia. You tell me; and then I'll let you know how that agrees with what I think I've noticed."

"The Exotics I've always known," said Hal, "were calm, intelligent, reasonable people, all of them. But nearly all of them also had a sort of philosophical arrogance underneath their gentle exteriors. It seems to me these people've had that arrogance planed off them; and they're almost a little surprised to find that the philosophy's still there. Like someone who's had a stand of large and valuable trees burned off land they own. Their first feeling is that they've lost everything. Then they realize that the earth they owned is still there and there's no reason the trees can't be regrown. Maybe even taller and stronger, because of the ashes enriching the soil."

Amanda smiled.

"I'd agree with that," she said. "Did anything about the occupying soldiers strike you, by the way?"

"I haven't seen enough of them to tell," said Hal. "They're sweepings—no good military commander would figure them worth having."

"Sorry," said Amanda. "I put that badly. I should have said—does anything about the way the soldiers react to the Kultans strike you?"

"I haven't really seen enough of that, either. But Marlo seems—they all seem to have made some sort of impression on the soldiers. I can't make out yet just what. Nothing specifically useful to the Exotics. Just a sort of moral ascendancy, which the troopers seem to be acknowledging whether they're consciously aware of it or not."

Amanda smiled again, and nodded. He smiled back at her and turned again to the kitchen as she went off to see about something clean and unused with which to make up Iban's bed.

When Hal came in there, after cleaning up in the kitchen, he found that she had covered the existing layers of bedding with extra blankets; and put down some more for cover, if needed. She was already asleep on the side of the bed against the wall when he got there. Now that he let himself feel it, a strong weariness was in him as well.

He laid himself down softly beside her and closed his eyes. He was ready to sleep; but once his body became inactive, a tribe of unanswered questions that had erupted into his mind at various times of the day came back at him like a mob, clamoring for attention. Ruthlessly, he pushed them from his mind; but they crowded in again.

The difference in the Exotics he had seen here must be only part of what was obviously in process of change about this whole world. Perhaps he should have gone down to Earth from the Final Encyclopedia, this last year, to see for himself how the people there were really changing; as Ajela and Rukh had seemed convinced they were. The coming of the Others appeared to have had a much wider effect on humanity than even he had given it credit for. . . .

He smiled to himself, harshly. Almost he had forgotten that he had given up trying to reach an understanding that would give him the key to the Creative Universe. With an effort he blanked his mind to all these questions and possibilities and, in the dark void that remained, the sleep that his body reached for came easily.

CHAPTER 12 ■

A touch woke Hal. He looked up at Amanda.

"Time to leave?" he asked.

"Yes." she said. "The gates'll be open in about twenty minutes. There'll be a crowd waiting to make the most of the day outside the city by getting out as soon as possible. We're safest leaving with them."

The day before had been cloudless. This one had scattered tufts of white moisture afloat, it seemed, just beyond arm's reach, with the mountains toward which they headed looming over all. The day warmed with the sun, but the road climbed steeply almost from the time they lost sight of the city gates in the vegetation behind them: and the air was thinner and drier than it had been on the previous day's walk.

"Not many people are headed this way," commented Hal, after they had been on their route for about an hour.

"Soil's not much worth farming as we get higher," said Amanda. "Look, you can notice the change in forestation."

Indeed, Hal had. And over that day and into the next, he watched the changes in their surroundings. From the scattered stands of taller timber and the plenteous bush and scrub trees of the uplands, they moved into more open woods of variform evergreens whose ancestral seeds had been imported from Earth; mixed, still, with some native varieties.

"By the way, I left Marlo some money so she could replace the food we ate without Iban being any the wiser; and also so she'd have a little extra for her own use."

"Money?" said Hal. He had had so little use for money, beyond the letters of interstellar credit he had carried in his younger years, when he was trying to stay one jump ahead of Bleys Ahrens and the Others, that he simply had not thought of money in connection with this trip to Kultis. "What sort of money do they have here?"

"Scrip issued by the occupying authorities, now," said Amanda. "Arranged to further put the squeeze on the native Exotics. Theoretically anything else—even interstellar credits in any form—isn't legal tender anymore on this planet and on Mara."

"Where'd you get scrip? I didn't see any when the guard at the gate dumped your bag to see what was in it."

"I'd picked some up on my earlier trips, and brought it out with me," she said. "At the Encyclopedia your friend, Jeamus Walters, copied me a large stock of it. Most of it's still in the ship; but I'm carrying a young fortune sewn into the hem of my robe."

She paused.

"Your friend Jeamus seems to be able to do anything."

"With the help of the Encyclopedia," Hal said.

"Also, before I went to sleep," Amanda went on, "I stole a small, but useful, amount from Iban. Not so much that he'll notice the loss, but enough to help out what I gave Marlo. A man who stuffs scrip into any pocket that's handy doesn't usually keep an account book in his head."

"That's true enough," said Hal.

"I could have given Marlo a lot more, of course," she continued, "but the Authority strictly limits the amount of scrip in circulation, to tighten up the shortages being forced on the people. If Marlo had a lot to spend, she'd stick out like a sore thumb. I can do a lot more good by giving small amounts to a large number of people, spread across a wide area."

Hal nodded. "How far is it to this Chantry Guild?"

"An easy day's walk from here to the Zipacas. Though this isn't a route I've taken lately," said Amanda. "From there, a short climb to the Guild itself—"

She broke off in midsentence. They had both halted reflexively at a faint sound that it was impossible to identify.

Amanda gestured with a hand toward her ear, in a signal to continue listening. Hal nodded. He had lost the noise and at first heard only the sound of the insects and the breeze in the trees around them. Then he became aware of an undertone that was a human voice talking steadily in a low, unvarying pitch. The voice was too far off for them to distinguish words; but it was undeniably the sound of someone speaking, steadily and without pause or change in emphasis.

"It's up ahead," said Amanda.

"Yes," said Hal.

They went on up the road, which here curved to its left through a stand of the local evergreens. Mounting a small rise, they looked down a short, relatively open, slope into a clearing that held the ruins of one of the former Exotic villas.

Vegetation had not yet encroached upon those ruins, but there was little enough left of the home that had been. Back some short distance from the road were the low remains of fire-destroyed walls, partly shrouded with vines and weeds. Most such places, and this one was no exception, had owned white walls; and the fire-blackening had oddly and arbitrarily seemed to paint what was left standing of these, so that the impression was of an end to the home that had come about by age rather than by flame.

Hal remembered that he had felt something medieval about the moment in which they had waited at the gates of Porphyry. Today, the ruins of the houses they had passed had struck him with a feeling from an even earlier period in history. They had made him think, for some strange reason, of how the ruins of Roman villas must have looked in ancient Britain, after the military power of that mighty but decaying Empire was withdrawn; and the barbarians flooded in to loot, slay and destroy what had been.

There was no obvious reason for such a thought to arise now. Nonetheless, it was strong in him as the two of them started down toward what was left of the home in the clearing, and the man they saw there.

He wore the ordinary penitential robe and had let his graying hair and beard grow. These were clotted into locks from lack of washing; and his robe, even from a distance, showed that it had not been cleaned for a very long time. He was a thin man, whose hollowed cheeks looked sucked in above the beard that mounted his face toward the cheekbones; and his arms and legs, protruding from the robe, were skin and bone.

He stood before what had once perhaps been a decorative fishpond in the forecourt of the villa. It was a round body of water with a red-tiled edging, some four meters across in size and undoubtedly quite shallow, since mounds of something peeked here and there above the surface. The breeze blowing across it up the slope toward Hal and Amanda brought a smell sick with the stink of organic decay.

The area around the pool itself, a circular terrace of gray stone with white stone benches and a stone pedestal about chest high to the man—before which he stood—had been meticulously restored, cleaned and cared for. Everything sparkled in the clear upland light, with two exceptions, besides the appearance of the man himself.

One, was the dark opaque waters of the pool, which seemed to swallow all light falling on it; and the other was a row of decorative flowerpots all around its edge. Those in the flowerpots to the man's right held many-branched plants of some sort, that had been stripped down to bare branches and twigs, as if in the depths of winter.

The contrast of these with the potted plants on the man's left was startling. The latter were of the same size and shape, but bore small, heart-shaped green leaves, and a profusion of flowers in a variety of reds and pinks, the tiny petals of the cup-shaped blossoms curving upward together to make a bouquet that in that case of each plant made it look like a Horn of Plenty made of fine, tinted lace. These gleamed in the sunlight, the soil at their base black from recent watering.

On the pedestal in front of the man was one of the pots with the flower-bearing plants in it. As they approached he stood there, continuing to talk—apparently to it, since there was no one else in sight—in a steady stream of words so run together as to be individually indistinguishable and incomprehensible.

As he did this he slowly, delicately and methodically, one by one, took hold of petals from the blossoms of the plant on the pedestal before him and tore them off, dropping them into the decay-smelling waters of the pond before him.

Hal and Amanda came into the forecourt itself and walked up to him. But he took no notice of them; only went on methodically destroying the plant before him. As the final petal of the last blossom fell to the dark water below, he began stripping and shredding the leaves of the plant, one by one.

"*Fugga, mugga, shugga . . .* " he seemed to be muttering.

Understanding woke suddenly in Hal's mind and, turning to Amanda, he saw that the same comprehension had come to her. What the man was intoning was a litany of obscenities, so many times repeated that the syllables of the words had run together to the point where the words themselves had lost all meaning.

"Hello," said Amanda clearly, almost in the man's ear.

He took no notice of her. Whether he did not hear, or whether he heard but paid no attention, was impossible to say. His robe was so grimed and worn that Hal had paid little attention to it originally; but now he made out the fact that at some time in the past, the word DESTRUCT! had been painted on it, both front and back.

As they watched, the man finished stripping the last leaves from the flower bush he had been denuding. He fell silent, turned from it, still ignoring Hal and Amanda, and went down to the end of the last of the pots with the stripped branches. He picked this pot up and carefully carried it back into the ruins of the house.

They followed him.

He went completely through what had been once the closed rooms of the dwelling, and came out into an open area which was filled with scores of plants in pots like his current burden.

They were in all stages from utterly bare of leaves and flowers through the buds of new leaves and flowers to full-blooming individuals. Still ignoring them, he found a place to set down the pot holding the stripped plant, then went to another part of the area and chose a plant overflowing with blossoms. Carrying this as carefully as he had carried the stripped plant, he went back toward the front of the house, out into the forecourt, and put the blooming plant at the end of the line of those on the left of his pedestal.

He dusted the palms of his hands together as he went back to the pedestal. He lifted on to it the nearest of the row of blooming plants, putting it side by side with the one he had just stripped. Leaving them there, he began moving over, one by one, the other pots of unharmed plants, then the row of bare-limbed ones. Finally, he took the plant he had just stripped and lifted it down into the vacant place now available just to the right of his pedestal.

He straightened up and began stripping the petals from the nearest bloom of the fresh pot before him, dropping the petals into the thick water of the pond. The stream of nonsense syllables came again from his lips. All through the time they had been beside him he had never once shown any awareness of Amanda or Hal.

"There's nothing we can do for him," said Amanda. "We might as well go."

They turned away and went on toward the mountains. But gazing at those toward which they traveled it occurred to Hal for the first time that if, as Amanda had said, the edges of the rock forming the valley floor had been uptilted by the molten, interior rock rising from below, then it was very old rock that now essentially plated the new at the base of the mountains. As his mind reached out to conceive of the possible millions of years of difference between the two ages of rocks combined into one single entity that was the range, a strange and unexplainable shiver ran on spider-light feet up his spine. And then was gone.

But the memory of its passing stayed in the back of his mind, even as the image of the man they had just left displaced it in his present thoughts and continued with him as they went. Hal saw the image in his mind, only. There was nothing interfering with his physical eyes, which took automatic note of his surroundings; including the road that now had dwindled to a foot trail of packed earth, and had begun to follow the contours of small, but fairly steep, hills as it continued to work its way upward.

Their surroundings now varied from open patches to heavily forested slopes, both above and below their way. The open spaces were covered with knee-high versions of ferns; and for the first time Hal was conscious of these being stirred by the passage of occasional small animals. He pointed the movement out to Amanda.

"Rabbits," said Amanda. "You remember I mentioned them? The Kultans imported a variform to be farmed for meat protein, for those of the Exotics who weren't on purely vegetarian diets. Some got loose . . ."

She waved her hand at the forest about them.

"You see the result," she said. "No natural predators to

keep them in check. They spread over this whole land mass. At any rate, they've turned out to be a boon to the locals as the major source of meat available; and since protein isn't easily got by any but the military, the native population's become meat-eaters out of necessity, to balance their diet."

Hal nodded, and turned his mind to other observations of their surroundings. Procyon was high in the sky above them and the last of the puffs of clouds seemed to have burned away in the heat of the air at this upper altitude. He saw all this, but his thoughts were not on it. He had returned to trying to imagine himself in the mind of the man they had just seen.

This business of imagining himself as being someone else he had met had begun as a game when he had been a child, and grown from there to a practice, almost to a compulsion. He had come to count it as a failure when he could not imagine himself seeing all things as any other person might see them.

It was more difficult to put himself in the other's shoes than it would be with almost anyone else. The man was obviously insane. But he should be able to do it with sufficient effort.

He had probably been driven into that state by whatever the Occupation soldiery had done when they destroyed his house: and it was because he was so plainly mad that they had not bothered to move him away from the ruins into the town, since then, as they had with the other Exotics.

Hal focused his inner vision now on the thought that it was he himself standing there, plucking the blossoms, destroying the flowers. It was slow . . . but the image of the scene took shape in his mind's eye at last.

It was always necessary to understand; and to really understand it was necessary to actually feel himself being somebody else. A complete empathy. Empathy was a good word for the process of other-being. Good . . . and necessary. Complete empathy produced in the end complete responsibility. Complete responsibility became in the end universal and instinctive—an automatic consideration before any action involving other human beings.

With full and instinctive responsibility in all humans, James would not have died, Tam would not now be at the brink of death with three men's deaths still crushingly upon his conscience.

Now, to himself, he was the madman; and to him, the destruction of the plants was the destruction of what had destroyed his sanity. Bit by bit, he was trying to balance the books, to climb back to where he had once been. But the path he had chosen was circular. He would never get there.

Unless, perhaps unless, Hal could unlock the Creative Universe for him, along with all other people.

Somehow the mad man, Iban, the Exotics, the Encyclopedia, the war, Old Earth, the Younger Worlds—they all came together like lines converging to a point. He could all but feel the convergence right now as a living thing, held in his hands, like the willow twig of divining rod. Oddly, he felt it in his mind as if it converged toward this place he had never seen, the place toward which he now moved. The new Chantry Guild.

Strange how the one person it was at once easiest and hardest for him to be was Bleys.

His inner eye watched the thing of greater importance, the thin fingers dropping the torn petals into the dark water. His mind went far, far back into his childhood as Donal Graeme, a century before.

"You're thinking," said Amanda, after some time.

He started, broken out of his thoughts into the world about him again.

"Yes," he said. "That man back there . . . I was like that, once."

They continued walking. His eyes were on the trail ahead of him, but at the edge of his vision he saw her head turn and her eyes look at him gravely.

"You?" she said. "When?"

"When we got the news of James's death—my youngest uncle. I told you, once, didn't I?"

"Yes," she said. "You were eleven years old; and Kensie came and found you in the stable, afterward—in a cold rage. What would you have done, even if you'd had the man responsible there, in that stable? Try to kill him—at eleven years old, as you were then?"

"Probably," said Hal, watching the mountains ahead. "Pure destruction is a circular action. It trapped me then, as Donal, and I've spent all my time since growing out of it."

"I know," she said softly.

"You see," he said, looking at her, "it's got no place to go but back upon itself. It can only replace, the way that man replaces his plants, over and over, never adding to what's there. Creativity's the opposite, a straight line projecting endlessly forward. The trouble is, the urge to destruction is a racial instinct, useful for testing the individual's ability to control his environment. Children vandalizing a school are doing exactly the same thing as that man we passed. It's instinctive in each new generation, as it becomes conscious of time, to want to sweep away everything old and make everything new. It's instinct in them to feel that all the past went wrong; and now they're going to start the race on the right path from then on.

"But the circularity of destruction traps everyone who does that; and they end up blamed, along with the rest of all history, by the generations that follow. That's why, even with the historic forces endlessly seeking a balance, Bleys and the Others have to lose eventually; because they'll be left behind while the creative people move forward. And evolution happens when that takes place."

"You're saying," said Amanda, "that Bleys is out to destroy Old Earth and the best products of the human Splinter and other cultures, as nothing more than some sort of surrogate for what he really wants to destroy? Like the man with his flower petals?"

"Not exactly," said Hal. "His philosophy's sensible enough if you accept his premises; primarily, that humanity in the past let technology run away with it and went too far, too fast, too soon. No, it's not a ritual, instinctive reaction that moves him, but faulty reasoning—because he lacks empathy, and therefore a sense of responsibility. It's just that he could have gotten started toward it from the same sort of targetless fury as I did, like the man back there maybe did. Bleys could have begun turning into what he is, out of rage at a universe that gave him everything— brilliance, will, mental, moral and physical strength—and then, like the uninvited witch at the christening in the children's story, capped it all with the fact he could never find any other human being to share what he made with him."

"You think so?" said Amanda.

"I don't know," answered Hal. "But it could be. And it might be important."

Almost, he had become lost in his thoughts again. What brought him out of them this time was a glimpse he thought he had, momentarily, of an expression on Amanda's face. He came back to his surroundings and looked narrowly at her.

"Were you smiling?" he asked. "Why?"

"Was I?" said Amanda, her features now perfectly composed. She tucked an arm through his and squeezed it. "If I was, it was because I love you. You know, it's time we stopped somewhere along here to eat. Help me look for a good place."

CHAPTER 13 ■

They found such a spot, shortly. A small, fern-carpeted open area where a tiny stream of cold, drinkable water crossed the trail, from among the bushes and trees on the route's upper side. Seated there, they looked down a clear space of hillside to a heavily treed valley a hundred or so meters below. Amanda unpacked dried fruit and pieces of cornbread. The other food consisted mainly of sandwiches, the taste of which carried the flavor of the pith Hal had eaten before. They went well with the icy water of the stream, which must have its source in the mountains above.

They spent no more than twenty minutes at the most, eating. Procyon was already only an hour or less from the tops of the mountains that could be seen towering above the treetops ahead of them. The mountains looked only a few hundred meters ahead in the clear air, when they must be much more distant than that, Hal thought. He and Amanda went on their way.

"We haven't seen anyone else, except the man by the pond, for hours," said Hal. "Aren't there any people at all up this way?"

"Not as far as I know. That's why the Chantry Guild is back in here. There's nothing much to support a population," answered Amanda. "Oh, there're mountain meadows that could be used for grazing animals, but the Exotics were never herdsmen, even in their early years here; and of course the living's so easy, particularly here at the edge of the tropics, that they've never had any need to. Even before the Occupation, you'd have found it empty up here, except for an occasional traveler. But now the Occupation doesn't let natives make trips without special reason—and special permits. So from here on until we hit the Chantry Guild we shouldn't run into anyone."

Hal was ready to believe her. The road had long since become a foot-track, which had in turn become a trail, and now was nothing at all. It was as if Amanda was setting her course across open country, by memory or some other unseen means. Hal watched the ground carefully as they covered it. Tracking had been one of the many skills drilled into him by his tutors, so his eye was skilled enough to pick up even small signs of others having passed this way. In fact, he did so, from time to time—things as small as a scuff mark, in the dirt or a broken twig—though those were few and inconspicuous.

He ceased to look, therefore, for sign and let himself simply enjoy the walk through the open country.

Enjoyment was there, to anyone raised in the mountains—and Hal was doubly so. As Donal he had grown up in the mountains holding his home, Foralie, on Dorsai; and as Hal he had been raised until he was sixteen among the Rocky Mountains of North America, on Earth. Being among them now brought an exhilaration to him that no other kind of country could evoke. Unthinkingly, his head lifted, his eyes read the lands and heights around him, his nostrils sniffed the clean, clear air . . . and his stride lengthened.

"You can slow down now," Amanda said. "We'll be following along a stream course for a little distance, and it's almost level."

"Oh. Was I pushing the pace?" said Hal. He was embarrassed.

"Not for me. But we've got a way to go yet and the last part's a literal climb. Better take it easy."

Even as she said this, they were already among the unbroken strip of trees and bush, interspersed with leafy stalks of bright green fern, a meter or more in height, that filled the nearly even floor of earth between two steeply upward-sloping and wooded hillsides.

Here, for the first time in some while, the trail they were following became once more visible as it wound between the trees. Obviously it was in regular use, to have had enough traffic to keep it from being overgrown. What was it doing here, in a region that did not usually host ordinary travelers—

A faint touch on his left arm brought him back to his surroundings. He looked at Amanda, and she briefly brushed the outside corner of her left eyebrow with a forefinger, as if some small insect had landed there.

This was one of the "signals" from the "short-language and signals" she had asked him if he remembered, back when they were about to leave the courier ship. She had just signed that something was watching them and paralleling their course on the side indicated. Whatever it was, was doing so deliberately, for it was at once keeping up with them, and keeping out of sight among the trees and brush off to their left.

Without looking directly to his left, Hal set himself to seeing what he could pick up out of the corner of his eyes. It took a little time, but eventually he became aware of whatever it was more by the faint noises and small movements of the ferns and branches it pushed aside in its passage—though it was apparently trying to move as quietly as it could—than by actual sight of it.

He glanced at Amanda and questioned her with a raised eyebrow.

Amanda shook her head in puzzlement, and her hands moved in small movements, quick but unobtrusive signals.

"It's human—a child, or child-sized, I think," she said in this silent fashion. "It's interested in us for some reason. There's an open spot of nothing much more than bush and fern just ahead. Let's sit down there as if we're taking a break and try to tempt it out into the open."

Hal blinked a signal of agreement at her, and a few moments later when they had emerged into the open area she had referred to and reached close to the center of it, she yawned, stretched and stopped. Hal stopped with her.

"Let's sit down a bit," she said clearly. Whoever was shadowing them could not have failed to overhear. "There's no hurry."

She had stopped by a small bank overgrown with fern— a tiny variety rather than the larger growth that had been interspersed with the trees earlier. This was, in fact, a natural stopping place. It occurred to Hal that these would make an excellent bed for Amanda and himself to stretch out on, together. They sat down on the bank now, cross-legged and facing each other.

"Chit!" said Amanda. "Reelin."

She had switched now to the audible "short-language." On the Dorsai a number of code words were generally known by everyone, since these could come in useful if two Dorsai on a foreign, planet wanted to exchange information within the hearing of others when they did not wish to be understood. In addition, each family tended to have its own private code of made up words; and the members of the Morgan and the Graeme families, growing up and playing together as children, knew most of each others' private codes. As youngsters, there had also been a particular pleasure in being able to exchange secret information under the noses of nonunderstanding adults. So the codes were always improved upon by each new generation.

In effect, what Amanda had just said was, *"Let's talk in a way our shadower can't understand. Maybe we can trick whoever it is into coming closer to try and hear better, and figure out what we're up to."*

"Right," said Hal. There was no particular reason not to use a plainly understandable word in answer, and a few understandable words might increase the temptation of the listener to come in close and hear enough of them to make out what the tenor of conversation was.

"Muckle minny cat," he added.

He was pointing out that there were two of them, and since whatever or whoever it was that had been shadowing them was not large, one of them ought to be able to catch it while the other blocked its escape in this direction. Implied was the question of who should chase and who should block.

Amanda smiled, slightly but firmly.

"One! (*I'll be the one to chase*)," she said. "Home snap-back (*you stay here and get ready in case whoever we're chasing doubles back this way.*)"

"R," he said, agreeing. She would be faster and more agile at broken-country running than he. "Mark!"

The last word was to remind her that their listener had crept close enough so that now an effort might be made to catch him or it.

"R," said Amanda. "One-C."

The last code word reasserted the fact that she was in command; and as the chaser, she would pick her own moment to begin pursuit. Meanwhile, with their gazes apparently only upon each other, they were both using their peripheral vision to try and observe something about their watcher, who had indeed slipped closer to them to try to understand their strange conversation.

"Whisper stonewall (I've heard some talk about this person, but I could never get any definite information)," said Amanda. They both had their shadower plainly in view out of the corners of their eyes now. "Y'un."

That she was a "young-one," a half-grown girl, was inarguable, since—except for a length of what looked like dark green, dried vine, with half of a split open pod in the middle of it, knotted around her waist—she was completely unclothed—naked was not a word that suited, since she wore her lack of clothes as unselfconsciously and naturally as an animal wears its pelt of fur. The vine seemed more an ornament than any attempt at a piece of clothing; although at the moment she was apparently using the split-open half of the pod as a sort of pocket for carrying what looked like small rocks, about half the size of her own fist. She was certainly under the age of twelve or thirteen, unless she was a case of arrested physical development.

"Carry!" said Amanda—which broadly translated into "*We've got to get her out of here and to some place where she can be cared for!*"

"R," said Hal.

His agreement was automatic, while waiting for her to start the pursuit—and in fact he had hardly got the last codeword out before she had sprung to her feet and dashed off in pursuit of the little girl.

Amanda was fast—very fast. But the child was almost literally like the wind. Also, plainly, she knew every foot of the ground. She zig-zagged like a hare in flight, leading the way through openings in the forest growth large enough for someone her size to slip through, but too small for one of adult size. In seconds they were both out of Hal's sight among the farther trees.

The sound of their passage, however, turned once more

in his direction, and he suddenly caught sight of the little girl backtracking at full speed. She looked likely to cross the trail some twenty meters ahead of Hal. He jumped to his feet and ran to intercept her.

She zigged and gained on him, zagged and made it back and across the trail after all. He followed her out of sheer stubbornness for perhaps fifty meters, and then accepted the fact that she had been gaining on him with almost every step and was plainly now lost beyond question. He walked slowly back to the trail and Amanda, catching his breath as he went.

Amanda was standing waiting for him on the bank where they had been sitting.

"It'd take a hunting party of a dozen, with nets, to surround that one and get her," Amanda said as Hal came close. She had already gotten her wind back, which was more than he had. "The climate's mild year 'round at this altitude. But still, how she's survived by herself, God knows. She couldn't have gotten this wild and skillful in just one summer. She's like an animal—maybe more animal than human, by this time. One way or another, it's the Occupation that's responsible for this, too. In Exotic times, she'd have been found and brought in long before this."

"R," said Hal, trying not to pant. He was once more annoyingly conscious of how unfit he was, in spite of his daily exercise sessions at the Final Encyclopedia; and being lashed in the face by branches that were just at the right height to be run under by the child, but not by him, had not made him any happier. "I suppose we might as well be getting along."

"Might as well," agreed Amanda.

They took up their way in somber silence. The streambed they had been following had been inclining more and more steeply with every step they took these last few minutes. Suddenly, they came through a small, thick cluster of trees and there was the face of the mountain itself; a near-vertical brown limestone wall of rock looking as if it had grown up suddenly through the ground before them, to tower on up and back, until it was out of sight.

The forest came almost to that wall. Amanda led Hal forward and he saw that the lower part of the near-vertical rock was pitted and indented with concavities.

"This way," said Amanda, leading him to one dark opening, which they had to bend double to enter. Hal followed her in thinking that they were moving into a cave, which made no sense—but suddenly their way turned under the rock and he saw light before him. They came out, into sunlight once more, somewhat higher up, into a sort of gouge in the steep rock face itself.

Hal noticed as they emerged that a large, semi-round boulder was perched to one side of their exit. It looked as if it were balanced so that it could be rolled to fall with its bulging side into the place where they had just come out, like a stopper into a bottle. Amanda led him into the gouge, and they continued upward, now climbing as much as walking, working their way around bosses of the naked brown limestone. They stopped to rest for a while on a small level area.

"How much farther?" asked Hal, shading his eyes to look up the rock face they were climbing. "I can't see any sign of anything built up there; and"—he switched his gaze to Procyon in the west—"the sun is going to be behind those peaks in a hurry—I'd guess no more than another fifteen minutes."

"You don't see anything because nothing's supposed to be seen," said Amanda. "But you're right about the fifteen minutes. We'll make it."

Hal looked up and for the first time saw, only a dozen meters or so higher up, that what he had assumed to be an unbroken, steep slope above them, actually ended in the lip of a ledge. The ledge ran off out of sight on either hand around the bulge of the mountainside. Its rock had blended in appearance very well with a slope behind it that he now realized must be at some distance from the edge he saw.

He had not noticed it before because the light of the descending sun had added to the illusion of a single, unbroken, upward face of rock. Now the sun was down enough that shadow lay on the rock face under an overhang of the upper slope beyond, as it lay on the two of them, here. The ledge itself must still be in sunlight, for what had caught his eye at last had been that its lip was now rimmed with light.

Seeing it, and aware of the waiting level just above them, the reality of the place that was their destination became suddenly solid and undeniable in his mind. His thoughts moved together into an undeniable conclusion, and he knew that finally he must have the answers he had wanted from Amanda earlier.

"Wait!" he said.

He had stopped; and now, ahead of him, Amanda stopped and turned to face him.

"What is it?" she asked.

"This may be my last chance to talk to you alone for a while." The words seemed to sound stiff and awkward even as he said them—but they had to be said. "When Tam Olyn told you to have faith back at the Final Encyclopedia, what was he talking about? And what was it you turned back to say to Rukh and Ajela, just before we left?"

She gazed down at him for a long moment with an unusual intentness, as if she was trying to search for something deep within him.

"Tell me," she said at last, "are you going on up? Or are you turning back, even at this point?"

"Why should I turn back?"

"Would you—now?"

He thought about it for a moment.

"No," he said then, "I wanted to come here. I still do."

"Good," she said, "because you had to come here of your own decision, your own free will. Because you wanted to come."

"I did. You know that."

"I had to make sure," she said. She hesitated for a second.

"You see," she said, "when I stopped to talk to Rukh and Ajela, it was to tell them it would be all right now, that there was hope you'd find the Creative Universe after all."

He stared at her.

"How could you promise them something like that?" he said. "I've no guarantee there's hope—you knew that. And even if I did, no one can know certainly, one way or another!"

"Oh, Hal!" She threw her arms around him suddenly, pressing her head against his chest. "Don't you understand? You've worn yourself thin trying to get through a wall at a point where there was no way in. Back at the Final Encyclopedia, you could see how everybody else had been worn thin; but you wouldn't face it in yourself! You've got to step back from the problem and wait for another way to come to you. That's why you had to come here! And as for the other question: I only know what Tam saw. He was seeing more than I ever had, because, just as he said, he was halfway through the door to death. But when he told me what he'd seen, I could see it, too—a time in which I'd need to believe in you, and why. Because you'd have won after all—but at a greater price than any of us had ever imagined. And the way to that's *here*; I can feel it!"

"What price?" He was almost glaring at her, he knew, but he could not help himself.

"I don't know!" she said, still holding him. "I said it was beyond imagination; for me—and I think even for Tam. He only knew the fact of it. But when he told me, I could feel it the way he did; and I understood something else— that I couldn't tell you, until you'd committed yourself by actually coming here."

She stopped, as if she had suddenly run out of breath.

"What else?" he demanded.

"Your next step on the road to what Tam made me see. You've committed yourself now by coming to the Chantry Guild here, of your own free will and choice. If I'd told you before this, it might have affected what you keep calling the Forces of History."

She let go of him then, but kept a hand on his arm as if a living connection was necessary for the message she still had to reach him with.

"Hal," she said, "listen to me! Tam has to die completed if you're ever to do what you first set out to do. You *have* to find the Creative Universe before he dies. Only that'll justify his life in his own eyes; and he must die justified. If he doesn't, you'll never find it!"

He stared at her.

"Don't ask me why!" she said. "I don't know why! I only know what Tam believes; and—I know he's right."

Hal's mind clicked and slid, from premise, to odds, to conclusion. Now that his intuitive logic was given what it needed to work with, it was offering up answers where it could offer none before. What Amanda said made sense.

Until the Final Encyclopedia should be put to its final, practical use, the shape of that use would be undefined. It had been passed on, undefined, as no more than a dream, from Mark Torre to Tam and from Tam to him. The chain of cause and effect of this unreal and as-yet-unshaped, but powerful, cause could break at Tam's death, if he believed he had died without it reaching at last to its goal. It would mean to him that all his life, and everything effected by it, had been a wrong working of the developing historical fabric; a working to a dead end, that now would be abandoned.

Hal felt suddenly weak, with the weakness of shock. It had just been shown to him that he alone, of the three of them, had been in a position of choice. Neither Torre nor Tam could have turned from their work once they had taken it up. He could have—had to have been able to, before being given the chance to find the answer they all had sought—or else there was no free will. Otherwise, the fabric of future history was pre-determined.

And it was not. Not fixed. Only the past was that. So he alone had had the power of choice—and he had almost chosen wrongly.

No, *never that!* Succeed or fail; but to give up as he had thought himself ready to do was unthinkable after the torch had been carried this far. Fail, if he must, but the only decision he could live with was to stick with it to the end. Otherwise, all he had ever believed was false and useless.

He turned his face again to the ledge above them and felt Amanda's hand slip down his arm to take his hand. Together they went up into sunlight.

CHAPTER 14 ■

The sunset exploded in their eyes as they came up over the rim onto the ledge, for a moment all but blinding Hal as his eyes struggled after the dimness of the shadowed slope below. His legs felt strange and weak to be once more on level ground. Gradually, visual adjustment came and he began to make out what was around them.

They had stepped up onto a level space that ran back a hundred meters or so before the mountain face resumed its upward thrust. The ledge was at least five times as wide as it was deep and it was a crowded, busy place.

For a moment, still dazzled by the rays of the setting sun, Hal could not make out the details. Then his vision made a sharper adjustment, and all that was there seemed to stand out with a particular depth and clarity, as if he was seeing it in more than three dimensions.

There were several openings in the mountain face at the back of the level space; whether to caves, or interior continuations of the ledge, it was impossible to tell from where he stood. He and Amanda stood only a little way to the right of a small pond, fed by a stream which angled across the flat rock of the ledge floor from a near waterfall spilling down the farther face of the mountain. The pond must drain from its bottom, he thought, since there was no other obvious exit, and the water probably emerged elsewhere on the mountainside or as a spring in the forest below.

Directly ahead, on the right of the tiny stream as Hal looked toward the back of the ledge, were three large buildings. The one farthest in was slightly larger than the one next to it, and the one closest was a structure so small that it seemed hardly more than a cabin by comparison with the other two.

All three buildings had been built of logs. The face of the mountain behind was in the process of being quarried for blocks of brown limestone, and some of these blocks had already been set up on the other side of the stream, marking the outline of what promised to be a greater structure that would eventually fill and use all the space at the back of the ledge. Away from the stream on both sides, and otherwise in lines about the ledge as well as against the upslanting rock walls of the mountain—so steep their upper branches touched the stone—were numerous variform pine, with a scattering of native evergreens. Pine needles were scattered everywhere and made a carpet over all the ledge itself.

People in robes were moving purposefully everywhere, along paths under the lines of trees. The only exception to this, in the sharp sunset light, was a ring of individuals walking in a circle, a little beyond and behind the pond. They walked, one behind the other, chanting; a chant that Hal now realized some acoustical trick of the rock below the level of the ledge had kept him from hearing until this moment. But now it came clearly to his ears.

They intoned it as they walked, but it carried no clear message to him in this first moment. But for a reason he could not identify, something about it rang a deep note of certainty in him. It was right.

The last of the sunset was disappearing with the swiftness that was to be expected on a world under such a tiny seeming circle of light. The star was, in fact, far from Kultis and Mara—Procyon was a much larger, as well as brighter, star than Earth's Sun. At the distance from it that

Earth was from its Sun, a world like this would have been uninhabitable.

The evening shadow seemed to fall across all the world at once; and as it did so, Hal's mind finally registered the sense of what the walkers were repeating. That what they repeated had taken this long to become intelligible to him had not been because the words had not been spoken in Basic—Basic was what everyone on all the human worlds normally used nowadays. Nor was it because they had run the words together, or in any way sounded them differently.

It had only been because of their method of chanting. They intoned the phrase they used, not in chorus, but as if each one was repeating it solely to himself or herself. Sometimes the voices blended on the same sound at the same moment; and sometimes they did not. But at any rate, now he clearly heard and understood them. There were only eight words to what they repeated.

> *The transient and the eternal are the same . . .*
> *The transient and the eternal are the same . . .*

So suddenly did they become understandable to him, that it was as if they had abruptly been translated from some language he did not know into one he had spoken from his earliest years.

It was not so much the words in themselves that registered so strongly on him, but the burden of their meaning; which he could not identify clearly, but which stirred him strangely. As unfamiliar music might move him unexpectedly and strongly even at the first hearing.

It was like a sound heard around a corner and out of sight, striking some powerful meaning in him; but exactly what and why was not immediately clear. Still, for the present it did not matter. The knowing would come, at its own pace, but in time to be useful. All that mattered now was realizing that it rang a deep chime of truth in him.

It continued . . .

The transient and the eternal are the same . . .
The transient and the eternal . . .

. . . and so it went, on and on, echoing in him as if his mind was one great unlighted cavern and it was speaking to him with the voice of all the universe at once. Echoing and speaking, echoing and speaking. . . .

His body tensed to make an instinctive step toward the circle; then checked. He held back, his eyes focusing for some reason on one walker with a long, white beard, silky on a thin, bony face beneath oriental eyes. The man he watched had just completed the turn of the circle, after having been facing away from Hal, but now came back toward him. For a moment his features were clear in spite of the steadily deepening shadow that seemed to wash the colors from the walker's patterned robe of thin, smooth cloth, unlike the rough garments the other walkers wore. Hal turned to Amanda. He saw her face looking up at him, concerned. He looked back down and smiled to reassure her.

"You were right," he said. "I needed to come here."

"Good," she said, the concern relaxing from her eyes. "Come along then."

"Where?" he asked.

The face of the ledge was busy with people moving to and fro between its buildings. Some of these smiled at Amanda; but none seemed surprised to see her. They extended their smile in a welcome to Hal himself in a manner so like that of the Exotics as Hal remembered, that he felt a sudden, small pang of sadness. Amanda was leading the two of them toward the smallest of the buildings.

"First you've got to meet the one in charge here," she said, "an old friend of yours."

"Old friend?" He tried to think of Exotics who might fit that description. "Nonne?"

Nonne had been the Exotic representative—theoretically to the Final Encyclopedia, but actually, as both the Exotics and Hal had clearly understood, to Hal himself, since he had been the one who had won their allegiance to the cause of Old Earth in a debate against Bleys, broadcast to both Exotic worlds.

That had been at the time of the movement of the Dorsai people to Earth's defense, and it had resulted in the donation of Exotic wealth and knowledge to the same end. The time of the activation of the phase-shield. It was also the fact that Nonne had been sent with him to voice any objections the Exotics might have to Hal's later arrangements, as a kind of single last voice of the Exotic Splinter Culture.

Nonne had stayed the first year with him at the Final Encyclopedia. But it had become more and more obvious that Hal was concerned, not with the management of Earth's defense, but only with the work he pursued alone in the carrel of his suite. So she had gone home, leaving the actual uses of Exotic funds and skill to Ajela; and the actual execution of that defense to the Dorsai.

She had ridden out through the phase-shield with one of the Dorsai advisors, like Amanda, who had been returning to the Exotics after a brief, necessary visit to Earth. Hal, at least, had heard nothing of her since.

She had been a waspish, angry woman by nature, very nearly the exact opposite of what other cultures thought of as Exotic. But Hal had appreciated the sincerity and single-mindedness of her point of view; and her sharp-faced, middle-aged image rose again in his mind now as he said her name. It had not struck him until this moment that she might be the one he should come to meet here in this place.

"I'll let you find out for yourself," was all Amanda answered. She led him on toward the entrance of the first, and smallest, log building.

However, before they reached it a figure that was not Nonne's but even more familiar to Hal appeared around the edge of the building. Walking beside him was a man as large as Hal. Both wore the penitential robes. But Hal's eyes fastened on the small body and wrinkled face of the smaller of the two, who had been his closest companion during the time when he had been struggling to bring the

Exotics to give all they had to the cause now fought for by Earth.

"Amid!" he said. "But you're not at the Final Encyclopedia anymore?"

He corrected himself.

"No, of course not," he said. "Forgive me. I've been so out of touch with people this last year, even at the Encyclopedia, that I forget. That's right, about eight months ago one of the advisors from Kultis, here, brought word your brother was sick. You left to go to him, didn't you? But I didn't realize you'd stayed."

A smile energized all the lines in the face of the little man so that he seemed to shine with good humor.

"Hal!" he said, hurrying forward to take Hal's hand with both of his own. "I'd hoped—but I didn't really think there was a chance Amanda could bring you here!"

Hal smiled back. It would have been next to impossible not to.

"As you see," he answered. "But you found a job to keep you here?"

"I'm sorry. Seeing you—" He broke off. "I suppose I ought to explain that Kanin wasn't actually a brother of mine, by blood—the way the word's used on other worlds. In my generation, we still ran to large communal families. But he was as close to me as if he had been, physically, my sibling. Perhaps closer. And I called him brother. So of course I came back here as soon as I heard."

"And stayed, obviously," said Hal.

"Yes." Amid let go of Hal's hand, but continued to beam up at him. "For one thing, he'd died by the time I got here, and I was needed. For another, for a long time I'd been bothered. I was sitting there, safe and useless behind the phase-shield, in the comfort of the Encyclopedia while my people were suffering."

"So your brother was one of the people here?"

"He was Guildmaster," said Amid. "Now, I am. By default, more or less."

"That's not true," said the tall man. "No one could have filled Kanin's shoes, his brother's shoes, but Amid."

"I'm sorry," said Amid. "I should have introduced Artur, here. He's Assistant Guildmaster. Artur, you know Amanda. This is Hal Mayne."

Artur extended a hand and Hal clasped it, feeling from the sudden heartiness of the grasp confirmation of what his instinctive perceptions of emotion in others had already suspected. Artur was an impressive-looking individual; nearly bald, with a narrow waist and massive, smooth-skinned arms and legs showing beyond the short sleeves and the hem of the robe he wore. But he would far rather have been a smaller man.

Hal had been aware that, in the first moment of their seeing each other, Artur had automatically measured himself physically against Hal's size and apparent strength. However, it had been a reflexive, unwilling measurement. Artur was undoubtedly strong, even in proportion to his height and weight, but he apparently was one of those who found the gifts of both size and strength as only crosses to be borne.

Like certain other large men Hal had met, Artur clearly had an unhappiness over the attitudes of those smaller, who assumed that because of his size he did not suffer from their fears, their sensitivities to the pains and dangers of life. He felt that everyone expected him, because of his size, to do more, to endure more, to enjoy what they thought of as an unfair advantage. An advantage he, himself, would happily have foregone if he could only be treated as no different than everyone else.

It was an unhappiness which Hal had been lucky to avoid, largely because of his upbringings, both as Donal and Hal. Also because with the Dorsai, just as physical training and skill could more than compensate for differences in power, they also rendered unimportant any advantages of extra size. Strength, there, was irrelevant, in comparison with the will and soul inside the person—large or small, old or young, man, woman, or child—on whom others might have to depend; and the Dorsai culture took for granted an understanding of this.

"Come in. Come in and let's talk!" Amid was saying.

He stood aside to let Amanda go before him and then followed her through the doorway of the small building. Hal was about to follow, when Artur spoke behind him.

"Hal Mayne?"

"Yes?" Hal turned.

"I'm sorry . . . you're the Hal Mayne, of course. I should have recognized you at once. Amid's talked about you often."

There was embarrassment, but also relief in Artur's voice; and Hal understood. Artur could not be expected by anyone to compete against someone with Hal's reputation.

"Recognizing anyone right away from nothing more than verbal descriptions is pretty good," said Hal.

He turned and went in, hearing Artur behind him.

Inside, the building seemed almost entirely given over to what appeared to be a single meeting, eating, and working room. The last of the sunset was almost gone behind the rocky peaks almost directly over them, in just these few minutes. But the lingering brightness of the sky still glowed into one side of the large room they had just entered, touching it through a number of the small, square windows spaced evenly around the walls. Interior lighting was just beginning to supplement this.

The artificial light came from a combination of candles, and three of the common, portable, hundred-year lamps, affixed to the rafters which openly crossed the space overhead under the steeply pitched roof.

Solar-charged lamps like these would be left over from before the coming of the Occupation Forces to Kultis, which brought an end to what relatively little manufacturing the two Exotic worlds had done for themselves. In addition, there was an open fireplace, contained within a square of four knee-high walls of reddish brick. There was a hood over it of some metal which looked like, and well might be, copper; undoubtedly likewise salvaged from earlier days on this world. The hood reached up to a chimney pipe of the same metal.

The fire already burning in the fireplace gave little light of its own; but what there was of it softened the rather harsh illumination from the hundred-year lamps, which were originally designed primarily for outdoor and commercial uses.

In the partition wall opposite the door they had just come in were two other doors, both partially open at the moment. One gave a glimpse into a small bed area, and the other, a bathroom. Around the large room were wooden chairs, homemade obviously, but padded and comfortable; and one large table end-on to them, that had its farther end piled with papers.

The four of them moved instinctively toward the chairs closest to the fireplace, for though the sun had been hidden for only a few minutes, it seemed that a chill was already penetrating into the building from the open air beyond the front door.

"These are my quarters," said Amid as they sat down, "but I've also got another office in one of the two dormitory buildings, which can double as a bedroom. I'll let you two have that for the night, if you like, since we aren't set up for guests in the ordinary way of things. But sit down, sit down! You've come just at dinner time. Will you eat with me?"

"We'd be glad to," Amanda said. Artur got up again, hastily.

"I'll take care of it," he said, and went out.

"He's a good Assistant Guildmaster," said Amid, as the door closed behind the big man. "If I hadn't had him to help me take charge here, I don't think I could have managed."

"Do you mind if I ask why you did take over?" Hal asked. "I can see you staying, for the reasons you gave a moment ago. But why take on the job of Guildmaster?"

"I was drafted into it, in a manner of speaking," said Amid. "Those who'd known Kanin wanted me simply because I'd been his brother. They seemed to think there was something in common between us that fitted the job. And, to tell you the truth. I did know something of how Kanin thought in many ways. Even though we hadn't seen each other for fifteen years. I flattered myself my decisions would be his decisions. Because he made this place work. He didn't found it, you understand—or has Amanda told you all about the Chantry Guild already?"

"I've told him nothing," said Amanda.

"I see." Amid looked at Hal. His lined old face was shrewd. "Why did you come. Hal?"

"Because Amanda said it was something I should do. She was right," said Hal.

"You just wanted to see it?"

"Originally, it was probably more of an excuse than a want," said Hal. "But now, if you'll have me, I'd like to stay awhile."

"I take it," said Amid, "you might want to walk in the circle then?"

"If that's allowable," Hal answered.

Amid grinned. He did not smile, he grinned.

"For anyone else there'd be a period of observation first, a sort of apprenticeship; and a vote to be taken at the end of it, on him or her by all the members here," he said. "But I think we could do without that, since you're who you are."

He sobered.

"In fact, no one but Artur and I knew you might be coming. It's probably best to keep your real identity secret as long as we can—which won't be too long. I think the other members will let you walk on my recommendation alone, if that's necessary."

"No," said Hal.

"Yes," said Amanda. "Amid, Hal doesn't know Kultis as it is now. Hal, you'd be doing the people here a favor to at least give them the excuse that they were never told who you really were."

Amid nodded, looking over at Hal.

"She's right," he said. "Besides, it's not as if your coming in on the Guildmaster's recommendation alone was something otherwise unheard of. We've had people before this who were deserving, who've been let into the circle incognito. But—"

He turned back to Amanda.

"It won't be more than a matter of weeks before they'll have guessed who he is, anyway. Secrets aren't easily hidden in a place as small as this ledge."

"In a matter of weeks, the situation could be entirely different," said Amanda. "For now, let's do what we can to protect everybody concerned. Will Artur have spoken to anyone about who Hal is, when he went out just now to get the dinner?"

"No, no. Not Artur," said Amid. "He volunteers no information. Besides, he's a highly intelligent individual; and even one who wasn't would have the sense to know the danger to Hal—and to us all, as you say—if it were known he was here on Kultis."

"In any case," said Hal, "I won't be here too long. But— Amanda, you were right. There's something here for me to find, in that circle. You were going to tell me about the one who started it?"

"Yes," said Amid. "It was a Maran Exotic you'll never have heard of, named Jathed. He was a student of historic philosophy to begin with. He was ahead of his time in speculating that we Exotics might have gone astray from our original path. He spent twenty years, after he finished studying at various of our universities, examining our beginning—the Chantry Guild of Walter Blunt in the twenty-first century. How much do you know about that?"

"A fair amount, as it happens," said Hal.

"Good, then I won't have to go into too many details for you," Amid went on. "You know a chantry was a place, or an endowment for a place, where prayers could be said for a dead person, or persons; and that Walter Blunt chose this name for his organization back in the twenty-first century because by its very nature a chantry implies a relation of past, present, and future?"

"Yes," answered Hal.

"Well, it was that relationship as Blunt applied it that attracted Jathed. As I say, he spent his life studying the original Chantry Guild. You can see how the idea of a connection of past, present and future, now and forever, could lead to the concept of the transient and the eternal being the same. Jathed even went to Old Earth for a while. When he came back, he set himself up more or less as a hermit on the outskirts of a little town near here called Ichang—"

Hal looked at Amanda.

"It's about forty kilometers from Porphyry," Amanda said. "We could have come through it on our way here, instead of through Porphyry; but Ichang's not a garrison town. I mean, it doesn't have a garrison of Occupation troops. The Porphyry troops have a contingent quartered there, but that's all. I wanted you to see what a garrison town on the Exotics, under the Occupation, was like."

"This with Jathed was some years before the Occupation," said Amid mildly. "As I say, he became something of a hermit. You're probably already aware it's quite possible to live off the country in areas like the one just below us. There's enough insect, animal, bird, and vegetable life to keep anyone alive with just a couple of hours of food hunting a day. That's how Jathed lived. He deliberately wanted solitude to 'think through,' as he said, the proper direction of what should have grown from that original Chantry Guild."

Artur came in, followed by two men and a woman, all carrying loaded trays. Artur directed the setting of these at the far end of the table as Amid went on.

"Now, of course, since the Others, and particularly since the Occupation," he said, "every one on our two worlds has necessarily begun to rethink the direction we Exotics took in our attitudes and our thinking after we emigrated to these planets. But Jathed was considerably in advance of them all. At any rate, he moved farther and farther back into the woods, to get away from even casual contact with people; and eventually—we don't quite know when—he found his way up to this ledge here.

"—By that time, he'd acquired a few—disciples, let's call them. Yes, Artur?"

"Everything's ready on the table. And hot."

"We'll be right there. Wait—" For Artur had turned to follow those who had come in with him out the door. "You're to eat with us. That's an order. I want you to be a part of everything we decide with Hal, here. By the way, just to reassure us all, you didn't mention who Hal is to anyone?"

"Of course not, Guildmaster!"

"That's his way of reproving me," said Amid to Hal and Amanda, "when he calls me by my title. The reproof is for even needing to ask. We'll be at the table in a moment, Artur. Meanwhile, come and sit with us; and if I forget to tell Hal part of the story of Jathed, break in and fill the gap, will you?"

"If you'd like me to," said Artur. "Thank you."

"No thanks needed," said Amanda. "You should have taken the invitation for granted."

"I'm sorry," said Artur, seating himself with them.

"And no apologies are needed, either," said Amanda. "Go on, Amid."

"Where was I?" said Amid. "Oh, yes, Jathed had started the walking down in the forest. He continued it up here, specifying the rules under which it was to be done, particularly the rule about how they were to chant. They were not to chant in unison, or try to walk in step, unless these things happened by accident. The idea was that they should be studying by themselves, even though they were in company. Above all, they were to utter nothing but the Law—about that last he was most emphatic. You'll have to remember that at all times, Hal. It's not a 'mantra' you're hearing from those people outside. Not a prayer, hymn, or incantation of any kind. Jathed hated the word 'mantra' and wouldn't allow it used by anyone around him; and he was a violent man about getting his own way."

"He used to drive people off with a staff," put in Artur, "though he did that more when they were down in the forest—or have you told them about the earliest Chantry Guild in the woods below us, Amid?"

"No. I mentioned it, then went right to the ledge," said Amid. "Now you see why I wanted you here? Jathed's first incarnation of his Chantry Guild was, as Artur says, down in the wild country below us; close to these cliffs, but not overly close. He already had a number of disciples by that time, and he set them to walking the circle he, himself, had earlier worn ankle deep. Of course, there were new people coming every day wanting to join. But as I say he wasn't easy to get along with. One mistake and the would-be member was out—chased out, in fact. Jathed walked around with the staff Artur mentioned, and anyone who showed what he considered 'incomprehension'—but particularly the fault of calling the Law a 'mantra'—got chased out, with Jathed running behind them hitting them with his staff to keep them going at a good pace."

"He called it a Law?" asked Hal.

"Yes." Amid looked penetratingly at him for a moment. "He called it a Law and he meant it to be a Law, as clearly acknowledged as he Law of Gravity. And he was furious with anyone who wanted him to teach them. He claimed all that was needed was for each of them, individually, to study the Law."

" '*The transient and the eternal are the same*,' " said Hal.

"Yes," said Amid. "I don't fully understand it myself, either, Hal; but like many people who've come into contact with the Law, I can feel there's a power there; and I think Jathed was right, too, about the fact it can't be taught. Whatever's in it has to be found by individual effort to understand its meaning. You know, he said a strange thing. He said that in two generations everyone—and he meant everyone in the human race, not just those here on Kultis—would know the Law, and many would already have started to put it to use."

He shrugged.

"One generation of those two has already gone by; and there's few enough even among us Exotics who ever heard of it or Jathed; and it hardly looks like that'll change in the next twenty years or less. But that's what he said."

"Now is a time of change," said Hal thoughtfully.

"True. But for something like the Law to be accepted, let alone put to use, under present conditions where the human race is at civil war with itself . . . the Others certainly aren't going to take to the Law in any case; and wouldn't, even if it came from some other source than an Exotic. You realize the Others are literally out to kill us off—all of us on these two worlds? The only reason they don't simply bring in armed soldiery and shoot us down is because a massacre like that couldn't be kept secret from the other Younger Worlds and it might give rise to anti-Other attitudes out there."

"I know," said Hal. "In fact, I had Bleys Ahrens tell me about his goals, once."

"The only thing that's forced Bleys to try to accomplish his ends here by genteel starvation and casual individual murder by his Occupation troops," said Amid, "is the fact that there're only a handful of Others, a mere few thousands, to control all the Younger Worlds. We here at the Chantry Guild have been overlooked, rather than specifically allowed to survive. But, back to Jathed and the history of this present incarnation of the Guild—"

"Amid," said Artur, "might I mention the dinner again? The food's getting cold, as I said. We could talk as we eat."

"Of course. Of course, you're right!" said Amid. "I'm getting more single-minded every day. Let's move to the table, everybody."

They moved.

CHAPTER 15 ■

"At any rate," said Amid a few minutes later, when they had started to eat from a number of dishes of vegetables, the contents of which, cooked and uncooked, were in large bowls on the table before them, with chopsticks laid out neatly at each seating place, "as Artur reminds me, it wasn't until perhaps three years before the Occupation began that Jathed moved the walking circle up here to the ledge and shortly after that, he died. Kanin was one of his disciples—"

"The Master's leading disciple," said Artur.

"Well, well, perhaps," said Amid. "Jathed didn't assign ranks to his followers. At any rate, Kanin, foreseeing something like the Occupation, moved everyone connected with the Guild—not just the walkers—up here and started building for permanent occupation of this place. Then, last year, he died . . . and I've already told you how I came to be with him—too late, and was asked to take over as Guildmaster."

"The only possible choice—" began Artur, but Amid interrupted.

"Perhaps, as I say. But what you need to know, Hal, if you're going to stay here awhile, is that we're an open democracy in this place, everybody having a vote on everything and the majority ruling. In practice the Guildmaster has a veto over anything voted, but—"

"In practice," put in Artur firmly, "no one would think of questioning the Guildmaster's veto, or an order by the Guildmaster."

"Well, well. The point is, Hal, you'll be moving in as one of the members of the Guild. That means you'll have a

vote, of course, but I'd suggest you wait until you understand this place better before you begin using it. You'll
stay in one of the dormitory buildings, in the singles' quarters. There are rooms for couples here as well, but they're
all full right now and we haven't had time to build more;
that's why I suggested you use my office as your room for
tonight."

"Thank you," said Amanda. "We appreciate it."

"Yes, indeed," said Hal.

"The office would only be empty otherwise. I sleep
here, nights." Amid made a dismissing gesture with his
chopsticks. "Now, about the circle itself. Every Chantry
Guild member, which means everyone on the ledge, has a
chance to walk in it, in regular rotation. He or she can pass
up the turn when it comes, if they want. Both Artur and
myself have to, most of the time, because of the administrative work to be done. For the rest, it's a matter of each
one waiting for his or her turn, then joining the small group
of waiters beside the circle—did you see the group of those
waiting their turn as you came in?"

Hal thought back. There had, indeed, been a handful of
men and women on the far side of the circle of walkers, but
he had thought they were simply people who had stopped
for a moment to watch.

"The rule as laid down by Jathed, you see," went on
Amid, "is that once you begin to walk the circle you can
keep walking as long as you wish. The circle goes twenty-
four hours a day, every day of the year, so if it was physically possible, a single person could hold his or her place
in it indefinitely. But in reality, exhaustion would eventually put an end to anything like that; and the truth is, even
those walking normally seem to reach a point far short of
exhaustion, at which they decide to step out and let someone replace them. I don't mean they stop as a matter of fair
play or good manners; but simply because something in
them feels it has accomplished, or absorbed, or whatever
you want to call it—what it set out to do. As if a good
day's work had been done and they were satisfied with

what had been achieved after the time and effort expended."

"Can they tell you afterward what it was that made them decide to stop? What it was they'd accomplished?" Hal asked.

Amid glanced at him suddenly.

"That's an interesting question," he answered. "No. They can't. But they'll tell you that they feel . . . completed. In fact, that's the way I've felt after walking."

"I see," said Hal thoughtfully.

"What this means," said Amid, "is that while I can recommend your immediate access to the Guild members, you'll still have to go out there and join those standing by, and wait your turn when it comes. Unless someone ahead of you offers you his or her turn; and of course, this assumes that those in-between you and the one offering don't mind you going before them, too."

"No one, I think, would object to Hal being given priority," said Artur. "In fact, even not knowing him, they wouldn't object if a fellow Guild member wanted to trade places backward."

"Well, in theory they've got a perfect right to object, and I want Hal to understand that."

"I do," said Hal.

"In fact," said Amid, almost fiercely, "what you may actually find when you join the waiters is that they'll each offer you the chance to step ahead of them, so that you may be the first one to take the next opening in the circle. But that's up to them. They'd have to do that. I can't, in conscience, even recommend it."

"I understand," said Hal.

"Guildmaster," said Artur, "I think you may be leaning over backward a little in all this. Hal should also be reminded that it would only be showing a proper appreciation to accept if anyone offers him a chance to move up."

"Well, yes," answered Amid. "You're right of course. I'm sorry if I seemed to imply that you shouldn't accept if anyone offers, Hal."

"You didn't," said Hal.

"Good, then," said Amid. He turned to Amanda. "Amanda, you've hardly said a word. Now what, now that you've brought Hal here? Will you be staying, too? If so, there'll be a question of quarters. I'd gladly let you have my office for an indefinite number of nights, but sometimes we do need to work over there, when I've got a lot of our people doing some large project or other here; and in any case—"

"In any case," said Amanda, "I'll be staying only a few days to see how it works out for Hal. Then I'll be getting back to my own work in the district below."

"Whatever you want. Although," said Amid, "I'm old-fashioned enough not to like the idea of your teaching Exotics to physically fight for their rights."

"Only if they ask for it," said Amanda. "You should have understood by this time that what I teach them mainly is survival—how to survive if hunted, how to survive under the noses of the garrison troops. Your Exotics are never going to rise and drive off these invaders. On the other hand their own culture, given a little help in some instances, arms them with ways to deflect trouble, avoid trouble or defend themselves, if trouble unfairly comes looking for them."

"I'm relieved to hear that," said Amid. "As far as your staying temporarily, we won't be needing the office evenings and nights for several weeks, anyway; and in the case of your coming back for a few days unexpectedly, we can always work out something. But you haven't anything to say about what we're talking about? About Jathed and the history of our Chantry Guild here?"

"I'm interested—but this is Hal's area," said Amanda. "I'll just go on listening, if you don't object."

"Object? Certainly not. This isn't a place where people object to things. Also we're not discussing anything at all secret."

Amid turned to Hal.

"And since the subject of your area's come up," he said,

"I ought to admit to you, Hal, that we've got a selfish motive for having you with us; particularly since Amanda can't stay. The Occupation Forces would wipe us out in a moment if they suspected we were here. We avoid their finding out as much as possible by having contact with only three people from Porphyry, who come up this way every so often on the excuse of gathering fruits or berries from the wild plants. But there's always a danger that something might cause the local garrison to investigate this area. It'll be a relief to us to have someone with some military training on hand, even though the chance of their hearing about us up here is remote. We'll sleep a little easier until you leave."

"I'm afraid," said Hal, in a colder tone that he had intended, "you're under a misapprehension. Maybe Amanda could be some real help to you, but I'm no Dorsai."

He avoided Amanda's eyes directly as he said these last words but he was aware her gaze was on him. She said nothing.

"Oh, you aren't, we all know that," said Amid swiftly, "but I understand you had a Dorsai as one of your tutors and you're a good deal closer to one than anyone else on the ledge here—except Amanda, of course. But if the soldiers find us and it comes to an actual conflict—"

"Oh, that—" Hal shrugged. "Certainly, anything an individual can do, since I'm your guest. Of course."

He smiled a little, not happily.

"It's a good thing you didn't ask me that a couple of years ago," he said. "At that time my answer would have been that I'd become a little like the rest of you, in that philosophically I'd moved away from the area of violence. But now I'm free to be useful to you up here in any way I can."

"Ah," said Amid gently, "of course, you're entitled to live by your beliefs, just as much as the rest of us. If it'd be imposing on those—"

"No!" said Hal, and was surprised by the sharpness of

his own voice. More gently, he added, "it's perfectly all right. I'm at your disposal, body and mind."

"We appreciate it," Amid answered.

Amanda still said nothing, and Hal thought he was aware of an aura of disapproval emanating from her silence.

"Tell me more about Jathed," he said, to change the subject.

"Give Amid a chance to eat, Hal," Amanda spoke finally, "then you can ask all the questions you want."

"No, no. That's quite all right. I eat very little," said Amid. "About Jathed—what specifically do you want to know about him?"

"If you don't mind, Guildmaster," said Artur. "I've been sitting here just eating and listening; and I've pretty well finished. Why don't I answer while you eat? If there's anything important, you can always speak up. But you should eat."

"I'll eat, I'll eat!" said Amid. "You'd think I was a prize goat the way they're always trying to stuff more food down me!"

"I'm sorry, Guildmaster. We do overdo it, of course—"

"Never mind. I'll eat. You talk," said Amid. "But if there's anything I want to say, I'm not going to let a piece of fried root keep me from it. All right. I'm sorry. You're right. Talk. I'll eat."

He began taking pieces of food from the various serving bowls and putting them on his plate.

"If Jathed didn't believe in teaching, what did he do?" asked Hal. "Did he walk in the circle, himself?"

"Not in the memory of anyone who became a disciple of his," said Artur. "Apparently he had for years, all those years he was alone in the jungle living like a hermit, because, as I may have mentioned, there was a rut—in fact, you might even want to call it a ditch—worn outside the hut he'd built for himself by the time he began to admit disciples. In fact, it was already so deep that they'd shortly have worn it down until they were walking around out of sight below ground level, if some of them hadn't started to fill it in surreptitiously when he wasn't around. He came and caught them at it once, but didn't object. So they filled it back up to ground level, and kept it that way. You could never tell, apparently, what he was going to approve of or object to."

"But he, himself, had stopped walking by the time anyone began to live with him?" Hal asked.

"He said he didn't need to, any longer. That the Law was in his mind all the time now—it had worn a rut there as well as in the ground. That was one of the questions he answered from someone, once, instead of simply shouting '*Stupid!*' and chasing whoever it was off with his staff."

"But what did he do, if he didn't teach and he didn't walk?"

"In his later days," said Artur, "after he had acquired disciples, there were lots of times when he talked to them. I don't want to give the impression he was unreasonable all the time. In fact, most of the time he was pleasant, even witty, and perfectly willing to discuss things. The only problem was that if you made a mistake you got chased away for good."

"Someone he ran off couldn't come back later?" Amanda asked.

Artur shook his head.

"There weren't any warning shots, any second chances," he said. "Evidently if you asked the wrong question you were showing you didn't belong there, and out you went. Some of the people he chased away tried to form their own groups, but none of them got anywhere."

"Jathed could be, and was," interrupted Amid suddenly, "not only informative but charming. It didn't take a question to get him talking. A bird, a falling leaf, anything or nothing at all, might bring a comment from him and he'd go from that into a sort of informal lecture. Theoretically, as Artur just told you, asking the wrong question got you thrown out; but his disciples noticed that during one of these informal lectures of his, questions were a lot safer to ask. Then, he seemed more willing to explain than at other times. Some of these 'lectures' were recorded by those there at the time—Jathed didn't seem to object to that, either, under those conditions . . . Artur, where's that control pad? I thought I had it on the table, right here, unless I knocked it off. . . ."

He was searching around the end of the table.

"I'll find it, Amid," said Artur. "I think I saw it over by that chair you usually sit in."

He went back to where they had all been sitting around the fireplace, lifted a transparent glass paperweight, showing a small, green pine cone, about the size of a hen's egg, and took a control pad from underneath it to set it down by Amid.

"Thank you," said Amid. "My memory's as good as it ever was, except for little things like this."

"You work too hard, Guildmaster."

"I do what has to be done—never mind that, now. Ah, I've got it!"

He had been fingering the pad. Suddenly a surprisingly resonant, pleasant, deep bass voice sounded in the room.

"*. . . different universe. My universe is not your universe. For example, in my universe I will now get up— watch me—walk across the room, up the wall and stand head down, talking to you as I am now. That's because in my universe it's possible for me or anyone else to do that.*"

There was a long moment of silence, finally broken by a somewhat timid-sounding, young male voice.

"*Jathed?*"

"*Yes, Imher?*"

"*Pardon me . . . but it seems to me . . . that is, you're still sitting in your chair. You talked about moving but you didn't move.*"

"*Of course not—in your universe. But in my universe, I did exactly what I said. You didn't see it because you're not in my universe, you're in your own. Make an effort and*" *step into my universe, and you'll see me standing on the ceiling talking down to you."*

There was another pause.

"You can't do it?" said Jathed's voice. *"Of course not. You don't believe in yourself enough to believe that you can enter someone else's universe. But there're people even on the inhabited worlds today, Imher, who have enough faith in themselves to step into someone else's universe. Faith and—yes, courage—which you also lack, all of you here. Am I correct that none of you see me standing on the ceiling at this moment?"*

There was yet another pause.

"Well, speak up, speak up!"

A chorus that was very close to a shamefaced mutter of "no's" answered Jathed.

"But I can! I can, just now. It just happened. Jathed, I can see you up there."

"Do you indeed, Imher? Very well, as reward for your faith and courage, you may come up and join me. Come on up."

"Come up?"

"Wasn't that what I said?"

"Yes, Jathed."

There was a moment of absolutely soundless silence.

"I . . . I made it."

"LIAR! Out! Out! Out of my sight! Out of this place and never let any of us see you again! Go! Go!"

There was a thump, a scrabbling noise and the sound of shod feet running away. A door slammed.

There was a further lengthy moment of silence, then the voice of Jathed again, now a little breathless.

"Intolerable! Outrageous! Now, where was I? Oh, yes, on the ceiling. I'll just go back up there . . . try to watch me this time and see me. Now, here I am again, hanging head down; though of course it's not head-down to me, all the rest of you are wrong-side up-ah, but what have we here? Someone who actually has courage and faith. Well, don't

sit there on the edge of your chair, trembling! If you think you can do it, Reho, come up and join me."

"Should I?" said a different voice, doubtfully—female this time.

"Of course I think you can, numbskull! Would I invite you up if I didn't see you were in my universe? Come at once!"

"All right . . ."

Silence again.

"I'm here!" said the voice, full of wonder.

"Where did you expect to be? Now, for the benefit of all those below us who still lack faith and courage, to prove to them you're actually with me, reach back into your own universe and break the ceiling light just to your right, there."

A hesitation. Then the smashing and tinkling impact of light fragments on a hard surface.

"Very good. We'll go back down now. That's right."

"I . . . I'm afraid of heights. I didn't stop to think before I came . . . being upside down with nothing to hold me—"

"NOT IN MY UNIVERSE! You are not afraid of heights in my universe, Reho! Do you hear me?"

"Yes, Jathed."

"Good. Go down."

Silence again.

"Well?" said the voice of Jathed. *"Now that Reho and I are back in our seats, none of you saw anything at all out of the ordinary—except the inexplicable breaking of the light unit, two meters above your heads?"*

"No, Jathed," said the chorus.

"Well, you all have something to hope for, then, Each one of you pick up a fragment of that broken ceiling light and take it away with you to help you study. Ponder. Think. Do that successfully and you, too, may one day become aware of your own universe as distinct from others."

"Jathed?" It was yet another female voice.

"Yes, Katchen?"

"We didn't—I mean I didn't—see you go up the wall to the ceiling in your universe. But when Reho broke the light in her universe, we all saw it break. Why could we see something that happened in her universe but not in yours?"

"Think! Answer your own question. Why? Think! Can't you think of the answer yourself?"

"No, Jathed."

"You didn't see Reho break the light in her universe—that's the answer!"

"But . . ."

"But what?"

"But the light's broken. We can all see its parts on the floor there. We all saw it break."

"Where?"

"Where?"

"Don't parrot me. I said 'where?' Now you tell me—where did you see the light break?"

There was an extended silence.

"You each saw it happen in your own universe, you idiots!" snapped Jathed. "You didn't have the faith and courage to believe that I could walk up a wall and stand on the ceiling, in your universes. That's impossible. But you could believe that a light could be broken. Because lights break. That's poss-ee-ble!" He drew the last word out sarcastically. "When I, Jathed, told you that the light would be broken, so that you'd all have evidence Reho had been with me on the ceiling. THEN you believed! Numbskulls! Reho broke the light in her own universe, only. You—each of you—because for a moment you believed it was possible—broke it yourselves in your own universes, to make what I promised you actual."

He stopped talking. No one else said anything.

"All right. Understand then, that you have a universe, that you can do with it what you will—look at the piece of broken light in your hand, those of you who've already picked a piece up—the rest of you pick one up and look at it. Think. You did that, without getting up from your chair, without even walking up a wall and standing on the ceiling!

Do you understand now? Do you comprehend how your universe is a place where you can do anything you want, if you've got what's needed to do it, the faith, the courage— and the knowledge, which in this case is the knowledge that a light will break easily? If I'd said Reho would punch a hole in the ceiling, you might not have been as quick to believe and make it happen in your own universe."

"—Would you turn it off?" said Hal.

"Well, do as I say, pick up—"

The voice of Jathed broke off abruptly.

"That's curious," said Amid. "Why did you want the recording stopped, and stopped just there, Hal?"

"Because he said something very interesting. As you just remarked." Hal smiled at the older man. "I'd like some time to think about it."

"And what was it that was so interesting in particular, if I might ask?" Amid said.

"What he said about everyone being in their own universe," said Hal. "Don't ask me why just now, if you don't mind. The only answer I could give you would be too long and complex and right now I'm not even sure it'd be satisfactory."

"If you wish," said Amid. "This tape, and others of Jathed, are here any time you want to listen to them."

"Thank you," said Hal. "Now, since dinner's over—for which, thank you—perhaps Amanda and I had better make our move over to that office of yours, for the use of which, also thanks. It's been a long day, all of it uphill."

"I can imagine," said Amid. "Good night, then. It's very, very good to see you both. You particularly, Hal, since I hadn't been sure, until Amanda talked to me about bringing you, that I'd ever see you again after I'd left the encyclopedia."

"No meeting is ever impossible," said Hal.

"True. Good night, then, as I say. Artur will show you where the office is, and make sure you're properly settled there. Won't you, Artur?"

"Of course," said the big man.

CHAPTER 16 ■

Amid's office-the Guildmaster's office, as Artur somewhat apologetically explained it should be referred to, when they spoke about it to anyone but Amid—was large enough for two work positions, and that was about all. It did, however, have enough floor space to allow the folding down of an old-fashioned mattress, which during work hours folded up against one of the walls. It was a generously sized double mattress, for which both Hal and Amanda were thankful, having had to do with a few ordinary-sized beds in their time.

"Well," said Amanda, sometime later and just before they fell asleep. "Do you want to tell me why that recording of Jathed made you feel so good? I could feel you radiating cheerfulness right across the dining table. I probably could have felt it clear outside that room."

"It was what I told Amid, what had struck me in what Jathed had said," Hal answered, "about there being a universe for every individual person. I haven't lacked for evidence. I was on the right track in my search for the Creative Universe. But I haven't had any new evidence for several years now; and, suddenly, along comes a man who agrees with me."

"How agrees with you?" said Amanda. They were lying on their backs in the darkness, side by side, with all of the cloth covers with which the bed was furnished laid aside, since they were both rather sweaty. They were also holding hands. "He talked about a lot of universes. You've always talked about just one."

"It doesn't matter," said Hal. "One big universe with room in it for everybody to create what he or she wants, or one universe each in which to create what each one wants. It amounts to the same thing——"

He broke off suddenly.

"What is it?" asked Amanda.

"Just hearing myself say that both *conceptions* amounted to the same thing. *The transient and the eternal are the same.* The likeness reminded me of Jathed's Law, that's all. Anyway, Jathed evidently had hold of a corner of the same blanket I've got a corner of. It does cheer you up to have your findings corroborated."

"I'm happy for you then." Amanda gave his hand a squeeze. "But to be truthful, I still don't follow that business of the broken light. Would it be 'not-broken' to someone who hadn't been there, who just walked into the room, afterward . . . or what?"

"I don't know," said Hal. "Maybe that's why I'm right about it being one large universe with room for unlimited creations to be built in it, rather than an unlimited number of private universes, like Jathed said; and that's what's wrong with his theory, the fact that the question you just asked can't be answered. Or it may be that he was right in that some things done in the Creative Universe acquire existence in this one——for example, a painting's made in the mind of the artist, but it appears in what people will probably always call the real universe."

"But you know why it appears in the real universe. You can watch it being painted."

"No," said Hal, "what you watch are materials of various colors being applied to an even, vertical surface. When do you see the painter put into the painting whatever it is that makes those colors have a profound emotional effect on you? Or take music for example——"

"Never mind," said Amanda. "I see what you're driving at. I'm still glad you find him corroborating you; but the fact is I wasn't too impressed with him. He seemed more interested in showing off than anything else."

"Still," said Hal, "he was using the Creative Universe consciously and deliberately, which is something I can't do. He was entering it. All down the centuries, these artistic examples I'm always giving have been cases of creativity being used only on the unconscious level. It's as if the artist can reach through into the Creative Universe with his arms and hands only in it, and has to work there by touch alone. I want to go into it completely—step into it as if it were another place to be stepped into. I have to do that, to make a battleground where the Enemy and I can finally have it out; and to make an opening so that other people can enter after me, wholly and consciously, to work with it in the future. But you're right about miracles being a bad way to teach anything, let alone this. I rejected that method of teaching its existence the first time I discovered the Creative Universe—but I've told you about that."

"I wish," said Amanda, "you'd stop telling me you've told me things that you haven't told me. You've never said anything to me about when you discovered the Creative Universe."

"I'm sorry," said Hal. "I do a certain amount of going over things in my mind, with you there in imagination—effectively bouncing problems off you; and unless I deliberately stop to remember when I did that on a specific topic, I get the imaginary talks with you mixed up with the real ones."

Amanda turned her head on the pillow and kissed his cheek.

"What was that for?" he asked.

"Nothing. Go on," she said. "You're going to tell me, actually this time, when you first discovered the Creative Universe."

"It was back when I was a Donal," said Hal. "You remember I showed you Sayona the Bond back at the Encyclopedia? It was some time before then. I'd just quit being War Chief for the two Friendly worlds after a rather unfriendly scene with Eldest Bright, who was head of the United Council of Churches for the Friendlies—in fact, he threatened me with summary trial and execution. I had to shoot three of his guards he ordered to arrest me; and remind him that his capitol city was full of enough of my mercenaries, who could appreciate the bloodless victory I'd just given them, to make it unwise for him to try doing such a thing. He'd accused me of being bought by the Exotics, over whose forces I'd just given him the victory; and it turned out he hadn't wanted it bloodless. He'd wanted blood and lots of it, specifically Exotic blood.

So he had to let me go; but his last words were that I should go and look for work with the Exotics. I'd already decided to do just that, anyway; and so I contacted them. That led to an interview with Sayona, who hired me, but also made the suggestion I become an Exotic. One of the things he said was that he, at least, believed I was the kind of person who could walk on air if I really wanted to. I turned him down on being an Exotic, but . . ."

In the quiet office-turned-bedroom Hal could hear his voice echoing differently from the walls, now, as he remembered how it had been, being Donal. It was Donal's voice in his present ears; and it brought a strangeness over him. Telling Amanda about it, he found himself reliving that time, now more than eighty years in the past . . .

  . . . *deep in thought, he had returned to his own quarters in the city of Portsmouth, on Mara, which then held the Military Command Base for the two Exotic worlds. Portsmouth was in what on Old Earth would have been the temperate latitudes; but the nature of Procyon, the same sun that shone on Kultis, was such that the night which had just enfolded that city as he came back was tropical.*

  The soft illumination of his room had come on automatically as he entered; but it was so adjusted that it failed to white out the overhead view of the stars. These shone down through the open wall of the loggia that was his bedroom.

  Standing in the center of this loggia, his mind still full of the conversation with Sayona, Donal frowned. He gazed up at the gently domed roof of the loggia, which reached its highest point at two meters above his head. He frowned again and turned to search through the writing desk in the room until he found a self-sealing signal-tape capsule. Then, with this in one hand, he turned to look toward the ceiling again, and took one rather awkward step off the floor.

His foot found purchase in the air. He stepped upward, putting his weight on it. Slowly, step by step he walked up through nothingness to the high point of the ceiling. Opening the capsule, he pressed its self-sealing edges against the white surface of the ceiling, where they clung. He stood there a second in the air, staring at them.

"Ridiculous!" he said suddenly—and just as suddenly, he was falling. He gathered himself with the instinct of long training in the second of drop and, landing on hands and feet, rolled over and came erect like a gymnast against a far wall. He got up, brushing himself off, unhurt—and turned to look up at the ceiling. The capsule still clung there.

Suddenly he had laughed, cheerfully and out loud.

"No, no," he said to the empty room. "I'm a Dorsai!"

"You rejected it," said Amanda in the darkness. "Why?"

"I handled all things by intuitional logic, then," said Hal. "I ran the probabilities forward and found they went nowhere—at least as far as going where I wanted to go, which was to lead the human race to a time when none of them would ever do the sort of thing that had caused the death of my uncle James. But you do see—"

He turned to look in her direction. Although there was some light leaking around the door that led to the interior of the building and the bathroom facilities, there was not enough to read the expression on Amanda's face.

"—how I'd entered the Creative Universe, and used it, I'd had to, to be able to put that message capsule on the ceiling. From that, I realized there must be an aspect of things I'd never taken into account before; and the concept of the Creative Universe grew from that."

"But you turned away from it then?" she said.

"My first thought was that it was only good for parlor

magic tricks. It never crossed my mind it could be useful. Remember, at that time, as I say, I still believed in the way of getting physical control of all the worlds and making the people on them live by laws that would end the sort of situation that'd killed James. At that time I didn't see any reason it wouldn't work."

He hesitated.

"But that was the first time I'd entered the Creative Universe," he said more slowly, "and, like everyone else since time began, I did it unconsciously. I said to myself, 'let's see if I can't walk on air,' and tried it; and found I could. The potential of that came back to me once I got control of all the Younger Worlds and found laws alone wouldn't change human nature."

He laughed.

"Breathtaking discovery, wasn't it?" he said. "At any rate, then it occurred to me for the first time to go back to the twenty-first century and change the *direction* of history. My full appreciation of what the Creative Universe could mean for the race was born in my search for a way to do that. To begin with, it offered me a way to put my mind back into the past—and bring it back eighty years later than when it had left, in a two-year-old body."

He lay for a moment without saying anything. Amanda waited patiently.

"But even then I was making use of the creative forces largely unconsciously, without really understanding them. It was only when I had to recognize the Others as a result of the changes in intent I made in the established—frozen by time—historic forces of the twenty-first century, that I began to see the real shape of the job I had to do. It was then I really looked at the Creative Universe; and saw its ultimate possibilities, and the absolute necessity for them."

"Tell me," said Amanda thoughtfully, "you don't use intuitional logic anymore?"

"No;" said Hal. "It doesn't help what I'm doing now and hasn't helped much with anything I've done for a long time. It's a Donal-style tool, about as useful as the ability to do calculus instantly in your head. Idiot savants have done things comparable to it for centuries without giving the race a chance for improvement; let alone helping it grow, the way I hoped——"

He stopped, on a note in his voice that left what he had been saying uncompleted.

"But while my mind was back in the twenty-first century," he said, "under the influence of Walter Blunt and what the Chantry Guild was then, as well as by my own will, I entered the Creative Universe deliberately. Earlier, I'd just passed through it to get back in time. It was because I was there that I could be, and was, struck at by the Enemy. Otherwise, I'd never have begun to see what the conscious, willing entry into that universe promises everybody."

"But there's no way you can use intuitional logic to see your way to the Creative Universe?" Amanda asked.

"It doesn't work for that sort of problem. It's essentially a tool of the real universe, bounded by logic. It can't jump gaps—only go through the logical steps faster. I know I've been saying I have to find the way to the Creative Universe; but perhaps what I ought to be saying is that I have to *make* a way to it. If there was already a way, the kind of way I need, to the Creative Universe, intuitional logic could find it. But there isn't one yet, and intuitional logic not only can't find what isn't there, it can't make anything on its own."

"I understand then," Amanda said thoughtfully. "You're saying you can't see ultimate consequences to anything?"

"That's right. I can't. All that's visible to it is what ordinary logic would predict if ordinary logic had all the elements of the problem and unlimited time to work them to a conclusion. Intuitional logic not only doesn't work in the creative area, it doesn't work in the personal one—for instance, I can't see my own death; because like all reasonably healthy persons, I can't, on the unconscious level, conceive of myself as dead and the universe going on without me——"

Amanda did not move physically. The years of her upbringing, both as a Dorsai and as the protégé of the Second Amanda, held her still. But her profound emotional reaction reached out to Hal with shocking impact, through that same channel by which they could touch each other across light-years of space. Swiftly he gathered her into his arms, holding her tight against him. She lay still there, too, but now he could feel the trembling inside her.

"Amanda!" he said. "What is it?"

"I don't know. I can't tell you . . ." she said between teeth clenched tight. "It's as if the edge, just the edge, of some terrible sadness brushed me. Oh, my love—hold me!"

"I've got you," said Hal.

"Tell me you won't go away, ever!"

"I'll never leave you," said Hal.

"Oh, thank all heavens, all gods . . ." Amanda clung to him. He held her tight; and, in time, they slept—still close together.

CHAPTER 17 ■

Dawn through the uncurtained windows of the office woke them both. They dressed and found their way to the dining hall of the dormitory building they were in. They were seated across from each other at an end of one of the long picnic-style plank tables, having breakfast, when Amid joined them.

"Someone told you we were here," said Amanda, as the old man sat down next to her. He looked more diminutive than ever side by side with Amanda, Hal noticed. It was as if the last year or so had shrunk him even further, only without harming him. He was a little kernel of a man, but hard and alive.

"Quite right." He beamed at her. "I'd left word with those on kitchen duty in both buildings to let me know when you were up for breakfast."

He looked over at Hal.

"I thought I'd take you out and see you started in the circle myself," he said.

"Isn't that possibly going to mean a long wait for you?" asked Hal.

"Ordinarily, yes," said Amid. "But it seems things are out of my hands. Word about a visitor here is already around; and those currently waiting have all volunteered to let you go first. We'll only have to wait until the first person to step out of the circle after we get there does so. Then you step in; Amanda and I go about our business."

"Your business?"

Hal looked from Amid to Amanda.

"Well, I about my business," said Amid. "I was merely using the expression. What Amanda's immediate plans are, I've no idea. I assumed you'd know."

"I'm staying for a day or so," said Amanda, "so I can watch Hal at the start. I'll just wait around—unless you've got something I can do to help pay our way with you here? I know everyone on this ledge works at something or other."

"You're our guest," said Amid. "That rule doesn't apply to you or Hal unless you want it to."

"As I told you," said Hal, "I'll do my share of whatever's to be done."

"There you are," said Amanda. "That takes care of him. Now, what have you got that I can be useful at?"

"Thank you, then," said Amid. "All right, you can drop by our infirmary, if you want to. We don't have much sickness here, but small accidents will happen. Old Man is walking right now, so we could use someone who knows something about acupressure for pain relief and such—the sort of thing you Dorsai all know."

"A place like this, on an Exotic world," said Hal, "and

you need the skills of a Dorsai for battlefield-style medical handling?"

"Amanda radiates the will to recover more than most, as I imagine you know," said Amid. "We have one person here, as I just mentioned, who calls himself simply 'Old Man,' he does the same thing; but even he's not as good at it as Amanda."

"Oh?" said Hal. "I'd like to meet him."

"You'll see him when you get out to the circle," said Amid. "He's got a sort of aura about him that seems to make people heal themselves faster and more comfortably. Actually, his name is Laoren, which, I gather, is Chinese in origin. But when he came here he asked us to simply call him by its translation in Basic, which is 'Old Man.' He's somewhat unusual; an Exotic from a family that had preserved their ethnic purity for more than a century and a half. You know how, on these two worlds of ours, we've always approved rather of mixing ethnic strains than keeping them separate."

"I believe I saw him, as we came in," said Hal. He frowned with the memory of the sunlight flooding his eyes.

"It wouldn't be surprising if you had," said Amid. "He does rather stand out. Also, you probably noticed he wasn't repeating the Law aloud as he walked. That's another thing about him. He only speaks when he has to and we've gathered he appreciates people not trying to draw him into conversation. I don't mean to suggest he's withdrawn, socially. He's probably one of the most genuinely merry people I've met. But he just doesn't talk much."

Hal and Amanda finished their breakfast and they all went outside. In the fresh mountain air of the new day, Procyon beamed down at them out of a cloudless sky and the temperature was rising with that swiftness that promised a warm, if not hot, afternoon.

"Come to think of it," said Amanda, with a glance at the sky, "have you had a solar radiation shot in the past three years, Hal? Because Procyon's not like Sol—"

"I'm up to date," said Hal. He glanced at her exposed arms and legs, normally so pale, that were now a smooth, light tan. "How about yourself? You look as if you might be letting the local star get to you."

"Oh, I'm up to date, too," said Amanda. "I wouldn't slip up on that. It's just that I'd stand out like a bright light among all these Exotics if I'd stayed my usual skin color. So I amended it, to help me fit in."

Ahead of them, the circle was moving as it had been the evening before, and Hal now particularly took note of the small cluster of men and women off to one side, who were obviously the waiters. There were no more than half a dozen or so of them.

"Do those in the circle deliberately cut their time short, if they see a lot of people waiting?" Hal asked.

"They could, of course," said Amid. "But I don't think it happens very often. Once in the circle and once in the proper frame of mind; you see what's going on around you but it doesn't seem to have much, if any, importance—I can tell you that from personal experience. I think we've got one or two in the waiting group there, though, that are just out here to see you."

They had been walking toward the circle as they talked.

"You're sure word of who I am hasn't been mentioned?"

"I'd be the first one any of the people here would come and tell, if they thought you were who you are," said Amid. "Some may have seen a picture of you; but if so, since you haven't been announced, they're doing the polite thing and keeping it to themselves."

"A picture of me?"

"Yes," said Amid. "It's been spread all over the Younger Worlds as part of the Others' propaganda against Earth. I don't mean they've published it separately. But there've been references, of course, to you, Ajela, Rukh and some other people, as charges against them were publicly made. Not you so far, Amanda, by the way."

"Good," murmured Amanda. "I'd just as soon my picture wasn't too well known."

"Yes. But I'm afraid, in your case, Hal," said Amid, "there's a whole generation of children on the Younger Worlds growing up who're being taught to spit after saying your name. You're supposed to be the evil sorcerer crouched spiderlike in your lair in the Final Encyclopedia, cooking up evil things for good people on all the Younger Worlds."

They had joined the waiting group by the time Amid had finished saying this; all of the people in the group, with typical Exotic politeness, avoided looking directly at Hal and Amanda, or in any way appearing to attract the attention of the newcomers. As those walking passed, Hal had time to notice individuals. There was a drinking water fountain just beyond the far end of the circle, and three small buildings that were obviously personal waste-disposal units for the walkers.

"Three?" Hal asked Amid, pointing at them.

"Yes. Oh, I see what you mean," Amid laughed. "No, it's not that we've got three sexes around here, but you'll find when you get in the circle that you don't think of stopping for anything until something reminds you. Then you may be in a hurry. What we've found that tends to happen here is that someone will make a comfort stop and inadvertently set off what you might call a chain reaction. Jathed would have sneered at such niceties as drinking fountains and chemical waste-disposal units here; but my brother thought otherwise—by the way, there's Old Man turning the far corner, now."

Hal looked and saw the oriental-appearing walker who had attracted his attention when they had first arrived, the day before. As Amid had said, Old Man was just now coming around the far end of the circle, on its side that was closest to the waiters, so that he was now walking toward Hal and the rest of the waiting group.

True to what Hal had been told, the eyes of those in the

circle—and Old Man was no exception—seemed to take in all that was visible before them, but show no particular interest in it. Old Man's eyes looked at and through Hal as he strode toward him.

"Has he been walking all night?" Hal asked.

"I believe so," said Amid. "You saw him in the circle when you came in?"

"Yes," said Hal.

It was hard to believe Old Man had been at this for hours. He moved with a particularly light and springy step, as if he was about to leap into the air with the next stride; and Hal guessed that for all his long white beard and white mustaches, the other could run like a deer if he had to. In fact, in spite of his skinniness and the evidence of his age, there was an impression of power and youth about him. It was startling, for in appearance alone, he was almost frail. He was hardly taller or heavier than a twelve-year-old boy, except for the largeness of his hands and a surprising width of shoulders under the robe he wore, which Hal now saw figured with white blossoms upon a background of a red color so dark as to almost seem black. Old Man's hair was as white as his beard and so sparse that the skin of his round skull under it was visible in the sunlight.

"He's in remarkable physical condition," Amid was saying, beside Hal. "He has a sword of sorts he brought here with him; and he exercises with it when he isn't otherwise occupied. It's very graceful. It looks as if he's dancing, when he does it."

They fell silent. There was something about the words, repeated and repeated in their ears, that not only made conversation unnecessary but drew their minds, if not their bodies, into the circle of those who moved before them. Hal found his thoughts running over the oriental schools of martial exercises with the sword that he could remember. He made a mental note to watch Old Man at his exercises the first chance that made itself available.

Hal was still at this when one of the walkers left the circle. He was a younger man with close-cut reddish hair and a fuzz of reddish beard. He had been walking with all the appearance of normality, but after taking several steps away from the circle, he stumbled and his feet dragged, like those of someone exhausted, but still driving himself to move. One of those waiting was almost immediately at his side and helping him toward one of the nearer of the two dormitory buildings.

"In you go, Hal," said Amid.

"I'm waiting for Old Man to come around," said Hal. "I'd like to walk behind him."

"If you like," said Amid.

Old Man came around and Hal stepped in behind him. The next walker in the circle fell back a little distance to give room. Hal followed Old Man and, opening his mouth, began to repeat the Law:

"The transient and the eternal are the same . . ."

Almost immediately the rhythm of the walking and the intoned phrase took him over.

It was as if he had stepped on to the back of some powerful bird, which now took off with him. The words were like a living thing that lifted him and carried him away. The beating of his heart was in synchrony with the heartbeat of the bird; and a pressure he had not been conscious of feeling, but which had pressed down on him before, was suddenly released, so that he felt light and free.

He ascended within himself on the wings of the feeling that bore him, that had been outside him to begin with but which was now working itself inward on him, staining into him. He felt the words resonating in his throat and all through his body. He could not say what they meant, any more than he had understood more than their ordinary, everyday meaning before. But he felt something additional in them now, even though he could not reach through to something of deeper import yet—like a vast mountain in the distance, somewhere beyond him.

It was as Amid had said. He did not lose sight of, or

■ *Gordon R. Dickson*

touch with, his surroundings. He saw Amid and Amanda still standing, watching him for a little while before they turned and went off together, leaving only the small group of those who waited their turn in the circle. He saw and felt all that he ordinarily would have seen and felt, but it was irrelevant to what he was experiencing with his own movement and the repetition of the words.

The bird carrying him was his image and he let himself go with it. He felt the softness and warmth of the back feathers under him, felt the vibrations through them of the powerfully pumping wings, saw far distant on the horizon the triangular, mist-white shape of the Grandfathers of Dawn mountains that was his destination. The clean, thin air of the heights drew deep down into his lungs, searching out their very bottom crannies and corridors. And, without warning, he understood.

He understood that the weight that had dropped away temporarily from him as he stepped into the circle had been the weight of defeat. It had accumulated, layer by layer, day by day this last year, surrounding him, but held off from closing in on and crushing him by his strength of will, which grew and toughened like muscle in response to the demand placed upon it. So that his lack of success and his strength of will had increased together—until at last the limits even of his will were approached; and he had begun to give under the weight.

So despondency had finally begun to touch him. He had fought well and won, fought and won, again and again—and again and again victory had left him with the decisive encounter yet to be. Fear and its stepchildren, self-doubt and self-hatred, still tore and destroyed in the innermost parts of all human beings. He had conquered one wall only to find another, and another after that, and after that another, with his foe still alive and protected . . . until there seemed no end to the walls, and he felt the beginnings of an end to his strength.

He was aware that others had taken up this challenge in times before him, and all had failed in the end. But like

■ 180

each of those who had gone before, he had said, "We have come so far. We have won this much. Now, finally, we ought to be ready to reach the final battleground; and put an end to what plagues us."

Donal had won . . . and the final battle had turned out yet to be fought. Paul Formain had won . . . and the final battle still awaited. Hal Mayne had saved what must be saved of the human race, safe for a little while until the final battle could be fought—and the final battle was still beyond the horizon, still out of reach.

There must be an end, as there must have been a beginning. For the first time he wondered about the moment of beginning of the historical forces that had brought him and the human race to this moment. He had used the Creative Universe for the first time, as Donal, to go back to where he thought he could set up the forces that would bring about a final encounter. As Paul Formain he had found them in the twenty-first century. But neither then nor now had he ever thought of trying to reach back and find the absolute beginning of that last battle in which he would be a solitary warrior.

He reached out, mentally, now, to find that moment of beginning; and it led him to a place and a time, to a scene in which he became an Englishman in armor at the lowest point of his own life's long battle. It was a day of victory for the Black Prince of England, the battle of Poitiers; and its sights, its sounds, its feel came to Hal not only through this knight who had been his unconscious forerunner in this centuries-long contest, but also from a dying soldier of the other side. Hal was both men; and looked through the eyes of each to see the face of the other.

. . . *Sir John Hawkwood had fought the long day's fight, and fought well—but none of rank or worth on his own side had been there where he had fought the best of the other side, to note what he did. He had taken a prisoner, but it was a prisoner who was a French knight of small holding; and the ransom would not make Sir John rich. As*

*ransoms had made rich Sir Robert Knolles, and the notice
of the Black Prince had made famous Sir John Chandos.
He was weary and the anesthesia of the wine from the
night before, and of the early morning before the battle,
had long since worn off, leaving him weary and wasted
inside. Aimlessly, on a battlefield on which the main action
was over, he rode up one side of a little rise; over the top of
which, on the farther downslope, lay the tanner's son.*

*The tanner's son lay dying in the bright September sun-
light. About him was the odor of crushed grass and the
stink of the blood and the intestines of a horse who had
been disemboweled and lay nearby. The tanner's son was
a crossbowman from Lombardy. He wore leather hose and
a leather smock of sorts to which chain links had been
sewn. He was tall and lean, with a swarthy face and
straight black hair. He was in his early twenties and still
had most of his teeth. His mouth was wide and mobile. He
had an English arrow completely through his right side
under the ribs; and he had worn the feathers completely off
its shaft, since he had gone out of his head unsuccessfully
trying to draw it out the way it had entered. He had bled a
great deal; but in spite of that he continued to lie supporting himself on one elbow with such a wild look on his face
that none of the English archers or men at arms had
paused to cut his throat. Besides, he lay off to one side
himself where there were no wounded French knights or
such worth taking prisoner; and the battle had gone away
from him.*

*His eyes no longer focused on the field. Occasionally he
would cry out weakly in the dialect of his native Genoa,
forgetting he was now in the foreign fields of France.*

"Help! Help for the tanner's son!"

*Beyond him, at some little distance, the bearded, blood-
daubed English archers and other foot-soldiers hurried by,
rooting among the dying and the dead for a prisoner worthy of ransom. There were slim pickings here, for the more
adventurous of their fellows had already covered the
ground, cutting throats with quick boarlike jerks of their*

knives, when a candidate proved worthless or too wounded to promise to live. The wild, calling crossbowman, with the lank black hair falling half over his face, they had passed by out of a sort of instinct—two or three had even crossed themselves in passing. For, by a trick of its entering angle, the arrow appeared to anyone from a distance to have driven squarely through the crossbowman's heart. It seemed that he must already be dead; but still propped up and calling; whereas he was actually only dying, like all the rest.

Beyond the unfocused eyes of the crossbowman was part of the field of Poitiers, in the midwest of France. Up a slope behind him was a rubble of hedges and new-dug mounds, considerably torn about and beaten down now, which had been the original position of the English. Out beyond in the other direction was the little valley with the wood of St. Pierre to his left. In another part of the field, at the edge of that same wood, the banner of Edward of England, the Black Prince, was flying from a tall tree, to serve as a rallying signal for those English pursuing the French retreating to the moment of their slaughter below the prudently locked gates of the city of Poitiers. Below that flag, the tent of the Black Prince had been pitched; and in it, the Prince, Sir John Chandos and some others were drinking wine.

In a farther section of the field Geffroi de Charny had just been killed, and the banner of France, which he was holding, tottered to the ground. Behind him, King John of France, his dead lords about him, his fourteen-year-old son Philip beside him, felt his weary arms failing at the effort to lift and strike with his battle axe once again. The English were crowding close, eager to capture a King, shouting at him to surrender. He turned to one strong young man, pushing toward him, who had called out to him in good and understandable French. The moment of his capture was near.

Meanwhile, unknowing of all this, the crossbowman wept a little from his unseeing eyes, propping himself on his elbow, and called out to the great pain in his body and the sun, like a brilliant furnace at high noon over his head in the cloudless sky:—

"Help! Help for the tanner's son . . ."

And so he cried—as he had cried for a long time without any response, but more weakly as time went on. Until, from somewhere he heard the approaching thudding of hooves that came to him, and stopped; and a following thud as two mailed feet came one after the other to earth beside him. For a moment nothing happened; and then a voice in an English the crossbowman could not have understood even before he got an arrow through his body, spoke above him.

"Who's a tanner's son?"

A couple of iron-sheathed knees came to earth beside the crossbowman. The crossbowman felt the weight of his upper body lifted off the supporting elbow. Through the delirium of his pain, a feeling of being rescued penetrated to him. He stopped crying out and made a great effort to focus his eyes.

A circular shape peaked at the top steadied and unblurred before his eyes. He looked from a distance of inches up into a lean, rectangular-jawed face, unshaven and surmounted by an iron skullcap with a cloth skullcap showing dark blue and rather ragged edges underneath the metal edge. The face of John Hawkwood had a deep-set nose, fine blue eyes under straight brown eyebrows, and a straight, angular nose that had never been broken. The face had the clear, even color of naturally blond skin tanned and dried by the sun until its surface had gone into tiny, premature wrinkles around the corners of the eyes and indented deeply around the mouth. The mouth itself was thin-lipped but level of expression, the nostrils thin— and from them came a strong exhalation of breath laden with the odor of wine gone stale.

"Who's a tanner's son?" repeated the lips, this time in the mixed argot of the military camps. But the crossbow-

man now comprehended nothing but the dialect of his childhood. He understood only that someone had come to his aid; and because the man who held him was clean-shaven he thought, not of a knight who might need to breath unencumbered inside his clumsy headpot of a helm, but that the one who held him was a priest. He thought the priest was speaking to him in latin and exhorting him to confess.

"Forgive me, Father, for I have sinned . . ." he whispered.

The man who held him had been able to make out the business of the tanner's son; but this further whisper in the Genoese dialect left him at a loss. Vaguely, he caught the sense of the word "sinned" but that was all.

"What the hell," he said, in the camp argot, a little thickly, "we're all sinners. But we aren't all tanner's sons."

He sat back on his heels and lowered the head of the crossbowman on to his knees. He lifted the cloth and metal skullcaps of the bassinet off his head together and wiped his forehead with the back of his hand. "I'm a tanner's son, myself."

He broke off and looked down, for the crossbowman had begun to speak again; and the rhythm of the phrases of the confessional were familiar.

"Well," he said in English, "I can do that much for you. One Christian to another, eh?"

He put the bassinet back on his head and listened, though what the other said was all but incomprehensible. The crossbowman was trying to remember his sins; but he confused the pain in his body with the pain of disease, which he associated with the evilnesses of his relations with women. To describe these, he had of necessity to use words more common and understandable to the man whose knees he rested on—and who nodded, hearing the words.

"That's it," said the man. "That's it. Not much like that

*in Hedingham Sibil, in Essex where I was a tanner's son—
or wherever you hail from, I suppose. But enough of it
here."* He listened awhile longer. He noticed the lips of the
crossbowman were darkened and dried.

"Use a little wine, here," he muttered. "None with me
though, damn it. Go on, go on . . ."

But the crossbowman had finished his confession; and
now he had begun to weep once more. He had thought
that, having confessed himself, he would find himself forgiven and the pain taken away. But it was still with him. He
plucked feebly at the now smooth end of the arrow.

"Help!" he husked, once more, in a barely audible
voice. "Help, for the tanner's son . . ."

"Damn you!" swore the man holding him, blinking his
own eyes suddenly and pulling the plucking hand from the
unmoving arrow's nocked end. "What do you want me to
do for you? That's no good."

The crossbowman wept. His mind had wandered again;
and now he imagined he was a boy again and the pain was
because he was being punished for something.

"You made your peace," growled the man holding him.
"Get on with your dying." He looked at the arrow. "A hard
way out is it?" He blinked again. "Poor filth. All right,
then."

He reached down and drew a short, heavy-hilted dagger
from a scabbard on his swordbelt.

"Misericord," he said. "God forgive this wretched sinner, and give him quick relief from payment for his sins,
amen."

He leaned over with his lips close to the crossbowman's
right ear, thinking perhaps it would give the sinner the
good feeling of a little pride before his death. "A knight
kills you, man."

But the crossbowman did not in any way understand the
words. A deeper understanding had come to him. He had
finally understood that he was dying. His mind had fled
back to imagining he was with a priest again; and when he
saw the insubstantial, glittering shape of the misericord

*lifted up before his eyes, he thought it was the Cross being
given him to kiss, and he felt a holy joy.*

*"I am ready to die, Lord," he thought he prayed. "Only
let it be fast."*

It was fast.

CHAPTER 18 ■

Hal woke to find himself stumbling over the level ground,
which seemed to heave and billow under his feet like the
ocean surface. From the position of Procyon, overhead, it
was midmorning; he was no longer in the circle. Amanda
held him by one arm, supporting and guiding him. Old
Man held and supported him on the other side with equal
strength. As Hal turned his head to see the other, Old Man
looked up, smiled fleetingly but warmly and then looked
ahead again to the dormitory building containing. Amid's
office, to which the two were taking Hal.

"What is it?" said Hal. "What's wrong?"

To his own surprise his voice came out like a whisper.
His throat was raw from repeating the. words that still
thrummed in his mind.

"You walked for twenty-three hours, Hal!" said
Amanda. "I think you'd have killed yourself the way a
horse can run itself to death, if we hadn't pulled you out
of the circle. Now, lean on us. We'll have you in bed in a
minute."

Suddenly, he felt a longing to be where she had promised. Horizontal, on a flat surface, in the darkness of a
quiet, closed room. Consciousness of the exhaustion of his
body flooded in on him. His knees gave at every step and
his legs wobbled with weakness. He staggered on between
Old Man and Amanda to the dormitory building and the

outside entrance that led directly to the office, to the bed . . . and onto it.

"Thank you," said Amanda to Old Man. He smiled back at her, then went softly and swiftly out. She took a blanket from the bed and hung it over the windows on a rod above them that had not been there when Hal had last seen them. The blanket did not completely shut out Procyon's intense light, but it dimmed the room and Hal luxuriated in the dimness.

Amanda went around to the other side of the bed and lay down on top of the bedcovers beside him. She put her arms around him.

"Now, sleep!" she commanded.

He closed his eyes, and sleep swooped down to carry him away.

When he woke, the room was totally dark. Amanda slumbered beside him, now tucked in under the covers in ordinary fashion. She opened her eyes as he stirred. He laid his hand on her shoulder, lightly.

"You sleep," he whispered. "I'll be back in a while."

He got up, found his clothes—Amanda or someone had obviously undressed him while he was still too deep in sleep to notice—and let himself into the outer air on the other side of the office door.

Beyond the walls and the blanket that served as a curtain over the window, he found the first faint light of dawn. He guessed it at about four in the morning. He must have slept for nearly as long as Amanda had said he had walked. His body worked better now than it had on its way to bed from the circle, but it still held a feeling of having been used and overused. He was not so much weak as drained of strength.

A few lights were on in the two dormitory buildings, particularly in the part of each one which held kitchen and dining facilities. The mountains to the east were a distant darkness beyond the lip of the ledge, and a few figures moved about the area with the intentness of those on duty of one kind or another. But in the near distance, where two lights still could be seen burning, paled by the approaching day's illumination, the circle still turned. Those in it still chanted and four people stood in a small group, waiting their turn.

He walked away from the building, toward the circle and those who waited. But he stopped back a little from joining the waiters; and stood, merely watching them and those in the circle for a few moments. Then he turned and went on, parallel with the stream beyond them, toward the edge of the ledge. At the point where the stream emptied into the pond, he found a level space of ground beside it and sat down; looking across it toward the end of the ledge, only some five meters beyond, and at the black ridge of the Grandfathers of Dawn, distant, their upper edges now a jagged, glowing line from the ascending sun hidden behind them.

Slowly, as he sat watching that glowing line, he found himself beginning to understand how Tam's dying, with his guilt still unexpiated in him, could stop Hal from ever finding the Creative Universe.

Amanda had been right. The way he searched for was to be found out here among people; rather than back there in that artificial, if valuable and special, atmosphere of the Encyclopedia.

What would happen if Tam died unfulfilled, in his own mind unforgiven, for his responsibility for the deaths of his sister's young husband, David Hall, of Jamethon Black, who had sacrificed himself to stop the attack that Tam had mounted against the whole Friendly culture, and the assassination of Kensie by a political group on Ste. Marie as a direct result? Unless Hal found the Universe in time to prove to him that, if nothing else, these things had had a purpose to a good end, for all the race? Lacking that, plainly, Tam was determined to leave life as the legendary King Arthur had, in sadness and remorse.

If Tam died that way Ajela would die with him, in spirit; and that part-death would make her unable to continue running the Final Encyclopedia, precious as it had always been to her, as to Tam. If that happened, who else was there who could guide and order it? Rukh had helped out to a great degree, these last months, but it was not her job.

Rukh's job was the kindling of a faith in the new future to be, in the people of all the worlds; and that was a larger, more important duty than steering the Final Encyclopedia. He, Hal, should not, because his job was also elsewhere, leading those who would be the pioneers into this new untouched infinity of potential that the Creative Universe would be—if he ever achieved it. But if Ajela could not, Hal must. It was a special trust, handed into his keeping by Tam, who had gotten it from Mark Torre in equal trust. And that would be an end to his search for the Creative Universe. As Amanda had now shown him, the way to that was to be found not in special places but out among people.

Sitting, waiting for the dawn, he was aware of the presence of Tam, keeping him company. It was not an unpleasant awareness.

The sky had brightened, though the sun was not yet in sight above the Grandfathers of Dawn. Below, the valley was a deep lake of white mist hiding everything, but thinning as he watched. Slowly, as he sat with the daylight growing stronger all about him, he felt himself gradually enclosed by peace. Behind that peace came the order and reason he realized now he had needed for some time.

Just as his frustration at the Final Encyclopedia had made him blind to Tam's completion being necessary to the completion of his own search, so he had been blind to the obvious fact that what had blocked him in his search at the Final Encyclopedia must have been implied in the historic beginnings of that search.

He knew of the man he had envisioned while walking the circle, from his military studies as Donal and his readings as the young Hal. And he doubted that any histories held the moment he had relived while walking the circle. That had been a creative reconstruction of his own imaginative unconscious. He had not been able to enter the Creative Universe, except in his dreams; but he had been able to reach into it from the circle to build something that must fit closely with the known facts.

Historically, therefore, his fight against the Enemy had had its roots in the chronicled life of a man known to history as Sir John Hawkwood, citizen of fourteenth century Europe, and English knight in the early years of the Hundred Years War between England and France. A man destined to become one of the earliest of the great *condottieri*—professional military captains of the fourteenth to seventeenth centuries in Italy—and the individual some later military historians were to call "the first of the modern generals." The circle and the Creative Universe had at last led him to this man. Not to Hawkwood's whole life; but that special moment of it, on a field of victory, which paradoxically had been the lowest point of the dreams and hopes in Sir John's life—as the past year had been Hal's lowest.

At Poitiers, Sir John had been entering into middle age, a knight with only a modest name as a military captain and no fortune to show for the scars of twenty years in arms and armor. And with the final defeat now of the French, let alone the capture of King John of France which Hawkwood at that moment had not yet known about, the war that had promised him a way to better himself was apparently over. He had stood empty-handed in the middle of his life and looked, it seemed, nowhere but downward into old age; penury and oblivion.

But from the chroniclers, Hal knew, as Sir John then had not, that from here the knight would go over the mountains into Italy, entering not only into more wealth than he had ever had before, but into the pages of history. Unknowingly, at this moment on this battlefield where his future looked most bleak, ahead of him lay his marriage to Donina Visconti and the most important period of his life. His name would come to mean more at the English court, once he was in Italy, than it ever had during the long years he had been in France.

The only question now might be whether Hal's case was really comparable to Hawkwood's, as his vision had implied.

It must be. The parallels were too close. As the predawn light grew, Hal's belief strengthened with it. Even though he could no more see his own future than Hawkwood at Poitiers could have seen his, what he had just envisioned assured him, once more, that his coming here had been the way he needed to go. Just as going over the mountains into Italy, with the White Company of mercenaries, after Poitiers, had been the right way in which Sir John had needed to go.

Moreover, all this fitted together with, and was reinforced by, his own strong reaction to the circle and the Law, from the moment he had first seen and heard them.

As for Tam, the instinct in Hal that had caused him to associate the older man's state of mind with the lines from Tennyson's poem on the death of Arthur Pendragon, must be trusted as well. It fitted too well with the story and character of Jathed, and the Hawkwood episode. Part of Hal's error, he told himself now, had been to ignore Tam as still an important factor in the search for the Creative Universe, beyond the point of his retirement as Director of the Encyclopedia.

Even as Hal thought these things, the sun broke its top edge clear of the Grandfathers of Dawn, on the far horizon. Procyon looked blindingly over them at him for the merest fraction of a second before he could lower his eyes from that blazing tiny circle of light; and in that same fraction of a moment he realized what he must do. What was necessary to him here was Jathed and Jathed's philosophy, even though Hal instinctively felt it was not entirely correct. What was here, that was nowhere else to be found, was the Law.

Hal could walk the circle and say the Law, as the others did. But it was not enough to use it as a tool to put himself into flights of exploration of his inner mind. What he must do was understand it—completely understand it.

"The transient and the eternal are the same . . ."

He knew what the words said. But what, in their completeness, did they really mean?

He did not know—yet.

There was an understanding needed here that must be made by the deeper parts of his mind, by his creative unconscious. Sudden excitement lifted him to his feet. It might be that in this greater understanding was exactly what he had sought for so long, a way into the Creative Universe. Certainly, it had let Jathed through; and Jathed had not the reason to go there that Hal had, nor the vision of what going there could make.

Filled with wonder, the first direct rays of the sun already warming his back through his robe, he went lightly and swiftly as Old Man might have gone, back to the office where he and Amanda had spent the night.

CHAPTER 19 ■

He reached the office and found it empty, the blanket down from the window, the bed made and tilted up into its storage position against the wall. There was something finished and over with about the room that brought a sadness like the pain from the thrust of a dull knife, deep into him. He turned and went through the office's inner door and along a corridor to the dining area of the building the office was in.

Amanda was not there. The room was all but empty of breakfasters.

"Friend?" The server on duty behind the counter with its trays of breakfast foods called to him. Hal turned.

"You're to go to Amid's Reception Building," said the

server. "Amanda's waiting for you there, with another new visitor."

"Thanks," said Hal.

He left and went to the small building which had been the first he had entered here on the evening of his arrival. Amid was there, seated with Amanda, and not only Artur, but Simon Graeme as well, around a fireplace that now in the growing warmth of day held no fire in it, only a few blackened ends of wood and the ashes, cold and gray, from the previous night's blaze. The pine cone paperweight gleamed on the desk in the daylight.

"There you are," Amanda said as he came in. "Come sit by me, here."

He went to the empty chair beside her and sat down. She put out a hand to him and for a second he held it and then their grasp fell apart.

"How do you feel?" asked Amid.

"A little washed out," said Hal. "Nothing another night of ordinary sleep won't cure."

He looked back at Amanda, and Simon just beyond her.

"Hello, Simon," he said. "You look a little washed out yourself."

"Hello, Hal." Simon smiled, a little ruefully. "Mountain climbing, even down-mountain's, not something I'm in training for."

Hal's gaze turned on Amanda.

"You're leaving?"

"If I can trust you to take care of yourself in that circle from now on," said Amanda. "Simon can go back to the near vicinity of Old Earth, and fire off a millisecond message to the Final Encyclopedia telling them how we're settled, then immediately jump clear of the Solar System and come back to stand sentinel over us from orbit. I've got a full district I ought to be covering locally, since no one's seen me since I left to go back and get you. It'll take a month to cover it all, but I'll never be more than a couple of days' march from here. So if you need me, signal Simon with our cloth display system; and he'll either go get me, or pass the word to me to make it back here. What about it? Do you think you might need to stay as long as a month?"

"I could, very possibly," said Hal. He looked at Simon. "Where's the ship?"

"In a crack back up in the mountains, out of sight from here or anyone below," Simon answered, his heavy-boned Graeme face under its dark brown, thick hair lit up with a wry smile. "Amanda put out the signal late yesterday and I landed last night; but I had to wait for near day to climb down to you if I didn't want to break my neck in the dark."

"How much of a climb is it back up to it?"

"A couple of hours, at most," Simon answered. "Slower up than down."

Hal nodded. He reached out for Amanda's hand again, and felt her fingers close with his.

"I hate to see you go," he said.

"I know," she answered softly. "But I'm not needed here, and I am out there."

He nodded.

"I guess that's it then," he said. "If anything changes or develops for me, here, I'll call you back."

"And I'll not waste any time coming—oh, before I forget it again," said Amanda, turning to Amid, "I've been meaning to mention this. A few hours' walk from the bottom of our mountain, here, there's a wild little girl in the woods who came out to take a look at us but was too quick for us to catch. Someone ought to be looking after the child. Do you suppose some of the people from here could go down there and catch her? It'll take a dozen at least. She's fast, and woods-wise."

"Hmm," said Amid. "Maybe I'd better let you answer that, Artur?"

The big man shifted uneasily in his chair as the rest all looked at him.

"You see, Amanda," said Artur slowly, "we—I know all about that girl. Her name's Cee. Actually, she's my niece."

"Your niece?" Amanda was staring at him. "Then why haven't you done something about her before this?"

"Artur has, and does—" Amid was beginning, but Artur lifted a hand.

"I'd probably better explain it all," he said. "My sister, her husband, and Cee—Cee was only seven years old, then—lived fairly close to here. In fact, where you saw Cee probably wouldn't be too far from where their home was."

His face clouded and he clenched one hand into a heavy fist with which he beat softly on the arm of the chair he sat in.

"The trouble was, I was so bound up in the Chantry Guild—we'd just begun to use the ledge here, but we hadn't yet really moved up to it—that all those first seven years of her life, I hardly saw my sister's house, and Cee . . ."

"There's no point in blaming yourself for what's past," said Amid. "We've discussed that a number of times."

"I know. But if I'd just dropped by half a dozen times a year, just enough so that the girl would realize I was one of the family . . . only I didn't; and you're right, it does no good to keep going over and over that fact now."

He hesitated.

"The point is," he said to Amanda, "Cee never got to know me. I've never been anything more than a stranger to her; and she doesn't trust strangers. With good reason."

" 'Good reason,' have anything to do with our friends, the Occupation troops?" asked Amanda.

Artur looked at her brilliantly.

"I thought you might guess that," he said. "Yes, just after we'd hidden ourselves up here on the ledge, the Occupation went around killing all the relatives of people known to belong to the Guild. There was no warning for any of them. One day up here, we heard explosions and, using a scope screen, we found troops in the woods less than half a kilometer from here. Some of us went down to the place where my sister's home had been—this was before they destroyed all the country homes and moved people into town—but there was nothing left but a pile of rubble. We found enough of my sister and her husband to know they had been killed by the explosions that destroyed their house. We searched for Cee, found nothing there or anywhere near; and when she didn't show up, we checked and made sure there was no one alive under the rubble. The soldiers were going back and forth below us frequently in those days. It wasn't practical to really dig into the rubble without giving away the fact we'd been there. So we assumed she was dead under it somewhere. So we gave up temporarily; and then, some of us, slipping into the towns nearby for things we needed occasionally, began to hear about a wild little girl in the woods up this way."

He stopped. Beads of sweat were standing out on his forehead.

"It wasn't until nearly a year later that I began to believe that the stories were anything more than that, and that the wild girl might be Cee. I went down to find out; and I soon found you could look forever and not locate her, because she'd be seeing you long before you saw her and keeping out of your way. So I started going down there and just sitting. I sat; and after a number of trips, when I was sitting. I began to catch glimpses of her, getting just close enough to watch—and gone at once, if I turned my head to get a square look at her."

He beat his fist softly on the chair arm again. He was looking past Amanda now, at nothing unless it was his own memories of those times he had sat, hoping that the little girl would move into his field of vision.

"I kept that up. It was incredible she'd survived, all by herself that way; but as you know, you can live off the country, here, the year around. And we've got no real winter. The temperature hardly varies. The only problem is rain, which isn't a problem unless it comes in the winter months and then it comes down pretty steadily. But all she'd need would be some place to get in out of it; a cave, or even a hollow tree. Anyway, it was true. My little niece had become like a wild animal."

"She was old enough when her parents died to know

about other people," said Amanda. "You'd think she'd have gone looking for, if not you, for someone she knew who'd been a friend of her parents."

"They hadn't—my sister and her husband weren't hermits by any means," said Artur. "But they believed in being as self-sufficient as possible; living off the land and making what little money they needed out of their wood carvings—they were both sculptors. Also, like me, my sister tended to tie into an idea and see nothing but that. They didn't have any close friends, they were off in the woods by themselves—and I really think that their deaths, the way it happened, did something to Cee. She's not really sane, I suppose. Still . . ."

He fell silent.

"Go on," said Amid gently, "tell them the rest of it."

There were beads of sweat still on Artur's forehead. Aside from that, his face showed no particular expression. But now his hands clenched on the ends of the chairarms beneath them.

"I sat for weeks," he said, "and gradually she began to come closer to me, a little at a time. She'd stay at a certain distance for days; and then, one day, she'd be just a bit nearer. I'd learned by that time not to watch her, except out of the corners of my eyes; and I never showed in any way that I knew she was gradually closing the distance between us."

He laughed, a little shortly, but his forehead was still damp and his hands still gripped the ends of the chairarms.

"I got to be very good at pretending not to notice—so good I could almost convince myself I wasn't the least bit interested in her—and all the while, day and night, I was carrying around a load of guilt because I hadn't searched harder for her after the explosion that killed my sister and her husband. I got very good at listening. I could hear her, quiet as she was, when she started to get very close behind me. And still I never moved, I didn't give her any cause to suspect that I was just waiting for her to get within arm's reach."

He stopped and wiped his brow with the back of one hand.

"She finally came right up to me," he said. His voice had acquired a strange deadness, as if what he was starting to tell them now was beyond emotion. "She came up right behind me, and I felt a touch—oh, what a light little touch it was—against the back of my robe. Just a moment's touch, and no more. But still I didn't move. I was still waiting; and, after a long while I began to see something out of the corner of my left eye. She was inching around to look at my face up close. And I let her come . . ."

He stopped.

This time Amid said nothing. They merely all waited. After a long moment, he went on.

"She came around. She was moving by twitching her heels a tiny distance sideways, then twitching the front ends of her feet next, in the same direction. I didn't move. I hardly breathed. When she came around by my left knee, so that she was in plain view, just inches away, I still kept staring straight ahead, as if she was unimportant, as if she wasn't there. And so she came all the way round in front of me, so that I had to look into her face or move my eyes. And we looked at each other . . ."

He broke off.

"Go on, man. Tell them!" said Amid, as the silence went on and on.

"Wonderingly—" The word came out like a gasp. "She looked at me so . . . wonderingly, as if she was searching my face for something to find that she'd know. I never should have tried what I did. I should have known better. From the beginning I should have realized it'd take someone more patient. Old Man could have done it. He'd have waited. He knows how to wait. I've seen him put the tip of one of his fingers slowly under a moth perched on a twig and pick it up on that finger, off the twig, so softly and easily that the moth doesn't fly away. But she belonged to me . . . she was my niece, all that was left of my sister's family."

He stopped talking for a moment. Then brought his gaze back to focus on Amanda, and went on.

"And so," he said, "when she finally stood there in front of me, right in reach, searching my face with those eyes of hers—hazel eyes they are and large—without really thinking, supposing that somehow she'd come to understand later and everything would be all right once I'd brought her up here—I reached for her. I grabbed at her."

He hesitated, but just long enough to draw a deep breath, this time.

"She was fast," he said. "I can't believe how fast she was. I could have sworn no human being could come that close within my reach and not be caught. But my hand barely touched her. And she was gone."

He stopped. He breathed, another sigh that this time was so deep it seemed to empty him, and his large body slumped in its chair.

"And since then, she won't come near you," said Amanda.

He nodded.

"I sit—I've sat for two years since then," Artur said. "And she comes. Sometimes I just catch a glimpse of her, but whether I see her or not, I know if she's there. But she's never come within ten meters of me, since. And sooner or later, something'll go wrong. Something will bring soldiers by; and one of them—she always comes to look at anyone who goes by—some soldier'll shoot her. Or she'll get sick and hide herself in some hole where no one can find her, and die. She's all alone down there—"

He broke off on a single, hoarse, dry sob that shook his heavy chest.

"I can't do anything," he said. "She won't come near me."

"Of course not," said Amanda gently. "What do you expect? When you reached for her that way, you just confirmed whatever it is that makes her what she is. She'll never come close to anyone as long as you're around."

"What can I do?" Artur looked at her. "I can't just forget about her and leave her alone down there!"

"Send a woman," said Amanda. "Didn't you ever think of that? I'd guess even your Old Man wouldn't have a chance at her now. Also now that I know what her story is, it's plain my idea of a group taking her would be the last thing to try. It'd probably destroy whatever chance there is of her becoming halfway normal again, if she was taken by force. But a woman, starting from scratch, could get close enough to make friends with her. Note, I said make friends with, not grab. The day she'll come home to you safely will be the day she comes up to this ledge of her own free will, holding the hand of someone she trusts."

Amanda stopped. Artur stared almost blindly at her.

"I'd do it myself," said Amanda, "but I've got other responsibilities; and she's still only one life, while there're hundreds of lives within two days' walk of here who can use my help. It'll take time to do, probably, time I can't spare for that alone, in any case. But there must be a woman member of the Guild who could help you."

She reached out to put a hand on his arm.

"The hard part for you," she added, "is going to be staying away while the woman makes friends with her."

"Yes . . ." Artur's face twisted, then straightened out. "A woman! I'd never thought of that."

"You should have," said Amanda. "The soldiers were probably all men, judging by what I've seen of the Occupation forces. And she was well enough up in years to know the difference and what she is, herself. You can try it."

"I will. Thank you, I will." His face twisted again for just a second. "But it'll be hard not going down to see her, day after day, just as you say."

He stood up.

"Never mind. That's what I'll do. If you'll excuse me, Amid, I think I'd like to go and look for someone to help me with Cee right now."

"Just a second," said Amanda. "Before you go, can you tell me what the idea was of that vine around her waist, and what it is she carries in the pod in the middle of it?"

"Rocks," said Artur. "My sister, Mila, and Petay, her

husband, used to hunt rabbits as part of their food. Petay could throw a rock accurately enough to kill a rabbit from some little distance. He'd wait until one sat up with its head above the ferns to look around and then aim at its neck. If he was a little high he'd still get the head: if he was a little low he'd still strike a shoulder area and slow the creature down so that he could run it down and catch it."

"They weren't pure vegetarians, then, your sister and brother-in-law?" Amanda asked.

"No," said Artur, "luckily for Cee. She's got no access to diet supplements. Mila preferred to use a sling—you know like the sort of sling they used on Old Earth in very ancient times. Whether Cee learned from the two of them, or practice made her good at hunting since she's been on her own, I don't know, but she kills rabbits regularly for her own eating, both ways. She can throw very hard and accurately with a sort of sidearm swing; or she can use the vine and pod, or something else as a sling, to kill from a greater distance. When you tried to catch her, did she make any motion to use the vine, or take one of the rocks out of it?"

"No," said Hal.

Artur nodded.

"She wasn't too frightened of you, then. She must have been sure she could get away. But she does know what she can do with those rocks—as I say, whether she had lessons from Mila or Petay or not—and I've always been afraid that if soldiers came up here and chased her she might try to use the rocks on them. Then they undoubtedly would shoot her!"

He turned abruptly to Amid.

"Forgive me, Amid," he said, unusually brusquely for an Exotic, "but the sooner I find someone as Amanda suggests, and tell them what needs to be done, the better I'll feel. If you don't mind—"

"Go ahead, go ahead!" said Amid. When the door had closed behind Artur's back, he turned to Amanda. "I don't

.think you'll ever know how much of a help that suggestion of yours was to Artur, just now. Well, never mind that, now. How soon had you planned to leave?"

"Right away," she answered. "Both Simon and I'll be going our separate ways."

She looked at Hal and smiled a little, regretfully.

"Let's step outside and have a word by ourselves, before you go," Hal said to her. "Amid, Simon—you'll forgive us? We won't be more than a few minutes."

"By all means," said Simon, "we've got all the time there is. Take what you want."

Amid simply waved them out.

Once in the open air and the sunshine beyond doors, Hal began to pace toward the ledge. Amanda walked along with him. Their hands joined automatically. They walked without speaking until they came near the edge and turned, so that they walked along it, with empty air on their left and the further vertical cliff-face of rock behind the ledge, some distance to their right.

"There's everything to say, and no good way to say just part of it," murmured Hal finally.

"I know. It doesn't matter," said Amanda. "You'll find what you want; and then I'll be back."

"And Simon'll take us back to the Encyclopedia, then we'll be apart again. Or will you even be coming back with me? There's no real need, if you're tied to your work here."

"If I can be of use, I'll go anywhere with you, my Hal," she said. "You know that. If I'm not really needed by you, though, I am needed in other places—but you still haven't told me just how you managed to make yourself regress to being a three-year-old child during your eighty years in space alone—was it eighty?"

"About eighty," Hal said. You have to remember I was three years old when I was rescued; and I was thinking like a three-year-old. It took me some years as I grew up on Old Earth to recapture my original memories and plans. Some have never come back to me yet. So I'm not certain how many actual years there were before I planned to be where I would have to be found. G'and all else that I'd planned would take its course."

"But years alone in interstellar space," said Amanda, "until you were found, alone in the couriership, and could begin your life as Hal instead of Donal Graeme—you're frowning. Do you know, I've never seen you frown before?"

"Am I?" he said. He smiled away the frown.

They had lain and sat awake most of the night before; while at her prompting he told her—this time in full—about his youngest uncle Stephen, killed by a false order from a message sergeant: who knew he had no right to send any order at all—even a correct one—to any of the Dorsai expedition. He knew that doing so was grounds for breaking the invarying contract with which the Dorsi always agreed to be employed in someone else's war.

But he had no longer cared. His message center was directly behind Stephen's Command; and he was wild to live; even if he spent the rest of his life in a Cetan military prison. So he had sent a message as if it was one hurriedly passed on from Dorsai Headquarters Unit—orders for Stephen and his command to hold their position at all costs.

What he dreamed sixty-five men, four groups only, and even of Dorsai, could do to delay a full enemy advance clear across a ninety kilometer front, with full heavy war machines, was inconceivable. But he was ready to do anything to have time to get away and save at least his own life before the advance caught up with him.

He had not succeeded, of course; and news of the death of Stephen Donal's youngest and dearest uncle—closer in age to him even than his older brother Mor, had changed and directed Donal/Hal's life from that day to the present. Stephen and all of his men—wasted—had taken over young Donal completely and changed the course of his life. There had not even been anything to bring back to Dorsai itself for burial. Their bodies had been ground into the Cetan earth and destroyed beyond recovery; otherwise—though only Gray Captains and unusual cases was that possible in the overcrowded spaceship transport that brought expeditions to and from their contracted work.

It had pointed the life of then Donal, and now Hal toward one end only—that such a thing should never happen again within the human race.

"—I know how I did it," he had answered Amanda's question in the night, "but we don't yet have the contexts and the words to explain it. It's like my taking over the dying body of Paul Formain, back in time when the Chantry Guild was hardly more than a money-making cult. I couldn't change history; but I could observe the beginnings of change and plot forward. Essentially you could say it was this faculty of mine for what's been called my intuitive logic—and there's really nothing new there, except my organization of it. It's elements are there in everyone. It's just been thought a sort of gift; as they used to think the faculty of artistic creativity was a rare gift owned by only a few people—no one else had it. But Cletus Grahame clearly put some elements of it to work in that mutli-volume work of his on Strategy and Tactics that made we Dorsai the useful professional soldiers we've been—"

"Yes," said Amanda, somberly, "but Dorsai has been built on our blood."

"Yes," said Hal. "But if I get it all done, what I've worked on for two lives now, the bloodshed may be over—or perhaps not when we venture farther into the universe. At any rate, the seed of development is there in every living human, and it's close. There's something about this Jathed that bamid was telling us about. Jathed may be fumbling at the doorlatch, even now, I'll try to find out. In any case, I'll complete my own job bringing it to everyone, on all the worlds."

"If Blyes doesn't finally overwhelm Old Earth, and kill you—let's talk about something else."

"Yes, said Hal; and for a moment neither said anything, then Hal went on.

"Yes," he said, again. They were out of doors now on the ledge where the Guild had been built, walking together in the short time that remained before she must leave. But the Guild members also outside were keeping a good distance from them; obviously so that they might have no fear of being overheard.

He had a sudden mental picture of how they must look to the Guild members who happened to look their way. The tall man and the tall woman, holding hands, their heads close together in conversation as they walked along the edge of the emptiness beyond the cliff edge.

"Somewhere, somewhen, there's got to be time for just being together. Time to shut ourselves away from anything else, without having to keep an eye on the need to go back to duties."

He searched her face with his eyes.

"Life ought to owe us that much for ourselves, shouldn't it?"

"Are you asking Amanda-who-loves-you, or Amanda-who-sees?"

"Both," said Hal.

"Amanda-who-loves-you promises, some day we'll have the rest of our lives together."

"And Amanda-who-sees?"

Her face grew very still.

"That's one thing Amanda-who-sees isn't able to see." She stopped and turned to face him. "Oh, but I trust Amanda-who-loves-you. Don't you trust her, too? She trusts you."

"Always." He smiled down at her. "I always trust her, first and foremost."

They went back to walking again.

"Do you have any idea at all of how long you'll be here?" asked Amanda after a moment.

He shook his head.

"I'm at the point now where I'm beginning to pull strings together in my own mind."

"Which strings?"

"I think, mainly, the strings to Western and Eastern thinking. In spite of the three hundred years the race has been on worlds beyond Old Earth, those two schools of human thought still need to be reconciled in lots of ways. Then, there're the strings to the past, to the present, and the future to be brought together: and the strings to the real universe and the Creative Universe. Many, many strings. Too many, actually, to hope I could pull them all together, here and now. All I can hope is to tie enough of them in with each other so I can move up the line and begin tying in the rest."

"But you do feel I was on the right track, bringing you here?" said Amanda.

"Yes," he answered. "There's something necessary to be learned in this place, at this time. Something I need, in this whole idea of a second Chantry Guild and particularly in Jathed's Law. I've got to understand that Law, understand it absolutely. But you know, there're probably other things I don't recognize yet as important to everything I work for, that are here, too, and need taking into account. There was a researcher once, long ago, who said that whenever a source or a reference was really needed, it'd manifest itself out of the continuum. And centuries ago, back in the old days of magazines, editors used to talk about the fact that all of a sudden a number of writers would simultaneously submit stories about the same idea—writers who in many cases didn't even know each other. Then, of course, there're the historical facts about important inventions, or technological advances, appearing at the hands of two or more entirely separate inventors or workers, at almost the same time—and arguments about who came up with what first."

"I don't see how simultaneity like that ties into your problem," said Amanda.

"Oh, sorry," said Hal. "You're the only person who has to suffer this from me—I get to thinking out loud around you. What I'm driving at is that I have to go on the premise that wherever I am there may be historically important forces at work in making me see what I see. Forces I should recognize—in things like Old Man. Artur, or even the little girl, Cee."

Amanda frowned.

"I don't see any connection, myself, between any of those people and what you're after," she said. "But now we're in your work area, not mine. Anyway . . ."

She stopped, turned to him and reached up to put her arms around his neck and kiss him.

"I've got to get moving," she said. "It's a good two days' walk to the little town I want to go to first; and part of today has already been used up."

"Does it make all that much difference?" said Hal wistfully.

"You, of all people, to say that!" replied Amanda, starting to lead them back to where Amid and Simon waited for them. "How would you like it if you got to a town just one hour too late to save someone's life?"

"Yes," said Hal. "Of course. You're right. But that can't be something that happens often—never mind. You're quite right. If it only happens once, that's reason enough for not wasting time."

He smiled at her.

"But there's a human limit to the amount of help anyone can give," he said.

"You say that?"

She linked arms with him and they went back in a shared silence that, though warm, was both deep and thoughtful; and still in it, returned to the small building that was the Guildmaster's main office.

CHAPTER 20 ■

Over the weeks that he had now been at the Chantry Guild, Hal's sitting by the pond to watch the sun rise when he was not walking in the circle at that time had become a ritual.

Seated, he unchained his mind to its own ways of abstracting his thoughts; ways that produced inner thoughts and visions also. Although those evoked as he sat by the pond tended to be of a different character than those he produced for himself in the circle.

One morning he had just seated himself while the world beyond the ledge was still lost in the grayout of predawn, when a figure materialized from the dimness at his back and also settled by the pond, not far from him and also facing the mountains over which the sun would rise.

It was Old Man. He and Hal looked at each other companionably. Hal, however, found himself vaguely disturbed. Not by the other's presence, but by something about it that felt not quite right. He puzzled over this feeling for several moments and then understanding came to him.

Old Man was sitting on his heels, quite comfortably but undeniably squatting, rather than seating himself cross-legged as Hal had; and if there was anyone on the ledge whom Hal would have expected to sit naturally in a cross-legged position it would be the white-bearded older man now beside him. Moreover, Old Man had obviously joined Hal and the natural thing would have been for him to signal the fact by taking the same posture.

But years had gone by since Hal's early training by the Exotics among the three tutors he had had as a boy; and the occasions on which a lotus position might have seemed appropriate for him to assume had become fewer and fewer. He had become careless. His legs were almost in the half-lotus position, but his toes were not tucked in behind the calves of the opposing legs the way they should have been. With an old-fashioned sort of politeness. Old Man had evidently taken the position he had to avoid seeming to go Hal one better by sitting down in a proper half-lotus himself.

Hal was out of practice, but not so much that the half-lotus was impossible to him. He tucked his toes in. Old Man dropped immediately into the same position with one fluid motion. Hal bowed gravely from the waist to him. Old

Man bowed as gravely back. They both turned their attention to the mountains over which would come the sunrise.

Hal's gaze went away beyond the cliff edge. For him, the Chantry Guild and the place it occupied had now effectively ceased to exist. He knew the names of the area that surrounded him as anyone would know his own, familiar neighborhood.

He sat on the eastern face of the range of the Zipaca mountains. Behind him, the thickness of that range ran eastward until it was out of sight. But Hal now knew it descended at last to high, nearly perpendicular cliffs overhanging the coastal forest, which was too steamy and hot to be more than sparsely inhabited. That forest was called the Tlalocan—the "land of sea and mist" in the ancient Mayan language of Old Earth. It reached to the shores of the Zephry Ocean, which stretched some thousands of miles onward to the next large continental mass of Kultis. At his feet lay the Mayahuel Valley, up which Amanda had led him to this place; and beyond where he sat now, the Zipacas continued, angling in so that they, and the Grandfathers of Dawn, opposite, became one range to the north, after the upland forest below had given way to high altitude desert. It was the Grandfathers over which the star Procyon would rise to bring daylight to the Chantry Guild and the people in the valley below.

Watching the far dark bulk of the distant mountains, as their details began gradually to emerge from the mist under the steadily brightening overhead, he let his mind flow in whatever direction might attract it, as water seeks its own way down a slope. This was not his way in the circle, where he deliberately turned his mind over to understanding the Law he repeated as he walked. Here and now, he only set it free like a hawk to soar with the waking day.

It had come to him some mornings since, seated in this place, that for the first time since he had been a young boy and dedicated himself to ending that which had killed his uncle James, he had a chance to step back and add up the gains and losses of his own lives.

They were part-lives, really; for Donal Graeme had ceased to be before middle age, so that he could become Paul Formain. And Formain had existed only a few years as a shell for him who had once been Donal, before he had been abandoned, along with the rest of the already-dead twenty-first century. From there, what was essentially both Donal and now Hal had returned to the courier ship of the twenty-second century: and to the timeless wait of eighty years that had passed before he became the two-year-old child who had grown into what he was now.

But all those lives had been armed and controlled by a single mind and a single purpose; and they had achieved some things and failed to achieve some others—so far, at least. It was ironic that at the Final Encyclopedia for three years, where he had had nothing to do but concentrate on his goal, that he had never found time to do this sort of self-survey. And now, immersed in walking in the circle, watching the sunrise, serving food, fixing, cleaning—he had been set free to do just that.

He had grown smaller in the eyes of his race and larger in dimensions where the vision of other people did not penetrate. It was as if to grow as a human being he had needed to give up more and more of what other humans had desired and admired. On all the worlds only a handful now knew him, in any real sense of that word; and nearly all on the Younger Worlds had known Donal, in Donal's later years.

He had started out to kill a dragon, and had ended up striving to climb a mountain others could not even see, to a doorway they had yet to imagine. And yet, to him his goal had become more concrete and infinitely more worthy and solid as it became progressively more invisible and inconceivable to others. Yet it was the same goal—only now, sitting here, he seemed for the moment to see it clearly; while in the beginning, like all the rest, he had seen only that false façade within the real universe that was a tiny part of it.

Now, all the universe had become his classroom; and

everyone and everything in it, subjects of his study.

The first isolated sparks of sunlight were beginning to find crevices in the top line of the mountains. He reached out to the limits of his imagination, now, then stretched on beyond the veil at the end of known limits, reaching through it metaphorically with both hands, into the Creative Universe he could not yet wholly enter; and with his hands hidden from him he molded the place he now sat into the place of its own future.

About him, in his mind, the ledge changed.

The few heavy blocks of stone that had so far been hewn from the mountains and polished, multiplied and fitted themselves together to make the finished structure for which they were destined. The House of the Chantry Guild, constructed of the warm, green-threaded marble of the mountain that contained it, was lifted up, roofed itself, and sent walls and pathways forward to enclose that space of the ledge not covered. The little stream ran now between narrow borders of native grasses and flowers to the pool, which had become enclosed by a rim of stone terrace. On that rim he sat, now in the far future. Behind him, he heard the timeless chanting of those in the circle. He sat, young and waiting for a sunrise, centuries ahead in time.

The surface of the pool now showed white flowers upheld on the surface of the waters by flat green leaves. Variform lilies, stirred only occasionally when their stems, reaching down underwater, were brushed by the passing of one of the fish among those living in the pool; raised there, then as now, to be part of the food for the Guild members. Then, as now, the sun had just joined together its sparks of light into one line of illumination marking the chain of the mountaintops.

He sat, in lotus position, waiting for the sunrise as he did every morning. Behind him the walker adults chanted and turned; and the brightening day drew his attention to the clouds of the sky and reflected in the pool beside him, and to a flower on its surface, almost within arm's length.

There was a particular spark of light from one white petal. Procyon had climbed high enough to strike a diamond glitter off a dewdrop on the blossom of a flower. There was something powerfully memorable about that, but he could not divine what it was. He looked away once more, back out to the crest of mountains itself, and watched the actual breaking through of the sun, its upper edge reaching at last over the barrier of the mountains to look directly onto the ledge at the Chantry Guild and at him. Then with one crescendoing upsurge of light it burst fully and directly into his eyes and made him blind to all about him.

He blinked and looked away. His eyes met the eyes of Old Man. They exchanged a smile, and got to their feet, parting as they went their separate ways into the daytime activities of the ledge.

Hal turned his mind from the sunrise just past, and back to the present practical requirements of life. He had now been here seven weeks, nearly double the time Amanda had asked if he intended to stay. In itself this should be no great time, but in his mind he could see the image of Tam, fighting off death, hour by hour, waiting, and he felt the urgency like a hand pressing always on his back.

He was to begin a walk in the circle again early this afternoon, but first, this morning, he was scheduled to go with a foraging party to collect edible wild fruits and vegetables growing in the forest below. The foraging group was to consist of six people and meet at Amid's reception building. He turned in that direction, accordingly, and the sight of it, together with the thought of the land below, brought back to his thoughts the matter of Cee. Ever since Amanda had first suggested it. Artur had let one of the female Chantry Guild members, a round-faced, brown-haired, cheerful young woman named Onete, go down to sit in the forest. But not seeing his niece—at least not being able to feel her presence there, and have direct personal evidence of the fact she was alive and well—had been painful to Artur.

The pain had been evident; but he had borne it with a quietness and patience that made no lessening of his usual activities in the Guild. It was behavior which had reminded Hal of something he had almost forgotten. The Exotics, for all their original apparent softness and tendency to surround themselves with that many thought of as luxuries, had proved to have the inner strength Hal had seen in them, that was even now making it hard for the Occupation to kill them off. It was a strength that had its roots in the constancy of their individual philosophies, regardless of how each one might and did interpret it, that was as characteristic of them, as unflinching faith was of the best of those on the Friendly worlds, and courage was of the Dorsai.

He remembered with a sudden pang of sadness and loss, even after all these years. Walter the InTeacher, who had been the Exotic among his tutors, as Malachi Nasuno had been the Dorsai and Obadiah Testator the Friendly—until Bleys' thugs had gunned the three of them down, that one warm, late summer afternoon in the mountains of Earth, years ago. Walter, who had ordinarily seemed the most persuadable of the three old men who had brought Hal up, had been in fact the most unyielding, once his mind was made up. So it was with the best of his fellow Exotics under the heel of the Occupation.

Remembering this, Hal found he had reached Amid's reception building and that he was in advance of his fellow foragers. There was no one else waiting outside. The thought of Cee returned to his mind; and, since he was here, he knocked at the door of the building.

"Come in—come in, anyone!" called Amid from within, Hal pushed open the door and went in, closing it softly behind him.

Amid was seated on one side of the fireplace, in which a small fire, probably built against the chill of the early hours, was now burning down unheeded to a few glowing coals. His chair had been pulled around to face two other chairs, in which sat Artur and Onete.

"Ah, it's you," said Amid. "I'd almost have bet it'd be you, Hal. Come join us. Sit down. I was going to call you in on this, anyway."

"Am I that predictable?" asked Hal, entering and taking a chair which he also pulled around, so that they sat in a rough circle, he and the three others.

"You sit out there to watch the sun come up every morning," said Amid. "As soon as the sun's up, you go to whatever duty you've got. That duty's foraging below, today. So you were bound to come here, weren't you?"

"But not necessarily to knock at your door," said Hal.

"You're ahead of time—watching the sun come up makes you that way," said Amid. "What are you going to do, stand around alone out there? Or am I so unapproachable? You know I like talking to you."

Hal smiled.

"When you've got time to spare," he answered. "But of course. I'd forgotten. You sit here all day doing nothing, just hoping for someone to stop and talk to you," he said. "As a matter of fact, I was going to ask about how things are progressing with Cee, and you've got the sources of information right with you."

"It's Cee we're concerned about," said Artur.

"What's gone wrong?"

"Nothing, as far as my trying to win her trust is concerned," said Onete. "But while I was down there, yesterday, Elian—one of the people from Porphyry—came looking for me. I've got in the habit of sitting in the same place down there every day; and the local people have come to know I'm there. He wanted to pass on the word that there was some interest, none of the townspeople knew why, about the Guild among the soldiers in the garrison."

"You see," said Artur to Hal. "we thought they'd given up looking for us long ago. No one knows the location of this ledge but the Guild members. Amanda and yourself. Even the local people below only know that we live out there, somewhere; and even they've got no idea how many of us there are or anything else pertinent about us. The garrison soldiery hunted for the better part of a year for us, after they first moved in here. But we stayed up on the ledge, except in emergencies, and they finally gave up looking—for good, we thought. Our guess was they'd assumed we'd left the district, if not this part of Kultis, completely, and scattered."

"But now, according to Elian," said Onete, "the soldiers are talking about some sort of new hunt of the area here for us."

"The trouble is," said Amid, "if the soldiers begin making an organized sweep through here, they're almost certain to catch sight of Cee, because she'll come to look at them. If she wanted to, she could probably dance all around and through them and none of them would know she was there. But she won't realize the danger of being seen. She won't realize that with enough people, acting in concert, there's a danger that she can be surrounded and caught."

"And there's no way for us to make her understand this," said Artur.

"Any thoughts on the matter, Hal?" Amid asked.

Hal shook his head.

"Short of our capturing the girl first, ourselves—" he began.

"No," said Artur and Onete simultaneously. "She'd never recover from that," Artur added. "Amanda was right."

"Then I haven't anything to suggest," Hal said, "at the moment, at least."

"We may just have to wait and hope," said Amid. "However, a little knowledge of what the present situation is wouldn't do any harm. You're the tactical expert here, Hal. I'd like you to go down with the foragers just as you were supposed to do. But don't stay with them. When they get down, break off by yourself and take a look around the area as far as you think you can in the time you've got to give it. You might consider delaying your normal turn at the circle so that you could put in the whole day down there?"

"Of course," said Hal.

"Thank you," said Amid.

"Thank you," said Artur, almost simultaneously.

"There's nothing needing thanks in that," said Hal. "As far as that goes, I'm walking the circle in the back of my mind all the time I'm awake anyway—and for all I know most of the time when I'm sleeping."

"Are you?" said Amid. "That explains why we now have two of you. Old Man and yourself, who walk the circle without saying the Law aloud as they go. It's interesting. That's exactly what Old Man told me, when I asked him why he didn't repeat the Law aloud as he walked. I'd been obliged to ask him because others in the Guild had asked me if it was correct for him to do that. Old Man said the same thing—he didn't need to say the Law aloud. It repeated itself in his head all the time, no matter what he was doing. Jathed would never have stood for either one of you walking in his circle and not repeating the proper words."

"But you will," said Hal.

Amid smiled.

"I will, because I think my brother Kanin would have Kanin had a tremendous admiration for Jathed—as I may have said, Kanin was his chief disciple. But Kanin, like any true Exotic, had a mind of his own."

Hal's ear had been picking up the slight sounds of voices beyond the closed outer door of the building.

"I'd better be going," he said. "It sounds like the others are ready, outside."

"I'll go too," said Onete, also rising, "since we'll be traveling the same way for the first part of it. Unless there's some reason for me to stay awhile yet, Amid?"

"No. Go ahead."

"Thanks."

Hal and Onete went out, joined the rest of the foragers and they all started down the mountainside.

"Where's your gathering bag, Friend?" one of the men in the mixed group asked Hal. It occurred to Hal that he had become so used to answering to the name "Friend" that he had almost not recognized his own when Amid had used it during the conversation just a few moments past. He had been planning to pick up a bag after speaking to Amid—but there was no point in doing that now.

"I've been given a separate job," he said.

"Oh."

They were too polite, both as Exotics still and as Guild members, to question him about what the task might be.

When they reached the forest below they split up, the foragers spreading out to the north and Hal and Onete going together southward, down toward Porphyry.

"I never did get to ask how you're getting on with Cee." Hal said once the two of them were alone.

"I'm making progress." Onete smiled. "What a magnificent little thing she is! I used to wonder how she could survive down there all by herself. But she really owns that forest. She knows every foot of it. I'll bet she could run through it blind if she had to. But what you want to know is have I got her to come really close to me?"

"That's about it," said Hal.

"I have," said Onete. "Oh, I don't mean close enough to touch, though if she'd stand still for it, she comes near enough to me, nowadays, so that I could probably stand up, reach out and touch her. But that's not what I'm after. It's curiosity that brings her close, you know. She wants to touch my clothes, and me, as much as I'd like to touch her, but she doesn't dare. She doesn't trust me enough yet. Artur grabbed at her, eventually—well, you know that; and of course she's expecting me to do the same thing. She's going to have to actually come up and touch me and walk away again without my moving, a number of times, before she'll begin to put me in a different category. Poor Artur!"

"Yes," said Hal.

"He couldn't help it, of course. He'd wanted to hold her

so long, that he just didn't have any patience left, when she came in reach. I can tell how he must have felt, by the way I feel myself; and she's not part of my extended family, the only part that's left. But I'll wait. I think if I wait long enough. Cee'll not only initiate the touching, she'll start to lead me around and show me things. Then, I can perhaps see if she'll let me lead her places; and so finally I can bring her up to the ledge and safety."

"But not before these soldiers come," said Hal.

"You think they'll really make a search through here?" Onete looked up at his face as they walked.

"Yes," said Hal.

He did not say to Onete what he had also not said to Amid, only because Artur and Onete had been there, which was that he was afraid it was because of him that the search would come.

CHAPTER 21 ■

Yes, thought Hal, Bleys would indeed come. The Other had his own, personal version of intuitional logic, as he had told Hal when the two had talked together briefly in the cold and misty tunnel through the phase-shield, soon after the shield had gone up. Intuitional logic, or its counterpart, would not tell Bleys where Hal was, but he would be able to read from the general situation that Hal was up to something and probably not on Earth. Undoubtedly, on all the Younger Worlds, right now, the police, the military and all other paramilitary under the control of the Others, were looking into formerly closed files and commencing to examine groups and areas left unexamined for some time.

Particularly on these two Exotic worlds. A little serious thought, let alone an intuitional logic, would rule out one by one the other worlds beyond Old Earth. Hal would not return to either of the Friendly worlds, where he was too well known. There would be no reason that was likely to take him to the mining world of Coby or the older worlds of Mars and Venus, which had been settled early and never fully developed. Newton, the scientists' world, almost alone among the Younger Worlds, held no groups actively resisting the Others, from which Hal could get aid and protection. Also, Newton and its counterpart, Cassida, were sterile for the purpose of Hal's aims, at this time in history. There were no strong historical forces among the populations of Ceta, Ste. Marie. New Earth and Freiland; and there was no point in Hal's returning to the all but empty world of Dorsai. By default, therefore, there were left only Mara and Kultis, either one.

There would have been a command, originating with Bleys, himself, and filtering down through the hierarchy of political and military authorities the Others controlled. It would have started the military and paramilitary forces on the two Exotic worlds searching for any group or people who could give shelter or assistance to someone like Hal. The important thing to Bleys would be not so much to find Hal as to find what it was that could have brought him out from behind the shelter of the phase-shield. Whatever Hal was after, by definition it would be something which Bleys would prefer he did not have. So the order would have gone out.

And the military in Porphry, like such organizations everywhere, would have begun by first searching what was easy to find and close at hand, going farther and farther afield as they found nothing, until their inquisitions brought them, finally, once more to this part of the valley, and possibly to the very foot of these cliffs.

Hal did not think they would find the hidden entrance to the ledge. They would pass by, and retire at last, empty-handed, to their garrison again. But meanwhile, anyone like Cee would definitely be in danger. What he must do now was find some evidence of how far out they had gotten in their searching and their planning to search . . .

As he had been thinking these thoughts, he had been carrying on a casual conversation with Onete; and now they had come at last to the soft, vine-covered hummock of decayed wood which served as Onete's chair during the time she sat and waited for Cee, who was possibly watching them at this very moment. Hal closed his eyes briefly and tried to feel if there were eyes watching Onete and himself at the present moment. But he felt nothing and opened his eyes again quickly enough so that Onete did not remark on his having closed them.

"Well," said Onete. "You'll be on your way, I suppose. I'll settle down here the way I always do. If you come back this way, you might be quiet and cautious approaching this spot, just in case Cee is being unusually daring or extending herself in some new way. We don't want to frighten her off."

"I'll be careful," said Hal.

So they parted and Hal took off through the forest, still in the direction of Porphyry, but now alone. As soon as he was well out of sight of Onete, he took off his sandals and hung them on a handy bush, leaving himself barefoot. Earlier, he had accommodated his pace to that of the foragers and Onete while he was with them, but now he would need to cover ground if he hoped to see as much of the local territory as he had planned, this day. He broke into an easy lope.

Like most of the other Guild members, he had fallen into the habit of walking the circle barefoot, and the soles of his feet were hardened to travel without footwear. Just as the weeks of work and walking up on the ledge had put him back into shape, physically. The best of the gym equipment for exercise seemed never to give the results that actual walking, running and hard hand-labor did.

He smiled to himself as he loped along, feeling the enjoyment of stretching his legs after . . . how long? He had done his running at the Encyclopedia on a hidden treadmill, with the illusion of a countryside unreeling about him at the pace he was traveling. It had been almost, but not quite the same thing. For one instance, his feet had come to know the artificial irregularities and bumps of the illusory path beneath them. Here, they were continuously new and real.

Privately, he would have liked to go down to the valley below to do distance running, but it was plain the Guild members avoided leaving traces of their presence below as much as possible; and although he was sure Amid would have given him permission to go, he did not want special consideration. The members of the Guild had gotten used to seeing him at his various exercises about the ledge; and, being Exotics, would never have dreamed of anything but accepting whatever was his personal choice of a way of life. He smiled again, thinking of the Guild members. With them, during these few weeks, he had come closer to understanding Exotics than at any other time in his lives. Like so many individuals of the other Splinter Cultures, and like nearly all of the people on Old Earth, itself, he had taken the Exotics' nature and their philosophical search for an evolved human pretty much for granted.

He had not realized what that search had meant to them in terms of an active pursuit, or how much it had altered them as a people. For the first time he saw their culture for what it was and realized the real change it had made in them. There was no doubt in him now that it was equivalent to the changes the Dorsai had made in becoming what they were, and the Friendlies in becoming what they had become.

That change was not just a matter of surface manners, politeness and consideration. These people actually saw life from the standpoint of their philosophical search for an improved human race; and strove to find the materials for that improvement in themselves. Thinking back now, he realized his first actual acceptance of that fact had been in what he had seen in those around him on the road to and in the town of Porphyry. They had been subjected, but not changed. Even oppressed, all but a very few of them had remained the Exotics they had been before the soldiers from off-world had come.

It had been a great discovery. He felt now, for the first time, that there was something to learn; something that—although it might be that in following it up he was going away from his problem—might in the long run end by bringing him back to it by a better route. The Exotics wanted an evolution in humankind, per se. What he, himself, wanted was specifically a moral, an ethical, evolution in humanity. Surely the two desires were close, if not united in purpose?

But it was his survey of the land down here he should be thinking of now. He began by swinging to his left in an arc that brought him back to a path. It was not really a path, here, but a trail which could be followed by woods-wise eyes, the trail that he had taken with Amanda when she had first led him to the ledge. He followed this barely perceptible trail backward toward Porphyry, accordingly, still at a lope; and it was not long before it grew into what was a visibly used path.

In this early stage it could even be a path worn by larger animals, who, like humans, took the easiest route on their first time through unknown territory and then tended to repeat their steps on subsequent trips. Of course, there were no such wild animals on this world. He had been thinking too much as Hal, who had seen such game trails on Old Earth. Younger World troops would not think of anything but human feet having made such a trail, when they came across it.

After a while the trail gave way, in small stages, to a regularly maintained road, even though narrow and unsurfaced.

So far he had seen no evidence of recent passage this way by soldiers, or by any group of people, organized or unorganized. There was no possible way soldiers, particularly the poorly trained troops of the Occupation, could have gone up the unsurfaced trail without leaving sign of their passage in the way of bootprints and damaged vegetation, on either side of it. No more could they have come up this road in some days without leaving sign of their passage, to Hal's eyes at any rate, in its soft surface. The early part of it he traveled, accordingly, must also be territory to which they had not penetrated for some time. It was not far down the road, however, before he rounded a curve, descended a small slope and came upon not merely sign, but a deliberate announcement of their recent visit this far from Porphyry.

He had reached the home of the madman who spent his days stripping blossoms from the rapidly growing plants he cultivated in pots around the pool before his house and in the space behind it.

But the man was not plucking blossoms now—and plainly had not been for a couple of weeks, at least. Local scavengers had been at his body. What was left of it now swung in the light breeze, suspended by the noose from which he had been hung.

Below him was a printed sign showing large block letters in red on white.

DO NOT TOUCH OR REMOVE, BY ORDER OF THE COMMANDANT OF THE GARRISON.

Hal was suddenly reminded of such executed corpses dangling from makeshift roadside gallows in Hawkwood's time, with similar notices. The idea then, of course, had been that the body of the individual who had been hung should serve as a warning and a deterrent to other criminals. Here, where deterrence was not the object, the sign was simple savagery and sadism on the part of the Occupation troops.

Hal did not touch the body. There was no use, and to do so would merely serve as an announcement to any soldiers returning this way that others besides the madman existed in this area. He turned and headed back up the road at the same pace he had used since he had parted with Onete.

Only the morning had gone by. He decided to use the rest of the day in generally surveying the terrain, not only so he would know it in the future, but so he could make some informed guesses as to how the troops would spread out and move through it, when and if they came.

Accordingly, he now made side excursions to right and left out from the trail. The soldiers, under the impression that the Chantry Guild would be in the forest rather than above it, would look for evidence of signs of traffic to and from the location of its headquarters. Not even they would expect an obvious connection of trails linking that head-quarters with the visible footpath he now followed. They would be likely to simply follow the footpath as far as it seemed to them to exist. Only after it had disappeared would they then probably form a skirmish line and begin to sweep through the greenery area beyond; which they would have divided on their map into blocks of territory, running right to the foot of the cliffs.

It was well that Onete had chosen a place to sit for Cee that was some distance beyond and off the line of the trail toward the cliffs. It was not so good that she had chosen a spot relatively close to the entrance under the huge boulder, leading up to the ledge.

There were advantages in such a close position, of course. She, like the foragers, could literally be watched from the ledge, using a viewscope adjusted for distance viewing; in fact, lately, Artur spent what moments he had to spare during the day doing just that, to catch what glimpses he could of Cee. Also all Guild members, when they were below, were trained to glance up at regular intervals to where they knew the ledge to be.

Although the ledge was invisible from the lower ground, to someone who knew where its outer edge should be, it was still easily locatable; and if whoever was below saw a bush growing on that edge where normally no bush grew, the warning to get immediately back up to safety was clear.

Even Hal himself had been checking the position of the ledge, hourly, without being more than barely aware he was doing so. Reminded of the warning bush now, he looked for it, even though the most recent hour was not up; but there was no bush there.

No, Onete's location was admirably suited from the standpoint of Onete's own safety. But if the soldiers had anyone among them who could read even the most obvious of sign, the marks of Onete and Cee's visits to that location would tell whoever it was that people had been there, recently. The soldiers, accordingly, would search more carefully in the region about that spot, including up to the cliffs, the boulder and the secret entrance.

Hal did not really think that even such a tracker, if they had one, would suspect that the apparently small shadowed hollow under the great boulder was anything more than that. The slope of loose rock just below that entrance did not hold the marks of the goings in and out of Guild members, who were always careful to move some distance on the rock, along the base of the cliff, before they left it individually at different points to enter the jungle.

The chances of the soldiers finding their way to the ledge, consequently, were slim. But unfortunately the evidence of Onete's meetings with Cee would still have directed attention to this area; and if there were some of the Others on the Exotic worlds they might have the imagination the soldiers lacked—to direct a search closely along the cliff-front, investigating every nook and cranny until they crept in under the boulder and found the route to the ledge. To Bleys Ahrens, himself, the evidence of Cee and Onete's meeting would simply suggest immediately the likelihood of a secret dwelling place on the cliffs above.

However, there was no quick way now to hide that evidence. There remained the business he was engaged in now, which was putting himself empathically in the boots of the soldiery; and from their point of view working out how they would go about covering the terrain he was now surveying.

He had automatically gone back to his training as the young Donal, and that of the young Hal under the tutorship of the Dorsai, Malachi Nasuno, on Old Earth. For the moment everything else had been put aside and he thought and reasoned only according to that early training. As a result something connected with that way of thinking came automatically to his mind. It was a part of the multivolume work on tactics and strategy, which had been the lifework of Cletus Grahame, Donal's great great-grandfather.

"*. . . the importance of knowing the terrain where encounters with enemy forces are likely is impossible to underrate,*" Cletus had written in the volume titled FIELD USE OF FORCES. "*The commander, whether he expects to have to operate defensively or offensively over that terrain, gains a tremendous advantage by knowing it personally and intimately. It is not merely enough to glance at a visible area and relate it to a map displayed in a viewer. Large elements, such as rivers, gullies, impenetrable undergrowth and such, are obvious features to be committed to memory—but this is only the beginning of the advantage to be derived from the Commander's going out in person to cover the area.*

"*If this is done, then a great many smaller, but infinitely useful bits of knowledge may be acquired that may well make the difference between success and failure in any action. The quality of mud on the riverbank, the exact depth of a gully, the character of the impenetrable undergrowth—such as a tendency of part of its vegetation to stick to the clothing of enemy passing near it or attempting to penetrate it—all these are items of information that may be turned to account; not only in helping to build a picture of how the enemy will be channeled and directed, delayed, or aided in moving through the area, but in deciding how the enemy forces may be led or forced into a situation where they must surrender, or may be easily taken prisoner, giving the bloodless victory that is the hallmark of the fully capable commander. . . .*"

Hal frowned for a second as he loped along, his eyes noting and his memory automatically cataloging what he saw as he wove back and forth through the jungle across the route the soldiers would be led, by conditions of the terrain, to come.

Something was nagging at the back of his mind. There should be something more to the passage from the text than that. Something that was of importance, not to the present moment, but to his larger, lifetime search; and yet, he had the page of the ancient text from the Graeme library on Dorsai clearly in his mind's eye and those paragraphs were the extent of what was pertinent there to what he was doing at the moment. He made a mental note to search his memory again on that subject when he had leisure and turned his whole attention back to the business of studying the ground he was covering.

He was almost to the cliffs by this time. The next pass would take him past the foot of them. He broke off his traveling to and fro to make a turn back to where he had left his sandals on the bush. Since this took him close to where Onete was sitting, he swung wide in his approach, and covered the last hundred meters or so silently and cautiously so as not to disturb Cee if she were there.

He had seen no sign of Cee, however, by the time he had retrieved the sandals. Instead of putting them on immediately, he gave in to the temptation to move with unusual care closer in to where Onete would be sitting, and after a few moments he came within sight of the spot and saw her.

Cee was indeed with her, standing directly in front of Onete; and, it looked to Hal, well within reach of Onete if the latter had wished to reach for the girl. As Onete had said, however, she plainly had no intention of doing so; and Cee apparently now trusted her in this, because she stood relaxed before the grown woman, almost as if they were in casual conversation—as perhaps they were, in one fashion or another.

It occurred to Hal suddenly that, if only there were the materials up on the ledge to fashion a quick-acting tranquilizer of the kind used to immobilize wild game, he could easily have delivered it at the point of a dart or arrow, into the little girl, from his present position or one like it. With the proper sort of tranquilizer, Cee would never know what had hit her until she woke up in the women's section of one of the dormitory buildings, with Onete still with her.

She might react strongly to finding herself enclosed; but Onete's presence would be reassuring; and if the worst came to the worst, it might be better than leaving her here for the soldiers to discover and catch.

Of course, in argument against doing such a thing there was the fact that even a large contingent of soldiers might not be able to catch her—which they would probably try to do before they tried shooting her. If she could get away from Hal and Amanda, these Occupation troops were not going to find her easy to deal with. Then, once they had shown any sign of doing such things, she would make it a point to keep out of their sight.

Hal faded back from the clearing where Onete and Cee still confronted each other. When he was a safe distance away, he put on his sandals and made his last sweep of the ground at the bottom of the cliffs. Then he returned through the entrance under the boulder, up to the ledge. Amid was at work in his office, with a tray holding some crumbs of bread and the remnants of some sort of vegetable stew in a bowl perched precariously on the corner of a table otherwise piled with papers.

"I'll take that back to the kitchen when I go shall I?" asked Hal, nodding at the tray after knocking on the office door and accepting Amid's invitation to come in.

"What? Oh, that. Yes, thank you. Sit down," said Amid, looking up from the plans for an additional log building—one which would be in between the dormitories and his reception building in size. "What did you see? And what did you think? You're back earlier than I expected."

"It didn't take as long as I'd have thought, either," said Hal, sitting down.

He told Amid about the hanged madman and about his

idea for possibly tranquilizing Cee and bringing her up to the ledge that way.

Amid looked uncomfortable.

"I'm sure Artur and Onete won't like the idea," he said. "Even if we could do it. Oh, I don't doubt you could creep up close enough on her to get a dart or something into her; but even I don't like to imagine how Cee'd feel, waking up locked in one of our small bedrooms, even if Onete was with her."

"It's just a suggestion," said Hal.

"Then there's the problem of the tranquilizer itself. We've got a number of drugs in the clinic here, of course, but . . ."

"I know," said Hal. "As I say, it was just a suggestion."

"Well, well, I'll talk to our pharmacist and if anything like that's possible, maybe you'd be willing to make the suggestion yourself to Artur and Onete. They and we could sit down and discuss the chances of it working."

"I'd be glad to," said Hal.

"All right, then," said Amid, "as soon as we all have some free time at the same moment. I can call in Artur at any time, but Onete's still down below, isn't she?"

"Yes," said Hal.

"And you're about to take your turn at the circle?"

"I could put that off."

"No need to, particularly since we have to wait for Onete to get back up here."

Amid sighed, a sigh that was more than a bit weary, pushed away from him the plans he had just been examining, and sat back in his chair.

"Well," he said, "now, about the matter I wanted you to look into down there. When do you think the soldiers might come out here? And what might they do when they actually come?"

CHAPTER 22 ■

"I can't begin to give you even guesses by way of answers," said Hal, "until I get some information. How many soldiers are there in the garrison? Have you any idea how many of those would be free enough from other duties to make up a search party large enough to comb the district out here? Do they have a tracker among them?"

"Tracker?" Amid frowned.

"Someone who can tell whether people have been moving through wild country like that below us by reading sign—recognizing part of a footprint, or what a broken branch means, and so forth."

"Ah! I see," said Amid. "I don't know if they have or not."

"There must have been other searches, in this district and others. Did they ever use anyone like that to try to locate the people they were hunting?"

"Not to my knowledge," said Amid. "No, I'm sure they didn't. In fact I doubt they've got someone like that. It would be common knowledge if they did."

"If it isn't, it only means they've got no one outstanding in that sort of ability," said Hal. "It doesn't necessarily rule out the fact that some of them may be a little more knowledgeable about the woods and quicker to notice a footprint or other sign, that's open and obvious. For example, there'll be no hiding the fact that Onete's been sitting in that little clearing for some weeks now, and meeting Cee there."

"No. I've been worrying about that, but I don't know anything that could be done to erase the marks of their being there. Do you?"

"I haven't been able to think of anything so far," said Hal.

"I'm particularly concerned—not merely for Cee, but for the Guild as a whole," said Amid. "We've been safe until now up here; but there's no getting around the fact that if they find the entrance under the boulder and follow it up, they'd have us all in a trap."

"No weapons up here, I suppose?" Hal asked.

"Here?" Amid looked at him sternly. "Certainly not. We're Exotics! I suppose you could count Old Man's sword as a weapon, if he'd let someone else use it that way. He won't hurt anything or anyone, himself."

"Too bad," said Hal. "The soldiers would be very vulnerable, climbing up here after they got past the boulder. For all practical purposes they'd have to come single file. With even a few weapons, you might be able to ambush the whole party on the way up and take them prisoner. Of course you'd have the problem of what to do with them, once you'd captured them. I take it for granted you wouldn't be able to bring yourselves to murder them in cold blood, even if some of them have done just that, effectively, to people like that insane man down the road."

"No, we wouldn't hurt them, of course," said Amid. "And as I say, we've no weapons, anyway. Is there any way we could take them prisoner, if we had to, without weapons?"

"I'd strongly advise against trying it," said Hal. "The Guild members probably outnumber any search party that'd be sent by at least two to one. But barehanded against soldiers like that—"

He grinned.

"Now, if you were all Dorsai," he said. "Or even true, faith-holding Friendlies . . ."

"Please," said Amid, "let's be serious."

"Serious is that you simply can't afford the search party's discovering the entrance under the boulder."

"Yes." Amid frowned down at the drawing on his desk for a moment, then raised his eyes again to meet Hal's. "Only about five of all the Guild members even know it," he said, "but besides the boulder that's there beside the opening now, we long ago cut a second piece of rock of the right kind into the necessary rectangular shape and buried it just beside the boulder. The spot where it's buried has been grown over, since, just like the other spot near it that holds a block and tackle and levers for moving the block. We can fit it into the opening and it'll look, and feel, like part of the cliff behind the boulder. In fact, the block's got weight and mass enough so that even a couple of searchers—and there isn't room under the boulder for more than two at a time—couldn't push it backward and out of their way by hand, even if they suspected it of blocking a way through. But there's no reason they should."

"Very good!" said Hal.

"What it means, of course," said Amid worriedly, "is that once it's in place they can't get in, but we can't get out; except for those who know enough about mountain climbing to go down the open rock face. We've got a few who could do it. Not that we'd want to get out while there're soldiers down there."

"You're vulnerable to being seen from above," said Hal. "I know the brush you've got growing on the roofs of the buildings and the rest of the camouflage hides the fixed elements of what you've brought to this ledge. But a satellite in orbit looking directly at this area on its scope, or even a ship in orbit, could see people moving about if they made the effort—the circle, for example, always has people in it; and even if it was empty you'd have to cover the worn area of ground with something. And with all that, even if you knew they might look, and hid everything and kept everybody inside, a close study by an expert of a picture taken of the ledge in daytime would find evidence of human occupation here."

"You're telling me we're going to be found, eventually," said Amid unhappily.

"Only if they look. As long as none of them ever think of the possibility of your being up here, you can last forever. That's why making sure they don't find anything below to make them think of it is crucial."

"Yes," said Amid. The deep wrinkles of his forehead were even deeper than usual. "I know. We'll talk some more with Onete about what that Elian from Porphyry told

her. He may have said something that would give us more
information about the character of the search party, how
large it might be, when it might come—and information
about the garrison troops generally, their number and so
on. Meanwhile I'll also try to locate anyone else among the
members who's talked to someone from Porphyry lately;
and if they've got anything of value to tell you, I can bring
them in to talk to you. Meanwhile, you were going to walk
in the circle today, weren't you? You might as well go
ahead and do that. You won't mind if I interrupt your
walking if I feel I need to talk to you before you stop of
your own accord?"

"Of course not," said Hal. "Anything I get mentally
occupied with there, I can always get back into at a later
time."

"Good."

Hal went out, picking up the utensils of Amid's lunch as
he went. These reminded him that he, himself, had not yet
eaten today. When he got to the nearest of the dormitory
kitchens, he found it, now in the early afternoon, almost
empty. He ate a quick lunch and went on, out to the circle.
There were only two people waiting there, a thin, tall, elderly man named Dans, with dark brown eyes that always
seemed to give him a stare, and a small, athletic young
woman with blond hair, known as Trekka.

"I think duty took you out of your normal turn Friend,"
said Dans. "Trekka's first, but would you care to go
before me?"

"Before me, as well, Friend," said Trekka.

Hal grinned at them.

"No, you don't," said Hal. "I can get put in your debt
like that once, but I'm too clever to be caught twice. I'll
follow Dans."

As it turned out, however, several of those currently
walking were very close to the point where they wanted to
stop. Hal and the other two were all walking the circle
within five minutes of his arrival.

As always, when he began this, Hal shed his concern

with daily matters as he would drop a winter cloak after stepping into a building's warmth. There was nothing special about the circle to facilitate this, or even anything metaphysical about it, since he had been able to do it since childhood. It was no more than the extent to which anyone lets go of their pattern of directed thoughts, when he or she slips off into daydreams.

But on this occasion, the urgency of the possible coming search by the troops and its attendant problems may have lingered a little in his consciousness and directed the otherwise free flight of his mind; for he found it once more occupied with the passage from Cletus Grahame's work on tactics and strategy that he had called up form memory in his reconnaissance below. Once more he felt tugging at him the feeling that there was more to the passage than he had read off the printed page in his memory.

Now, freed by the movement and voices of the circle to go seeking, he traced down the source of that feeling. He was a boy again, the boy Donal, back on Dorsai. There, in the big, shelf-walled library of Graemehouse, filled with old-fashioned books of printed and bound paper, there had been a number of large boxes on one shelf which had held the original manuscript of Cletus's writings. As the boy Donal, once he had mastered reading, which he had done so early that he could not remember when he had first started to read, anything written was to be gobbled wholesale.

Those had been the days when he could so lose himself in reading that he could be called to dinner by someone literally standing at his side, and not hear the voice of whoever it was. During that period of his life he had ended up reading, along with everything else that was there to be read in Graemehouse, the manuscript version of Cletus's work. It had been handwritten on the grayish-white, locally made Dorsai paper, and here and there, there had been corrections and additions made in the lines. In particular, in certain spots whole passages had been crossed out. Notes had not been made by Cletus on the manuscript, usually, when such a passage was deleted; and Hal had often played with trying to figure out why his great great-grandfather had decided not to include it. In the case of the neatly exed out section of the remarks on terrain, the note in the margin had said—"of utility only for a minority of readers."

Of utility only to a minority? Why?

Hal had puzzled over that reason, set down in the time-faded, pale blue ink of Cletus's round handwriting. He remembered going into the office which had been Cletus's to begin with, and that of the head of the family ever since, and sitting down in the hard, adult-sized, wooden swivel chair at the desk there, to try if by imitating Cletus as Cletus had worked, he could divine the meaning of the note.

Why only a minority of readers? As a boy, the phrase had seemed to threaten to shut Hal out. What if he would be among the majority who would not understand it? He had read the deleted passage carefully and found nothing in it that could conceivably be useful; but there was, unfortunately, no way for him to test himself with its information in practice until he was grown up and an officer, himself, facing a specific terrain to be dealt with.

He had not even asked any of his elders about the passage, afraid that their answer would confirm his fear that he might be among those who could not use what Cletus had originally planned to include in his work.

Later on, when as Donal he had been grown up and an officer in fact, the deleted passage had become so deeply buried in his memory that he had almost forgotten it, and, in any case, by that time he had evolved intuitional logic, which in every way that he could see did all and more that Cletus's passage had promised.

The deleted passage itself was short and simple enough. Now, walking the circle, Hal had left awareness of the ledge and the Chantry Guild far behind: and he found himself, as in the earlier case with Sir John Hawkwood, being both Cletus, seated at his desk and writing that passage, and someone watching the slim, unremarkable man with his sleeves rolled up, writing away.

"If, having fully surveyed and understood the terrain," the deleted passage had read, "the officer will concentrate on it, resurveying it in memory, and imagining enemy troops or his own moving across it, eventually he will find the image in his mind changing from a concept to a vision. For the purposes of which I write, there is a great difference between the two—as any great painter can attest. A concept is the object or scene imagined in three dimensions and as fully as is humanly possible. But it remains a creature of the mind of the one imagining it. It is, in a sense, connected with the mind that created it.

"But a completed mental picture, once brought into existence, has an existence entirely separate from the one who conceived it. A painter—and I speak as a failed painter, myself—can paint anything he has conceptualized, adapting or improving it as he wishes. But with a completed mental picture it will have acquired a life of its own. To make it otherwise, even in the smallest degree, would be to destroy the truth of it. He has no choice but to paint it as it exists, which may be greater than, or different from, his original concept. I would guess that the same phenomenon occurs in the case of the writers of fiction, when they speak of the story as taking control of itself, taking itself away from the author. Such situations in which a character, for example, in effect refuses to be, say, or do what the author originally intended, and insists that he or she will be, say or do something else instead.

"As painters and authors come to have such completed mental pictures and learn to trust them, instead of holding to their original conceptualizations, so a fully effective field officer must learn to trust his own tactical or strategic visions, when they develop from his best conceptualization of a military situation. In some way, more of the mind, spirit and capability of the human having the vision seems to be involved with the problem; and the vision is always therefore greater than the mere conceptualization.

"For example: in the case of the management of available terrain, the officer may find the ground he has sur-

veyed apparently hanging in midair, in miniature, like a solid thing before him; and he will be able to watch as the enemy forces, and his own, move across it. Further, as he watches it, these envisioned characters may create before him just the tactical movements that he needs to bring about the result he desires.

"This is an ability of almost invaluable use, but it requires concentration, practice and belief, to develop it . . ." The crossed-out section ended.

Now, suddenly, nearly a hundred years after he had read the handwritten manuscript, as he still watched and was Cletus under the influence of walking the circle, Hal understood what he had not, before.

In his own time, Cletus had needed to achieve some actual successes in the field to prove to the experienced military that his theories were something more than wild dreams. Those tactical successes were a series of bloodless victories achieved where his superiors would have considered them impossible. Hal had studied these, years ago, to see if Cletus had been using an earlier form of intuitional logic, and had concluded that Cletus had not. He had seen his way to the unexpected tactical solutions he achieved by some other method.

Just what method, Hal had never been able to determine until now. Hal himself knew that his intuitional logic was not unique to him. Chess grandmasters had undoubtedly used versions of it to foresee sequences of moves that would achieve victory on the playing board for them. What he called intuitional logic was only a somewhat refined and extended activity of that same pattern of mind use.

Cletus had clearly made a similar extension of the artistic function he used in painting. His description of the miniature battlefield hanging in midair and the tiny soldiers acting out a solution to a tactical problem, apparently on their own, could be nothing else than a direct application of the unconscious mind to the problem. In short, Cletus, as well as Walter Blunt of the original Chantry

Guild—and Jathed, and who knew how many others whose names were lost in history—had been making déliberate use of the Creative Universe to achieve desired ends. Like Blunt, and possibly Jathed, Cletus had used the Creative Universe without realizing its universality, but only the small application of it to what at the moment he wanted to do. But it was startling and rewarding to find further proof of what Hal himself, sought—and on his own doorstep, so to speak.

At the same time, he realized he still lacked a sure answer to the question of why Cletus had deleted that passage. Hal was suddenly thoughtful. Since Cletus himself had set down the way, why couldn't he, Hal, use his own creative unconscious to try and ask him?

He looked hard at his own vision of the man who was seated at the desk, writing. Cletus was lost to time. There was no way of actually reaching the living man, himself. But if the transient and the eternal were indeed the same— even though he, Hal, had yet to feel that fact as an absolute, inward truth—then it ought to be possible to talk to the spirit of his great great-grandfather by the same creative mechanism Cletus himself had described.

Hal concentrated . . . and although the solid-looking, three-dimensional figure he watched continued to sit and write, a ghostlike and transparent version of it turned its head out of the solid head to glance at Hal standing by the desk. Then the whole ghostlike body rose up out of the solid form of Cletus at the desk and walked around the corner of it to face Hal. It was Cletus, as much or more than the solid figure was; and, as Cletus, it sat down on the edge of the desk, folded its arms on its chest and looked at Hal.

"So you're my great great-grandson," the spirit of Cletus said. "The family's put on some size since my time."

"In my original body as Donal Graeme," said Hal, "I was only a little larger than you. This was the size of my twin uncles, who were unusually large even for my time. But you're right. As Donal Graeme, I was the small one among the men in my family."

"It's flattering to hear I'll have descendants like that," said Cletus. "Though of course I'll never really know of it, since you and I are at this moment just a pair of minds outside both my time and yours. You understand, I'm not just a projection of your own self-hypnosis, as your dead tutors were when you evoked them to advise you as a boy in the Final Encyclopedia, when you first started to run from this man called Bleys Ahrens. I, the Cletus you're looking at now, am actually more alive than the one seated at that desk, writing. He's a product of your imagination. I, since you brought me to life in what you call the Creative Universe, have a life of my own. I'm Cletus Grahame, not Hal Mayne's concept of Cletus."

"I wonder," said Hal soberly. "Maybe I've done you a disservice. What happens to you when I go back to awareness of my own world and time?"

"I don't know," said Cletus, "any more than you do. Perhaps I go out like a blown-out candle. Perhaps I wait for you in the Creative Universe until you find your own way there, as you should, eventually. I'm not worried about it. You wanted to know why I deleted those few paragraphs of my writing on the use of terrain?"

"Yes," said Hal.

"I deleted it because I wanted as many people as possible to read and benefit from my writing," said Cletus. "No one's completely without unconscious prejudices. If, in reading, someone runs across mention of something that offends one of these unconscious prejudices, they tend to find faults to justify a rejection of the writing, whether the faults are actually there or not. I didn't want my work rejected in that way if it could be helped."

"Why should they find fault with your idea of a vision being something more than a concept?"

"Because I was speaking about something that's supposed to be a sort of magic that takes place only in great artists—writers, sculptors, painters, and so forth. The majority of the race, unfortunately, tends far too often to have given up on the possibility of creativity in themselves; either without even having tried to make use of it, or after early failure. Once something like that's been rejected by an individual, he or she tends to resent anyone who tries to tell them they still have it. Because of that resentment, they find or make some ground to reject any suggestion it still exists in them; and that rejection, being emotional, would probably force them to reject my writing as a whole; in order to get rid of the unwanted part. So, I took out the passage."

"What about those who could have benefited from it?" said Hal. "Those who wouldn't be looking for an excuse to reject the idea?"

"They'll find it eventually on their own, I'm sure," said Cletus. "But if a man puts a patch over one eye and goes around trying to convince not only everybody else but himself that he was born with only one peephole on the universe, I've not only got no duty, but no moral right, to pull the patch off and force him to face the fact he's wrong."

"History could force you to do it," said Hal.

"History hasn't required that of me, in my time," said Cletus. "If it has of you in your time, I sympathize with you. Brace yourself, my great great-grandson. You'll be hated by many of those you give a greater vision to."

Hal smiled a little sadly, remembering what Amid had told him about children on the Younger Worlds being taught to spit after saying his name.

"I already am," he said—

. . . A hand had caught Hal by the arm; and at the touch his attention returned suddenly to the circle, the ledge and the outside situation. It was Amid.

CHAPTER 23 ■

"I'm sorry to interrupt you, as I told you I might have to—" Amid was beginning, with relentless Exotic courtesy, when Hal cut him off.

"It's quite all right, as I said it would be. Don't be concerned," said Hal.

The sun was just disappearing behind their own cliffs; and the mountains he watched at sunrise were now lost in night's shadow. Below them, the jungle was losing itself in twilight; and the ledge itself, to its outer edge, was in the last rosy light of the sunset.

"What is it?" asked Hal.

"A search party from the garrison will start combing through the jungle below, tomorrow," said Amid. "Elian visited Onete again this afternoon to tell her, while she was visiting with Cee. Cee, naturally, disappeared just before Elian showed up; and since Onete knew the news was important, she didn't wait around to see if Cee would be back, but came directly up to the ledge and me. I've had them dig up the barrier stone to block the way in under the boulder, and it's set ready to be put into position at a moment's notice. Onete, Artur and Calas—you know Calas, of course?"

"Of course," said Hal. Calas was a wiry little man who had been one of the original Guild Members with Artur, back when Jathed was still alive.

"We're gathered in my reception building, making plans. I'm afraid we need your advice."

"Anything I can do . . . " said Hal. Amid was already leading him at what, for the small and aged man, was almost a trot toward the reception building; which now, like the two dormitories, had blackout curtains over its windows.

Within the building, an evening fire had just been lit in the fireplace and the people Amid had mentioned were seated in three chairs on one side of it. Overhead, the ordinary artificial lighting that was powered by stored sunlight from collectors on the mountainside above them in the day, was on a setting so low that its radiants, shaped like upside-down cones, glowed no brighter than candles. There was an empty chair between that of Onete and the chair Amid always occupied. Amid led Hal to it and all but pushed him into it before the Guildmaster seated himself.

Whatever the other three had been discussing, they had broken off. They sat silent as Hal and Amid came in and found their chairs.

"Here's Hal," said Amid to Onete, unnecessarily. "Tell him what Elian told you."

"He said ... " began Onete. A product of Exotic schools, she had naturally been taught what the people of Mara and Kultis called Perfect Memory. In effect, this was a mnemonic system that, when learned, gave virtually total recall of information gained through any of the senses— the equivalent in ear, nose and sense of touch of an eidetic memory for anything visual. " 'I just found out at lunchtime that the garrison's definitely sending out a search party for the Guild, tomorrow. My cousin heard Sanderson, the corporal who's quartered on her and her husband, talking to the private he uses as an orderly. They were outside the house, but just outside the front door. She heard them through the door—a little muffled, but clear enough. That's the first thing Elian said when he reached me. He was out of breath. He'd barely made it outside the town before the guards would have looked suspiciously on anyone that late in the afternoon; and he'd come as fast as he could once he got out of sight of the walls."

She paused and looked at Hal.

"Did he say how many soldiers were coming?" Hal asked.

"No. He probably didn't know."

"Did he say at what time they were leaving town in the morning, so we can make an estimate of when they'll get into this area?"

"Well, no," said Onete. "Actually we talked about how

terrible it was they'd search for us after all this time; and I thanked him for coming to tell us, and then I came right back up here to tell Amid."

"Did he say anything," asked Hal, "this time or at any time earlier, about how the soldiers might be armed what rank of officer would be leading them, whether they knew their way around in the jungle up here or had maps of any kind? Did he mention that any of the soldiers would be ones who'd searched this area before?"

"No. As I said," said Onete, "we just talked . . ."

She looked unhappy.

"I made a mess of it, didn't I?" she said. "I should have asked him useful questions like that, or at least anything I could think of that would let us know what we were up against. I'm sorry. My first thought was to thank him for taking the risk to come and warn us. That's us Exotics, polite and considerate before anything else! I might just as well have chatted with him about the weather!"

Her voice ended on a bitter, self-accusatory note.

"Don't let it bother you," said Hal. "Exotics aren't the only ones who wouldn't know what to ask in such a situation. Just about anyone without the proper experience or training wouldn't."

"I'll bet Cee would have asked him some of the right questions, if she'd talk; and if she'd trusted him enough to stick around!" said Onete, still bitterly.

"Never mind," said Amid, "we'll all make mistakes like that before this thing is over, probably. Our Exotic training is exactly the wrong sort of training for handling situations like this Occupation."

"Don't devalue yourselves," said Hal. "Remember, that same Exotic training of yours centers around making life more comfortable for those who have to deal with you. Just having to live with you has brought these same soldiers more peace of mind and comfort than most of them have ever had in their lives before. Whether they admit it to themselves or not, it's hard for them to deprive themselves of that comfort by killing you all off; in spite of the fact they're aware that's essentially what they've been sent here to do. Almost unconsciously, you've been countering the directives under which they operate. So—don't blame yourself for not asking questions only a professional soldier might think to ask. To each his own way of fighting."

"Well, in any case," said Amid to Hal, "as far as the number and equipment and so forth of the soldiers in Porphyry is concerned, Calas here can answer some of the questions for you. That's why I have him here—"

The door to the reception building suddenly banged open and there strode in—there was no other proper word for the way she moved—a Guild member whose name, Hal remembered, was R'shan. She was no taller than Onete and slim enough to look as if she was barely more than a girl. But as Hal had seen, she was incredibly strong for her size. He had seen her tossing fifty-kilo sacks of variform sweet potatoes around in the Guild storehouse, apparently without effort. At the moment she was in work trousers and a somewhat ragged shirt. Her short-cropped blond hair had dust and woodshavings clinging to it. Underneath the hair two bright blue eyes sparkled out of an attractive, sharp-featured face.

"Sorry to be late," she said, coming on in and throwing herself into the empty chair just beyond Calas. "I was up in the crawl space just beneath the roof of Dormitory Two and over the third floor ceiling. Amid, I found that leak up there. All that repairing they did around the kitchen chimney didn't do a bit of good. The crack in the roof's a good half-meter off from the chimney's flashing. I could see sunlight coming through—"

"Forgive me, R'shan," said Amid, "but we can talk about the leak in the Dormitory Two roof later. We've just gotten word the soldiers from Porphyry are sending out a search party to try and find us in the jungle below here. We've got to make plans."

"Oh? Of course!" R'shan sat up in her chair. "You'll want to know how we're supplied—"

"Yes," said Amid, "but in a moment. Hal's the only one

here who knows anything about the military and how they might go about searching. He's asking the questions."

"Ah. Friend, here, you mean?"

"Of course. Friend. Forgive me," said Amid, looking apologetically at Hal under R'shan's correction.

"My name doesn't matter either," said Hal. "Let's stick to the situation under discussion. You, first, Calas. How do you happen to know more about the Occupation Troops than these others?"

"I was one of them," said Calas. His voice was slightly hoarse, and it struck Hal suddenly that he had never heard the man speak before. "I was caught in a rock slide one day when half a dozen of us were out chasing an escaped prisoner. The slide buried me and those other bastards just pawed around a little and then went off and left me. Wrote me off. Some Guild members were out foraging and saw what happened. After my so-called mates were gone, the Guild people came, dug me out and carried me back here to get well. I had a broken arm and leg, as well as other things wrong with me. The Guild saved my life. So I stayed here. I'll help you fight those sons of bitches any day."

"Fighting them's the last thing we want to do," said Hal. "Whether the Guild lives or dies depends on the soldiers never finding out it still exists. You say the soldiers with you gave up digging for you after just a little effort to find you?"

"Yes. It was a hot day, but that's no excuse. Excuse enough for them, though."

"You're a Cetan, aren't you?"

"Yes." Calas stared at him. "How did you know?"

"It's too complicated to explain at the moment," said Hal. "Basically, the way you talk rules out your having grown up on any of the other worlds. Tell me about the garrison. How many are there in it?"

"When I was there, counting officers, a little over two hundred. Only about thirty of them women and most of those worked at inside jobs like administration."

"How large a search party do you guess'll be sent out tomorrow?"

Calas shrugged.

"Who knows? There's five Action Groups of twenty bodies each. The rest of the garrison people are officers or have regular jobs. The five Groups rotate on duty so that there's always one on active duty—it's like guard duty, except you don't do anything but sit there and wait for something to come up, like chasing an escaped prisoner from the Interrogation Section cells. Then there's another Group on backup, which means you have to be able to report for duty within five minutes—and they come on duty if the duty Group goes out on some job. The rest are off duty, until their own duty turn comes up. Duty's twenty-six hours. A day and a night."

"Correct me if I'm wrong on this," said Hal. "Effectively they've got a hundred active-duty soldiers, and the rest are support only?"

"That's about it," said Calas.

"All right, give me your best estimate of how many bodies might be in the search party we'll see tomorrow, how the party'd be officered, whether they'll have maps and how they'll be armed and equipped."

Calas frowned.

"No telling how many there'll be. If they're really serious, they'd use two full Groups; but that's only if they weren't searching anyplace else at the time or had anything else going on. More likely one Group."

"What would two Groups add up to in numbers, rank and so forth?" asked Hal.

"Two Groups," answered Calas. "That'd mean forty privates, four team-leaders, two groupmen and maybe two force-leaders—but probably just one of those, in command. They'd be Groups that were off duty to begin with, and they'd have the usual needle guns—just a few power rifles—and field equipment—helmets instead of caps and so on. The non-coms and officers carry power-pistols instead of long guns. And that's about it."

"No power slings for casting explosives? How about portable explosives? No power cannon that might be able to blast holes in the ledge here, if they found it?"

Calas shook his head.

"Hell, I don't know anyone in that whole outfit who'd know how to load, direct, or fire a power sling or power cannon," he said. "As for portable explosives, I don't think they've got anything like that, except for grenades and fixed charges that they can slap on the wall of a house to blow it down—and there's only one groupman I know of who'd know how to use that without blowing himself up. Besides, they wouldn't bring explosives up this way. There's nothing they know of here to blow up, but jungle; and no profit in blowing up that."

"Good," said Hal. "Anyone in the outfit know how to track?"

"Track, Friend?"

"Read sign. Follow people through the jungle by seeing where they'd stepped or the undergrowth they'd broken through."

Calas shook his head.

"Not that I ever knew of," he said.

"Even better," said Hal. "Any technological equipment—sniffers, for example?"

"I don't know what sniffers are," said Calas.

"Neither do any of the rest of us," said Amid. "What's a sniffer, Ha—Friend?"

"Equipment that can be set to sense particular odors at a distance. Body odors, cooking odors."

"Not that I ever heard of; and I'd have heard about anything like that," said Calas.

"They'd have scopes?"

"Scopes?"

"Viewing scopes—for getting a close-up picture of what's distant. You might have called them telescopic viewers, on Ceta."

"Oh, those," said Calas. "Every non-com and officer'll have one, and there might be some issued to a party of the bodies if they're going off someplace to look at things by themselves."

"Good. That ties right into what I was going to ask you next. Any searching that's done is likely to be either with individuals strung out in a skirmish line, or with small units of something like two to a dozen individuals, setting up a center point and working out from there, until the specific area assigned that unit for search has been gone over. In light forest like that below us, where ferns and scrub brush fill the spaces between trees at times, two men could lose track of each other easily within a short distance; they'll probably figure to use a group working out of a center point. If so, what's your guess as to the size of the units the search party'll be broken up into?"

"Six to ten bodies," said Calas.

"Giving us two or three units from each group?"

"That's right."

"Good . . . and bad," said Hal. "Now—"

"Why do you say both 'good' and 'bad,' Friend?" asked Amid.

"Good, because it adds to the evidence that they're not expert trackers or searchers. It also means they're either lazy, or don't expect to find anyone; so for their own greater comfort and pleasure, they'll stick together in large units to have company and make easier work of the searching. It's bad, because they'll be taking longer to search over the same amount of ground; and that means they'll be around here longer. I covered most of the area that concerns us in about six hours, earlier today. They could take almost as many days to do it if they stay in large groups and loaf on the job."

"That's exactly what they'll do, too," said Calas.

"Right," said Hal, glancing out the window at the deepening gloom of the night. He turned to Amid. "Do you have someone who could climb high enough on the mountain behind us to see the road past the madman's place, using a scope? Whoever it is would have to be in a position where they could not only see the road, but also where they could be seen from down here. I want someone ready to signal us below here when the troops come in sight. That way we can leave the block out of place at the entrance under the boulder until the last minute."

"Of course," said Amid. "There's a number of us who could do that. If I were twenty years younger—"

"They'll have to climb in the dark. I want whoever goes up to be in place by dawn."

"Hmm," said Amid. "Yes, I think we can even do that. There are some fairly easy routes up, ways some of us already know about. Even in the dark they should be safe to climb."

"Fine." Hal looked at R'shan. "How about supplies? We've got water from the stream. How long can we live up here on stored food alone?"

"Six months," said R'shan, staring levelly at him.

"You see," said Amid, "we've always considered the possibility of being kept from leaving the ledge for an extended time."

"Six months!" Hal smiled and shook his head. "You've done well in that department. Now—" He looked at Amid steadily. "Did you talk to your pharmacist; and to Artur and Onete here, about bringing Cee in the way I suggested?"

"We can't do it," said Artur.

"Really, we can't," said Onete. "She'd go wild once she woke up here and found herself locked in, even if I was with her. From what little I can gather from her, my guess is that the soldiers that destroyed her family home must have caught her parents outside and deliberately put them inside before blowing the house apart; and Cee saw that. She trusts me a lot now, I think, but anything that held or enclosed her . . . she'd go wild and hurt herself trying to get out!"

"You see," said Amid to Hal, "otherwise, the pharmacist says it'd be perfectly possible to make such a tranquilizer dart."

"That's good," said Hal, "because they may turn out to be useful in other ways. Would you have him make up about a dozen of them and find me people who can shoot a bow or use a sling with enough accuracy to deliver them?"

"I can do that, yes," said Amid. "How were you planning on using them? Because that may make a difference in how he makes them."

"I don't know, yet. It's just that such darts would give us a silent, nonlethal weapon. Maybe, on second thought, you and I had better go over and talk with him or her, now—"

"You stay here!" R'shan was already on her feet. "I'll go get him. People are supposed to come to the Guildmaster, not he to them—remember, Guildmaster?"

She looked sternly at Amid, who in turn looked slightly embarrassed.

"Sometimes it's quicker—but you're right, you're right," said Amid. "I think he's still in the pharmacy, R'shan."

"Since you're going to get him, then," said Hal hastily, "would you get whoever's going to climb the mountain with the viewscope and watch for the soldiers on the road?"

"Missy and Hadnah," said Amid. "Bring them both, R'shan."

"Right." The door slammed behind her, giving a brief glimpse of the new darkness outside.

"We'll also want to cover or camouflage the circle and anything else that's evidence of people here on the ledge from an overhead view; just in case they do take a look from above at this area," said Hal.

"I really don't think they can," said Amid, smiling a little. "I'd forgotten when you first mentioned it; but of course, when all the wealth of our two worlds went at your request to Old Earth, we couldn't afford to keep on the payroll all the technicians and experts from other worlds we'd been used to employing. Most of the staff on the satellite system, which was primarily a weather-control system for whatever world the satellite was orbiting, were other-world meteorologists. When they left, the few Exotics who were there in the station left too; but before leaving they made a point of effectively sabotaging the equipment aboard."

"Good!" muttered Calas.

"Those the Occupation Forces sent in," continued Amid evenly, "were soldiers only. They might have had a few people among them who could use the equipment on the satellites, but they hadn't any who could repair it. The satellite system's gone unrepaired ever since, as the weather patterns show. I really don't think anyone can get an overhead view of us without actually flying a space-and-atmosphere ship over, and it'd be prohibitive in cost to do that for every little group like us they're trying to search out on both Kultis, here, and Mara."

"There's still the possibility of the searchers sending up a float-kite, or balloon with a scope aboard, to relay images back to the ground," said Hal. "We should cover up, anyway, and keep everyone out of sight from above, particularly in the daytime."

"Oh, we'll do that, of course. I didn't mean to say we wouldn't," said Amid. "It's just that it's amusing that they can't use the satellites because of a situation they helped bring about, themselves."

There was a moment's pause in the conversation, broken by Artur.

"I don't know what to do about Cee," he said.

Onete put a hand on his thick forearm.

"She'll stay out of sight, I'm sure," she said. "It's true she's always curious; but that many people together, and particularly if she remembers the uniforms of the soldiers who killed her parents—and I'm sure she does, even if she won't talk much about it—she'll be frightened and hide from them. If she really wants them not to see her or know she's there, they're about as likely to get a glimpse of her as they are to catch a sunbeam in a box and carry it away."

Artur turned his head to smile at her, but his face was still troubled in the shadows cast by the firelight. He got to his feet.

"I'll get busy right now organizing the camouflaging of the ledge," he said. He went out, walking heavily.

Since they had a few moments on their hands in which to do so, Hal had Onete repeat her full conversation with Elian, word for word; but what she had said earlier was correct. There was nothing more Hal could learn from it.

Amid began an explanation to Hal of how at least some weeks' supply of food for those in the Guild was always stored ready in precooked form, or was of such a nature that it could be eaten without cooking. These ready-prepared foods were used up in rotation as part of their regular daily diet, and regularly replaced. Other foods, such as root vegetables, were also used up in rotation, being replaced by more recently acquired supplies of the same food.

The door opened to let in a tall, thin man with white hair and an unusual erectness, considering his obvious age.

"Hal, you've met our pharmacist, Tannaheh?" said Amid. "Tanna, this is Friend, an honored visitor among us for a while."

"I think I'm probably the only Guild member you haven't met, Friend," said Tannaheh. "I'm honored, of course. I've heard all about you from the others."

"And I've heard about you," said Hal. "Honored, in turn."

"Tannaheh is really a research chemist—" began Amid.

"Was a research chemist," said the thin old man.

"At any rate, he's our pharmacist now. Tanna we just got word through Onete that a search party from the Porphyry Garrison is on its way here tomorrow."

"I've been told," said Tannaheh. "In fact, everyone on the ledge knows it."

"I suppose," said Amid, with a faint sigh. "Well, the point is, Friend's original need for a tranquilizing drug to be delivered in the form of a dart isn't going to be used for Cee, as we originally thought we might use it. But he thinks he might have other uses for such drugged darts. Do you want to explain, Friend?"

"It might be possible to use something like that against the soldiers if some of us have to go down to deal with them," said Hal. "What I've got in mind for that purpose, though, isn't just something to put a person to sleep, but something that would leave them physically helpless, but awake and—in particular—susceptible to hypnosis. Do you have the materials to give me something like that?"

Tannaheh put the tips of his long, thin fingers together and pursed his lips, frowning slightly, above them.

"You want them more or less incapable physically," he said, "but awake enough to be put into a hypnotic state? I assume you're able to put someone in such a state yourself; and that's what you plan to do after the medication's taken effect?"

"That's right," said Hal.

"Hmm," said Tannaheh. "It's a bit of a problem. You're really asking for two things. A muscle relaxant that would simply leave them too limp to stand up would give you the physical state you want them in. But you also want something that would leave them receptive to hypnosis but—I assume—not in a condition to be alarmed by you or give the alarm. I suppose the idea is that if you have to knock one of them down with a dart, you want to use hypnosis to make that person forget what happened to them?"

"That's it," said Hal.

"Forgive me for interfering in the tactical area, where I'm not experienced," said Tannaheh, "but if you're able to hypnotize, you ought to be aware that a post-hypnotic command to forget something isn't likely to be effective for very long after the subject comes out of the state you've put him in."

"I know it," said Hal, "that's why there's one more requirement. The drugs used have to be compatible with alcohol. I take it for granted you've got alcohol among your supplies?"

"Yes. Actually, I pick up the local homemade rotgut the

soldiers themselves drink, and redistill it for my own purposes. I've got a connection with one of the Porphyry people. I meet her down in the jungle on certain days and trade mineral supplement pills for the drink."

"Mineral supplement pills?" echoed Hal.

"Why, yes. I make a powder that can be mixed right into the food for us up here; but the people down below find it easier to distribute and take their mineral supplements in pill form. Also, they seem to feel there's something special about such pills made by a professional chemist. It's needed in their diet, as it is in ours. You do know that these worlds of Mara and Kultis are naturally deficient in the heavier metals, being progeny, so to speak, of an F5 star like Procyon?"

"I'm sorry," said Hal. "I did know. I'd forgotten."

"We used to make our supplements in central manufactories, using metal imported from worlds like Coby," said Tannaheh. "But naturally there's no importation now and the Occupation trashed the factories. Of course, there's still plenty of the metals scattered around these worlds. It wouldn't be hard for anyone to find a piece of iron, say, and reduce it by practical methods to a form that could be ingested, although they'd need to know the proper amount to take . . . anyway, I do have alcohol."

"Have you got some of the original rotgut, as you call it, still in its original containers?" Hal asked.

"Certainly."

"That may be particularly handy," said Hal. "My idea was to dart them; then, under hypnosis, get them to drink a certain amount of alcohol, and leave them unconscious with another drug and the post-hypnotic idea that they'd drunk themselves insensible."

"Very good. I can handle the drug and syringe part of it for you—a syringe that drives the needle in and makes its injection with the force of impact. I suppose?"

"That'd be fine."

"Very good indeed. I'll take care of that as soon as I

close up the pharmacy, which I was about to do for the night, anyway. I'll take some of the bottles of local drink up to your room. You're in Dormitory Two, aren't you? How much rotgut?"

"Do you have as much as a dozen half-liters?"

"If I haven't. I can make some up. You see, as I say, I normally distill the stuff to get something I can use in the pharmacy. I can dilute some of the high-proof alcohol I've already distilled out and mix it back in with the original to get the amount you need."

Tannaheh got to his feet. "So, if either of you want me, I'll be either at the pharmacy or in my room. If I'm asleep, don't worry about waking me. I wake easily, but I can go right back to sleep again without trouble."

He went out.

"Forgive me if there's some reason it's not a good idea," Amid said, "but shouldn't your Dorsai with the spaceship be signaled so that he can take you off in case we do get found and taken, up here? Old Earth and all good people can't afford to lose you."

"The signal to Simon is the laying out of a cloth," Hal answered. "We don't want to do that now, just when we're trying to make this ledge look uninhabited from the air. There's no need to worry. He was to shift in for a quick look once every twenty-four hours, in daytime. He's got sense enough to know something's up if he sees the ledge suddenly looking as if there's no one here and never has been. I'd guess he'll land in the mountains tomorrow night like he did once before, and climb down to us the morning after to see if he's needed."

"You can be sure of that?"

"Reasonably sure," said Hal with a grin. "Just as I'm reasonably sure that word is bound to leak to Amanda, wherever she is, and she'll know whether and when to come back here, herself."

"I'm pleased," said Amid. "I feel a responsibility, having you here."

"You shouldn't," said Hal. "I came of my own free will, on my own decision."

"It's a great advantage to us, having you with us when something like this happens," said Amid. "We'll be deeply indebted to you."

"Nonsense!" said Hal. "I'm indebted to you; and I'll be more so when I've got what I want out of Jathed's Law."

"Jathed's Law is available to anyone who can use it. In no way could you be considered to be indebted to us for that . . . however," said Amid, clearing his throat, "as far as Amanda Morgan's concerned, you're quite right that she'll hear about the search very shortly. There aren't enough soldiers to keep our people from going to and fro with word of anything interesting, between our small towns."

He looked at Hal and blinked.

"They never were really towns, you know, in the ordinary sense," he said. "Most of us preferred to live out in the countryside with space around each of our homes. But there were some who liked to be close to their neighbors; so we had these small clusters of homes, and a few stores or necessary offices naturally sprang up where they were. But our 'towns' were still essentially just clusters of homes."

He cleared his throat again.

"It's at times like these, with soldiers coming," he said, "that I remember, almost in spite of myself. The little clumps of homes with their balconies over the streets, and the flowers growing on the balconies; and the houses in the countryside, our white-walled houses, now most of them with only a few blackened sides standing where there used to be spaces that were half room, half garden, filled with sunshine . . ."

His voice ceased. Looking across the flames of the fire, Hal saw Amid's eyes glittering in their light.

"I knew of course, more than any of us, that this was coming—back in the days when I first met you and later when we decided to give away everything we had to the fortress you've made of Old Earth. I knew; and, in a way, I helped bring the present on us. But at times like this, I remember . . ."

He turned his head away.

"Forgive me," he said. "I'm an old man now and I cry easily."

Hal got to his feet, stepped around the fireplace to Amid's chair. He put one hand gently and briefly on the other's shoulder as he passed on his way to the door.

"I'll go out and check on how everything's getting done," he said softly; and went.

CHAPTER 24 ■

Hal woke at his usual time, something less than an hour before dawn. He had only had some five hours of sleep, but that would be sufficient for the day to come. He rose, showered and dressed, out of the habit ingrained in his boyhood as Donal, in completely clean clothes. Any morning with the chance of battle meant a clean body and clean clothes if that were possible. Many other things besides needle guns could make wounds; and soiled clothing pushed into a wound could carry infection deep into the body. There was little to no chance of his being hurt this day, but old habits had been triggered.

They made him sad and the sadness wrapped around his shoulders like a cloak as he began the day. There was no respite. From the time word of his uncle James's death had come to him in Donal's boyhood, until the present moment, the birth of each day had brought a dragon to fight. Long since, now, he had thought he would have found the nest in the human soul from which such dragons came and have destroyed it, ending them all. But still they came. Once again he was at a morning on which he dressed with the possibility in mind of having to fight for the lives of himself and others. It was as if nothing had been accomplished from his youngest years until now.

Perhaps there was no such thing as ending it. Perhaps the best he could settle for was to meet each new dragon each day, do the best he could with it, and count that as victory. At least he would have fought the breed while he could. He would have done his duty. But what was duty, if that was all that was done?

Back into his mind came a book he had read when he was young. He remembered a verbal exchange in Conan Doyle's novel *Sir Nigel*, written at the beginning of the twentieth century and laid in the fourteenth century. The fourteenth century had been a time when "duty" was a common word among the upper classes, in its French form of "devoir." The words he had just remembered were part of a passage in which there had been an angry exchange involving Sir Robert Knolles, the leader of the group of English men-at-arms and archers to which Nigel Loring, then still only a squire, belonged. It was a dispute between the experienced Knolles and a hot-headed but inexperienced young knight, Sir James Astley, concerning a skirmish into which Astley had gotten himself and those with him.

" '. . . I have done my devoir as best I might,' said Astley. 'Alone, I had ten of them at my sword point. I know not how I have lived to tell it.'

" 'What is you devoir to me? Where are my thirty bowmen?' cried Knolles in bitter wrath. 'Ten lie dead upon the ground, and twenty are worse than dead in yonder castle . . .' "

No, to fight another dragon every day might make a good show, but it made no difference. Because as long as the nest remained, the number of dragons would be endless. To fight anew each day showed responsibility, but nothing else; and yet, responsibility was part of the whole answer he sought. Just as the Law of Jathed was also part of it, if only he could grasp the full depth of its meaning. The Law rang again in his mind now, as it had rung when he had first come to the ledge here and heard it; but still it rang far off and muffled, not with the close, clear message that would signal an understanding of it, within him. Not yet—for that.

Dressed, he left his room and headed on his customary route toward the lip of the ledge and the sunrise to come. Not yet—the understanding. Only a dragon.

It was still full, moonless dark outside and the air was not merely chill, but icy, with that greatest coldness that comes just before dawn. The soldiers would not be leaving Porphry until after the sun was well up. They would not even be coming into view of the lookouts above them on the mountain for several hours yet and there was nothing more in the way of preparations that could be made. Meanwhile, it would be reassuring for the Guildmembers to see him following his normal pattern of activity, as if the danger now threatening was not all-important. The ledge had originally had its trees cut so as to provide corridors for people to move about, shielded from overhead observation. But there was no need to follow those corridors yet with the sun not yet risen.

Like all the other Guild members, now, Hal had come to know the layout of the ledge in darkness the way he knew his own room with the lighting off. He went toward his usual position near the front edge of the ledge but chose a spot a little way from it, under a tree that would hide him when the sun had risen. He sat down in lotus position.

In a little while the sky began to lighten; and shortly after, like a carven figure emerging out of darkness, he saw Old Man, already there and similarly seated, under a tree a few meters away. They bowed to each other and then directed their attention toward the sunrise that was coming.

The day lightened the landscape around and below them; and Hal's mind once more slipped off into the scene of himself, seated like this in the Guildhouse of the far future, completed of polished stone. He sat beside a pool now rimmed with polished granite, in which fish swam and waterplants floated their white flowers.

Once more he searched out a plant close to him, with its white blossom, on one petal of which was a drop of dew, that might catch the light as the sun rose.

He found a dewdrop; and again this morning, it did.

Once more, as the light was suddenly reflected from the speck of water, for a fraction of a second he felt the closeness of the understanding he sought here, but had not yet grasped. It was all but within his reach. . . .

But he could not close upon it. As the sun pushed more of itself into visibility above the far mountains, and regretfully, he returned to the needs of the moment. He exchanged bows again with Old Man and, like the other, rose. They went their separate ways under the shelters of the corridors of trees.

Hal's way led him by force of habit toward the kitchen of his dormitory—building number two. He was a good third of the way toward it, his mind full of how close he had come to some sort of understanding, back during the sunrise, when older habit caught up with him again and he turned away.

It was old Dorsai training. Clean body and clean clothes the morning of a battle—and no breakfast. To miss one meal was unimportant. But to have the stomach empty might be helpful, in case of body wounds. Also there was the feeling—possibly an illusion, but he like others had felt it nonetheless—that the mind was keener and more awake on an empty stomach; just as he would not have thought of eating just before watching a sunrise or walking in the circle.

He went instead to Amid's reception building, sure that

in spite of the early hour, he would find the older man there. There, Amid was indeed, sitting at a table surface between the fireplace and the front door, set up in the space vacated by a number of the chairs that had been pushed back against the wall. Spread out on the table surface was a map of the immediate jungle area, from directly below the cliffs holding the ledge to where the road past the former madman's place turned into a trail.

The map had evidently been printed up from data records in sections, and fused together into one large sheet, overnight. On it, at Amid's right elbow, sat a table-model scope with a permanently exposed, 30-millimeter-square screen. The sight of it made Hal automatically reach to his waist to check that he had his own, 10-millimeter-square field scope folded up and hooked on there. It was.

"Hal!" said Amid, looking up as Hal came toward the table. "I'm glad you came directly here from watching the sun come up—but, wait, you haven't had breakfast yet?"

"I'll have something later," said Hal.

"Don't forget to eat—that's what they're always telling me; and at your age you need the fuel for your energies more than I do," said Amid. "Hal, look at this map. Will you show me the way you think the soldiers will do their searching?"

Hal came up to the table surface beside him.

"As I told you yesterday," said Hal, "they'll come up the road, here, to the end of the trail. There, they'll drop off a couple of soldiers to set up a post; unless the officer in charge of the search is lazy or for other reasons decides to set up his own headquarters there. Either way, there'll be some of them there, in direct phone contact with their headquarters back in Porphyry.

"The rest . . ." His right index finger traced routes on the map. ". . . will probably continue on as two separate, equal units, to the two center points of equal halves of the area to be searched. Once at those center points each unit will set up secondary headquarters, under the command of sub-officers, keeping at least a couple each of the soldiers with them. My guess is that one alternative then is that the soldiers of each unit will be sent out to form a skirmish line at the farthest extent of their part of the territory; and make a sweep through it until they meet the skirmish line of the other unit coming from the farthest extent of their territory. If by the time they meet they've found nothing, they'll travel back together to the head of the trail and withdraw to Porphyry. That's unless their plan is to break up into smaller units."

"Yes. I see," said Amid, nodding. "Now what about them breaking up into even smaller units?"

"It's equally possible," said Hal. "An alternative, once the secondary posts have been set up, is that they'll divide the soldiers not kept at the secondary headquarters into, say, five-person units. These units will then be sent out to search a specific piece of the territory that's to be examined by that particular sub-group. In short, the original search party will still divide into two equal units, but then the two units will each divide again into a number of smaller units, each with the responsibility of examining a small part of the total territory to be searched. Those small parts will probably be defined for them by specific coordinates on their maps, which we can learn by watching how they move."

"And which way do you think they'll do it?"

"I've no way of knowing," Hal said. "The choice'll be made on the basis of what kind of soldiers they are and what kind of officers they've got over them. For example, if the officer in command is afraid his sub-officers are going to lie down on the job once they're out from under his eye, he or she may prefer the skirmish line. On the other hand, if the commander's in good control and/or the sub-officers are responsible and have good control of the soldiers under them, the commander may prefer the individual group method as being more likely to make a close and careful examination of the area they're assigned to search."

"How long should it take them to get into position to search?" Amid asked.

"Probably, judging from what I've seen and what I've heard about them, they'll take all of today just to set themselves up," said Hal.

"Yes . . ." Amid rubbed his hands together worriedly. "I suppose we've nothing to fear, really, until tomorrow. I was wondering whether to send word to block the entrance yet."

"Any time. I'm a little surprised you haven't done it before now," Hal said. "There's none of the Guild people off the ledge, are there?"

"No, no Guild people," said Amid. He looked up at Hal. "But Artur hates to see that block go into place. You understand."

Hal shook his head.

"Cee's not going to come through that entrance of her own accord," said Hal. "Even if she knows—and I'd bet she does—that it's where all the Guild members vanish to. She's undoubtedly followed Artur, Onete, or some foragers back to the boulder and seen them go under it and not come back out, before this. I'll even bet she's actually come in through the entrance when no one was around, and possibly explored the way beyond, even as far as the ledge."

"Well, there you are," said Amid. "Artur feels the way you do. That she knows. And he hates to give up on the thought that if she's really frightened by the soldiers she might prefer us to them and come in. But once that block's in place no single adult, let alone a child, is going to be able to budge it—particularly from the outside. It weighs as much as three men your size."

"I'd close the entrance now, if I were you," said Hal. "Your first responsibility's to all the people up here; and Artur's feelings are only Artur's feelings."

"Yes."

Amid was clearly unhappy. He pointed to the desk

scope. "Did they tell you—Missy and Hadnah—they were going to try to set up a tight-beam link between their observation post and a repeater down here on the ledge?"

Hal nodded. He had a great deal of confidence in Missy and Hadnah, although he had not known that they made a bobby of rock climbing until the present problem had come up. They looked enough alike to be brother and sister, although evidently they were not related. Both were short, well-muscled, blond-haired and young; and they even acted alike—being, as far as their Guild duties and the circle-walking allowed, always in each other's company.

"Well, they did it." Amid touched a stud on the desk repeater and it chimed as its screen lit up to show a bulging mass of cliff-face. A second later Missy's face blocked out most of the view of the rock.

"Yes, Amid?" her voice said. "There's no sign of soldiers yet."

Amid moved aside to let Hal look into the screen and be seen above.

"I just wanted Friend to see you'd made the connection."

"Right. Good morning. Friend. I hope you slept well."

"Very well," answered Hal. There was nothing to be done with Exotic manners but live with them. A polite inquiry about his last night's sleep was as out of place in her situation and his in the present moment as a tea party in the midst of an earthquake. "I had five hours. How much did you two have?"

"Hadnah's taking a small nap now," said Missy. "After that he can keep watch for a while and I'll take one. Thank you for asking. We're not tired at all, really."

"I'm glad to hear that," said Hal. They two must have climbed the better part of a kilometer, vertically, during the night. "Focus your scope on the end of the road for me, now, will you?"

"Right." Missy vanished from the screen, and the view of the overswelling rock face above her was replaced by a view from what appeared to be only a dozen meters above the point where the road gave way to a trail.

"Pull back your focus," Hal said. "I want to see that spot in relation to the ground around it."

"Right. Say when," replied the voice of the now invisible Missy. The scene on the screen seemed to move away from Hal and Amid, taking in more and more ground area as it went, until it showed not only the connection of road-end and trail-beginning but an area of a size that could have been occupied by four city blocks on a side.

"Stop," said Hal.

The withdrawal of focus halted.

"Let it sit with that view," said Hal. "I'm going out to the edge of the ledge now and I'll be keying my belt scope into the circuit from your repeater down here. You've got up to half a day before any soldiers show up. Take another nap, yourself. If we really need you, we can call you with the chime on your scope."

"I'm really quite all right," said Missy, still invisible.

"You may not be five days from now, up there," said Hal. "Rest while you can. We'll call you if we need you."

"All right, Friend. Thank you."

"Don't thank me," said Hal. "I'm just protecting myself against having two overtired observers sometime later on."

"Right."

The last word was followed by silence from the scope on the table surface. Hal looked at Amid.

"Where's Calas?" he asked.

"I can have him found," said Amid.

"Do that. Have him come and join me out at the edge of the ledge," said Hal. "Send out Old Man, too."

"But Old Man never was a soldier," said Amid, frowning.

"I didn't suppose so," said Hal. "But he's a very insightful sort. Tell him I'd like him to join me, if he would."

"Oh, he'll be glad to, I'm sure," said Amid. "I will. And you're right. He's a very insightful individual."

"And get some rest yourself, when you can," said Hal. "Remember what I just told Missy. This could last five days or more; and we may need to be in the best possible shape at the very end of it."

He went out, and followed the closest corridor of trees to as close to the lip of the ledge as he could get and still be hidden by tree branches overhead. There, he seated himself in the tree's shade, unfolded his scope and keyed it into the view he had asked Missy to set up from above. The end of the road—and as far down as he could see it before it vanished under the foliage of the treetops that intervened because of the angle of the view—lay alien, intrusive and empty in the jungle, beneath the rapidly warming rays of the brilliant, white pinpoint of sun rising ever higher in the sky overhead.

He looked away from the scope and at the scene as his unaided vision saw it. It would be some time yet, as he had reminded Missy and Amid. He decided to follow Cletus's advice and let his conscious mind run freely over the terrain while waiting for his unconscious mind to produce some process for using it to the advantage of the people of the Guild.

In this case, that meant his remembering the ground as he had covered it during the first part of the previous day. He stared at the greenery below and the ground, together with the growth he had passed on it, began to unreel in the eye of his memory, stride by stride. He was on his third survey of the pattern he had covered when someone dropped down beside him, breathing a little heavily from the hurry in which he had come.

It was Calas.

"You wanted me?" said the small, wiry ex-soldier. His black hair was disordered on his head.

"How much sleep did you have?" Hal asked.

"I didn't fold up until about an hour after you did. But I've slept until now," said Calas. "That's where they found me with the word you wanted me."

Hal considered him.

"You're from Ceta," he said. "Where, on Ceta?"

"Monroe—I don't guess you ever heard of it," Calas

said. Hal shook his head. "It's a tiny state, out in Czardis-land Territory."

"Were you in any kind of military outfit there?"

"Local militia," said Calas. "Hell, all we did was shoot at targets, parade and get drunk together. We had uniforms, though."

"And you got picked up for military under the Others and sent here, because of that experience?"

"Yes," said Calas. "I should have said I was a rancher—variform sheep. I was that more than I was a soldier. Born and raised on a sheep farm."

"Have you any idea which officers and sub-officers might be sent out?"

"No," said Calas. "It could be any one of the five force-leaders, any of the groupmen and team-leaders of the active forces. Well now, wait, if the Commandant really wants results, he's most likely to send Force-leader Liu Hu Shen. Liu's the one Force there who really gets a job done. That means at least one of the forces would be his, and two of the groupmen and four team-leaders—all of them pretty strong on getting things done right, simply because Liu won't have anyone who won't do what he tells them. But the other force-leader and his sub-officers could be anyone—if there is another force-leader. Commandant Essley might just add someone else's force to Liu's. Not that it matters. Any other force-leader sent out is going to be second-in-command to Liu."

"Is Liu just a better soldier than the others," Hal asked, "or does he happen to like hunting down and killing Exotics?"

"Likes it, I think," said Calas. "But he's a good officer, too. Probably the best in the garrison—though nobody likes him. With him, it's always done by the numbers. Everything in line of duty, that's Liu."

A faint sound on Hal's other side made them both look and see Old Man now sitting there. He smiled at them, and Hal smiled back. It was a contrast, he thought with approval. Here was Calas, wound up to the tightness of a piano string;

while Old Man was his usual self. In fact, a sort of relaxed, almost grandfatherly, warmth seemed to radiate from him as he sat there; and Calas was already perceptibly less tense.

"Thank you for joining us," said Hal, and suddenly realized he was talking like an Exotic.

Old Man smiled and bowed slightly from his sitting position.

"I didn't ask you to join us," said Hal, "for any specific reason. I'd just like the benefit of your opinion on anything about the situation that you think might help. If you don't mind staying here with us, we'll watch the soldiers as they move in and perhaps you'll have some suggestions to make after you've seen them and the way they act."

Old Man nodded and smiled. He looked out over the jungle below in the direction from which the soldiers would come. Hal turned back to Calas.

"You don't have to stay with us now, if you'd like to get breakfast, or some such thing," he said. "In fact, if you came directly here after they woke you and haven't eaten, I'd suggest you get some food into you. It may be a long day's watch. I won't need you back here until after the soldiers are in view on the scope, close enough so that you can tell me who the important ones are and how they might act—or react."

Calas nodded. It was an abrupt, rather ungraceful movement after the nod Old Man had given. He got to his feet.

"I'll go eat," he said, "then I'll come back."

"Take your time," said Hal. "It'll be three hours yet, anyway, before I expect to see the soldiers—and that's even if they left their garrison at dawn. They wouldn't be likely to leave before that, would they?"

Calas gave a grunt of laughter.

"No," he said. "Under anyone but Liu, they wouldn't leave even then. They might not get off until noon."

He turned and went.

Hal and Old Man sat together in a silence that held no need to be broken. The sun moved up into the sky. The hours passed. After a while Calas came back. It was nearly noon by the time a line of four combat vehicles made their way up the road to the end of the trail and stopped there, letting the search party out.

"Liu," said Calas. Hal saw the one he meant.

"Porphyry itself hasn't any atmosphere to space ships, or any other above-surface vehicle they could use overhead?" Hal asked Calas.

"Not Porphyry," said Calas. "They could call some in from Omanton."

"Perhaps that's what they'll do, then," said Hal. He turned to the scope, on which the soldiers were now visible at close range, and pressed the chime stud. The voice of Hadnah spoke to him.

"Yes. Friend?"

"If Missy's not awake, wake her," said Hal. "Both of you forget the scope for now and watch for the approach of any kind of atmosphere ship. Each of you take half the visible sky to watch. It ought to be coming here in no particular hurry, but as soon as you see anything in the air, even if you're not sure it's headed this way, let us know below here. Amid, are you listening?"

"I'm listening for Amid. He's lying down for a bit," said the voice of Artur.

"Good. Make him rest as much as you can. Have everybody make sure they're under cover, starting now. We may have aerial observation at any moment from now on. Calas says they may get air assistance from Omanton. I don't know where that is, but it's got to be close as above-surface travel goes."

"I'll have someone check to see everyone's hidden, right away, Friend."

"Good," said Hal. "I'll let you go now."

Artur sounded as if he was in control of himself, Cee or no Cee, Hal thought as he turned back to closely examining the soldiers shown in the scope. He touched the controls to move his own picture to a closer view of the soldiers who had just got out of their vehicles and were forming up in units.

"All right," he said to Calas, "Liu is obvious, with that force-leader's insignia on his lapels. Tell me about the sub-officers."

"Right. See that thin groupman in the tailored uniform, with the black, black eyebrows, right by Liu, there?" said Calas. "That's the Urk. Sam Durkeley. He's Liu's pet. That groupman just getting out of the cab of the second vehicle, and the one forming up the first unit of men, are new since I was there. I don't know them. The other groupman just beyond the Urk is Ali Diwan. The only team-leader I know is the one backing the first vehicle off the road to turn it around, so it's ready to head back. That's Jakob . . . can't remember his last name. He's pretty decent, compared to most of them. There's more I don't know than I thought. I forget how long it's been since I joined the Guild."

"It looks as if Liu is setting up a command post just off the end of the road there," said Hal. "They're putting up a shelter. Do you suppose Durkeley'll stay with him?"

"He wouldn't be wearing that tailored uniform if he'd expected to go slogging through the jungle," said Calas. "No, the Urk'll be where Liu is, you can count on it."

"And Liu is obviously staying at the end of the road," said Hal. "That ought to mean he's got enough confidence in his sub-officers to let them make the search out of his sight; since you said he was the most capable of the garrison's force-leaders, he wouldn't be letting them do it on their own simply because he was lazy or unsure of himself."

"Right," said Calas. "He's either got them scared, like old Jakob there, or trained like the Urk. That doesn't mean he won't come on in, himself, if they find anything, or run into any trouble. Or he might show up when they don't expect him just to keep them wound up. That's the way he is."

The search party continued to get out of their vehicles, form up and move off into the jungle.

"Calas," Hal said abruptly, "have you any idea how

many more scopes we have that aren't in use at the moment?"

"No," said Calas, "I don't."

He scrambled to his feet.

"I'll go find out," he said.

"If there's three more that can be spared, will you bring them out here to me?" said Hal. "From the way they're deploying I'd guess they're going to follow the plan of dividing up the area and putting a team in each section. We may need to keep track of several different parties simultaneously."

"I'll be back as quick as I can," said Calas, and went off at a run down the corridor of trees, Hal's eyes met those of Old Man and Old Man smiled gently at him. The scope before Hal chimed.

"Craft approaching by air at three o'clock," said the voice of Missy, off screen.

CHAPTER 25 ■

The craft was a surface-to-orbit shuttle bus, completely unsuited to surveillance of the sort it was being put to here. The Occupation was clearly hard up for space-and-atmosphere craft, since the Exotics had given away most of these with their spaceships to Old Earth, before yielding to control by the Others.

Very probably its pilot knew that this trip was simply a waste of its time and his; for the craft made two explosive, supersonic passes over the area where the troops were, far above the speed at which any naked eye observation would have been possible. Pictures, of course, could have been taken; but even if they had been, Hal doubted that they would be subjected to the time-consuming, careful

examination that an expert would have to make to discover evidence of human occupation anywhere on them.
The time-cost of such expert attention to all the small
areas probably being searched at the same time would be
prohibitive.

The chance was still there, of course. But it was so small
that he thought they could afford not to worry about that
until it proved to have some substance.

Having made its passes, the shuttle bus disappeared.
Hal, with the other two, went back to watching the deploy-
ment of the soldiers below into their various assigned areas
of search.

It was a slow dispersal, and the soldiers were not driving
themselves to accomplish it with anything more than casual
speed. As the units departing the roadhead broke up into
smaller and smaller units, their pace slowed progressively,
until by the time they were down to the four individuals
that seemed to be the team number for an individual section
of territory, they were literally loafing along; and when at
last they reached the area that was to be theirs alone to
search, they put themselves first to the leisurely business of
setting up temporary camps.

Meanwhile, Procyon moved across the sky overhead
and the day wore on. Hal and Old Man sat still, engrossed
in the developing situation as shown on the screens of the
four scopes that now sat in front of them since Calas had
rejoined them. None of the soldiers, as yet, were close
enough for naked-eye observation. But Calas became more
and more restless as the day wore on. Hal could feel the
tension in the wiry little man growing with the passing
hours.

"Why don't they get it done, damn it?" exploded Calas
finally.

"Do you know about the battle of Thermopylae?"
asked Hal.

Calas turned to look at him.

"No," Calas said.

"It happened on Old Earth, nearly three thousand years

ago," Hal said. "Persia, a huge empire of that time, set out to conquer the city-states of the Greeks on a peninsula reaching down from the southern part of Europe into the Mediterranean Sea. Xerxes, the Persian ruler, attacked the Peninsula with a vast army. His forces clashed with seven thousand Greeks on a narrow strip of coastline with the sea on one side and steep cliffs on the other. The sea was barred to the Persians by Greek ships. The seven thousand Greeks on land were mainly from Sparta, a city that produced the best hoplites in the world then—men armed with large shields and long spears, fighting in close formation."

Hal paused. Calas was, at least, listening with every sign of interest.

"For three days of fighting Xerxes tried to get past the Spartans. But Leonidas, King of Sparta and their commander, with his troops, who were mostly Spartans, held them. Then a Greek traitor showed the Persians a narrow footpath up over the cliffs. They started to go up and around the Spartans to take them from behind. Leonidas, learning of this, sent most of his soldiers off in retreat. He, himself, and three hundred of his Spartans with some of the allies from other cities, stayed and defended. They who stayed died fighting; but what they did allowed those sent off to get away safely."

He paused again, this time glancing at Calas.

"The place where they fought the Persians and died," he said, "is called Thermopylae; and after, there was an inscription put up there. It said *'go, stranger and tell the Spartans we lie here in obedience to their command.'* "

Hal stopped; he reached out and enlarged the view on one of the scopes.

"And?" said Calas. "What has all this three-thousand-year-old history to do with what we've got down there?"

He jerked his hand at the valley below.

"Just that Leonidas knew what he was deciding to do when he chose to stay and die—and those with him knew." Hal looked directly into the eyes of Calas. "We only have one life; and at its end, there's one important question only. Whether what we did praises or condemns us in our own eyes. And judgment can rest on any moment's decision or action, from all our years."

Old Man bowed as only he could from a seated position, toward Hal. Hal looked at him.

"Now, why?" he said to Old Man. "I only put a truth into words."

"It was the truth I bowed to," said Old Man; and smiled.

"All right, all right . . . " muttered Calas, peering into his scanner, "you don't have to underline it. Maybe I know what you mean better than you think. Don't forget I figured myself for dead, under the rocks of that slide, when I heard those mates of mine taking off without digging for me."

But from then on he watched the screen before him closely, continuously and without fidgeting.

By the time the sun began to set, the soldiers below had all made their individual camps. A few of the separate teams had even made a brief search of part of their assigned area. But most had simply spent their time setting up shelters and building a fire. They sat around the fires as darkness grew, talking and drinking from their canteens; and when, at last, there was nothing to be seen from the ledge but deep shadow where forest foliage had been visible, the numerous firelights flickered and twinkled like echoes of the stars that grew into brightness overhead.

"Friend?"

Hal had heard the footsteps coming up behind them; but, still caught in his long day's observation of what was below, on identifying them as the footsteps of Artur he had merely noted them, and returned to his concentration on what was lit on the screen before him by the light of one of the fires below. Now he roused and answered.

"Yes?" he said.

He got to his feet, cramped by the long watch. Beside him, Calas and Old Man were also rising.

"I thought I could take over for you here," said Artur. "At night, there's not much need for a skilled watcher; and you'll need rest."

"True," said Hal.

The darkness was deep enough so that the two men were standing close together. Hal caught the faint sour odor of nervous perspiration from the other. Fresh sweat raised by the body in response to physical effort did not have that smell.

"I'll head back in, then," he added. "Calas, Old Man, come along. Amid's probably going to want to talk to us about what we've seen."

He stepped around Artur, making it a point to pass so closely his elbow brushed lightly for a second against the shirt of the Assistant Guildmaster. Sure enough, Artur's shirt was soaked through with sweat.

"Make sure you get enough sleep yourself," Hal said to Artur as he passed.

"Don't worry about me," Artur's voice came, controlled and level behind him. "I'm wide awake."

"Good," said Hal.

He led the two with him to Amid's reception building. Within, Amid was talking, also by firelight, but artificial illumination as well, to Onete.

". . . All right," said Onete, breaking off whatever she had been saying as he came in the door. "I'll be going."

She smiled at Hal and the others as she passed them on her way out. The door shut behind her.

"Come and sit down," said Amid.

They did so. There was a rough circle of chairs to one side of the table where the map was laid out, in one of which Amid sat. They took others facing him.

"You put in an extended watch," Amid said. "How are you all?"

"Myself," said Hal, "I'm still a little stiff from sitting that long. But it's something that'll work itself out."

"I'm fine," said Calas—but there was tiredness to be heard in his voice. Old Man smiled and nodded.

"What were you able to figure out about them, and their plans for searching?" Amid asked Hal.

"Most of what I saw just confirmed what I told you earlier," said Hal. "They've clearly divided the area into small sections they're going to search in no great hurry, with units of four searchers to the section. Thanks to Calas, I understand more about some of their officers than I did. But before we get into that, you know that Artur's taken over as night guard, replacing us?"

"Yes," said Amid. His wrinkled old face squeezed up in a frown that would have been almost comical if it had not been so concerned. "He knows it doesn't do any good, but he feels better out there, where he can watch where Cee must be, even if he doesn't know exactly where she is and couldn't see her down there, even if he knew. There's no great need for him to be doing anything else. I thought he might as well be busy at what he wanted, so I agreed to let him take the night watch. There's no problem with that, is there?"

"Not from the standpoint of safety," Hal said. "How much sleep has he had?"

"He told me he'd had over six hours last night," said Amid. "I've only got his word for it. What is it? Are you afraid he might fall asleep out there on watch?"

"No," said Hal. "But you can be wide awake on very little sleep and still not thinking straight—even though you think you are."

"I'm not sure I believed that about the six hours, but I believe him when he says he couldn't sleep now if he tried," said Amid. "Why's it important? The soldiers certainly won't do anything during the night?"

"No," said Hal. "They can't search in the dark; and they're not the type for night exercises, even if they were trained to it, which I doubt."

"I never got any training in night exercises, when I was with them," said Calas. "Garrison people, that's all they are."

"But what did you learn, then?" asked Amid. "Anything that can help?"

"That surveillance craft possibly took pictures of the whole area," Hal said, "but as we agreed last night, it's doubtful they'll be studied by anyone able to pick up the small signs that'd show we're here, under the cover and camouflage you've set up. Chances are more likely some officer'll just run an eye quickly over them to see if there're any obvious signs of people—and that, they won't find."

"Yes, but the soldiers," said Amid. "How likely are they to notice some sign of our presence, down there in the flatland? After all, we do have foragers down there often; and there's the spot where Onete's been meeting Cee."

"I'd hate to promise anything," Hal said, "but even if they do recognize some signs of people, from what I saw today I think we'll be fairly safe if we just sit tight up here. That ought to include, by the way, not making any noises that could be reflected down into the valley. As we sat on the edge of the ledge, I could hear the sounds of the Guild people moving about here, reflected off that cliff-face above us. Sound rises rather than falls; but we should still keep things quiet until the soldiers are gone."

"We can do that," said Amid. He made a note. "I'll see to it."

"As far as the soldiers themselves go," Hal said, "they all moved clumsily through the forest, making harder work than they needed to of getting places in it. They've got the city-bred tendency to try to push their way through undergrowth with main strength, rather than slip through at the best place for it. Also, very few of them set up camp in the best places available. The few who did, I think, did it by accident. They're certainly not woods-wise; and they're probably not too happy to be here. That attitude'll help make them careless when they start searching."

He paused.

"Those are the most certain points about them I picked up today; that and the information Calas was able to give me about certain officers. Basically, from what Calas says, we've got to deal with a commander who's something of a martinet, leading poorly trained and motivated troops. What that adds up to is that he'll probably be used to clubbing them—metaphorically speaking—to get results. Which in turn means they'll slack off the minute he's out of sight, no matter how much they might be afraid of him finding out about their doing that, later. I'd guess that unless something favors them, we're pretty secure up here. Cee, even, should be fairly safe down there, unless she literally walks into their hands."

He stopped and looked questioningly at Old Man.

"Anything to add?" he asked.

"They'll sleep poorly tonight," said Old Man with one of his gentle smiles. "They're people of bad conscience trying to rest under unfamiliar conditions. Their sleep and their dreams will be bad; and tomorrow they'll be more tired than usual, and so more likely to miss seeing things they might notice otherwise."

He fell silent and, with Hal, looked at Calas.

Calas cleared his throat.

"Me?" he said. "You want a report from me on them?"

"Certainly," said Hal.

"Well, I wasn't really watching them the way I should have, earlier in the day. I didn't really look at them—then. Friend, I have you to thank for making me try to actually see them; rather than just sit up there and swear at their being here."

"What did you see when you did look closely?" Hal said.

"A lot of them're new since I was there. Not that there's any I really knew well; but the faces of the ones who were there when I was there, I'd recognize. You know? So, most of them are faces I never saw before, which means they're new; but they're going to be just like we all were. Most of them'll have come out with something to drink—liquor, I mean—in their canteens or hidden in the equipment they're carrying; and so most of them'll be drinking tonight. I'd have been drinking, even though I wasn't that much of a drinker when I was with them; just to help me sleep out here and make it more comfortable. More'n a few'll have hangovers, tomorrow."

He paused a moment.

"Some won't drink at all, of course," he said. "We've got some Friendlies and others who've got individual reasons for never drinking. Anyway, that's one thing."

Hal, Amid and Old Man waited.

"Something else, though," said Calas, "I didn't think of it until you told me about decisions, but friends tend to stick together, and the groupmen and team-leaders usually let them. Because that makes it easier for the sub-officers. That means in most of those units of four, there's almost sure to be at least two who're side-by-siders. That means those two'll stick together and the other two'll have to tag along with them. Also it means that one of the two is the leader of the two. So you've got one man in each four-man unit who'll probably end up making up the minds of the other three, whenever there's something to make up minds about. I don't know just how knowing that'll help; but maybe you, Friend, can see some use in it."

Hal nodded slowly.

"It may apply," he said.

"Apply to what?" Amid asked sharply, then immediately softened his voice to its usual gentle tone. "I'm sorry. Do I sound bad-tempered? I don't mean to. It's just that it's been a long night and a long day—"

"You don't sound bad-tempered," said Hal, "and to answer your question, there's something about what I saw of their dispersal down there today that bothers me. There're patterns to everything that humans do, and there's something about the pattern of the way they've set up for their search that bothers me, only I can't put my finger on just what it is. I've got my own system for figuring out cause and effect, which generally helps with problems like this; but right now it doesn't seem to have enough information to work with. I'll be able to tell you more tomorrow, when they begin actively searching."

The door to the building banged open and Onete entered, followed by two men wearing the large white kitchen duty aprons everyone used on that job. All three were carrying trays heavy with cloth-covered dishes. Amid popped to his feet and whisked the map off the table as Onete led her companions to it.

They set the trays down on the table and began unloading the dishes.

"You haven't eaten, any of you, all day," said Amid. "I asked Onete to go for food as soon as you got here. I may not be able to get Artur to eat, but I can make sure the rest of you are fed."

At the sight and smell of the food in the dishes, Hal became aware of how hungry he was.

"Thank you," he said, pulling his chair up to the table as Old Man and Calas joined him.

After they had eaten and the others had gone, Hal stayed behind at Amid's request.

"I'm worried about Artur," said Amid. "As I said, he's not eating. I don't really believe he's sleeping, either. He acts just the way he does usually; but I know him well enough to know he's tearing himself to pieces over this business of Cee being down there with those soldiers. You see, he feels responsible."

"Yes," said Hal, "that would fit his pattern."

"He shares your belief, as we were saying," Amid went on, "that Cee's probably followed one of us back under the boulder and right up to the ledge. That she knows where we live. He's afraid that if the soldiers catch her, they may assume she's one of us and try to get her to tell them where we are.

"Yes," said Hal, "that would fit their pattern, too."

"So, if they threaten to hurt her to make her talk, she'll have no choice but to tell them. Then, when they find the stone in place, they may think she's lying and doesn't really know; and then they'll kill her. On the other hand we can't leave the way open; so in a way we—and he—will be responsible for her death; and she's just a little girl."

"Never try to predict what an individual will do under torture," Hal said. "It's not a matter of will power. The individual doesn't even know himself until the time comes. The bravest can crack and people you wouldn't expect it from will die without saying a word. She might simply refuse to talk at all."

"But then they might torture her to death, to try to make her talk!" Amid seemed to shrink. "We can't let that happen!"

"You can. You must—if there's no way to avoid it," said Hal. "It won't save her to throw away the lives of everyone else in the Guild—and what the Guild might mean for the rest of your Exotics, someday. But keep your mind filled about how horrible Cee's situation could be, and sooner or later you, or Artur, or somebody else'll try some scheme that doesn't have a chance of succeeding, one that'll dump all of you into the soldiers' hands."

"Even if we could—" said Amid. "Even if we could accept sacrificing her, Artur never could. Never!"

"Then lock him up," said Hal, "until the soldiers are gone."

"We can't do that!"

"He'd hate you for it," said Hal. "But it may be the kindest way of dealing with him."

"I'll speak to him," said Amid. He did not wring his hands. They lay still in his lap, but he might as well have been wringing them. "If he can convince the rest he believes Cee will be safe—"

"You know yourself that's not good enough, even if he could do it," said Hal. "Your fellow Guild members are almost all Exotics. They're too empathic to be fooled just by his pretending not to be concerned. He's actually got to face the chance that Cee may die; and, by his example in facing that fact, lead the rest of the community into facing it, too. Anything less than that won't work. More than that, it'd be wrong."

"Wrong?" Amid sounded shocked.

"Yes," said Hal, "because you'd be letting a situation that's out of your control upset your people at the very time when this community needs to keep its morale as high as possible, and its thoughts as clear as possible. I promise you, if I see any hope of doing anything at all for Cee, I'll let you all know and I'll do it myself, if that's what's best. But until a real chance to help her appears, two things need to be done; and they're very hard things, especially for you Exotic-born Guild members. One, the members have to accept the fact that whatever is going to happen to Cee will happen, and they can't do anything about it, as things stand now. Second, Artur has got to face that fact himself, and show the rest of the community that he's done so."

There was a long moment before Amid answered.

"It'll be hard enough for us," he said. "For Artur—impossible."

"Then lock him up, as I say."

Amid did not answer.

Hal got to his feet.

"I'm sorry," he said gently, looking down on the old man who seemed to have shrunk within the confines of his chair until he was no bigger than child-sized himself. "Sooner or later everyone reaches a day on which he or she has to face things like this. It does no good to pretend such a day won't ever come."

He waited, a moment longer.

"It's your decision," he said. "If you think of some way I can help, call me. I'm going to get some rest now, while I can."

He went out.

The following morning he watched the sunrise as usual with Old Man and then took his position on the ledge's lip with the scopes. Calas joined them shortly thereafter. But it was a good three hours after that before the first of the searching groups down below began to go to work; and at that time some of them had just wakened.

Hal leaned forward suddenly and turned up the magnification on one of the scopes.

"Calas," he said. "What's that they're putting on the

ends of their needle guns? Something like an explosives thrower."

Calas looked.

"Oh, that," he said. "They're catch-nets. They use them a lot when chasing escaped prisoners—or taking any prisoners they'll want to question before they shoot them. You know how a needle gun works?"

Hal smiled. "Yes," he said.

As he had learned, growing up on Dorsai, the riflelike needle gun was a universal favorite as a weapon for field troops mainly because its magazine could hold up to four thousand of the needles that the weapon fired.

Each of the needles could be lethal if it hit a vital spot; but a spray of them was almost certain to bring down a human target, one way or another. The needles were slim little things, hardly bigger than their average namesakes that were used for ordinary sewing. A kick from a machine-wound spring unit or from a cylinder of highly compressed air flicked the needles clear of the muzzle of the gun and started them toward their target. But each needle was like a miniature rocket. A solid propellant, ignited by the needle's escape from the muzzle of the rifle, drove it up to three hundred meters in a straight line toward whatever it had been aimed at. All needles fired on the same trigger pull formed a spiral pattern that spread as it approached its target, like shot from the muzzle of an ancient shotgun.

The advantages lay, therefore, in the amount of firepower from a relatively light weapon; plus the fact that the needle gun was almost invulnerable to disablement through misuse. You could drag it through the mud, or recover it from being under half a mile of water for six months, and it would still work. Moreover, the fact that it could be used in poorly trained hands to spray the general area of an enemy like a hose, made it extremely popular.

It also could deliver a number of auxiliary devices, kicking them clear with spring or compressed gas, to be self-propelled toward a particular target. But this catch-net device was one Hal had never encountered before; probably because, as Calas had said, its design fitted it rather for police than military use.

"They've got seeker circuits in the noses," said Calas. "Once fired, the catch-net capsule homes in on the first human body it comes close to—combination of body heat, bodily electrical circuitry and so forth, I understand—and when it gets right close to them; it blows apart and spreads a net that drops over the body. As I say, they use them for recapturing prisoners and things like that. In fact, I think the catch-net was designed in the first place for prison guards and police crowd control. That sort of thing."

Hal checked the other scopes. All the soldiers who were ready to begin searching had the catch-net capsules perched like blunt-nosed rockets on the barrel-ends of their needle guns.

He sat back to see how the search would develop.

As the sun mounted in the sky, this second morning, all the individual search units were finally at work. Hal checked the command post at the roadhead and saw that Liu was still there, with the sergeant Calas had called "the Urk" in attendance. Outside Liu's shelter an operations table with map screen in its surface and permanently mounted scopes stood in the daylight. One of the vehicles in which the searching party had come out was still there and parked by the table, undoubtedly generating power for the table, as well as the comforts of the command shelter, on tight-beam circuit.

Old Man reached over suddenly, just before noon, and tapped with his finger on the screen of the scope before Hal. Hal looked, but saw nothing to explain the other man's drawing his attention to it. Still, the slim, yellow fingertip rested on the screen, which was now showing a mass of forest undergrowth just beyond the two soldiers they had in focus there at the moment. Hal kept his eyes on that area of the screen, waiting; and, after a moment, he too saw what had caught Old Man's eye—a flicker of movement.

He watched. A small, slim, brown body was moving

parallel to the searching soldiers, at a distance from them of perhaps ten meters. Hal continued to watch and for a moment she was fully in view, before the greenery hid her again. It was Cee, with, as before, nothing but the length of vine with its split-open pod shape a few inches to one side of her navel.

"I don't think they've seen her," said Hal.

"No," answered Old Man.

"Seen who?" demanded Calas. Once more Old Man's finger tapped and held on the screen. Calas stared at it. After a long moment he whistled softly and sat back. He looked at Hal.

"What should we do?" he asked.

"What would you suggest we do?" Hal said, meeting his eyes. Calas stared at him for a long moment and then looked away. Hal softened his voice.

"For now," he said, "you concentrate on that screen. Try to keep Cee in sight, but watch particularly for any sign either of those soldiers've spotted her."

"Yes. Yes, I will," said Calas, fixing his gaze tightly on the screen.

Hal flicked the controls on another scope so that he had a view of the whole area. A few more finger-taps overlaid the picture of the land below with a ghostly map of that same area, but divided into sections, with small bright lights in each section, each representing one of the searching soldiers.

The pattern in the process of search which he had not been able to find but which he had sensed was in the making there still bothered him. The troops below were equipped not only with their weapons but with all other ordinary field equipment, including helmets that would have built-in communications equipment, putting them in verbal contact with their fellow searchers, their immediate sub-officer, and even the command base. He wished for a moment he could tune in on what was being said over that communications network. That reminded him of another, earlier, wish, which was that the Guild, in addition to what other equipment they had possessed, had seen fit to equip themselves with a long range ear gun—a listening device that allowed the one using it to pick up even a faint noise from a specific spot no larger than an adult human hand and a kilometer or more distant. As it was, he had a view of the searchers, but no idea of what they were saying. With the ear-gun he could have overheard conversations even back at the command post where Liu waited. But to want what was not available was a waste of time. He put both desires from him and considered the pattern of ghost map and lights once more.

With intuitional logic he should have been able to track down what he felt immediately. The fact he could not meant that to intuitional logic the pattern he sensed was not there. Either there actually was no such thing, or a necessary link in the logic chain that would relate it to what he saw at the moment was missing. A word overheard from one of the searchers might have filled that gap. Particularly since he had known Amanda, he trusted his instincts more than ever before, and now his instincts were positive that there was a pattern to the development of the situation below him that he could not yet see.

He learned forward sharply to peer at the screen he had been watching.

"What is it?" asked Calas. He glanced up to see both Calas and Old Man watching him.

"Is Cee still following those two soldiers?" Hal asked.

"Yes." Calas nodded emphatically.

"Has either one of them seen her, as far as you can tell?"

"Not as far as I could tell."

"Or I," said Old Man unexpectedly.

Hal looked back at the screen before him.

"What is it?" said Calas again.

"They may not be as inept as I was thinking they were," said Hal. "Perhaps some of them've had some field training after all."

"Some'll have had training rounding up prisoners before," said Calas. "That's all."

"That may be enough," said Hal. He pointed at the screen before him with the ghost map and the lights. "Or they may be wearing some special equipment—heat sensors or such that would warn them Cee was following. Those two soldiers just began searching outside their own area."

"Outside . . . ?" said Calas.

"They're still moving in a straight line, and it's taken them over into the territory of another search unit—as best I can judge where the boundaries of the territories are—"

He broke off.

"There it is," he said. "I see what they're doing now."

"What are they doing?" asked Calas.

"Those soldiers Cee's following have spotted her after all. They're leading her on. Take a look at the screen. The other search teams are changing their pattern. The team leading her is keeping on going forward, to lead her into position, and gain time for a good number of the others who're close to move into a circle around her. Then, as they move in, using their helmet communication, they'll draw the circle tighter around her. When she finally begins to suspect and makes a break for it, it'll not only be these two, but a lot of the others, who ought to have a good shot at her with those catch-nets of theirs. Unless she stops following these two now, I think she's virtually certain to be captured."

There was the sound of feet on the gravel-like soil behind them. They all turned. Onete came up and stopped before them all. But it was to Hal she spoke.

"Artur's gone," she said breathlessly. "Evidently, he left last night. Rolled the boulder aside and rolled it back in place after him. He left a note by the boulder."

She paused to catch her breath.

"He said he was sorry, but he had to go down to do what he could to protect Cee. He asked them to leave the boulder in place as long as they could before they felt they had to replace it with the rock plug. Just in case he was able to bring her back up to safety after all."

CHAPTER 26 ■

"And it's been left?" asked Hal.

"It's been left," answered Onete. "Everyone wants it that way."

There was nothing they could do from the ledge but watch. Onete left them again. In the next three-quarters of an hour as Procyon climbed brilliantly into a clear sky, Cee shadowed the two soldiers and was drawn into a semi-open area with short but vertical, near-unclimbable cliffs on two sides of it; and with now more than two dozen of the following members of the Occupational Troops closing in behind her to shut off escape back the way she had come.

She clearly heard them moving in on her, as they drew close; but the sounds must have come from all directions, so that she turned, ready to flee one way, then hesitated, turned to run in another, and hesitated again.

The hesitations were what doomed her. If she had raced full tilt for their line at the first noise, she would have had some chance, at least, of dodging between two of them, twisting, ducking, evading their grasps and so getting away. But at her first betrayal of the fact she had heard them, they all burst into a run toward her, so that when she began to run, herself, they were already closing in on her.

She checked and stood, legs spread apart, one in advance of the other. She had evidently been carrying something cupped in each hand all this time; and she now threw these two things, whatever they were, at the men most directly before her.

The throws were delivered with the kind of power and accuracy that could only come from long practice. With a sidearm motion her whole body sent the missiles on their way, and to the surprise of those on the ledge as well as that of the soldiers, the two men she had thrown at went over backwards and down, while she dashed forward again at the gap in their line she had now created.

Almost, she made it. But the others were too close. Nets exploded into existence in the air above and around her, dropped and enveloped her; and a moment later her net-swathed body disappeared under the swarm of adult figures.

From the ledge it was still plain, however, that she was not easy to subdue. The huddle of soldiers' backs, which was all those on the ledge could see, heaved and moved for some time; and it was only the sudden appearance of Liu Hu Shen and the Urk that stopped one of the soldiers who had finally reversed his needle gun, raised it, and seemed about to use it as a club.

The huddle struggled a bit more and then went still. Hu Shen clearly was issuing orders right and left. There were now between twenty and thirty of the uniformed men in the clearing, and at last the group holding her stopped its struggle, indicating she had finally been held and immobilized.

In remarkably short time the power pistol which the Urk had been carrying had been used to cut down a number of trees, large and small, to enlarge the clearing; the cut-down upper parts being hauled off to one side by teams of the men. Left standing were two trees about ten meters apart. By this time three dome-shaped battle tents had also been erected. The moment the first of these were up, the huddle of men carrying Cee, invisible in their midst, moved into it, to come out of its entrance a little later by twos and threes with every sign of relief. Clearly Cee had been left, tied down or otherwise secured, somewhere within.

"Bastards!" said Calas.

Liu, who had been generally overseeing the work being done, now for the first time went into the building where Cee had been taken. He was inside for only a few minutes, however, before he came out again, crossed the clearing and entered one of the other structures, into which his men had been bringing various furniture, such as chairs, a desk and a cot. They had brought the furniture folded up in carrying cases; and once the furniture was inside, they reclosed the cases and carried them into the third dome.

Calas's gaze, however, was all on the structure into which they had taken Cee.

"They could be working on her in there right now!" he growled.

"I don't think so," said Hal. "My guess is Liu just stepped inside with her long enough to see if she'd answer him, but not really expecting her to. When she didn't, he left her tied up; or however she's restrained, in there, for now."

"That's your guess," said Calas mutinously. "I know the kind of shithouse sweepings they've got in that outfit!"

"I believe you do," said Hal, "but I also believe they won't dare do anything they aren't ordered to do by that commanding officer, from the way you've described him. And he won't want any of them touching Cee—just yet, anyway."

"Another guess?" Calas said.

"No. Look down there for yourself," said Hal. "If he'd wanted to question Cee physically, the obvious place for it would have been back at his base, in Porphyry. They've undoubtedly got the equipment for it back there—"

"That's true enough," said Calas, under his breath.

"But back there, he'd have superiors who might take not only control away from him," said Hal, "but whatever glory there might be in catching the famous little wild girl. It just might be, too, that Liu has a pretty low opinion of the officers over him."

Calas nodded.

"You mean, he's right in feeling that way?" asked Hal.

"Unless they've got some brighter ones in since I was around," said Calas. "Right up to the Commander, the rest are all the sort that want to get to their desk at eleven in the morning, sign half a dozen papers, then go to lunch and take the rest of the day off. You're right, as long as he stays out here, he's the one in charge."

"Yes," said Hal, "and he stands to gain more credit; which none of his superiors can take away from him, if he comes in, not only with the girl, but with as many more strays and outlaws as he can pick up and bring back. As I say, take a look down there. Don't those two tents and the cut-down trees make it look like he's planning to stay a day or two, at least?"

"Yes," said Calas, somewhat grudgingly, looking at them.

"It's a good guess, then," said Hal, "he's been looking beyond Cee's capture all along. He'll be pretty sure she knows who else lives around here, and he'll want her help in finding them."

His eyes met Calas's brown ones.

"You mean he knows about the Chantry Guild?"

"Guesses, at least," said Hal. "He may have picked up bits of information from townspeople he's questioned, and gotten enough out of them to at least suspect there's some kind of community of free Exotics up here. That's why he'll be in no hurry to get his men back to barracks: and that's why he won't hurt Cee, to begin with at least. He may even try to make friends with her."

"Lots of luck!" Calas cleared his throat, and spat, deliberately, over the edge of the cliff before them. "If she wouldn't answer when Artur tried to talk to her and she'd barely answer Onete, Liu's chances of making friends with her . . ."

Calas ran out of figures of speech, into silence.

"But it's still all just your guesses, all the same," he said, at last to Hal.

"Old Man," said Hal, turning to the silent figure beside them, "what do you think?"

"I think you're probably right." said Old Man softly. Calas turned to stare at the white-bearded, thin face. "He'll need the child in good physical shape to lead them to who-ever else is here; and if he's got any experience at all with managing prisoners, he'll know she'll be more willing to help him if she believes he doesn't plan to hurt them when he gets them. So I'd think he'll begin at least, by making her as comfortable as possible; while at the same time making sure she doesn't run away. Also, he'll try to give the impression that it's just a matter of time before he finds the other people, whether she helps or not, and a leisurely attitude to the situation is going to help along that illusion."

As usual, when Old Man talked at any length at all, the Guild members had a tendency to listen attentively. Calas listened. When Old Man fell silent again, he nodded, slowly.

"Right," he said. "It makes sense. But what happens if she still doesn't answer him? He's going to run out of patience sooner or later."

"We'll have to watch, wait, and hope some kind of opportunity comes up for us to do something about the situation, without risking discovery of the Guild," said Hal. "I don't know what other option we've got. Do you?"

After a long moment, Calas slowly shook his head again, and turned back to watching the screens showing where Cee was being held. Missy and Hadnah had followed the action of the chase closely and now held the area of the three buildings and the clearing in a good-sized picture. Calas sat unmoving and watching, but now he watched the way a wolf might, at a rabbit hole.

It was midafternoon when he suddenly exploded into speech.

"By God, they've got him!"

It was unnecessary to ask who had been meant by "him." Artur was the only one down there likely to be brought in as a captive. By rights it should have been Missy or Hadnah who first caught sight of the large man and his two captors, benefiting from the higher angle of their post of observation. But evidently the approach had been under the cover of treetops, which were more an obstacle to those viewing high on the mountainside than Hal and the other two with him.

"He doesn't look very mussed up," Calas went on. "You'd have thought someone like him who could move that boulder at the foot of the path out of his way and then roll it back could have put up more of a fight before they took him."

"He's unarmed," said Hal. "What would you do if you were faced with a needle gun—and both those soldiers bringing him in have them?"

There was a pause.

"You're right," said Calas; but he said it grudgingly.

Artur had plainly given his clothing some thought before he dressed to leave the ledge. He was wearing green shorts and shirt, and boots made of rough leather tanned a light brown. He would not have been easy to spot among the growth below unless he moved. On the other hand, Hal guessed that Artur knew less than nothing about moving inconspicuously through the high-altitude forest below.

Cee, on the other hand, could have given any one of them lessons. If it had not been for the heat sensors, or whatever other technological aids the soldiers had been carrying, Hal would have been willing to bet she could have moved around and between them all day long without being spotted.

As the two guarding Artur brought him into the camp, one of the dozen who had stayed around after the three shelters had been set up ducked into into the other tent, the one holding Liu. A moment later the commanding officer came out and stood while Artur was brought face to face with him.

They stood looking at each other. The screen showed their lips moving. Hal's ability to read lips had become rusty over the last few years and the angle at which the screen showed the two had Artur's back to him and Liu's face averted to the point where he could see only the left corner of his lips. He could not make out what either man was saying. However, they talked for no more than a few minutes.

The conversation ended with Liu abruptly turning around and re-entering his shelter. The two escorting soldiers, apparently having been given their orders by their disappearing commander, took Artur to one of the two trees that had not been cut down. They tied him to it, in standing position with his back to the tree trunk, enclosing him with what seemed an excessive number of turns of rope around his body and the tree. He stood with his back to the tree, unable to move even in small ways.

"Now what?" asked Calas.

"I believe," said Old Man in his soft voice, "that the officer has decided to leave him there to think his situation over."

"Does Artur know they've got Cee, do you think?" asked Calas, looking from Old Man to Hal and back again.

Old Man said nothing.

"I don't think so," answered Hal, "any more than I think they've let Cee know they've got him. Liu's probably planning to spring the news on both of them when the time's right to get the most shock value from doing it."

That may have been the commander's plan, but in any case he seemed in no hurry to carry it out. Procyon descended in the west and the stars came out. The forest below became one dark, mysterious mass, with the exception of the two small spots. One was where a blaze of artificial light lit up the clearing in the distance where the trucks were still parked. The other, closer, was more directly below the watchers, where Artur stood, still tied to the tree, and with Liu still out of sight in his shelter. From one of the other domes trays with covered dishes were carried into the tent that was Liu's, and it was perhaps three-quarters of an hour afterward that he finally made an appearance.

The Urk hurried up to him and was told something. The tall, thin underofficer in the tailored uniform went off to the shelter that held Cee and re-emerged a few minutes later, followed by two soldiers with the little girl held between them, her hands tied behind her.

She was making no effort to walk under her own power. Her knees were bent and the two soldiers were forced to carry her to the other tree that had been left uncut, where she was roped into the same upright position Artur had been tied into. After a few moments, she unbent her knees and took the weight of her body on her feet.

Her face had that blank look of a child's which could indicate anything from an extreme of terror to complete incomprehension. Her eyes followed the Urk as he went to speak to Liu.

Liu and the Urk came toward her. Behind the two men, in the center of the clearing, a large open fire was being built. It was not an unreasonable thing to do. At night, because of the altitude, even here at the base of the mountains proper, the nights were cool, for all that they were almost on the equator of the planet. But it did not get so cold that a fire so large had any real utility. Cee, herself, was obviously used to the nighttime temperatures, which she faced unclothed.

She was still unclothed now, more so, in fact, because her vine-pod girdle had been taken from her. But, as Hal had noticed on first seeing her when he had been with Amanda, her nakedness was such a natural and unconscious state that, if anything, she made those around her in clothes look unnatural. Her expression remained blank as the two men came up to her, and Liu spoke to her. It was intensely frustrating to Hal not to be able to catch enough of the officer's lip movements to guess at least a word or so from him, or from one of the soldiers.

In any case, she did not answer. Only, now, she stared directly at Liu, instead of the Urk, with that completely unfathomable, completely observant, open-eyed stare of which only the young are capable.

Liu's lips moved again. The expression of his face grew stern. There was no movement of lips or change of appearance in the girl before him. He glanced at the Urk, beside him, and the Urk said something.

"I think," said Old Man unexpectedly, "he asked for confirmation of the fact that she actually knows how to speak, and understands Basic."

Hal looked suddenly at the brown eyes in the ageless face behind the white beard.

"You read lips?" he asked, almost sharply.

Old Man shook his head.

"No," he answered, "I only guess. But I think it's a good guess. And I think this Urk is reminding him she was six years or older when her parents died."

Liu turned away and went back past the fire to Artur. His face was now so averted in the picture shown on the screen before Hal that it was obviously useless even to try to read lips.

"I'd say your guess may have been pretty close to the mark," he told Old Man. "What do you think he's saying to Artur right now?"

Old Man shook his head a little slowly.

"It's guessing, only," he said. "I could be very wrong, but obviously this officer's deliberately waited until dark to let the two see each other. Plainly, the fire is to make the scene look even more threatening. He gives the impression of a man who hopes to make use of psychological as well as physical pressures. Watching someone else tortured to produce answers is one of the favorite ways of getting information since mankind started to use such methods. The idea, of course, is to weaken the will of someone who doesn't want to talk. Here he's got two prisoners. He can question either one with all kinds of painful means, with a double chance of getting answers—either from the one he questions or from the one watching and expecting the same thing. Either might break. Obviously, though, he expects to be able to judge the effect of his questioning better on a grown man, than on someone like Cee."

"He'll be threatening Artur with torture now, if Artur doesn't tell him how to find the other people who're around here? That's what you're saying, isn't it?" demanded Hal.

"I would guess," said Old Man simply.

Liu continued to talk to Artur several minutes longer,

but Artur's face, unlike Cee's, showed anger and defiance. Liu pointed at Cee several times and Artur shook his head. Most possibly, Hal thought, the big man would be denying any knowledge of the little girl; although it remained impossible for Hal to read the movements of his lips. Eventually, Liu turned away from him and went back across the lighted clearing into his shelter, while the Urk, with two of the soldiers, got busy with the physical questioning of Artur.

Calas began to swear in a low, monotonous tone, and his voice went on and on, as if he were talking to himself.

Mercifully, the angle of vision both from the ledge and from higher up on the mountain with Missy and Hadnah was such that the bodies of the three men were in the way of any camera view of exactly what they were doing to Artur. However, the soldiers and their noncommissioned officer were careful not to block the view Cee could have had of what was going on.

But their efforts were wasted. After watching them for a moment until Artur's mouth opened in what was obviously an involuntary scream of pain, she took her attention off them. Her eyes, in that expressionless face of hers, turned instead to focus on the round, white shape of the tent into which Liu had vanished. They kept their gaze immovable upon the tent.

Old Man drew in an audible breath.

"He's made a mistake," Old Man said.

"He? You mean Liu?" asked Hal.

"Yes." said Old Man. "Artur denied knowing her and Cee told him nothing. The officer has no way of knowing she loves him, or he, her."

"She loves Artur?" Hal asked. "Amid told me she wouldn't let him get close to her, after that one time he tried to reach out and touch her!"

"True enough," said Old Man, "but all the time she must have remembered who he was an either loved him from before or come to love him when he tried to make contact again with her. She was just too frightened to come close to him. Look at her face now."

Hal reached forward to turn the screen's controls up to give a close-up picture of Cee's face. They saw it only slightly averted, staring at Liu's shelter off screen; but Calas's swearing broke off abruptly.

"Holy Mother!" said Calas.

Hal also was absorbing the shock of what he was seeing. It was strange, since in no easily visible way had Cee's blank expression changed. Only, the steadiness of her gaze seemed to have acquired a power of its own.

"God help that Liu if she ever gets her hands on him; and *him* tied up, or helpless!" breathed Calas.

Old Man nodded.

"But why do you say Liu made a mistake?" Hal asked.

"If she had not already, she has now identified him with whatever she saw done to her parents when they died. Liu Hu Shen thought to provoke fear in the child by forcing her to watch Artur being tortured. Instead he's unleashed hatred. A terrible hatred in her, against him."

After a long moment of silence, Old Man added:

"Who would have thought one so young could hate so much? But then life has made her more than half wild animal; and the actions of that man have now made her wholly so. . . ."

CHAPTER 27 ■

"I can't take any more of this!" said Calas in a thick voice. He got up abruptly and blundered off into the darkness. They heard the sounds of him being sick farther back from the lip of the ledge.

Hal and Old Man sat in silence for a while. Eventually,

Old Man spoke, raising his voice, but not looking back over his shoulder as he spoke.

"It's over for now," he said.

There was a pause, then the sound of footsteps coming back to them. Calas reappeared, a shadow in the darkness, and stepped around in front of Hal.

"We've got to do something about this." he said.

"We will." Hal looked into the screen. Artur sagged in his ropes, apparently unconscious. The Urk and the two soldiers had abandoned him when Liu had stepped out of his shelter and spoken to them, a few minutes earlier. As the three men on the ledge watched, they came back now, untied Artur from the tree, eased his unconscious body to the ground and re-tied it with the same ropes that had held it upright.

Cee, supple as a cat, had managed to slide downward not only herself but the ropes binding around her and the tree, until now she sat cross-legged on the ground at the foot of the tree. She looked almost comfortable. But nothing else about her expression or the target of her eyes, which was still either Liu or his shelter when he was inside it, had changed.

"We'll do something," said Hal. "I just had to know whether Liu was going to try to force the answers he wants tonight, or stretch the process out a day or two. Clearly, he's going to drag it out. Time doesn't seem to be a factor, or perhaps he has at least several days to find out what he wants to know. I was afraid he'd need to find out tonight whatever Artur or Cee could tell him, but that doesn't seem to be the case. Look, they're even covering Artur against the night cold."

It was true. On the screen they could see one of the soldiers throwing a blanket over the motionless form of Artur. Another soldier took a blanket over to Cee and tucked it around her shoulders so that it made a sort of small tent covering her body. Like the others, he ignored the fact she was now seated on the ground.

She paid no attention to the blanket being put around her, but when next they looked, it had left her shoulders and was a pool of darkness around her lower legs and on the ground. A soldier got up from among a group of them who were seated around the fire and passing a bottle around. He tucked the blanket into place again about her shoulders; but a few minutes later it was once more on the ground.

He started to get up once more, but the soldier next to him pulled him back into a sitting position. After that they ignored Cee.

"Missy? Hadnah?" Hal said to the screen.

"We're watching," the voice of Missy came back to him.

"Good," said Hal. "We're going to leave our screens down here for a council of war at Amid's. If you want me, that's where I'll be. You two can keep the watch going?"

"Count on us," chimed in the voice of Hadnah.

Hal got to his feet a little stiffly. His legs had adjusted to the morning sittings to watch the sunrise; but whole days seated on the ground were something else again. Old Man got to his feet lightly and easily, as if he had been seated there for minutes rather than hours. With Calas, they went to Amid's office.

He was busy dealing with a short, thick-set, and—for an Exotic—a remarkably pugnacious-looking man with bristly gray hair, cut short; about some matter having to do with the building on of extra dormitory space to provide larger units for copies, particularly couples with young children. The gray haired man was named Abke-Smythe, but that was all Hal knew about him except that he had some sort of responsibility for the group's housing. Amid started to interrupt this, to talk with Hal and the others as they came in; but Hal shook his head at the older man.

"We can sit and wait a few minutes," he said. "In fact one of your chairs would feel good."

He dropped into one of the larger overstuffed chairs, and both Calas and Old Man followed his example, except that Old Man, with a momentary, mischievous smile at Hal, took his position in cross-legged fashion upon the seat cushion of his chair.

Hal grinned back, momentarily, then let his mind go elsewhere. The fact was, as much as his body needed a rest from the position it had held all day, his mind now needed to switch gears from analyzing everything he had seen in the jungle below him since early morning and planning what was to be done with the night before him.

Without intending to, he fell asleep.

He blinked and woke, startled to find that time had gone by and things in the office had changed. A table had been set up with three straight chairs, and in two of them Calas and Old Man were already seated, eating. At another empty chair a place had been set which was obviously waiting for him.

"Take your time," said the voice of Amid. Hal looked over to see the head of the Chantry Guild still behind his desk, fingers busily tapping on some keys inset in his desktop. "We can keep the food hot."

"It's all right," said Hal. "I guess I just needed a moment to sort my mind out. I'll be right there."

He got up, went over and took the empty chair at the table. Calas passed him covered dishes, from which Hal began transferring large amounts of food to his plate. The fact was, he thought as he did this, that what he had just said was exactly the truth. The night before he had had a good night's sleep, and had not needed more now, but from long experience he recognized that his unconscious mind had wanted his consciousness out of the way while it addressed the problem he was facing now. It had worked. He had awakened with a solution clear to him.

He opened his mouth to start talking to Amid and the others, then closed it again. There was eating to be done and it would be some time into tomorrow's daylight before he would have a chance to eat again, probably. Best to finish his meal now, and have his discussion later. He went to work on the food, accordingly; in spite of his late start, ending up at almost the same second as Calas, who had continued to eat for some minutes after Old Man had finished.

"Thank you," Hal said, looking over at Amid.

"Now," said Amid, "what have you got to thank me for? Simply a share of our food, which we'd give to anyone who was here, let alone someone like yourself, who we count on to help us solve a situation like this."

"Don't count too much on me," said Hal. "In the first place, something might happen to me; and, in the second place, there are a number of people, including you and Old Man, who could do a creditable job of solving it alone. And in the fact, if Amanda was here, you'd be idiots not to use her for dealing with this, rather than me. She's had experience with this world, the soldiers, and a complete Dorsai upbringing."

"No doubt," said Amid. "But I think that if she, or anyone else, was here, she'd join the rest of us in choosing you to suggest what we need to do. There's something about you that carries a banner everyone rallies to."

"Including Bleys?" Hal smiled.

"I'm being serious," said Amid. "You know what I mean. All right, if you've finished eating, what have you got to tell us?"

"Not a lot that I haven't told you already," answered Hal soberly. "The trick's going to be to send these soldiers home thinking they've found nothing worth worrying about; and also to get Cee and Artur back alive, if we can. That's where those darts come in. By the way—"

"If you'll look on the table over in the corner there, under that white cloth, I think you'll find what you're asking about," interrupted Amid. "Tannaheh ought to have been here fifteen minutes ago—ah, here he is, finally!"

It was a little difficult to see why Amid should sound so sure, since he completed his sentence before the door to his "office" had swung wide enough to reveal who was coming in. But he was not wrong. Tannaheh was the one who entered, carrying a good-sized box which seemed to have been filled with long strands of grass, now dried to a golden brown color. Behind him was another man, a short man in his fifties or older with a long, straight nose and hands that were large for the rest of his body, as if spread and thickened by years of hard work. Under the thin, straight, gray hair the man's face was solemn almost to the point of sourness. He wore a jacket made of some material that looked like leather, over heavy, dark brown trousers and a checked shirt—a contrast to Tannaheh, whose slim body was dressed, as it had been earlier, in the gray wool sweater, white shirt, blue trousers and boots.

"Sorry to hold everybody up." said Tannaheh cheerfully. He carried the box over and set it down gently on the table covered with the white cloth. "I thought Luke was going to wait for me at his workshop with the belts and bows, and when I got there and didn't find him, I thought he'd just stepped out for a minute, and so I spent some time waiting there for him, until his son dropped in for some tool or other. He told me Luke'd already brought the things over here earlier and then gone on to the dispensary to wait for me. Anyway, we got together finally at the dispensary and here we are."

"You know Luke, don't you?" Amid asked Hal.

"Indeed, I do," said Hal, nodding at Luke, who was the Guild's chief craftsman:

"Sorry about the mix-up," said Luke, in a surprisingly deep bass voice.

"Well, well, it doesn't matter now you're here; and Hal and everyone's here," said Amid, getting up to come around his desk, rubbing his hands and holding them out to the central fireplace of the office, to warm them. "—Poor circulation in the extremities. Age. Well, show them what you've got."

"You go ahead, Luke," said Tannaheh. "The darts and the drugs in them'll need a little explaining."

"All right."

Luke twitched the white cover to the back of the table, revealing a number of items on the polished surface, including several bandoleer-like belts, with loops for ammunition. But what took Hal's eye particularly were five short recurved bows, no more than four feet in length, made of a milky-colored, smoothly glasslike material. Luke noted the direction of his gaze.

"Had the boys up all night, making these," he said. "The belts took hardly any time at all."

He picked up one of the bows and handed it to Hal, meanwhile reaching with his other hand for a rather stubby-looking arrow, apparently made of the same material as the bows.

The bow was already equipped with a string, tied tightly at one end and ending in a loop at the other. Hal had already placed the tied end on the floor and was putting his weight on the bow to bend it, as he slid the looped end up the shaft and into the notch prepared to hold it at the bow's far end. The bow, he saw, seemed to be made of a form of glass. Once strung, he held the bow up in one hand and ticked the string with the thumb of his other. It hummed musically.

The string was a little strange. It appeared to be made of the same milky material as the arrow shafts. Also there was a feel to it that was different from that of any bow string Hal had handled before. He plucked the string, listened to the musical note of it, hefted the bow and turned to pass it to Old Man.

"You know swords," he said, smiling. "Am I correct in thinking you know something about these, too?"

"Something," said Old Man, nodding as he took the weapon. "We used to shoot at a prayer target, blindfolded."

"Oh?" said Amid, interested. "Some form of divination? Or should we ask?"

"Of course you may ask," said Old Man. "But it wasn't divination. Hitting the target correctly was a test of control over the body and mind."

He was doing through the same motions with the bow as Hal had before, first unstringing, then restringing it—except that where Hal had placed an end of the bow on the floor and leaned his weight on it in order to bend it enough to slide the looped end up into its notch, Old Man merely tucked the bow under one arm and bent it against his body to string it.

"I don't think I'd be able to do that," said Hal, watching.

"Indeed you could," said Old Man earnestly. "It's only a matter of practice—and habit. Forgive me. I didn't mean to seem to be showing off."

"We all know you don't show off," said Amid. "What was that about shooting at a mark, blindfolded, though? Could you show us that?"

"If you'll forgive me . . ." Old Man looked around the room, then turned his back on it, so that he was facing the wall behind Amid's desk. "If one of you would fix a piece of paper against the far wall, then blindfold me and me and hand me an arrow—one with a sharp point, if you have one?"

"I'm afraid," said Tannaheh, "all the points are on the darts which fasten to the ends of the arrows—"

"That's all right," said Luke, "give me an arrow."

He took the blunt-ended, feathered shaft Tannaheh gave him, reached to Amid's desk for a pin from a tray which held such things, along with page fasteners and other small clips and devices. Hitching around from the back of his belt a case that held a number of small instruments, he clipped off the blunt heat of the pin with what looked like a needle-nosed set of pliers, then held the chopped-off point for a moment in the jaws of the pliers. Hal saw the blunt end of the pin glow red for a second before Luke used the pliers to sink it into the blunt end of the arrow shaft, which melted before it.

"That ought to give you point enough for wooden walls like these," Luke said. "I'll go put up a target."

He handed the arrow to Old Man, who received it without turning back to look at him. Luke tore off a sheet from the memo pad on Amid's desk, walked with it to the far wall and placed it against the wall at a point about level with his own eyes. By some means Hal could not see, he made it cling to the wall, then stood aside.

Meanwhile, Amid had been busy blindfolding Old Man with one of the napkins that had come with the food. When he was done, he stood back.

"All ready," he said to Old Man. "The target's up. Go ahead."

Old Man turned almost casually with the arrow already notched to the bow string. He gave the string the merest tweak, for the other wall was at most ten meters away. The arrow arced into the air and almost fell against the target, the pin in its end sticking in the very center of the paper, and plainly through it to the wood, for the arrow drooped, but did not fall to the floor.

"Now," said Old Man, "if you'll bring the arrow back to me and take down the paper."

Luke did both things, stopping halfway back to use one of his tools to straighten out the pin, which apparently had become bent. Once more Old Man fitted the arrow to his bow and sent it on its way. It stuck again, this time in the bare wall.

Luke walked over to retrieve it, reached for the shaft, then hesitated, staring at the place where it was stuck in the wall. He whistled.

"Just a few millimeters off from the first hole," he said.

He pulled the arrow loose and brought it back, as Amid took off the blindfold and Old Man laid down the still strung bow on Amid's desk.

"How could you do it?" Hal asked him.

"I listened to the rustle of the paper as it was carried across the room," said Old Man, "and aimed at where the noise stopped."

"But you hit the center of the paper!" Amid said.

Old Man smiled.

"There were only two sources of paper on your desk," he answered. "Notepaper, and the memo pad. They would rustle differently. Besides the memo sheets are glued together at the top. I heard Luke tear one loose: and when he pressed it against the wall to make it stick, the board made a small creak. I aimed at where that sound had been, with the memo sheet, and the wall, pictured in my mind."

"And then you did it again, with the paper gone," said Amid admiringly.

"Even more simply, I'm afraid," said Old Man. "The second time I simply used the bow exactly the way I'd done the first; and the arrow went to the same place."

He turned to Hal.

"These things are unimportant in themselves," he said. "I just wanted you to be sure I could be useful to you with the bow."

"You've made your point," said Hal. He turned to Amid. "Amid, we've got a record of all the scopes saw today, haven't we?"

"Why, yes," said Amid. "They're the usual sort of scope. They store images unless you set them not to; and we assumed you might want to check something or other."

"I do," said Hal. "Would you have someone check the records for everything seem in them today, to see if we've got any views of even parts of the interiors of the three structures Liu put up down there. Particularly, I'd like any views we might have of the building he's in, himself."

"I can do that right from here," said Amid.

He sat back down at his desk, punched a few keys, and looked expectantly at the screen of the scope on the desk that was now showing the brightly lit scene of the soldiers' camp below. The uniformed men around the table had dwindled to two and the bottle had disappeared. The extra men were spread around on the ground in sleeping sacks, unmoving.

"They were drinking when I last looked," said Hal.

"That under officer, whatever his name is—"

"The Urk," supplied Calas.

"Urk. Odd name," said Amid, "—looked out just before you came in here and they put the bottle away. He was in the center one of—what do you call those buildings?"

"Hutments is the military name," said Calas. "They're a kind of tent."

"—The middle one of those hutments," went on Amid. "The officer's in the one on the right of the screen as we look at it now. I caught a glimpse of what looked like a cooker and various kitchen furniture in that same one the Urk's in. Strange, but he and the officer are the only ones under shelter. Of course, at this time of year night showers are unlikely—"

"That's one of Liu's little military points," said Calas. "He never misses a chance to point up the fact that rank has its privileges. Making the ranks sleep on the open ground just drives home the difference between them and him and the Urk."

"A strange personality," said Amid.

"Not so strange, after all," said Old Man softly.

"Here we go!" interrupted Amid, as the scene on the screen changed to a still picture which showed Liu's hutment, with one of the two flaps that closed its front entrance folded back. A camp chair, an unfolded and set up desk and the corner of a cot could be seen, the cot already with bedding on it. "Seventeen more views, the screen says. Shall we look at all of them?"

"If you don't mind—" said Hal.

"Of course not . . ." Amid tapped his desk controls and they went, one by one, through the various views the scopes had been able to make of the inner area of Liu's hutment. It was furnished with what they had already seen, plus a sort of tall box that could be a filing cabinet or a food and liquor cabinet.

"All right," said Hal, when they had examined the last view. "Liu should be in that cot now and asleep. So should the Urk, in the center hutment. The two guards will probably be changed at intervals. Now—"

He turned his attention back to Amid.

"I'm going to go down there tonight," he said, "to try to get Cee and Artur back and leave those soldiers with the impression that they found nothing worthwhile. If I can manage the hypnosis properly, after disabling them with the darts, I'll hope to leave them believing neither Artur nor Cee had anything to tell them—that they both died under torture, and were buried up here—so that they'll go back thinking the whole thing was a wild goose chase. The question is going to be who I take with me."

"Me, for one," said Calas.

"Perhaps," said Hal. "We'll see. Now, Amid, who in the Guild knows the forest down there at night, and can move around in it in the dark, quietly?"

"Onete, of course," said Amid. "And there are four or five other foragers who like to do night foraging. There're some plants—some tubers particularly—that betray their presence at night more than in the day, by actions like opening blossoms or leaves, or—there's even a tuber that causes the ground above it to glow slightly, at night. But I'm wandering."

He pressed a key and leaned over a speaker grille in his desk.

"All those who're particularly adept at night foraging," he said into the grille, "come to my office right away, please."

"Good," said Hal. "How many of them, do you know, can use a bow and arrow effectively?"

Amid looked blank.

"I haven't the slightest idea." He appealed to Old Man. "Do you know?"

Old Man shook his head.

"Calas?"

"I haven't any idea," said Calas.

"By the way," Hal said to him, "you wanted to come. Can you move quietly through the jungle at night?"

"I've been out night foraging, too, if that's what you mean," said Calas. Then, on a more subdued note, he added, "I may not be the quietest, but I know enough to look where I'm putting my feet. No one down there'll hear me."

"And you can use a bow?"

"No!" said Calas explosively. "But we've got to have an

hour or two before we go down. I'll learn in that time."

He looked at Old Man.

"He can teach me."

Hal turned his gaze on the quiet, bearded face.

"What do you think?" he asked Old Man. "Could you teach him to use one to any good purpose, in just a few hours?"

"At short range, perhaps," said Old Man softly. "At any rate I could try. Perhaps you'll have to let me try teaching others along with Calas. Perhaps several people."

"I can use a bow," said Luke. "Shot one for years. Made my own first real bow when I was thirteen. I may not be as good as this magician, here"— he nodded at Old Man —"but I'm good by any ordinary standards. I'll say that and stand on it!"

"Then perhaps the two of you can do some teaching," said Hal. "When we finally go down, the six best shots will carry bows and darts. Old Man and I are two, that leaves four to be picked."

He turned to Amid.

"You might put out a call for anyone in the Guild who does know how to use one, night forager or not. And Tannaheh, while we're waiting, you might start showing me how the darts work and telling me about them."

"Of course!" said Tannaheh, on an explosive outrush of breath that betrayed his chafing at the delay in getting to discussion of this particular subject.

He led Hal to the box and reached down among the dried grass he had used as packing. What he came up with looked like an old-fashioned hypodermic of the kind used back before the human race had first settled the Younger Worlds, three hundred years before. There was a round, tubelike cylinder with a collar at one end that was threaded on the inside. At the other end was a slim needle of a rod, perhaps twelve millimeters in length, ending in a point that was so sharp Hal could not see it, except as a twinkle in the overhead light from the ceiling of the office. All of it was made of the same milky-appearing material as the arrow shaft.

"You're lucky I have a library," said Tannaheh, holding up the dart. "You're from Earth, Friend, as I understand it; and there they've still got zoos and refuges with wild animals in them. Consequently, they've got wild animals that need to be tranquilized so they can care for them when they're sick, or whatever. But Kultis hasn't any large fauna, native or introduced. The largest wild variform creatures we've brought in as frozen embryos from Earth have been some rabbits, and big birds, like hawks and vultures. The result was we haven't had any need for tranquilizer darts, or means to propel them into the animal. I had to go back into medical history, to the time of Earth's first ventures into space, to find the information I needed."

Hal nodded. Tannaheh gave every evidence of wanting to deliver a lecture, but it was too early to put the brakes on him, yet. He let the Guild pharmacist go on.

"I managed to dig up illustrations and information on what they were using then, and build on that; making do with substitutes, where necessary—which was in almost every phase of making the dart."

He reached into the box and came up with a machine copy of what was obviously a page from some old book. It showed a drawing of something very much like the dart he had in his other hand.

"You see," he said, "I've recreated an artifact from the past. But I had to use my imagination to duplicate almost everything about it. To begin with, our ancestors used metal projectiles. The body of the dart and even the needle itself was metal. We have some metal, but no way to machine it into this sort of shape."

"I understand," said Hal. "But clearly you found an answer to that."

"Quite right. I didn't have metal I could work with; but I did have glass that was as strong as metal and as flexible as I wanted to make it, something our ancestors of that time didn't have; and I could work with it more easily than they could work with their earlier version of glass. So this dart you see is made entirely of glass."

"Well done," said Hal.

"I'm glad you think so," Tannaheh went on. "But actually the problem of what to make the dart out of was small compared to finding the drugs needed to produce the effect you told me you wanted. Now, when the dart hits . . ."

He laid the drawing back in the box, fumbled around among the packing and came up with a small square of wood about three times as thick as his hand.

"The needle is pushed back into the body of the dart, this cylinder here"— he pushed on the dart and the needle shortened to perhaps four millimeters —"as you see injecting the drug. I'll be giving you a chart showing what parts of the body you should try to shoot the needle into for best results. Then, once the drug has been injected, the cylinder falls off, again as you see—"

· He let go of the body of the dart and it fell to the floor, leaving the needle still sticking in the wood with only a length of what looked like string trailing from it.

"The needle," he went on, "is coated with a sterilizing agent, which means you can pull it out without worrying about having started an infection. Not only that, but it's thin enough and sharp enough so that the person hit by the dart isn't going to feel much; and the only evidence that'll be left is going to be a small red mark on the skin surface. No blood, probably. Afterwards, the site of the needle entry is going to itch, rather than hurt, once the tranquilizing agent wears off; and this, together with the red dot, will make it seem like the person was bitten by some insect. No one should suspect."

"Good," said Hal. "Old Man, you and Luke had better try out the arrows with the weight of the dart on their ends. I assume," he turned to Tannaheh, "you've got some practice darts there without the drug in them; which can be used without our worrying about blunting the needles on something we're going to have to use later?"

"Of course," said Tannaheh. "I'll give them to you in just a second. But first let me tell you how I came up with substitutes for the drugs used in the old Earth darts."

"Go ahead," said Hal patiently. The hours of night were short, but he could give this man, who had after all done something absolutely necessary for them, the courtesy of listening to him for a little while longer.

"The original darts described in my books," said Tanna-heh, "used several drugs which weren't difficult to obtain back on Earth, even in those days, but impossible for me to get here. There were several mixtures. One of the very good ones was ketamine hydrochloride combined with xylazine hydrochloride and atropine. The atropine was there essentially to keep the subjects under, but breathing, after they'd been knocked down by the other two—which were very quick acting."

He paused, obviously waiting.

"I can see where you'd have a problem," Hal said.

"A large problem," said Tannaheh. "I had native sub-stances that could duplicate the knock-down effects of the two hydrochlorides, but they wouldn't mix with the closest native equivalent to atropine derived from one of our night-blooming plants. Mixed, they started interacting chemically, immediately."

He paused again.

"So what did you do?" Hal asked.

"Obviously the only solution was to have you inject the atropinelike drug after the earlier ones were already in the blood streams of your targets!" said Tannaheh.

"And so you made two kinds of darts?"

"That was the first thing I thought of," Tannaheh said. "Then I had a better idea."

He picked up the shaft which had fallen from the end of the dart head driven into the piece of wood.

"You'll notice," he said, passing the detached shaft back to Hal, "how the shaft is marked with a circle some twelve millimeters back from the end where the needle comes out? Break that end off."

Hal broke it off. It came free very easily, revealing another, somewhat shorter, needle projecting from what was now the new, effective end of the shaft.

"You see?" said Tannaheh. "You can shoot it from the bow again, or use it by hand to inject the atropinelike drug directly. Be careful of giving anyone a double dose, though. It's in very dilute form, here, but still dangerous. In its natural state, as part of the sap of the plant you get it from, it's a very effective poison."

"You've made whatever we can do down there possible," said Hal. "I think you know how grateful everyone is to you—"

"Nothing!" said Tannaheh. He waved his hand lightly. "I'd like to tell you, though, what you've actually got by way of chemicals there in these darts—"

"Is this something we need to know to use them?" interrupted Hal.

"Well, no. But—"

"Then, if you don't mind, you can tell us all about it later," said Hal. "We've only got so many hours of darkness to work in and a lot to do. I'm sure you understand."

"I—well, of course," said Tannaheh.

"Believe me," Hal said to him, more softly, "later, when there's time, we'll want to know. But right now there's a lot to be done."

"Of course. Of course," said Tannaheh, taking a step back from the desk with its open box of darts. "Forgive me."

"There's nothing to forgive." Hal turned to the rest of the room.

While they had been speaking, the door had been opening to let people in; and now there was a small crowd of them in Amid's office. They had lined up against the front wall of the office on either side of the door.

"Now," said Hal, "which of you are night foragers who can move quietly down there among the vegetation and rocks? Put your hands up so I can identify you."

Eight men and women to the right of the door as Hal faced it responded.

"And who's the best?"

"Onete," said several voices at once, with several more

following—all, in fact, but Onete herself, who had been one of those standing there and holding up her arm.

"Good," said Hal. "Which of you can use a bow and arrow?"

There was some hesitation. Those who had their hands up lowered them and looked at each other. Finally, two of them raised their hands hesitantly again.

Hal smiled at them, to relax them.

"I take it," he said, "this means you two can shoot an arrow from a bow, but you haven't much faith in yourselves as far as being able to hit the mark?"

The two arms went down and the heads above them nodded.

"Old Man," said Hal, turning to him, "and you, Luke, do you suppose you could take these two and any other two who want to volunteer—"

"Me," said Calas, quickly and stubbornly.

"All right," said Hal, "and one other volunteer, then. Take them to some inside space where there's light to see a target at about six to ten meters, and see if you can teach them something about hitting what they aim at."

"The corridors in the dormitories'd give us the distance," said Luke to Old Man.

Old Man nodded.

"And there are ways of hitting the point desired, that call for belief in self more than practice," he said. Both men began to move toward the door.

"Just a minute," said Hal. "In addition to the six who feel most sure about their ability to move in the dark quietly, we're going to need about six more who'll be needed to help carry. For the benefit of those of you who've just come in, what we're going to do is go down to that camp where Artur and Cee are, try to put the soldiers out of action, and bring Cee and her uncle back up here to the ledge. We'll need a stretcher for Artur, and that stretcher will need at least four people to carry it at any given time."

He paused to let that sink in.

"Bringing him up the steep slope is going to be the real problem. He'll have to be roped to the stretcher, so he doesn't slide off, and his bearers are going to have to be changed frequently. For those of you who've never done this—and I think that's most, if not all, of you—I can tell you that carrying even an ordinary-sized man on a stretcher up a steep slope is a very rough task, indeed. So we'll need at least three teams, so that the stretcher bearers can change off frequently. That's where you other eight come in. You can wait for the rest of us back out of earshot of the camp and help carry once we reach you with Artur and Cee."

"Will the girl come?" asked one of the men to the left of the door.

"I think she'll come if you bring Artur," said Old Man. "You should be careful how you handle him, though. If he cries out for any reason, she may assume you're just more people like the soldiers, as far as your reason for carrying him off goes."

"By the way," put in Tannaheh, "I've made up a medical kit with pain-killers and other first aid supplies for us on Artur, as soon as you reach him."

"Good," said Hal, "and thank you. I should have thought to ask you for that myself."

He turned to look at Onete.

"I think you better take care of the first aid," he said to Onete. "You may be the one person who can do things to Artur without Cee thinking we're simply harming him more."

"I can try," said Onete. "She just might trust me."

"Old Man's right, too, I think," said Hal, "in saying she'll follow if we take Artur—even all the way up here, where she's never come before. She won't trust him out of her sight in anyone else's hands."

He turned back to the people who had just come into the office.

"We've got until midnight to get ready," he said. "If for any reason some of you don't want to go, speak up now.

The rest of us'll start getting ready to go down. I want to move into that camp there as soon as both moons are down; and be back behind the boulder on our way up to the ledge before it starts to get light."

No one moved or spoke up.

"Good," said Hal. "Then, you four bow-people go with Old Man and Luke. Onete, you and the other night foragers gather around me, here. I'll explain how your part of it'll work."

CHAPTER 28 ■

Making the nighttime descent of the mountain from the ledge to the boulder beneath which they would exit had been almost like descending in daytime, from Hal's point of view. He had spent most of his life as Hal with Earth's single moon. Here, however, both of Kultis's moons could be in the sky at once—as they were at the moment—and both near the full. The combination of the two made not only for adequate light, but a near elimination of shadows.

The indescribable spicy odor of the alien semi-tropical forest had risen to meet them as they descended, and the clean mountain breezes were left behind, above them. At the boulder barring the entrance to the up trail, they had left the backup team of eight men and women, seven of whom stayed behind the boulder, which had been rolled back in place, and AnnaMist—the eighth—followed them through, but only as far as the other side of the boulder. It was to be her job to keep watch and, if necessary, pass the alarm back to those on the other side not to open up, if she got warning of anything gone wrong with the expedition.

Down in the forest, the moonlight was dimmer but still good, by the standards of Hal's Earth-accustomed eyes. However, the small and bright moons were fast-moving, and the smaller soon set. So the light dimmed, as they made their way toward Liu's camp. Eventually, it shut off completely, leaving them with only the starlight to help them see where to put their feet.

There had been some stumbles, and some who held to the person in front of them to make sure of the way. But Hal had sent Onete and the experienced night foragers ahead to lead. With these up front they made steady progress, until the line halted—so suddenly that Hal almost ran into the last member of the foragers, just before him.

A whisper came back down the line, passed from person to person for him, and he made his way to the head of the line. There he identified Onete by her general outline and body odor as he had become acquainted with the body odors of most of the Guild members in the last few months.

"We've found some new-dug soil that looks like two graves," she said in a whisper so low that no one else could hear it. "You don't suppose . . ."

"No," he whispered back. "It'd make no sense for Liu to get up a couple of hours before dawn to kill the two of them and bury them without the answers he was after—even if he'd had time to do all that since we left the ledge. Wasn't someone carrying one of the scopes? Let's take a look at the camp."

"The light from the screen . . ." began Onete doubtfully.

"How close to the camp are we?"

"A hundred and fifty meters. But you warned us against any light or sound once we left the boulder—"

"I think with a hundred and fifty meters of forest in between we can risk it, in this instance," said Hal. "Can you get it for me? The rest of you make a wall with your bodies between us and the camp."

There were a few minutes delay and then the closed scope was placed in his hands. He opened it and touched the controls. A tiny view of the camp they were headed for appeared in the center of the screen. The figures on it were almost too small to be recognizable, but one was clearly still Cee, seated on the ground, and one was clearly Arthur, still wrapped with rope and unmoving.

Hal turned the scope off, closed it and handed it back.

"Someone take this," he said. It was removed from his grasp. To Onete he added, "It'll be messy, since we've only got our hands to dig with, but we're going to have to see what's buried here, if anything is. Use the scope light, if you need to. That camp's got two men on watch, but they're only watching as far as the nearest darkness; and with those bright lights it must be like looking into an endless cave all around them."

Onete stopped him as he bent down to start digging, himself.

"Not you," she said, "you may need clean hands later on for some reason. Also, most of us know how to use the plants we pass to find materials to clean ourselves up with."

It was a realistic argument. Even his effectiveness in shooting the bow he carried might be hampered by badly grimed fingers.

"All right," he said and stood aside. He watched as shadowy figures labored in the soft earth of both dug-over areas. After some minutes, Onete's outline detached itself from the working group and came back to him.

"We've found a body," she said. "We're just finding out if the other grave holds a body too."

There was a subdued murmur from the working party, a few more motions, and then work ceased.

"I'll come take a look," said Hal. "Have you got that scope handy?"

"I'll get it." Onete moved away from him. He went to the group, which made way for him, and bent over the two half-excavated openings in the reworked earth. A hand pushed the scope into his grasp. He opened it, turned it on to show a minimum-sized picture, and directed the reflected light of the screen down into the opened holes.

A boot toe, the upper part of a body and the head of a soldier had been roughly cleaned of covering soil in one of them, the upper body and head of a second in the hole alongside.

The white, pale light of the scope, washing over the half-exposed bodies and their still dirt-streaked faces—eyes closed but featured staring up at the star-filled sky—was unpleasant enough so that a murmur arose from the group around the two graves.

"Quiet!" snapped Onete, with a tone of command Hal had not expected from her.

"But look at their faces—" said one protesting voice.

Hall reached down and brushed a little more of the loose dirt off the face and throat of the nearest body.

"They were strangled to death," he said. His fingers moved down to clear a little more dirt from the throat of the body before him; then pressed lightly on where the man's Adam's apple had been. The dead flesh yielded before the pressure like a loose sack of small fragments and there was the faint crackling of trapped air forced into the surrounding tissues. "His larynx's been crushed."

There was silence from around those around him.

"Does anyone here know," he asked, "was Arthur acquainted with any of the martial arts? I'm talking about those for bare-handed fighting."

The silence continued another moment.

"No," said Onete, "I don't believe he was."

"No blow from the edge of a hand did that," said Old Man's voice behind Hal. "It could have been done by a kick, a very skillful kick; but it's unlikely. The blow of a fist, perhaps though even Arthur would have to be lucky as well as powerful to strike that spot with enough force."

Hal squatted back on his heels, staring down at the nearest body.

"There's no good reason they'd kill two of their own

that way," he said, half to himself. He raised his voice
slightly. "We'll need to cover them up again so the graves
look undisturbed."

He got to his feet and watched as the shadowy figures
around him became busy, pushing the loose dirt back into
its original place. When it was done, they started out once
more through the forest with its root-cluttered rock-strewn
ground all but invisible under their feet.

It was not long; though before those in the lead halted,
and the line of people bumped each into the person ahead
of him or her, and stopped. Onete came back to Hal.

"This is about a hundred meters from the soldiers'
camp," she said.

"Thank you," he answered. "All right, here's the place
where we'll leave all of you except the six of us who are
bow-and-dart people and the other six night foragers.
Onete picked out as being able to move most quietly. I
want one forager attached to each of us who've got bows,
to get us to the edge of the illuminated area of the camp as
quietly as possible. According to Missy and Hadnah's
count, there's sixteen of the soldiers, counting Liu and the
Urk. Calas, I'm sorry you've got to be one of those to stay
behind, but you can't shoot and you can't move as well as
the people we're taking."

"It's all right," said Calas, his voice low and hoarse from
the black wall of bodies that now stood clumped around
him. "More than anything I want to see Cee and Artur free.
Just one thing—if we hear noises from the camp that sound
like they've woken up and may be taking you, can the rest
of us rush the camp, and try to help?"

Hal hesitated.

"You'd be smarter, all of you, to head back for the boulder and the ledge," he said.

"If they get their hands on six of you, anyway, they're
going to be able to make at least one show them the way up
to the ledge," said Calas.

"Yes," said Hal. "All right, if you're sure they're all
awake and trying to take us prisoner or whatever, come

along. You can rush the camp. But you'll probably just be giving them that many more prisoners, or dead bodies."

"That's all I want to hear," said Calas.

The small forward group moved off. They were close enough to see some glimmers of light through the trees ahead when Onete stopped them for the second time.

"About another twenty-five meters," she told Hal, "and you'll be just outside the clearing. They were foolish to put their lights up high that way. It means that direct illumination stops, for all practical purposes, at the edge of the area cleared. Reflection off ground and tree trunks will throw light farther back, but the eyes of those on guard aren't likely to pick up what it illuminates. Their sight is going ti be adjusted to the brightness of the area under the camp lights. It's so stupid to do things that way! Maybe there's a trap to it, somewhere?"

"I doubt it," said Hal. "I don't think they're really expecting us, or anything on the order of a try to rescue the prisoners. Those two men awake there, from what Calas tells me about the officers, are probably just part of Liu's spit-and-polish attitude. The rule book says post guards in situations like this, so he posts guards."

"Do you want to bow-people spread around the camp now?" Onete asked. "I can have the foragers position them."

"Not spread around," said Hal. "Old Man stays with me and I'd like you yourself to take the two of us down close to the hutments. Luke and the three other bow-people, take them over to where the soldiers are sleeping on the ground. Old Man and I will take out the two men on watch duty; and—Luke?"

"Right here," said Luke's voice from the darkness.

"The minute," Hal said, "you and the other bow-armed people see the two on guard drop, start shooting into the soldiers in the sleeping sacks. Old Man and I will be going after Liu and the Urk. Meanwhile, Onete, I want you to do what I asked you to do up on the ledge. Use that knife you're carrying to cut loose Cee and Artur. Then whistle in the other foragers with the stretcher to put Artur on it and start carrying him out of here."

He paused and looked around at them, so that his voice would carry to each.

"Remember," he said, "what I told you when I briefed you before we left the ledge. Once things start happening, each of you ignore everything going on around you and just do what you came here to do. This is to free Cee and Artur, get Artur on the stretcher and carried out. Onete, it'll be up to you to try to get Cee to understand we're not going to hurt him the way the soldiers did. She probably won't trust us at first sight, any more than she trusted them."

Onete nodded.

"I'll do exactly that," she said. "Don't worry about my part of it, just concentrate on your own."

Hal smiled at her, though he knew the smile would be hidden in the darkness; but perhaps it would color the tone of his voice enough for her to pick it up.

"I know you will. And we will." he said. "Let's go now. Onete, go around to everyone, pass the word to anyone who didn't hear or understand me completely, just now. Then come back and guide Old Man and me to our proper positions."

She did, and a few moments later saw the three of them ghosting like morning fog around the outskirts of the camp to the far end where the hutments stood and the table at which all the enlisted men had eaten. It was now occupied only by the two on duty. These two, deprived of their bottle, were seated at one end of the table and had found themselves entertainment in the form of some kind of gambling that involved dice. All their attention was on the movement of the small, dotted cubes.

Beyond them and close by. Artur lay silent and motionless under the blanket they had thrown over him. Farther off, Cee still sat cross-legged at the foot of her tree. She was wide awake, but her gaze was finally off the hutment that held Liu. Instead it was focused as plainly on Onete,

Hal and Old Man, as if it was broad daylight and she could see them clearly, in their movement around the camp.

"Can she see us, do you think?" Hal whispered as softly as he could and still be heard by Onete.

"Hears us, more likely," whispered Onete in answer.

"It's all right as long as one of those two soldiers doesn't take a look at her and get interested in what there could be out in the dark here to make her watch it," said Hal.

They stopped. Onete faced Cee squarely and shook her head deliberately, waving one hand past her face and deliberately turning her own gaze away from the little girl.

Whether Cee could not actually see them, or chose to ignore Onete's signal to stop watching them, was impossible to tell; but in any case, her gaze remained brightly following the three of them. Hal shrugged. They moved on.

"This will do," he whispered, finally, when they reached a point which put them at about the same distance from hutments and the two soldiers on watch. "Old Man?"

Hal had already taken his bow from his back and was stringing it. Out of the corner of his eye he saw Old Man doing the same. They each took a shaft from the quivers at their belts and a dart from a loop of one of the bandoleer-belts that Luke and his helpers had made for them.

In silence, together, they screwed the darts on to the ends of the arrow shafts. Old Man smiled, and—holding bow and arrow with one hand—held up the fingers of his other with the thumb and middle finger only a couple of inches apart to indicate the very short distance they had to shoot.

Hal smiled back and nodded. It was true. They were less than six meters from the soldiers. Even Calas, probably, could not have missed, at this close distance. Hal pointed at the farther soldier, the one across the table from them and whose face was toward them.

Old Man smiled and nodded, aiming at the other man.

They shot almost together. The soft twang of the bow-strings was loud enough to be heard by the two targets. Both men looked up from their gambling, startled, as the dart points went home, Hal's in the shoulder muscle of the man he had aimed at, Old Man's in the back of the neck of the soldier on his side.

Both the uniformed men reached with puzzled looks toward the points of irritation where the dart needles had entered, but the shafts had already dropped off the darts, clattering down and through the slats that made up the seats of the benches with which the tables were equipped. Old Man's target actually managed to close a couple of fingers weakly on the end of the dart which protruded from his neck; but Hal's never managed to touch his, before both men were falling backwards off the bench on to the ground.

Both Hal and Old Man broke off the ends of two more arrow shafts and shot another dart into each slumped body, a dart that would inject the atropinelike substance Tannaheh had equipped them with.

Now, for the first time, Hal took a second to look around the clearing. The soldiers in the sleeping sacks were still receiving dart-loaded arrows fired from the darkness beyond them. In the dazzling light from the overhead illumination, he saw Onete, knife in hand on her way to cut Cee loose from the tree to which she had been tied.

The twang of a bowstring close to his right ear brought his attention abruptly back to the Old Man. He was in time to see a dart-laden arrow penetrate the wall of the hutment in which the sleeping Liu was housed.

"I believe that lodged in a safe body area," Old Man said, lowering the bow and looking mildly at Hal.

"I thought you were going to wait until I could go and open one of the door flaps, so you could see what you were shooting at," said Hal.

"I know you made that offer, back up on the ledge," said Old Man, still softly, "but as it turned out it wasn't necessary. The still pictures on the scope were good enough to show us where his cot stood and how he lay on it—you remember there was one that showed him taking a nap with one of the flaps open, so that we could see him there in the shadow on the cot?"

"You're right," said Hal. He looked at the middle hut-ment. "We saw the inside of the Urk's hutment too, but without him on the cot. That's why you didn't put a dart through the wall of it into him?"

"According to my memory, his cot was almost com-pletely surrounded by equipment of one kind or another."

"I'll take care of it, then." Hal kicked off his boots. "I'll open a flap to let you see what you're shooting at; and if there's still no way you can get a clean shot at him, wave me on. I'll go in and place a dart in him by hand."

He glanced about, saw Onete busy now with the medical kit and Artur, stepped to the door of the middle hutment and pulled back the right-hand one of the two flaps that closed its entrance. Within, by the outside light of the clearing that was reflected inside through the open flap, it was possible to see a body in a sleeping sack on a cot between what looked like a temperature-controlled food storage box and a cooker. Hal was turning to check with Old Man when the soft twang of a bowstring was accom-panied almost simultaneously by the passage of an arrow by him. It lodged its needle in what looked like the upper body of the form in the sack.

The body lifted its head and shoulders as if to begin to get up; then fell back and was still.

"Here," said Old Man.

Hal turned to see the other beside him, the bow in one hand and the other holding Hal's boots, the top rims clutched together. Hal took the boots and put them on, as Old Man went forward, picked up the fallen shaft of the arrow, broke off its end and made the second injection into the drugged sleeper on the cot.

"Indeed, it's the one Calas called the Urk," he said. The hand that was not carrying his bow now held the power pistol the Urk had worn earlier. "This was in its holster, on a belt with the rest of his clothes, on a chair beside the cot."

"Thanks," said Hal, "you don't want to keep it yourself?"

"It's a machine for killing—nothing more," said Old

Man. "I've never killed, human or animal, and never will. These drugged darts are permissible."

Hal nodded and tucked the pistol into the waistband of his trousers.

He led the way back outside to the clearing. There the other bow-people were injecting the follow-up, atropine-like drug, mostly by hand, as they bent over the still forms in the sleeping sacks. Hal shook his head and smiled a little. For once, to confound practice as opposed to theory, a tactical plan had worked out as it had been planned.

Hal turned to the darkness of the forest and whistled. The sound went out into obscurity, and another whistle distantly responded.

A few moments later, Calas and the other Guild members they had left a hundred meters back ran into the clearing, carrying the various parts of the stretcher that had been part of their responsibility. As Hal watched they began to fit it together and prepare Artur, now unconscious from a drug in the medical kit but otherwise still alive, to be lifted on to it and secured there for carrying.

The sight reminded Hal of Cee. He looked back toward the tree to which she had been tied and did not see her, only Onete, hastening toward him. He went to meet her.

"Where's Cee?" he asked.

"I don't know. I don't have any idea," answered Onete. She sounded distressed. "She can move so fast . . . I cut her loose and had her with me, coming to join all the rest of us, here and something must have made me look away for a moment, because all at once she was gone. Maybe she ran off into the forest."

"Is that likely?" Hal said. "With Artur still with us?"

"But I don't know where else she would go—"

Hal did not hear the rest of what Onete said, because his ear was suddenly caught by a faint, but undeniable noise, a *wheep! wheep!* sound. He started at a dead run in the direction from which the sound had come, which was either right beside or in Liu's hutment. The image of the two dead soldiers they had unearthed was starkly in his mind, suddenly connecting itself with a memory of the two he had seen fall on the screen as the soldiers rushed Cee to capture her. He reached the hut and burst through the flaps; but he was too late.

Cee, holding one of Liu's socks in either hand, each sock with a heavy-looking lump in its toe, ducked under his arm and was out the flaps before he could turn around.

He did not wait to examine what he knew would be the corpse of Liu Hu Shen, but ran after Cee, almost catching her as she went in between the open flaps of the Urk's tent and actually catching her, a moment later, as she stood just inside the entrance swinging in her right hand a weighted sock that gave forth the same sort of noise that had attracted his attention a moment before.

He grabbed her from behind, wrapping his arms around both of her arms, pinning them to her body and lifting her clear of the ground.

She fought back fiercely, in utter silence and with incredible strength for one so young. She kicked back and up with her heels; but he had anticipated this, spreading his legs and holding her closely against him, so that those same heels, rock-hard after years of running unshod on all kinds of surfaces, could not reach his groin.

She tried to swing the weighted end of the sock up to smash his face or hit his head; but his grip was around her elbows and she did not have the freedom of movement and strength to rotate the heavy end through the air and upward to its point of aim. Meanwhile, continuously, she struggled to twist and turn in his arms, to win enough freedom from his grasp so that she could twist loose and escape.

But, fighting as best she could, she was a youngster pitting the strength of her small body against the large and powerful adult one. Hal held her fast and backed with her out of the hutment.

"Onete! Old Man!" he shouted.

He heard the sound of two pairs of running feet, but it was Old Man who first stepped around from behind him to face them. He twitched the weighted sock so suddenly from Cee's grasp that her fingers failed to hold their grip on it, and tossed it aside. Her gaze noted where it fell and returned instantly to glare at him.

"Child, child," he said sorrowfully to her. "don't you know that nothing is ever settled, nothing is ever gained, by killing?"

She stared back at him with savage, unrepentant eyes.

"Take her," Hal told him. "Hold her."

Onete had now joined them and was talking rapidly and soothingly to Cee, who ignored the woman completely.

"Old Man can hold her," Hal said to Onete. "You try and make her understand that we're here to rescue her uncle and take him to someplace where he'll be safe; but her killing Liu just now—"

"She killed the officer!" Onete said.

"I'm afraid so. I should have realized she might."

Onete stooped and picked up the officer's sock Cee had dropped, held it upside down and shook it. A short, heavy energy pack for a power pistol dropped out of the end of it.

"She must have got them from Liu's uniform belt," Hal said, "and thrown sock and pack together, the way she'd send a rock from her sling. Those two dead in the forest will have been her doing. The two he saw on the screen, who fell when they rushed in to catch her. But never mind that now."

"What are we to do with her?" Onete said, distressed.

"As I say, Old Man can hold her. It'll be up to you to make her understand that we're here to rescue her uncle; but she's already made a problem for us by killing Liu. If she kills anyone else, we may not be able to cover it up and send the soldiers away believing things that'll keep them from coming back. If they don't believe and do come back, they'll find and kill us all, including her uncle, after all."

Onete nodded.

"I'll try," she said.

"Don't just try. She's got to understand and go along with us. You've got to get through to her, somehow. She's got to understand that we have to take Arthur back up to the Chantry Guild to fix what the soldiers did to him; and she's got to help us do that, not hinder!"

"All right," said Onete.

"Take her, Old Man," said Hal, "but be careful. Loosen up for a second and she'll get away; and we'll never catch her."

With her weapon taken from her, Cee had stopped struggling in Hal's arms; but he was very sure she would explode into action the moment she felt any loosening of the grip upon her. He waited for Old Man to take the child into his own arms; but instead the other merely reached up and began to stroke the back of Cee's neck, meanwhile crooning to her, a wordless melody that consisted of the same series of musical phrases repeated over and over again.

"Artur told me about that," Onete murmured to Hal. "It was one of the things Cee's mother used to him when Cee was a baby and even after, to put her to sleep. Artur thought he could use it to make Cee trust him; but maybe he just didn't hum it right. Old Man must have learned it from him."

Hal nodded. The neck-stroking, he knew, was one of the physical aids to hypnosis.

In any case, he felt the tension gradually going from the small, tight body he held, growing less and less until eventually Cee hung almost limply in his arms.

Old Man stopped his crooning.

"I think you can let her go now," he said to Hal. He took one of Cee's small, hard and dirty hands in his own.

"Come with me," he said to the girl.

He led her off. Onete followed.

Hal turned back with a feeling of relief, mixed with urgency, to the matter of taking care of the soldiers, on whom the drug would act for only a limited amount of time.

The first thing to be done was to get the Urk up, and bring him out under hypnosis to ostensibly explain things to equally drugged and to-be-hypnotized soldiers. Hal's original story that he had planned they would carry back to their headquarters was to have been given them by Liu; and would have simply told them that both Artur and Cee had died under torture—the last stage of which would have been supposed to have taken place privately at the hands of Liu himself in one of the hutments; that the two had there-after been buried and, since Liu had learned enough from them before they died to be certain there were no other people around in this area of the forest, they would all be returning to headquarters.

Now, his story must not only be given by the Urk, which weakened it, the Urk being no more than a noncommis-sioned officer; also it must explain Liu's death, which would raise a great many more questions than if Liu, him-self, had returned with only two soldiers lost. Particularly when the loss could be blamed on the great strength of the adult they had captured. And it would be Liu's word that there was nothing more to be found up here.

In time, of course, that hypnotic memory would wear thin: and some memory of what had actually happened to each of them here tonight would have surfaced in the minds of all of them, officers and men. But by that time, the subject would have been closed and filed away some time since, and none of them, even Liu, would have any good reason to make extra work and trouble for himself by digging back into the records and looking for the truth of what had actually happened.

Hal stepped into the Urk's hut, still wrapped in thought. It was not until he actually opened the top flap of the Urk's sleeping sack and put his hand on the man's throat to both rouse him and begin the process of hypnosis, that the cool-ness of the flesh he was touching brought his attention back to what was before him.

The coolness was very slight, because of the shortness of time that had passed since they had reached the camp. But it was noticeable enough now to alert Hal; and now that he looked closely at the man under his hand, he saw that the Urk was also dead. Almost as immediately as he registered the fact of death and his eyes found what had killed the man, his memory clicked back with something he should have remembered but had not until this moment.

When Cee had dodged under his arm and out of Liu's hutment before he could catch her, she had been swinging *two* of the officer's weighted socks. There had been one in each hand. This, in spite of the fact that Liu had died of a crushed throat like the two dead soldiers they had disinterred on the way here. Since Liu presumably had been wearing only one sock on each foot, and had taken those off for the night, she had been able to turn them into weapons after she had stolen silently into his hutment. She would have loaded them with energy packs from the carrying loops in the man's belt. Then she must have thrown, and picked up again, the one she had used to kill the force-leader.

But when Hal had burst into the Urk's hut and wrapped his arms around her as she was just about to throw, she had been carrying only one of the socks with which she had left Liu's sleeping place. Somehow she must have gotten off one throw before Hal had caught her; and since it had been a hurried shot at the target, she must have been about to follow it up with a second cast when Hal had seized her.

There was an ordinary battlelamp on the chair holding the Urk's clothes. Hal turned it up and in the wash of reddish light that spread over the form on the cot the face stood out clearly. The right temple was plainly indented. The Urk must have died instantly from the first energy-pack loaded sock; but Cee, who had most probably been aiming at his throat as she had in all the previous cases, must in the dimness of light reflected from the outside of the hutment, have realized only that she had missed her target. So she had tried, but failed to get her second weighted sock thrown before Hal had stopped her.

He stood, head slightly bent under the low roof of the hutment, which had been tall enough for people like the Urk and Liu, but was not for him. Now, the situation was even more complicated.

Briefly, what he would now need to hypnotize the soldiers into believing, must be an ever greater distortion of what had actually taken place here in the forest.

He turned, went out of the hutment, and across to the group that was now strapping Artur securely onto his stretcher. A little off to one side, the drugged soldiers sat or lay still, watched by the other four bowmen; and a little beyond these were Cee, Onete and Old Man. Old Man's hand still rested on the back of Cee's neck. But it lay there with an appearance more like that of a comforting gesture, than a calming one. Onete's lips were moving steadily as she spoke to Cee; who in her turn was utterly unmoving and unanswering, but listened to the grown woman as if fascinated.

Hal reached the group by the stretcher.

"I'm sorry," he said, "but I'm going to have to make use of Artur before you carry him away. If he's ready to be moved, follow me. I want to bring him into the hutment on the far right where the officer in command was sleeping. Calas?"

"Right here," answered Calas, emerging from the crowd.

"Come along," said Hal. "I want to talk to you as we go. After Liu and the Urk, who'd be in charge of these soldiers?"

"Who? Probably him," said Calas as they walked toward the hutment. He pointed to a square-bodied, middle-aged man with thin, tousled hair on a round head, sitting beside his sleeping sack and staring at nothing. "He's a supply corporal; and theoretically he wouldn't command force-soldiery. But he's the senior in rank; and besides, he's one of the headquarters clique, one of the bunch that runs things and you keep in good with, if you know what's good for you. His name's Harvey. He'd take command here if Liu or the Urk couldn't. He'd like doing that—but it's not likely—"

He stared at Hal abruptly.

"Or is it?"

"Yes," said Hal bluntly. "They're both dead."

"Dead?"

Calas stopped in his tracks, then had to run to catch up with Hal, who had not paused.

"Cee got to them," Hal said.

"She did?" Calas broke into a smile. "How?"

The stretcher bearers, also close enough to hear this, turned their heads at Hal's blunt statement. But he did not answer. They continued to stare, to the point where they almost missed the entrance to the hutment at which they were aiming, before finally carrying the stretcher through it.

"So, as a result, we've got a problem on our hands," Hal went on. They were now inside the hutment that had been Liu's. Hal stood aside to let the bearers set down on the floor the still unconscious Artur.

"Take him off the stretcher," Hal directed them. "I want him laid, face down, sprawled out on the floor as if he'd fallen trying to reach Liu on his cot. When you're done with that, go to the hutment next door, dress the body of the Urk in his uniform, sidearm and all—find the power pistol—and carry him in here on the stretcher."

"Calas," said Hal, as soon as they had gone out, "how well could you imitate Liu's voice? I don't mean you'd have to be good enough to fool anyone under ordinary conditions, close up, but I need a shout or two, supposedly from him, to back up what I'm going to hypnotize the rest of the soldiers into believing. Did Liu have some particular way of speaking that was his alone? Everyone does; and most soldiers can imitate their officers' mannerisms."

"He had a high voice and a snappy, snotty way of talking," said Calas. "I think I could come up with something like it, if I'm to be yelling from inside the hutment here, where they can't see me and the hutment'll probably mess up the way his voice'd sound, some."

"Good," said Hal, "what I want you to yell is an order from Liu to the Urk to shoot. The idea will be that Artur's somehow gotten loose in here."

"Good," said Calas. "I can do that standing on my head. Anyway, I like the idea of Artur getting loose in here with the two of them. Or, I would if Artur would have actually done anything to them, even if he did get free."

CHAPTER 29

"Good," said Hal, in his turn.

He moved to the cot and began propping Liu's head up on the pillow beneath it, so that his throat was visible. The body was beginning to cool further, but still had not stiffened. He took the officer's pistol belt from its perch over the back of the bedside chair that held the rest of the man's clothes, and laid it on the seat on the chair, so that the power pistol in its holster was lying flat, with the pistol butt next to the bed. He stretched out the man's arm and curled the dead fingers around the butt of the weapon, half drawing it from its holster. He chuckled, with a rueful edge to the chuckle.

"What's the joke, Friend?" Calas's voice asked behind him.

"Only," said Hal—turning to face the former soldier— "the fact I'd just been thinking earlier that our plans for all this had gone off perfectly this time, exactly as we made them, up on the ledge. That was before I found Liu and the Urk had been killed—and everything had to be changed."

"You've got a different idea now?" asked Calas.

There was no doubt in the smaller man's voice. Clearly, he had complete confidence that whatever might have come up, Hal could adjust their plans to take care of it.

"I had it in mind to arrange things so that the two of them would take their troops home. Their report would be that both Artur and Cee had died under questioning. But that it was pretty clear from what they said that there was no one else living up here. They would have reported that they'd buried the bodies, the way they buried the soldiers that Artur'd have been blamed for killing earlier, then simply gave up and went back to the garrison."

"And now?" prompted Calas.

The stretcher bearers came in with the dressed and armed body of the Urk.

"Put him down just inside the entrance flap to the left,"

Hal told them. "As I was just telling Calas, we've had to change plans. Now when I hypnotize those soldiers out there I'm going to have to convince them that everybody killed everybody else. A taller story by quite a bit. Two dead soldiers, even a dead underofficer's one thing. A dead commissioned officer's something else—at least as far as paperwork is concerned. Their headquarters is going to be grilling these soldiers for details—that's right; take the Urk off the stretcher and pull him up so he's not quite alongside Artur. Now turn him nearly all the way over on his face, so that you can't see the front part of his body."

They did as he said.

"All right," said Hal, when they were finished. "Now, roll the stretcher up around its poles and lay it along the wall of the hutment, behind the cot, so it can't be seen. In a moment I want the rest of you to go out and join the others guarding the soldiers. Send someone to me at once if any of them show signs of coming out of their drugged state."

He knelt beside the unconscious form of Artur.

"Oh. Also—" he said, raising his head to look back over his shoulder at the stretcher bearers, "one of you go out and get me a length of the rope they had him tied up with. About a meter's length'll do."

The bearers looked at each other, and the one nearest the door went out. When he came back with the rope, Hal took it, tied Artur's hands gently together behind his back with one end of the rope.

"Anyone got a knife?" he asked, still kneeling beside Artur.

Calas and one of the stretcher bearers were the only ones with such items. Hal opened each of them in turn and tried the edge of the blade on his thumb. He chose Calas's. With it, he made various cuts all around the rope in an irregular circle, severing only the top strands. He pulled these cuts apart and cut deeper, pulling on the rope as he did so, so that when at last it parted, it showed a ragged end.

"There," he said, winding the rest of the rope around the central pole that upheld the hutment and had been mechanically driven deep into the packed earth under it. He left protruding about as much rope as would make one turn around the pole, with the ragged-looking end projecting into the air.

"There," he said. "That should look more like someone broke the rope with sheer strength, rather than its being cut. I think, under hypnosis, I can make them believe someone as big as Artur could do that."

"He probably could have," said Calas, accepting his knife back.

Hal shook his head.

"Have someone tie you with your hands behind you using ordinary string, sometime; and see if you can break it to get loose," he said. "If you've a length of it between you and what you're tied to, so you can snap the cord with a sudden jerk, you'll probably find you can't break even that. But it doesn't matter. I think under hypnotic suggestion we can make the soldiers believe Artur did it with this rope."

He stood up.

"Now," he said, "everybody out, except for Calas and one of you. Calas can use whoever stays with him as a messenger, if he needs to send me word of something. Come on."

He led them back out into the night and the bright overhead lights of the camp. A slow, damp breeze—a herald of dawn—had begun to blow. They had probably less than an hour before they would be able to see each other's faces without the artificial lights.

The prisoners were still either sitting or lying motionless, still under the effect of the drugged arrows.

"Set them up," Hal told the Guild members. "Including the two who were on watch and sitting at the table. Add those two to the back line of the others. I want them all sitting up with their backs to the hutments."

The Chantry Guild people went about setting up the resistless soldiers. Most of those they handled stayed put in an upright position, once placed in it, with their legs crossed. A few were overweight enough or tight-jointed enough that they needed support to hold that position. In such cases, a Guild member sat down with his or her back against the soldier who could not balance himself.

Meanwhile, Hal had been going down the line of men. There were two lines, since that was the way the sleeping sacks had been laid out on the ground. He squatted in front of each one in turn and spoke to the relaxed, apparently unhearing, man before him for a few minutes until he evoked an an answer to the question *"Do you hear me?"*

At a "yes," he moved on to the next one in line.

It took him nearly half an hour to get all of them to answer him. When, however, he had gotten a response from the last one in the front line, he turned to the closest Chantry Guild member, a slim, almost fragile-looking girl of eighteen, with a sudden dazzling smile that came without warning and invariably seemed to change her completely. Her name was Kady and she was one of Onete's picked group of expert night foragers.

"I'd like you to go to Calas now, in the hutment over there," Hal said to her. Her smile flashed in agreement. "Tell him that when you pass the signal to him, he's to call out in his best imitation of Liu's voice. What he's supposed to shout is *"Shoot, Urk! Now! Shoot him!"*

Hal repeated the words to be shouted, slowly.

"Now," he said to Kady, "you repeat them back to me."

"Shoot, Urk!" said Kady, in a thin, clear voice. *"Now! Shoot him!"*

"Good," said Hal. "You make Calas repeat it back to you, that same way, to make sure he's got it correctly. Then step outside and keep your eyes on me. When I wave, you stick your head back inside and tell him to shout. You've got all that?"

"When I see you wave at me I make Calas repeat *'Shoot, Urk! Now! Shoot him!'* " said Kady. "Then, what do we do?"

"I'll take care of the rest of it," said Hal. "You two leave the hutment and back off. Repeat that for me."

"Calas and I leave the hutment after he shouts and we leave the rest to you," she said.

"Right," Hal replied, "you're perfect."

She smiled again, and went toward the hutment. Hal himself turned back and walked around to face the two lines of seated soldiers, who now all sat facing the still dark jungle beyond the clearing lights.

His eyes picked out the man named Harvey, who was one of those able to sit upright, cross-legged, without any support at his back. He had a strong-boned face, softened by fat, and the bulge of his stomach was enough to reach between his crooked legs almost to the ground in front of him, leaning forward as he was; and probably helped counterbalance any tendency he had to fall backward. He would have looked pleasant and ineffective if it had not been for the hardness of feature under his facial fat.

On Hal's first pass along the seated lines, asking the individual soldiers if they could hear him, Harvey had been the single individual to whom Hal had said anything more. He had suggested then that Harvey might have to take on a position of decision for all the rest. With the others, he had merely made sure that he had fixed their attention hypnotically upon him and upon what he was going to tell them.

"Listen to me, all of you, now," he said, raising his voice. "You've all been asleep until just now."

He paused to remember something. He had asked the two men who had been on watch duty what their names were, and for a moment he had misplaced those names among the thousands of others tucked into his memory.

"All of you have been asleep," he went on, almost immediately, "even Bill Jarvis and Stocky Weems, who were on watch. That drink they had earlier tonight must have gotten to them. In any case, you were all asleep until just now. Isn't that right? Answer—yes!"

"Yes," muttered the two lines of men.

"You knew when you went to sleep that your force-leader, Liu, and the Urk were still at work in Liu's hutment questioning both the little girl and the big man you all took prisoner." Hal went on. "But you paid no attention to that until just now, when something woke you all. What woke you?"

He waited for a long moment of silence.

"I'll tell you what woke you," he said. "You heard a yell from the Urk, as if he was hurt or frightened. You don't remember what he said, but you do remember what you heard after that yell had woken you. You all remember that, don't you? Say 'yes' if you remember."

"Yes," said the seated men, again.

"That's right," said Hal. "From that moment on, you all remember everything, just as it happened, or as it was told to you. That's so, isn't it? Say 'yes,' you remember."

"Yes."

"You won't remember me or any of these other unfamiliar men and women you've seen here tonight. You'll forget that anyone was here but your own fellow soldiers and officers. Say 'yes.'"

"Yes," intoned the soldiers like a ragged, impromptu choir.

Hal walked forward among them until he stood before Harvey, in the second rank. He turned to the man on Harvey's right.

"You can't see me, or hear what I say to Harvey. You won't remember me at all, either from earlier or now. Say 'yes.'"

"Yes," said the soldier.

Hal turned to the man on Harvey's left, repeated his words and got another "yes" for answer. Hal turned his attention back to Harvey, squatting down so that he was almost face to face with the fat man wearing the corporal's tabs on the gray collar of his uniform. He spoke to Harvey, using a voice pitched so low that the two soldiers on either side would have had trouble hearing him even if they had been listening.

"Harvey," Hal said, "you hear me, don't you?"

"Yes," answered Harvey.

"You won't remember about this conversation, any more

than you'll remember seeing me or anyone but your own people and the two prisoners," said Hal. "You'll do this because I tell you to, but also because it'll be in your own best interests to forget. If you forget you'll get all the credit for getting these soldiers back to headquarters, yourself."

Harvey smiled, but the expression of the rest of his face did not change.

"In just a minute or two," Hal said quietly, "something is going to happen. None of the rest of the soldiers out here know it's going to happen; but you've been expecting some trouble of this kind to crop up from the moment you saw Liu and the Urk planned to question that very large, strong man, all by themselves, in one of the hutments, without a couple of the armed soldiers standing guard. You knew he was dangerous because he killed two men with his bare hands while he was being captured. But of course, it wasn't your place to say anything to the Urk or the force-leader, so you didn't. But that's why you've been ready to take charge of things if some kind of trouble does crop up. Isn't that right?"

"Yes."

Hal paused.

"That's why, not like the rest, you've been sleeping lightly; and so you woke up the first moment you heard anything our of the ordinary. Now, you're just about to hear it. I'll leave you for a moment, and then I'll be back beside you when you hear it, to tell you what to do; and I'll stay beside you until everything's under control. Understood?"

"Understood," said Harvey.

Hal got to his feet and moved swiftly and silently to Liu's hutment. He stepped inside to meet the inquiring gazes of Calas, Kady and the one Guild member who had stayed with Calas as a messenger.

"All set," he said to Calas. "Now, when Kady passes you the signal you've got two things to do. One is shout what Kady told you to shout. The other is to take the power pistol from the Urk's holster, and use it to blow the throat out of Liu. Can you do that, or have you got some hesitations about shooting a corpse?"

"I wouldn't shoot live people today—I hope," said Calas. "I felt like killing Liu after what he'd ordered them to do to Artur. But I don't think maybe I'd kill, anymore, except someone like him, now I'm a Chantry member. It's not going to bother me, though, to blow the dead bastard's throat out. I suppose you want to hide the fact of how he was killed?"

"That's right," said Hal. "If you hadn't wanted to be the one who used the power pistol, I'd have to, and I'd do the shout and the shot from here, before I go back to the soldiers. After you're done, put the pistol into the Urk's hand."

"Right," said Calas.

"Good," said Hal. He turned to Kady. "Come with me and stand just outside the door, so you can see me. I'll be waving soon after I get back to one particular soldier. When I do, you tell Calas, and run away from the hutments—fast. Orban, you come away now and get out of sight with the rest of the Guild members."

Orban was a slight man in his forties with very light-colored blond hair flat on his skull. He nodded.

Hal left the hutment, went back to the soldiers, and squatted down once more in front of Harvey. He looked about. All Guild members, as instructed earlier, were out of the line of sight of the hypnotized soldiers.

"Whatever happens," he said, looking back at Harvey, "it'll be up to you to lead all the rest of the men out of here and back to headquarters. You've got rank on everybody else; and the others'll follow you. All you have to do is take charge. I'll be right beside you all the time until you leave here, even though you won't remember that afterward, and the rest won't see or hear me when I talk to you."

He paused. Harvey watched him, listening with an attention that was so profound it was almost innocent.

"Now, in a moment, what woke you all up is going to go

on with more noise and trouble," Hal said. "You'll need to take charge of things at once. Order all the rest of them to stay put here while you go and investigate. Remind them you're the one in command, *Corporal*."

He watched Harvey's eyes closely on the last word, but they did not change. The ranks of groupman, force-leader, and team-leader, which Cletus Grahame had proposed in his massive work on tactics and strategy, had come into being as the jealousy guarded property of the actual fighting troops. The order ranks of corporal, sergeant, warrant officer and lieutenant had been kept only for those in support positions. Some who bore the older ranks were ashamed of them; some secretly pleased by the special access to privileges that went along with them. Harvey, it seemed, was one of the latter.

Nonetheless, most noncommissioned officers in his position secretly yearned for the authority to directly order and command combat troops. What Hal was suggesting hypnotically to Harvey now would give him not only that, but the approval of his superiors back at headquarters, when he took control of a situation in which his officers were dead.

Some men in his position might have found the prospect either forbidding or unpleasant. Harvey, however, gave no sign that this was the case with him.

Hal stood up.

"Now," he said to all the soldiers, "lie down. Sleep."

They all, including Harvey, obeyed. Hal turned to face the hutment that had been Liu's and the slim figure of Kady standing just outside the entrance flaps. He lifted his arm over his head and waved it back and forth, slowly, twice. He saw her arm go up to wave back and she turned to speak in through the flaps.

Turning back, she went off at a run toward one side of the hutments, where at the edge of the darkness, Onete stood with Cee. The girl had wrapped around herself another vine having a split-open pod, and the pod sagged down, heavy once more with what were probably more rocks of a size to fit the girl's closed fist. Her eyes were steady on the hutment in which were not only the dead Liu and Urk, but the still living Artur.

A shout, almost high-pitched enough to be called a scream, came from the structure, with the words Hal had directed Kady to pass on to Calas. They were followed almost immediately by the coughing roar of the power pistol, and almost as quickly after that, the figure of Calas slipped out through the flaps and headed off in the direction Kady and Orban had taken.

Hal clapped his hands together loudly.

"Sit up!" he shouted.

"All of you men! Listen! What's happening? What's going on in there?"

They were sitting up, most of them looking around, bewildered.

Hal leaned down swiftly and spoke in the ear of Harvey, who was also now sitting up, but looking toward Liu's hutment.

"Now!" Hal said softly. "Now, you take control of them, or it'll be too late. Tell them to stay where they are. You'll look into it!"

"Hold it! Stay put!" shouted Harvey, scrambling to his feet. "That's an order—from me! I'll find out what's happening."

A few of the soldiers who had already fumblingly started to rise, sat back down. Still groggy from the remainder of the drugs still in their bloodstream, but released from the deeper stages of hypnosis by the clapping of Hal's hands, they swore and muttered to each other, staring at the hutment—but they stayed put.

Harvey stumbled toward the hutment. His cross-legged position had evidently cut off the circulation of blood to his legs; and they were just now reawakening to normal flow. He was walking more normally by the time he reached the flaps of the hutment.

"Corporal Magson, sir. May I come in?" he called, and waited. When after a moment, there was no answer, he pushed his way inside, closely followed by Hal.

Under the silent interior lights of the hutment, the bodies of the obviously dead Urk and Liu Hu Shen and the unconscious figure of Artur lay still.

"They're all dead," said Hal quickly, standing behind the corporal. He spoke in a low voice, directly into Harvey's ear, as the fat man stopped, checked by the sight before him. "You can see what's happened. The prisoner must have been strong enough to break loose and start for the force-leader. Liu must have reached for his pistol, but since he'd been watching from his bed and the sidearm was in its holster on the chair beside the bed, he must have seen he couldn't get to it in time. So he shouted—we all heard him, just now—for the Urk to shoot. And the Urk must have—but not fast enough to save his own life. Look at that, his head's all crushed in. That big man must have been as strong as a giant! But the Urk did manage to kill him with that one shot."

"Yes. . . ." said Harvey, still staring, still under the influence of the hypnosis to the point where he heard Hal's words as if they were his own thoughts.

"And when the Urk shot the big man," Hal went on in a soft, persuasive voice, "the charge went right through him and killed the force-leader, too. They're all dead."

"Yes, that's it," said Harvey.

"You'll really have to take charge now," said Hal. "They'll think a lot of you at headquarters for handling this properly. You'll want to bring the officers' bodies back for burial, of course; but you can have some of the men scrape a hole and roll the body of the big man in it, next to where they buried the child, after she died from the questioning. As Liu himself said just an hour ago—remember? Liu said that there was pretty surely no one else up here to find; or either the child or the man would have talked by this time. But he said, remember, they might as well make sure by working on the man until he died?"

"Yes," said Harvey, "yes, I remember just how it was."

Hal paused.

"Actually, you know," he said in a lower, more confidential tone in Harvey's ear, "those two just wanted an excuse to have their fun with what they had left."

"Right. They would," muttered Harvey.

"Now, the first thing," Hal went on, "is to get a couple of the soldiers you can trust to remember what you say and do what you want. Get them in here with you to see what's happened, and then they can take the big man out and bury him. Also, you better record some pictures of how things were, here, while you're at it, to show back at headquarters."

"Now!" he said, clapping his hands softly together behind Harvey's right ear. "Remember. None of you've seen anyone but the big man and the girl. Now, get things moving!"

Harvey started, turned, and went out of the hutment. Hal followed. The fat man walked slowly back to the seated soldiers, and went around to stand in front of them.

"All right, listen to me now . . . " he began . . . and paused. Hal whispered in his ear and he spoke up again. "We've had a blowup. Both the Force and the Group are dead. That leaves me in command; so all of you snap to and do what I tell you! We've got to bury that prisoner, strike camp, and get the officers' bodies back to headquarters, right away. Ranj, Wilson and Morui, you three come with me. Bring a recorder. I want you for witnesses and to make some recordings of what's happened inside the Force's hutment. The rest of you get busy striking camp and making ready to move out. Come on, come on now! Move!"

Time was also moving, Hal noted. Dawn was very close. Both moons were long down; and the utter blackness just before day, at the ground level, denied the lightening of the sky beyond the lamps of the camp, when he looked straight up.

Back on the ledge, Hal had warned the Guild people to start getting back out of sight the moment he first clapped his hands, to begin the process of bringing the soldiers partially out of their hypnosis. They had faithfully faded back beyond the lights into the jungle dark; and, as the morning lightened further, they would move farther and farther off, until even under daylight, the forest itself would hide them from the view of anyone in the camp.

In the meantime Hal, continuing to remind the three soldiers Harvey had chosen and any others he dealt with, that he was not there as far as their perceptions were concerned, had supervised the picture-taking of the interior of Liu's hutment. Then, at his prompting, Harvey had picked up entrenching tools and taken the same men out into the darkness with a single handlight, to dig a grave for the supposedly dead Artur.

While they were involved in this task, he had the Guild bearers carry Artur, once more on the stretcher, with the straps securing him in place, to the edge of the excavation. The soldiers, digging and swearing at the hand labor, paid no attention to the bringers of the body they were to dispose of; and, having set Artur down, the Guild people melted back out of sight into the darkness.

Harvey had been supervising the grave-digging under Hal's instructions. When the diggers had gone deep enough into the soft forest floor, half mold, half earth, Hal had Harvey call them out for a break in their labors and take them aside. There, by the limited light of the single source of illumination they had brought with them, he brought them momentarily back into a more profound state of hypnosis, and gave them a false memory of having tumbled Artur themselves from the graveside into the grave; then begun to cover him up, before Harvey had called them out for a rest. Then he signaled the stretcher bearers to start back to the ledge with Artur.

As soon as they had faded into the darkness with their load, at Hal's prompting, Harvey sent the grave-diggers back to finish shoveling into the open excavation all that they had taken out. They did so; and Harvey took them back to camp. By now, all of the hutments and erected lights were down and packed, ready to move; and most of the soldiers themselves were in full kit, with their weapons, and ready to move out as well.

At the edge of the camp, Hal left the soldiery to complete the job of returning to their headquarters under Harvey's command. He had little doubt that from this point on, military habit would take them back there without further prompting. The hypnotic command he had given them would eventually wear off; but their memories of what had actually happened would remain confused, and there would be nothing for any of them to gain later by changing their version of what had happened, as they would have originally given it to their superiors.

He dropped into a lope over the now clearly visible ground, to catch up with the party from the Guild, who by this time would be halfway back to the entrance of the trail up the mountainside.

The day was rapidly brightening around him and his steady jog felt good. The ledge was small enough, and he had been deeply enough immersed in his other concerns, so that he had not deliberately walked, let alone covered ground at a run except for that one day, since he had left his exercise room at the Final Encyclopedia.

He was reminded again of what he had thought during that last run, a few days ago—even his running treadmill at the Final Encyclopedia, surrounded with the images and scents of an imaginary outdoors, had not been like this. This was real; and it brought back old memories of his runs through the forest near the estate in the Rocky Mountains where he had spent his second childhood; before the coming of the Others had sent him scuttling for a hiding place on the Younger Worlds.

For a moment, the image of the young gunmen with their long, slim-barreled void pistols, and Bleys Ahrens, as they had suddenly appeared at the estate, came back to him. Particularly Bleys, slimmer then than he was now—wherever on the Younger Worlds he might be at this moment, eleven years later. Slimmer, and seeming much taller; both because then, in that first sight, Hal had not himself reached his full adult height, which was to be the equal of Bleys'; and because of the last ten years of slight but noticeable aging and thickening of the other man's body.

A cold feeling like a breath of some stray breeze seemed to pass through him. He had let Amanda bring him here to Kultis and the Chantry Guild with no real faith that here he might be helped to find the Creative Universe. The impasse keeping him from that goal these last two years had been like some great, impossibly wide, impossibly thick wall of glass, holding him out. But now, over the past few weeks, he had come out of the despondency that his failure had built in him. Hope had stirred in him once again—but with hope, now, also came fear.

Time was passing. Tam's days were numbered. Even if they had not been, the force that Bleys was building to overwhelm even the phase-shielded Earth was moving to its inevitable completion. Time was on the march; and while he had refound hope—great hope, somehow, with this successful rescue of Artur—he had still not found a way past that impassable, glasslike barrier to his lifetime goal—

He glimpsed the figures of some of the Guild members through the farther trees before him and realized he had finally caught up with them. He checked his jog to a walk. It might worry them to see him running, might make them think that there was more urgency than there actually was now, to getting Artur up the mountainside to the ledge and proper care. Actually, it was only Artur's physical condition that still urged that time not be wasted. The soldiers of the Occupation Forces should not bother them for some little time to come.

He walked, but stretched his stride to cover ground swiftly without appearing to race. In a moment or two he was up with them. Artur, on the stretcher, was at the head of the traveling group, with a man on each of the four handles of the stretcher. As Hal had foreseen, Artur was proving a heavy load for his carriers, even across this level, if somewhat cluttered, forest floor. The extra people beyond the rock would be very much needed to get him safely up the steep trail of the mountainside to the ledge.

"How is he?" Hal asked Onete, who was walking beside the head of the stretcher, keeping an eye on Artur's face.

"He came to," answered Onete, without taking her eyes off Artur's face. "Tannaheh gave me several loaded syringes to use if he did that. I used one; and he went back to sleep. I wish Tannaheh had told me what I was supposed to be giving him. I don't like doing things like that without knowing."

"It probably didn't occur to Tannaheh," said Hal.

"It occurred to me," Onete said, "but he shoved them into my hand just as we left the ledge, after running after us to give them to me. I didn't have a chance to ask him, in the dark and all. Anyway, Artur's back unconscious or sleeping again, one of the two; and that's a blessing—"

She lowered her voice almost to a whisper, speaking out of the corner of her mouth, still without taking her gaze off Artur's face.

"Check to my right, about four meters off," she said, barely using her lips, "but don't turn your head to look."

He leaned over the stretcher as if to gaze more closely into the face of Artur, using the movement to disguise a tilt of his head to the right, so that out of the corner of his eyes, he could see into the forest on that side of them. His view picked up Cee, prowling along level with the stretcher and himself.

The vine with its pod no longer was around her waist. It hung by its vine-ends from one fist, with the weight of what was probably a single rock only pulling it down. Cee's other fist held a second rock ready. Her eyes were on him with the same steadiness they had held back at the camp when she had looked both at him and at Liu.

"She still doesn't trust us completely," Onete said, still in a barely audible voice, still with her lips hardly moving. "But particularly, she doesn't trust you. Liu gave orders to the soldiers and they did what they did to Artur. You give orders to us, as far as she can see; so you must be another like him. If she starts to rotate or to raise either arm, hit the ground, or get something between you and her."

"Thanks," said Hal, "I will. But don't worry about me. I know about slings—I can even use one myself. I'll be able to tell if she starts to use that."

What he said was true enough. His knowledge of slings as well as a number of other primitive weapons dated back to the early training of his first childhood on Dorsai. What he did not tell her was that it was going to be impossible for him to keep an eye on Cee at all times and meanwhile do whatever he might do to make sure they all got up to the ledge safely.

It was full daylight now; and they came at last to the large outcropping of rock under which it was possible for them to make their way to the boulder that had been set up to block the path beyond it on to the trail leading up the side of the mountain to the ledge.

CHAPTER 30 ■

Shawnee, a slightly stout, middle-aged woman, with her gray hair pulled back above her ankle-length blue robe and sandals, had the round, calm face of a typical Exotic and was on sentry duty just outside the entrance under the rock that led to the mountain trail.

"We heard you coming," she said, as the group reached her, "and got you on the scopes by relay from the ledge. The blocking boulder's moved back and the way's clear. You can take Artur through, and we'll block the way again behind you."

There was a short period of difficulty, for the bearers had to bend double to pass through the entrance and this made Artur an impossible load for the four of them. It ended up with seven people, including Hal, crawling through with the stretcher essentially carried on their backs, until they reached the other side of the rock face and the opening beyond where the path up the mountainside began. The large granite boulder, as Shawnee had promised, was off to one side.

They stopped to rest while the boulder was rolled back. Once in place, it cut off not only entrance, but any light from above. Now anyone crawling under the rock face would have no alternative but to believe they had come up against the solid mountainside and that nothing but stone was beyond.

"Amid said we shouldn't need to bother digging up the plug rock, if the soldiers were leaving," said Shawnee, "unless, you've got some reason to."

"No. No reason to now," answered Hal. He felt weariness, but with the warm hearth-glow of success at its heart.

But then began the labor of getting Artur up the steep slope of the mountainside track to the ledge. In spite of the Guild members' own experience with the way in, and the fact Hal had warned them the carries found they could only work in five-minute stretches before needing to be relieved. Hal stayed beside them all the way, on one side of the stretcher, ready to help catch it if one of the bearers should slip and fall. On the other side climbed Onete, her syringes ready, and beyond her, scrambling sometimes on all fours like a mountain goat, but with the sling loaded and its vine-ends caught up short, ready in one grimy fist, was Cee—her eyes continually on Hal.

There was one uncomfortable moment when Artur began to come to, and moaned. Cee was instantly upright, the vine-ends of her sling sliding down through her fists to their full length; and in the same moment Onete stepped up to the side of the stretcher, her body directly blocking Hal from any throw by Cee.

"He's all right! Hal's done nothing!" she snapped at

Cee. "I'm going to make your uncle comfortable and put him back to sleep, right now."

The stretcher bearers had stopped. Any excuse for a moment in which to catch their breath. Onete turned about, still blocking any throw at Hal with her own body, and gave Artur another injection. He relaxed on the stretcher.

"Let's get on," said Hal, taking his own grip on the side of the stretcher again; and they resumed their painful way upward.

When they finally stepped out onto the level surface of the ledge itself, everybody was at the end of their strength.

"We'll take him to a room in the clinic." Onete told Hal. "You can find him there later, if you want him. Tannaheh has some people trained as nurses and assistants. There'll be somebody with him all the time."

"Tell Tannaheh someone who's been through what Artur's been through is going to have to be brought out of it gradually," Hal said. "For a while at first after he comes to, he's going to think he's still in the hands of his torturers—but Tannaheh probably already knows that."

"I'll tell him anyway," said Onete. "You better get some rest yourself. You've been up more than twenty-four hours, haven't you?"

"Perhaps," said Hal, "anyway, I've got a few words I want to have with Amid before I call it done. I'll see you later."

He turned away from her and the stretcher bearers, who were now brand new at their job, being from among those who had stayed up on the ledge. Some of those who had helped the stretcher up the last few meters of slope had simply sat down, or lain down, where they had stopped, although to Hal's eyes none of them looked in need of more than an ordinary night's rest to put them back on their feet. He turned away and went toward Amid's office.

The heat of the rising sun of midmorning struck at his face and chest through his sweat-soaked shirt, and the level ground felt strange under his feet. He slanted across the open ground, approaching Amid's office from the front and side. He reached it at its right corner and walked along its front toward its entrance. As he passed, he glanced in one of the windows that were the best compromise these forest built structures could make with the former Exotic homes, where it had been hard to tell from one room to the next whether you were outdoors or indoors. It had suddenly occurred to him that the small, old head of the Chantry Guild might be somewhere else about the establishment, and the thought of a prolonged search for him on legs wobbly with weariness was not attractive.

But Amid was there. Hal saw him through the window, seated in one of the chairs around the now fireless central fireplace. In a chair facing him was Amanda.

Hal stopped for a second. Down below, he had forgotten Amanda might show up. He went on; but at the door, set open to the warming morning air, he paused and looked through its aperture at those inside.

He was not quite sure why he had stopped. It was as if an instinct had put out its hand to stop him for a second, to make him stop and think, first.

Perhaps, he thought, with sudden unnatural clarity, he did need to think before entering. A number of times in his life before it had been when he was most tired, after great and prolonged effort of mind and body, that his mind had taken on a strange, almost feverish clarity. The most important of those times had been some years back now, in the militia cell on Harmony, where he had been left burning up with fever, to die; and instead, in that moment, his mind had seen and worked clearly as never before.

Something like that was on him now, although he did not seem to be able to put it all together. But, out of the dull hopelessness from which Amanda had brought him, when she had led him here, he had finally climbed—to this.

But what was *this?* One thing was certain, it was not anything resembling his former despondency. He was alive again, and the feeling that the cause to which he had dedicated himself could not be lost was with him again.

Also, there were some new bits and pieces of understanding. But they did not fit together. More than ever in his existence before, he felt he stood on the brink of the answer he searched for, but could not quite see the final step that would take him to it.

Part of it was Jathed, that wild Exotic philosopher, who had preached a separate universe for each living individual. Part of it was Cee. Part of it was the fact that he had gone with the others and succeeded in rescuing both Cee and Artur, while sending the soldiers away harmlessly. And done it without harming anyone. True, Cee had killed. But Cee was no more to be held accountable as a murderer than a wolf who had killed in defense of itself and one of its cubs.

Somehow, all these things tied together; but also, somehow his mind failed at the moment to connect them. Particularly, it failed to connect them. Particularly, it failed to connect them with Amanda, who was part of the understanding. Amanda, from the moment she had met him on Dorsai, had made him the gift of that insight of hers. The full value of that gift he was yet to know, any more than he could yet appreciate the full implication of the connection of the other bits of discovery afloat in his mind. All he knew about the gift was that it had been a part of herself; and that it was something no one else could have given him, because no one else had it to give.

It was an awareness of that gift that had stopped him now. Stopped him, because it had made him more perceptive; and that added perception in him now rang a nameless dread of whatever she might have to tell him.

He remembered sitting in her kitchen in the Morgan homestead, Fal Morgan, on the Dorsai world, that first morning after meeting her. There had been a moment there in which he had had a chance to compare her with the telephoned picture of her sister. He remembered then that he had thought to himself that the sister was equally beautiful, but lacked something which Amanda possessed— something which in that moment he had called "intensity."

But it had not been and was not intensity. It was some-thing much more. Amanda went beyond. Part of her extended invisibly into another dimension, *lived* in another dimension. Everyone, it struck him now, had the potential to extend into that further dimension, but only particular individuals chose to do so, and only in some of these could it be seen in them by another individual—as he saw it now, where he had never been able to see it before. Now, remembering Rukh, he realized he had always seen it in her, and perhaps a little even in Ajela and some of the true faith-holders on Harmony, like James Child-of-God. It had been, now he thought of it, very clearly visible in Ajela, as it was in Tam Olyn; and it had been there in his three tutors—so that he now realized he had learned, partly at least, to recognize it from what he saw in them, without identifying what it was, but imitating it in his own life as he imitated the three old men in other ways.

But it was in other, more unlikely people, too. It was in Cee, surprisingly enough. And it must have been in Jathed. In fact, what he had come here to ask Amid, tired as he was, without knowing why he needed the answer, but knowing he could not sleep until he had it—was whether Jathed had, in those early years down in the forest, had some sort of contact with Cee. Perhaps he had visited her parents? Then the sudden discovery of Amanda here had all but driven the questions from his mind, until he real-ized, suddenly, that Amanda was connected to them, her-self a part of them, in fact.

He went in; and the other two turned at the sound of his boots on the wooden floor. Amid, he was now able to see, had his own extended element; and it came to Hal that both Amanda and Amid, as well as others like them, were not only part of what he had chosen to spend his life finding but part of what he had hoped for when he had let Amanda bring him to Kultis. She would not have identified this spe-cific element as one of the things he needed to discover; but, that strange, almost mystic part of her that had always set her family apart from other Dorsai must have sensed both his need and the location of this, among what else he reached for.

That sensitivity to his need and that which would answer it was part of what made her what she was. So that wherever she happened to be, as now in Amid's office, the perceived universe seemed to fall into order about her, to become sensible and clear of purpose. It was as if she shone with a light that, though invisible in itself, let those about her see more clearly.

He reached her and they held each other for a long moment without saying anything. Then, still holding him with her hands, she stood back a little from him and turned his face to the light of the nearest window.

"Better," she said, studying it. "Yes, you're better. But not all the way back to what you should be."

"I'm closer," he answered. "All the more close now that you're here."

She let him go, and frowned as he put out a hand to Amid's desk for support. He would have fallen otherwise. His legs felt as if they had no strength left in them.

"The grapevine brought me news of the soldiers coming up here to look around," she said. "I came as soon as I could, but I waited for full night to go up to that group you had guarding the rock blocking the trail in. I've been here since about an hour or so after you took your party down there. It was a temptation to follow you down, but if you'd planned what you'd planned without me, there was no point in my barging in and upsetting things. I've been waiting for you since—but you're ready to collapse."

"You could say that," he told her with a weary grin. "But I had a question or two to ask Amid before I folded up."

"Anything, of course," said Amid, getting spryly up from his chair and coming forward. "But do you have to have the answers right now? Amanda's right. You're exhausted."

"Two quick questions," said Hal. "Was Jathed around down there when Cee was living with her parents? I believe he was already dead when she began to run wild—but could they have talked to each other, somehow—would they have talked to each other?"

Amid frowned.

"I'm sure he was around, for a couple of years at least," he said. "And as for Jathed talking to her, what I've heard of him is that he would have talked to, lectured at, anyone—all in the same way, regardless of their age or situation. But whether he and Cee actually communicated—I'd have to ask some of the more longtime members of the Guild. I'll do that and let you know tomorrow. The question isn't going to be whether Jathed would talk to Cee, but whether they encountered each other—and whether Cee, young as she was, would be able to understand anything. But maybe she might. She might even have sensed he was no sort of threat to her, or even saw him as special—children can do that."

"That's what I wanted to know," said Hal.

He turned away from the desk, reeling as he lost the support of it; and being caught and held upright by the strong grasp of Amanda.

"Sleep for you," she said, "this way."

CHAPTER 31 ■

Hal woke to almost complete darkness relieved only by the faint line of light under the door to the bathroom. This alone told him that he was not in his own bed in Dormitory Two, but back in Amid's second office, in which he and Amanda had slept on his arrival at the Chantry Guild. There was someone beside him in the bed; and he turned his head to make out that it was Amanda, deeply sleeping, her hair spread out on the pillow.

It must be deep into the night. He lay there, trying to remember.

He had no recollection of getting here. He remembered nothing beyond Amanda catching him, holding him up, and telling him he must sleep. He had no memory of being brought to this bed. But now that he tried to recall anything at all after that, there came to him a few flashes from momentary wakings, as seeing a sliver of the rich daylight illumination of Procyon, that had managed to make its way here and there through the blanket she had once more hung over a rod to provide a near-perfect blackout curtain.

In each case he had awakened long enough only to recognize the fact that he was safe and comfortable, then fallen immediately and heavily back to sleep again. He had no memory of Amanda joining him. She would have been quiet so as not to disturb him, of course, as only she could be quiet. But how long had it been since she had come? How long since night replaced day outside his curtained window?

Some diurnal clock deep inside him told him that it had been a long time—that he had slept most of the night through, as well as the day; and dawn was near.

It had been no ordinary sleep. He had put in forty-eight hours of wakefulness under active conditions before this, without falling into such a pit of unconsciousness; and while he might be a few years older since then, and softer, in spite of his daily exercise in the Final Encyclopedia, neither time nor inaction could account for such a heavy, prolonged slumber.

There had to be another reason for it; and even as he formed the question the answer came. His unconscious mind had once more wanted his consciousness out of the way so it could work with perfect freedom, putting together all the things he had learned, one by one—those parts that now almost, but not quite, came together like the parts of a puzzle of many pieces, to give him a complete picture of his goal.

He felt a yearning to stay here, where he was, and put an

arm gently over Amanda, coaxing her gently back into wakefulness and the joining that they had always had so few chances for. But at the same time, there was a powerful feeling within him that now and only now the answer he sought, or at least another step toward it, was calling him outside this room. It was waiting for him with the dawn that would be coming; as it had waited all this time he had been here, but he had not yet learned enough to see it.

Quietly, as Amanda must have come to bed quietly, he left it, found his clothes, dressed and let himself out of the room. The corridor was bright-lit and silent; but outside, when he closed the main door of the building behind him, the ledge was in complete darkness. The night was empty except for the chanting of those who walked the circle, invisible to him. Both moons were down and the light of the stars was not enough to let him see his hand at arm's length before him.

But like the Guild members, he now knew the ledge well enough to find his way about it blindfolded. In addition, in this season of summer, even at this altitude, the wind blew toward the ledge across the land below.

Accordingly, he turned his face into the wind and, feeling the familiar slopes and pitches of the ground under his bare feet, went toward the edge.

As he went, his eyes readjusted to the darkness from the bright glare of the hall lights. He was able to see the treetops overhead occulting the stars, the trees that had been deliberately left uncut in patches and clumps so that part of one of them always hid any walkway below it. Almost unthinkingly, he oriented himself by those shapes of the treetops against the pinpoints of light in the sky, and as he got close to the edge he could see it as a line of demarcation where darkness gave way suddenly to deeper darkness.

He was out here earlier than usual and he did not expect to find Old Man here yet; and in fact, when he got to the place by the pool where he usually sat, the spot the Old Man usually occupied was empty. After all, Hal reminded himself his fellow watcher was no longer young, and also had just finished putting in much the same hours, at the same activity as had Hal. It would hardly be surprising if he did not show up at all.

Hal sat, therefore, waiting for the paling of the sky that would signal the approaching day and the sunrise. There was a strange blend of expectation and excitement in him.

In patches, where the native vegetation of the pond did not obscure its reflecting surface, the image of the stars overhead looked back up at him—as they also looked down on him through the clear, high-altitude air. He felt enclosed by them as an individual feels warmly enclosed by family or close friends at a gathering of those who were close. The sky about them was beginning to pale, but only beyond the line of the Grandfathers of Dawn in the far distance—that place from which the sunrise would come. Overhead, it was still dark enough for their lights to be clear and sharp against the deep dark.

As far as he could tell, none of those that he could see up there were stars that were suns over the other Younger Worlds, or Earth itself. Those solar bodies were at present in the wrong position to be seen from Kultis—or more accurately, this part of the planet was pointed in the wrong direction. But those he did see stood in for those he knew, in his imagination; so that it was as if they had come here at this important moment to watch him now from both above and below at once, waiting for him to take up his journey once more along the path he had chosen for himself that day of his uncle James's death.

It had been a ridiculously ambitious decision at the time on the part of a half-grown boy, to find and destroy whatever element it was in people that made them selfish and uncaring to the point of brutality and cruelty to each other. The shape of the answer he sought had emerged, little by little from the mists of things undiscovered as he worked his way toward it, trying one route after another, finding his way blocked but learning a little more each time, so that with each fresh start he chose his next route with more wisdom.

So, slowly, he had progressed. Slowly, his certainty had grown that there was a path to humanity's becoming a race of people who would voluntarily refrain from all harming of their fellows, by all actions, from literal killing, to the exercise of the little cruelties of words and sheer thoughtlessness that were so common in human society that they went almost without remark. But now, he was surer than he had ever been, that only a few thin veils—perhaps only one—hid it from him.

As Donal he had found that power and law alone could not force the change he wanted. But the discovery pointed to the road he himself must travel; and, after him, the race. As Paul Formain, back in the twenty-first century, he had found that part of the answer lay outside the known universe and its laws; but that this further universe—the one he had come to call the Creative Universe—was again, only part of the answer.

His last attempt had been the gathering of the best of what the Younger Worlds had gained—from the Exotics, the Friendlies, and his own world of the Dorsai—into safety behind the phase-shield he had caused to be set up, enclosing Earth and the Final Encyclopedia. He had been confident then, that at last, having done this, the next and last step to his goal would be obvious.

But it had not been. What he had achieved had only once more cleared the mists a little way, but left him with no understanding of what was to be done next. It had only shown yet a farther stretch of the road still to be covered.

He had not been wrong in anything he had done so far. Faith, courage, and the ability to think philosophically, all faculties of the human, developed from its animal forebears, and their extended forms, as embodied in the Friendlies, the Dorsai and these Exotics, had been part of the answer. He had not been wrong in that much; but now he saw what was needed was something still hidden by unknowns, still in shadow. He could only be sure now that it was somehow connected with the creativity in every living human.

In his disappointment and weariness, he had become blocked; and believed himself burnt out—a failure. So he had continued to think until Amanda had come to tell him he might find a new point of view here, on an Exotic world now wrecked and ground down by the forces of an enemy point of view that was trying to kill the growth element of the human spirit and destroy all that had been accomplished.

She had been right. He knew that now with a whole-hearted, instinctive certainty, as he sat here, waiting for Procyon's rise over the mountaintops.

Somewhere, with her and among the Chantry Guild members and with his recent part in the rescue of Artur and little Cee, who was of an age with the boy he had been when he had made his original vow, he had once more found a way to go forward. And now, now here, waiting for the sunrise, he felt perhaps only one more large step toward what he sought; perhaps even close at last to the doorway itself, through which he now knew he must pass to find what he sought.

The paling of the night's black sky and the extinguishing of the stars had spread forward from above the distant mountains as he had been thinking, and the light had grown stronger. He felt the approaching dawn like a hand laid upon him; and although the breeze was merely cool, it seemed to blow through his clothing so that he felt as if he sat naked and waiting, his legs crossed, his hands not in prayer position but laid, palms down, one on top of the other in his lap; as he remembered his uncle Ian's massive hands used to lie.

He let his mind go out to his customary imaginings of this daily exercise of body and mind: conjuring up the time of the far future of this Chantry Guild, when the ledge had been filled by a massive structure of stone blocks quarried from the mountain, its flat surfaces paved and gardened and this pool before him enclosed by a rim of pink-veined, light gray rock, with the native plants replaced by imported water-lilies spreading their flat, broad petals on the liquid surface to uphold themselves and their night-closed and sleeping white flowers.

Those flowers of his imagination which would be opening with the coming light of day.

As with some repeated meditation, the envisioned scene replaced the reality around him. His ears heard the chanting behind his back of the present and future walkers in the circle . . .

The transient and the eternal are the same . . .

Now, the chant seemed to pick him up and possess him. So that he resonated to it as a tuning fork resonates to being struck, with a single pure note. In the pool, the white blossoms were beginning to open as the light flooded forward and the day brightened.

His eyes ignored the unvarying green sweep of the high-altitude forest below him and focused on the distant range of mountains, the Grandfathers of Dawn. Always the mountains. Always the mountains and the sunrise. These belonged as much to the future of his imagined scene as they did to the present second in which he sat here. To the mountains and the sunrise, the years or centuries in between were unimportant, the moment of a single drawn breath in a lifetime of breaths.

The sun was not yet in sight from behind the range; but the brightness of the sky showed that it was close now, very close.

His eyes were filled with light and he felt the cool air passing in and out of the lungs above his motionless body as he sat. He looked down at the pond and saw that the white flowers were now fully open, some of them showing the drops of the dew that had collected in their tightly closed petal tips earlier. He felt as if some essential but nonphysical part of himself was lifted out of the rest of him and rushed through the airy space between him and the distant mountain range to meet the dawn, seeing nothing else.

At the same time his physical eyes looked down at the

pond and focused once more on a single flower, on one white petal of which a dewdrop sat like a blessing. The flower filled his gaze and like a wave through him came a great sweep of feeling, that anything should be so wonderful as the living leaf with the perfect transparency of the dewdrop upon it.

Feeling this, it was as if his flying, incorporeal self reached the upthrust giants of the land that waited, as they had always waited, for him in this moment; and, lifting, it and he saw the first blazing edge of Procyon, which was too bright to look at with the eyes of his body back on the ledge, appear in the bottom of a notch in the rock before him and send the first ray of direct light leaping across the space between range and ledge to touch the pond, to touch the flower.

It touched the dewdrop; and for one second too short for breath to draw or mind to do anything but hold in memory, the drop exploded, scintillating with light like a diamond, radiating off in all directions, including into him, where it shone unforgettable, from that moment on.

He sat, blinded by the vision. Behind him, the voices of the walkers chanted still. . . .

The transient and the eternal are the same . . .

And, suddenly, moving in to replace the wonder within him came the understanding he had waited for. Now, the words of the walkers engulfed him. Suddenly, at last, he understood the truth of what they chanted, what he had so often chanted; that it was not a matter of faith but of actuality.

For the transient and the eternal *were* the same.

He looked at the petal now and the dewdrop was already beginning to shrink, to disappear as the heat of the sun's ray drew it up. In a little it would be gone. The petal would be dry and it would be as if the dewdrop had never been there.

But the dewdrop was always there. Even as this one

blazed for a second with incredible light and began to disappear, somewhere in this infinite universe there was another dewdrop just beginning to scintillate, and after that another, and another . . .

And another dawn and another, and another mountain range and another, when this one should be worn down to level dust; and without a pause, another world, which would make another range through which a ray of light would come to another dewdrop on another petal—forever and forever, until time should end.

The dewdrop was beyond destruction. The moment of its brilliance was eternal. It was transient here, but eternal everywhere. Just so, all things were eternal, only waiting to be found, even the doorway to something that had only been his dream all these years.

The physical light of the present day was everywhere about him and the vision of the future was gone; but the moment of the sudden explosion of illumination from the dewdrop still filled him.

He got to his feet and went back, past the now fully visible circle of walkers toward the buildings beyond. He felt incredibly light-bodied. As if he could, with little effort, walk up into the thin air. A figure in the ordinary light workshirt and trousers, worn by the majority of the Chantry Guild members when they were otherwise occupied than walking in the circle, stepped out from behind some tree trunks to meet him. It was Old Man and he smiled up at Hal as they met and Hal stopped.

"You weren't there this morning," said Hal.

"I was there. I sat behind you," said Old Man. "Some things are best touched alone."

His smile grew and became almost impish. He reached into a pocket of his trousers and brought out a small mirror, which he held up to Hal's eyes.

Hal stared at the image of his own face. There was a difference in what he saw that he could not pick out at first.

Then he saw it—the pupils of his eyes were contracted almost to pinpricks of darkness, like the eyes of someone under drugs. For a fraction of a second the scintillation of the dewdrop seemed to leap out from those pinpricks and the mirror at him, making him feel light-headed, but happily so.

"How could you tell ahead of time, in the dark?" he asked, as Old Man put the mirror back into the pocket.

Old Man passed his hand from left to right through the air at chest height before him, palm outward toward Hal.

"I felt it," he said.

Hal stared at him, waiting for additional explanation; but Old Man, still smiling, merely turned and went away from him, back through the trees from among which he had emerged.

CHAPTER 32 ■

He went back to their room and discovered that Amanda had already risen and left. He found her having breakfast by herself at a small table in the building's dining room and joined her.

Actually, he wanted nothing to eat, and she, after a single wise look at him, said nothing, not even "good morning." Instead, she merely smiled and continued her own meal, leaving him to sit and do what he wanted, which was merely to enjoy the early day with her, along with the other breakfasters. He let himself be immersed in the chatter in the dining room and the sounds from the kitchen. The sun, shining in through the windows of the room to brighten all around them, wrapped him in an unusual sense of happiness.

When she was done, she rose. He went with her. Taking

her tray with its used utensils and dishes to the disposal slot, she pushed it through. Then, smiling again at him, she led him outside and parted company with him, going off herself in the direction of Amid's office.

He was left to his own devices, and found himself happy to be so. Kultis, around him, had never seemed more bright and fresh. Its colors stood out at him, as if just washed by a brief summer shower, from the sky overhead to the gravel of the paths underfoot.

He roamed about the ledge. There was a lightness to his body; and the sense of the illumination he had just received lingered within him. For once, he felt strangely free of purpose. It was as if his consciousness had been cut loose, like a towed dory from behind a small fishing boat, to drift at the whim of soft winds and gentle waves under a bright sun.

He smiled. The image of the loose dory pleased him. The implications of what he had found were too massive and momentous for his mind to handle logically, and so that part of him had been set free temporarily by the more capacious mental machinery behind it, that moved in creative and other areas where the conscious, with its rigid patterns and logics, could not go.

The day, accordingly, passed like a pleasant dream. Either Amanda, or Amid, or someone among the others must have passed the word to leave him to his own devices. None of the Chantry Guild members approached him or tried to draw him into conversation; for which he was grateful.

His thoughts slid between wonderings at small things in his surroundings—from the quaint shape of a pebble among the gravel at his feet to the living design of a variform leaf or blade of grass, or their native equivalents that he came upon. Architecturally, they were all beautiful; and he was a little surprised he had failed so utterly to appreciate them before.

Interspersed with these were other things observed, or remembered—bits and flashes of scenes from his past.

Images from his boyhood and manhood as Donal Graeme, from his brief life as Paul Formain and his present life as Hal; all these came and went in his head like bits of a serial recording.

Something within him guessed, but did not struggle to verify, at the possibility that these things he recalled were reflections of what his deeper mind was fitting into the matrix of his lifelong search, from what he had come to understand this morning. But he did not investigate this, did not question it; and it did not matter.

It was like being on a vacation. It occurred to him with a small shock of surprise that he had never really had a vacation, since he had been a schoolboy on the Dorsai. From the time he had left his home world he had never let go of his life's commitment for even a day. It was a strange feeling to be so cut loose now, even for a few hours like this; to be content with the distance he had come so far, when the end was still not yet reached. Though he could see it clearly, now.

As the morning grew into noon, he drifted toward Amid's office. When he stepped inside it at last, he was surprised to find it, for once, empty. Then it came to him that Amid, himself, might well have run short of sleep, these last forty-eight hours, and be in his own quarters, resting.

In any case, he had not come here to see Amid, but because of the memory of the recording of Jathed to which he had listened. He began to search both his memory and the office, and finally came across a filing cabinet with the name "Jathed" on it. There was a box of recording spindles in the second drawer from the top.

He took the box with him to Amid's desk and seated himself in a chair near it with the control pad Amid had searched for and found earlier. It was a standard desk unit and in a moment he had the first of the recording spindles in the control pad's magazine. Jathed's voice, apparently from several years earlier than the tape Hal had listened to before, sounded immediately in the room.

As he listened, he examined the other spindles. They were dated in order over a period of some twelve years. He started with the most recent ones and began playing them in reverse order to their dates of recording. Sitting in the empty office, he listened to the resonant, compelling voice of the founder of this reincarnation of the Chantry Guild.

He did not need to listen to more than half a dozen, however, before concluding that there would be little advantage to him in hearing them all. With the exception of two which were histories of Jathed's early life, dictated in an unfamiliar, elderly voice that might have belonged to Amid's brother, they were essentially repetitions of what were basically two or three customary lectures delivered by Jathed to audiences consisting of disciples, or others with an interest in what the cantankerous, but remarkable, man had to say.

In effect, the message of all of these was simple enough. Jathed believed that each person who had the necessary faith and self-discipline should be able to enter a personal, extra universe exactly like the physical one that surrounded him; except that in this other universe the will of the person involved could accomplish anything wanted by merely determining it should be so.

Furthermore, if that will was powerful enough, Jathed apparently believed that the effect produced in the extra universe could be duplicated in the universe of reality by convincing the minds of others that the alteration applied to the physical universe also.

In short, he believed in a personal, extra universe, and that the so-called real universe was no more than the product of agreement among the human minds existing in it.

It was in this latter view, about the real universe, that Hal found himself disagreeing with the other man.

It was true that when he had been Paul Formain, three hundred years before, he had experienced the night of madness brought upon a city by the original Chantry Guild of Earth, under its founder, Walter Blunt—that original

Guild which had become the parent of Kultis and its sister world and the whole Exotic culture. It had been a night in which he had seen a monument melting down like wax, a stone lion decorating the balcony of a building lift its head and roar, and a hole of nothingness appear in the middle of a street. A nothingness of such utter blackness that his eyes refused to focus on it.

That, and history was full of miracles witnessed by crowds, as well as smaller, so-called magics seen by small groups of people gathered in confined spaces for just that purpose.

And, finally, there was the sound of the breaking light on the first recording of Jathed Hal had ever heard.

Nonetheless, Hal held to his own view of a single, separate, creative universe that would be a tool, not just a box of conjuring tricks, for humankind.

The only strong point he shared with Jathed was that the other must also have experienced a moment of revelation in which the absolute truth of the transient and the eternal being the same became undeniable. But from that point they had each built different ways, if with much of the same material.

In any case, his mind would not work with the problem right now. It was a refusal, but a different sort of refusal than he had experienced at the Final Encyclopedia before coming here.

That had been a blockage, a painful situation in which he went over the same answers time and again, on each occasion finding them unworkable. This day was a pleasant moment of rest along a route that he now knew to be correct and to run straight to his goal.

But his mind would not wrestle with that problem—or any problem, just now. He put the spindles in their box back where he had found them, the control pad back on Amid's desk, and went out.

Later he was never able to remember, without a great deal of effort, how the rest of that day went for him. In part, he did not really want to investigate the memory, only recall it fondly as a sort of pleasant blur. At any rate, by the time night had fallen and he had at last taken something to eat and drink, he was back, seated in Amid's office in one of its few armless chairs, with a musical instrument in his hands.

The fire was alight in the fireplace and the instrument was someone's reconstruction of a six-string classical Spanish guitar. It was enough like the instrument he had played and sung with on his trips to Port, during the period when he had been a miner on Coby, to suit him.

The guitar had been offered to him, rather shyly, by one of the Guild members, who had said Amanda had suggested he might enjoy having it for a while. Indeed, he did. He wondered what part of the almost occult understanding in Amanda had prompted her to make such a suggestion.

In any case, he had ended up here with it, seated beside the fire in the evening.

The lights were turned down, so that almost the only illumination was from the fireplace itself. He was letting his mind and his fingers wander together, in whatever direction his memory took him, which for the last half hour had been to the ancient ballads and songs out of the past centuries of Old Earth. Songs he had learned there, as a boy, from books and recordings in the library of the estate where he had been brought up.

Amid and Amanda were seated in chairs before him, listening; and so, too, surprisingly, were a number of the members of the Guild, who had slipped in quietly over the past hour or so, taking more distant chairs—so that they were all but lost in the moving shadows cast on the wall by the flames of the fire.

Most surprisingly, among those there was Cee. He had not noticed her entering. He had only become gradually aware of her sitting with Onete in a couple of chairs against a far wall.

Since that first moment when he had discovered her, she had moved closer and closer to him; until now she was seated on the floor, almost at his feet. He had not caught her in movement once. She had made each tiny shift toward him at a time when his eyes were briefly off her, inching toward him, until she was where she was now.

He was careful not to look directly at her. But now it was not necessary. She was near enough so that he could examine her face out of the corner of his eyes. There was no more friendliness showing in it than there had been during the hard trek up the mountainside with Artur on the stretcher—but a great deal of wonder and fascination.

He had drifted off into the singing of old English and Scottish ballads, learned long ago out of the collection made by Childe in the nineteenth century.

How much such songs could mean to Cee, he had no way of imagining. The Basic tongue universally spoken nowadays on all the worlds was a descendant of the English language as it had been spoken during the latter part of the Technological Age, of the twentieth and twenty-first centuries. Its archaic word forms would be a little strange to the young girl, but most of it would still be understandable. Only, what she would make of the medieval Scottish and English accents with which he was pronouncing the words, and with those words which were in dialects now dead and forgotten, he could not guess.

He slid into Sir Walter Scott's Scottish version of *The Battle of Otterburn*, which was a little less loaded with unfamiliar words . . .

> *It fell about the Lammas time,*
> *When the muir-men won their hay,*
> *That the doughty Earl Douglas went*
> *Into England to catch a prey*
>
> *He chose the Gordons and the Graemes,*
> *With them the Lindsays, light and gay.*
> *But the Jardines wadna wi' him ride,*
> *And they rued it to this day.*
>
> *And he has burnt the dales O Tine*
> *And part of Almonshire,*

And three good towers on Roxburgh fells
He has left them all on fire . . .

This time Hal saw her move. It was a small shift, to only slightly closer to him, but the fact that she had allowed herself to be seen moving was enough to show that she had ceased to care about whether or not he would catch her at it. A new light of interest had come into her eyes. Clearly, this one was to be a song about fighting and destruction. Somehow, by chance—or was it by chance, entirely?—he had picked a ballad that particularly woke her interest.

She was motionless now, watching and listening. He continued to study her upturned features. It was a grim little face, in some ways. Again, he was reminded of the similarity between her protective reaction toward Artur, and his own reaction years before in that moment when, as Donal, he had heard of his uncle James's death. Perhaps his development since was an indication of the development to come in her. It was warming to think so.

He wished that there was some way that he could reach her with words, to tell her that the road she had been forced to follow so far need no longer be the way she must go. That he had followed one like it, himself; and, even though he had accomplished all he had set out to do in that direction, it had not brought him to the end he wanted.

But he knew that, even now, though she might listen to and enjoy his singing, she would probably not listen if he tried to talk to her—she would probably not even stay close to him if he tried talking to her. If he could stay here at the Guild for a long enough time for her to grow into the ways of the Guild members, the day might come when she would listen. But he could not stay here, just for that, just for her, no matter how strongly in this moment he might want to reach her with the truth. There were larger tasks calling him away. But his progress with them might in some way be a pledge for hers, into the new human future.

From covert glances around him, he read puzzlement

and some little consternation on the faces of some of the older Guild members there, listening to this story of iron and blood in this place where both by their heritage as Exotics and by their own choosing, they were committed to an attitude of nonviolence.

Just as it was with Cee, it was impossible to explain to them that the proliferating forces of history, conflicting, joining, altering each other's paths, had shown that the human race was not yet free of violence; that the laws, the authorities, the many ways that had tried in the past to end it, had overlooked the stark fact that it was something that must be dealt with inside each individual, herself or himself. And to deal with it, the individual had to understand it.

So he sang on, letting the verses of the ballad recount its version of that dark and bitter encounter between two armies of men; whose only excuse for fighting each other was that they wished to fight, in a place and at a time where neither land, nor anything else but who should win, was at stake.

He sang about how the Earl Douglas, son of the king of Scotland, having ravaged along the border, came at last to Newcastle, the home of Percy, the English Earl of Northumberland. It had been another Percy—called Hotspur—who had been immortalized as a character in one of the plays by Shakespeare.

At Newcastle, the Scottish force had been stopped. For all their numbers, they had had no way to take the fortification that the castle represented. But there was skirmishing just outside it . . .

> . . . *But O how pale his lady lookd,*
> *Frae off the castle wa,*
> *When down before the Scottish spear*
> *She saw brave Percy fa!* . . .

And some symbol—a pennon, a sword, something of symbolic value—was taken from the English to be carried back into Scotland as a trophy; something the Percy swore should not happen. So an appointment was made for the two forces to meet at Otterburn, some distance away in the Cheviot hills, where the Scots would wait for the English. . . .

> . . . they lighted high on Otterburn,
> Upon the bent so brown
> They lighted high on Otterburn,
> And threw their pallions down . . .

And settled in for the night. But during the deepest hours of darkness, an alarm was sounded to the young Earl Douglas.

> . . . . but up then spake a little page,
> Before the break of the dawn.
> 'O waken ye, waken ye, my good lord,
> For Percy's hard at hand!
>
> 'Ye lie, ye lie, ye loud liar,
> Sae loud I hear ye lie!
> The Percy hadna men yestereen
> To dight my men and me . . .

There was a small noise during a second's pause of the guitar's ringing and Hal's voice. The door to the office was opened from the outside as someone came in. But, caught up in recalling the lines of the song, Hal did not look to see who it was. For the next verse was one that had rung, echoed and re-echoed down the years, not only in his own ears but those of many other writers and poets . . .

> . . . but I have seen a dreary dream,
> Beyond the isle of Skye;
> I saw a dead man won the fight,
> And I think that man was I—

He broke off abruptly; and the vibrations of the guitar strings faded away into the silence of the room. For the per-

son who had entered stood cloaked and tall inside the doorway of the room, a darker black shape against the dimness
there; and though he could not see its face, Hal knew who it
was.

So also did Amanda, for she got up quickly, turning to
face the door.

"Forgive me, Guildmaster," said Old Man, slipping
around the figure to stand in front of it, "but this visitor
says he has come a long way to talk privately with Friend."

"Yes," said Amid, and the tone of his voice told Hal that
he, too, had recognized the newcomer. "I'm afraid we'll
have to end the entertainment for the evening. I'd suggest
the rest of you leave now."

"No reason for me to interrupt things," said the deep,
compelling voice of Bleys Ahrens. "I can wait."

"No," said Amid. "If everyone else will please leave?"

"I'll stay," said Amanda. "You might like to stay, too,
Amid."

"I'd prefer to," said Amid. "I have a responsibility to all
that happens here." He looked at Hal. "But I don't want to
intrude?"

There was a touch of humor in Bleys' voice as he threw
back the hood of his cloak and stood, a head and shoulders
above everyone standing around him. "Everyone can stay,
as far as I'm concerned."

But the Guild members were already moving out of the
open door behind the tall man. Only Cee stayed where
she was, ignoring Onete's beckoning. Cee's eyes on
Bleys did not hold the implacable gaze she had turned on
the Occupation force-leader and on Hal; but they held the
steady look of a wild animal ready to attack if it was
approached.

"Stay, Amid," said Hal, setting the guitar aside. "Come
in, Bleys. Sit down."

"Thank you."

He came over and settled himself in the chair directly
opposite. He threw back the rest of his cloak, revealing
himself in dark jacket, trousers and shirt, in every way

unremarkable except for the personality with which he somehow invested these clothes. Amid was still at his desk.

Amanda had moved back, into the fire-thrown shadows over by the exit door. Standing there, she was nearly invisible to those nearer the flames.

"You can come and sit with us, Amanda ap Morgan," said Bleys. "I'm not here to try to do any harm to Hal. He and I know that it'd make no difference to history if either or both of us died. The historical forces are in motion. We're only the aiming point of each side."

"Perhaps. Perhaps not," answered Amanda's voice. "I'll stay here, thanks."

"It's all right, Amanda," Hal said with his eyes unmoving on Bleys, "I don't think he'd try to kill me, here—even if he could."

"Come now," Bleys smiled, "do you think that if I'd come, seriously intending to do away with you, I'd have come at all unless I was sure I could?"

"If you were to try," said Amanda; and her voice had a curious, remote sound, almost an echo to it as if she spoke from a far distance, "you'd never leave this room, yourself, Bleys Ahrens."

"It's really all right, Amanda," said Hal, still without taking his eyes off the man opposite. "I'm safe."

"Perhaps now, if you say so," said Amanda. "Five seconds from now, who knows? I'll stay here."

Bleys shrugged and concentrated on Hal.

"Surprised to see me?" he asked.

"No," said Hal. "Clearly, the pictures taken by that fly-over were studied after all."

"Yes. You didn't really expect to leave the Final Encyclopedia for one of the Younger Worlds without my hearing about it eventually, did you?" said Bleys. "You can't shut off all traffic between the Final Encyclopedia and the surface of Old Earth; and no matter how reliable the people making the trip back and forth, information is going to travel with them. Information leaks; and the leakage reaches me, eventually; since we're always watching you there at Old Earth."

Amid got up from his chair and added a fresh couple of split logs to the fire, which flared up more brightly as the new fuel crashed down among the half-burned wood below it. With the gradual addition of other bodies to the room while Hal had been singing, the temperature had risen in the office; and then, when the door had been opened to let nearly all of them out, cooler air outside had swept in. There was a chill about them, now; and to Hal it felt even as if a breath of coldness had reached out to him from the folds of the cloak Bleys had just flung back.

Hal studied this man, leader of those who called themselves the Others, those who now controlled all that mattered of the Younger Worlds through their powers of persuasion—powers so effective as to seem almost supernatural, and which had set the people of those worlds to the task of conquering Earth.

He had met Bleys in person only at rare intervals in his own life, beginning with the time of the murder of his tutors and his own near capture by Bleys and his gunmen. The last time had been more than three years before, when Hal had first gathered nearly all the people of the Dorsai world, and the wealth and knowledge of the two Exotic ones, safely within the phase-shield Hal had caused the Final Encyclopedia's engineers to set up, enclosing and protecting it, and Earth.

But all those moments of confrontation were etched unforgettably in his memory—and he thought likely in Bleys' as well—for the two of them were oddly alike in many ways; and both had felt those likenesses, as though they might have been close friends if they had not been predestined foes.

So now, he noted the changes in the other man since their last meeting between the two walls of the tunnel opened in the phase-shield to let them meet. For either to have touched the milky whiteness of these walls, then, would have meant being drawn into it and destroyed, the touching body spread out evenly through the physical universe.

The impression of strength and burliness Hal had noticed for the first time then had developed even further in Bleys—even while in appearance Bleys' height and slimness were still the same. He had been almost elegant in that slimness, when Hal had first seen him, at the killing of Hal's tutors. He could not be called "elegant" now.

Instead, a force that was invisible, but very powerful, now radiated from him. It was strong enough that Hal could almost feel it, like the heat from the fire; and it challenged by its mere existence, challenged and attempted to dominate all those about Bleys.

For a long moment Hal was baffled at how such a thing could grow in the man he faced—and then he realized. Each time before that Hal had met Bleys, it had been obvious that the Other possessed great personal power. But the difference now was that he had taken a step further, the ultimate step. He no longer possessed nor controlled power. He *was* power.

Now most of the people of ten Younger Worlds looked and listened to him as if he was, in some way, superhuman. They did not merely obey his commands willingly. They rushed to follow the voice that would send them to die, if necessary, to destroy a Mother World they now believed had never given up an ancient desire to conquer and enslave them—an Old Earth, backed by the black magic of the Final Encyclopedia and ruled by the evil will of an arch-demon named Hal Mayne.

Hal reached for some compensating power within himself, but did not find it. He was not daunted by the strength now in Bleys, and he did not doubt that his mind, his will and imagination, was as strong as the Other's. But he could not feel a similar counterforce in himself. If it was there at all, it was as something entirely different, for all that he stood as Bleys' opposite number, the equal and countering chess piece on the board of History.

At the same time he was grateful that he had not met with Bleys, robed in power and certainty as he was, a couple of months ago when he, Hal, had been at his lowest ebb in the Final Encyclopedia. Or even, that they had not had this meeting before this morning's sudden explosion of understanding in Hal; the revelation that had come as the sun had risen above the mountains and the dewdrop burst into its explosion of light.

As it was, now he looked at Bleys from the viewpoint of eternity and found that which the other possessed to be infinitely small and transitory in that context.

"What brings you?" Hal asked. "You can't really be expecting any change of attitude on my part?"

"Perhaps not." Warmth now flowed from Bleys instead of the push of personal power. He could charm, and he knew it; even though everyone in the office at the moment knew that all but a fraction of his abilities in that respect were composed of hypnotic and other techniques developed by those same Exotics Bleys was now trying to destroy.

"Perhaps not," he said again, "but I've always believed you'd listen to reason; and I have an offer, one you might want to consider."

"Offer?"

"Yes. Let me establish a little background first. One of your tutors, who I most wrongly and mistakenly allowed to be killed—you'll never have forgiven me for that—"

Hal shook his head.

"No," he said, "it's not a matter for forgiveness. I can see now why it happened. At the time though, their murder triggered off the way I'd felt about another, earlier death. So I wanted to destroy you, then; as I'd wanted to destroy whoever was responsible, in that earlier time. It wasn't until I had to live through that sort of loss a second time, with you, that I started to understand retaliation's not the answer. No, forgiveness is beside the point, now. Which changes nothing as far as you and I are concerned."

Hal had seen Bleys' eyes narrow ever so slightly at the

mention of an earlier grief; and felt a touch of annoyance at possibly having betrayed himself to the Other's acute mind. No one could match Bleys in catching and pursuing an incautious slip. But then the annoyance evaporated. There was no way, even with Bleys' own self-developed equivalent of intuitional logic, that the man opposite him now could trace Hal back to the life of Donal Graeme.

"An earlier grief?" echoed Bleys now, softly.

"As I say, it's beside the point now," answered Hal. "What about my tutors?"

"One was a Dorsai. He must have made sure you learned something about military history, as far back as civilization tells us anything about it?"

Hal nodded.

"Did he ever mention a man who lived in the fourteenth century, one of the first military captains, *condottiere* as the Italians named them, named Sir John Hawkwood—"

Hal jumped internally, though he kept his face calm. What sort of black magic in Bleys had made him bring up that, of all names? Then his thoughts calmed. Their minds of necessity ran on parallel tracks toward a mutual end. It was not as unlikely as it might seem that they should both have considered the same historical character in the same short span of time. It could mean nothing at all that Bleys had happened to mention him now. Moreover it was Bleys' way to go at things obliquely. He would hardly have brought up his main purpose in coming, this quickly. Best to wait and see what was behind the mentioning of that name.

"Oh, yes," said Hal.

"I'm not surprised," said Bleys. "A sort of medieval Cletus Grahame, wasn't he?"

"I suppose you could say that. Why?" Hal said.

"There's a story about him—a bit of poisonous gossip, actually; only important really because it could be repeated and believed by some people who didn't know better, even after hundreds of years. I just wondered if you knew it—

about two of his soldiers he was supposed to have found quarreling over a nun they had caught—"

"—and he cut her in half, then said something to the effect that now there was part for each of them?" Hal nodded. "Yes, I know that particular bit of false history."

"I can't understand it." Bleys' tone was close to musing. "You'd think the sheer physical impossibilities involved would be enough to make anyone see through such a story. I suppose the reader is supposed to imagine that this man Hawkwood neatly divided the victim at the waist with one swipe of his sword, then delivered his single line of dialogue to the two soldiers and walked off, leaving them both stunned and deprived. None of those who repeated the story can have had the least experience with butchering animals for food. I had, as a half-grown boy on Harmony; and I boggle at the idea of hacking through that much flesh and backbone with one swipe of a fourteenth century broadsword. Even if the victim cooperated as much as possible by somehow miraculously keeping in place and on her feet until the operation was complete and the soldiers stood by with open mouths, it's humanly impossible. In real life it could have taken him minutes."

"More than a few minutes," said Hal, "given the mild steel of the weapons of that time; and the probable lack of edge left on his sword after whatever fighting they'd all been in. Since it was only with the soldiers drunk and blood mad after taking a city or castle, that even the worst of them would have indulged themselves in such license. But that's the least of such an event happening in real life."

Bleys looked at him amusedly.

"The least?" he asked.

"Yes," said Hal. The knowledge stored in the Final Encyclopedia was coming back to his mind. "Hawkwood isn't called the first of the modern generals for no reason. He was the most businesslike of the early *condottiere*. He knew the people he fought against today might be the people he'd be fighting for tomorrow. So he made sure his men never ruffled the sensitivities of local civilians, except under the conditions of outright war. That was one of the reasons for his success; apart from the sensitivities other elements of his life show. He kept a strict discipline over his hired soldiers; and hanged any one of them caught infringing even minor local laws."

"But of course," said Bleys, "as you say this must have happened during the sacking and looting of a just conquered city."

"In which case he wouldn't have been present at such an incident at all," said Hal. The memory of *being* Hawkwood as he walked in the circle had come to life again in his head. "He was a man of the fourteenth century and a combat professional. His actions and letters don't show him as the type of man who'd do anything as ridiculous as what that story has him doing; any more than a present day Dorsai would slaughter or torture prisoners."

The dry note in Hal's voice had not been enough to hide the emotion underneath. To his annoyance once more with himself, he saw Bleys had been quick to hear it.

"Torture and slaughter were involved in that earlier grief of yours, you mentioned?"

"No," said Hal.

Torture had had no part in the death of James. But evoked now by Bleys' acute question, the memory of Donal's older brother Mor, dead after torture at the hands of the deranged William of Ceta, had come inevitably back to mind. It was a memory he, Donal, should have foreseen arising out of any discussion with Bleys such as he was having now. He had been too deep in the wood to watch out for all the trees. He would never be able to escape the knowledge that he had been at least partly responsible for Mor's hideous death.

"In any case," he interrupted his own thoughts now, "Hawkwood wouldn't have been there in the city at that time under any circumstances."

"Perhaps you'll tell me why not." Bleys smiled. "As you know, my own military education is limited."

"I wouldn't have thought so," said Hal. "But, if you want me to spell out what might have happened—after months of besieging a city, after inaction and boredom, living for weeks on end in the mud and stinks of their lines, with a shortage of food and drink from a surrounding countryside, scoured clean of supplies so that they were almost as starved as the people in the city, the attitudes of the besiegers became as savage as the attitudes of wild animals toward the besieged. One hour after the city was taken, the rank and file of soldiers conquering it would have been roaring drunk and blood mad, on whatever wine or other drink they had managed to loot."

"Yes," Bleys nodded. "That sounds like the human animal I know. What was there to say that their commanders weren't equally drunk and mad among them?"

"The fact that when it was all over, in a day or two, those commanders would need to lead these drunken madmen again, as sober and obedient soldiers," said Hal. "But they waited until the drink was gone, the raping and looting was over, and the hangovers had taken charge, before they tried it. Raging wild in the conquered city, any of the troops, even the most loyal and trustworthy, were as likely to turn on their commander as sharks in a feeding frenzy. One of the earliest things a military leader learns, even today, is never give his subordinates an order they might not obey. So the medieval leaders stayed well outside wherever the looting and such was going on after a taking. They couldn't change what was going on in any case—"

He broke off suddenly.

"So," he said. His eyes looked directly into Bleys'. "It was a possible sacking of Earth you came to talk to me about."

"That's right," answered Bleys. "Don't tell me you haven't thought of that possibility; once—as it's bound to, eventually—the number of ships we can put into an attack is such they can make a simultaneous jump through the shield and smother any resistance, even that of your Dorsai. This, too, is a siege; and the same sort of attitude we've been talking about is developing on my side of the phase wall."

He paused.

"I'm willing to do whatever's necessary to put the human race back where it belongs, on Old Earth, for a few thousand years until it's had time to mature properly," he said. "But I don't like blood baths either; so I thought we should talk."

And he smiled at Hal.

CHAPTER 33 ■

Hal sat looking at Bleys for a moment.

"The crew and officers on your spaceships on patrol outside the shield," he said, "don't live in trenches or dugouts. They aren't sick, or starving. In fact, I'll venture to bet they eat better than their friends back on the home worlds they came from. If they're developing a siege mentality, perhaps it's because you've fed them full on the idea that the people living on Old Earth nowadays are something subhuman, that the Final Encyclopedia is an invention of the Devil, manned by devils, and I'm the chief devil of them all. It seems to me that an effort on your part put to taking those ideas out of their minds would also prevent any chance of a blood bath."

"Probably," said Bleys quietly, "but I'm not going to do that. And since I'm not—you'll admit you've considered the danger of such a blood bath?"

Before Hal could answer, he went on.

"Forgive me. That was an insulting question. Of course, you've considered all the possibilities, just as I have."

"Speculations waste time," said Hal. "You came here to make me some kind of offer. Make it."

"I'd like to call off the war," said Bleys.

"I'll be damned!" Hal said.

"Will you indeed?" answered Bleys. "In that case, try to get word back to me what it's like. No one's ever been able to send any messages back so far; but you might just be able to do it."

Hal hardly heard him. He told himself no one but the Other man could have startled him to this extent. For a moment he even found himself wondering if he had been wrong all along and that Bleys was far superior even to him after all; that the Other could read minds and see around corners. How else could he explain this sudden offer that would concede defeat just as Hal was about to move closer than he ever had been to winning the contest between them? Unless Bleys had somehow sensed Hal's breakthrough of just that morning?

Amid moved a little, involuntarily, in his chair; but no sound came from Amanda, all but invisible in the shadows by the door; and Hal did not move. In the fireplace a burned through log broke and fell into two halves with a soft crash; and the flames shot up above it suddenly, sending shadows dancing on the wall beyond Hal and Bleys.

Hal pulled himself together. There was a price, of course—some impossible price.

"In return for what?" demanded Hal bluntly.

"Well, you'll take down the phase-shield, of course," said Bleys. "And we'd want to settle some of the Younger Worlds' people on presently unused areas of Old Earth." He sat back comfortably in his chair. "There're tundra areas at both poles and sections of desert that Old Earth's ignored ever since its population stabilized, following the wave of immigration to the Younger Worlds nearly three hundred years ago. You see, I'm willing to leave the dispute between us, you and I, to the verdict of future history, without any use of weapons."

"Are you?" said Hal. "You know better than to think I

don't know what kind of Younger Worlds people you'd settle there. Their colonies would be enclaves, from which your colonists could work to convert as many as could be, of Earth's own people, to your way of thinking. The end result would be an Earth torn by a division of opinion—and ultimately a worldwide civil war—as much of a blood bath as the invasion you talk about. Why do you suppose I was instrumental in having the shield wall put up in the first place?"

"Instrumental's hardly the word," said Bleys. "The shield wall was all your doing. But think about it."

"There's no need," said Hal. "Old Earth's awakened to its danger now. It's building ships and training crews for them, with Dorsai help, in greater numbers all the time; and potentially it's still got more resources in materials, manufacturing and people than all the Younger Worlds combined. Let alone the fact it hasn't light-years of lines of communication to maintain support for its fighting ships."

"Yes," said Bleys, "what you say's all true, Earth's building faster all the time—but I think not fast enough. I think the Younger Worlds have too much of a head start. We'll be ready to come through the wall before you're ready to hold us off, let alone drive us away."

He stopped talking. Hal had made no effort to interrupt him and continued to say nothing, now.

"You disagree, of course," said Bleys, "or perhaps you don't. In any case, I've made the offer. You've no choice but to consider it."

"And I've told you," answered Hal, "what you know as well as I do. What would happen if Earth let you colonize like that."

Bleys nodded.

"But you know," he said, "that while you and I may ride the winds of history, we're not just completely helpless passengers. Of course what you say is right. But the result of those colonies moving in doesn't have to be what you suggest. Perhaps you can let them in and still bend the winds to your advantage. It's possible."

"Possible, not probable. What you suggest is a road downhill to what you want. But for we who want something else, all roads would be uphill if I agreed."

"The alternative's invasion and the blood bath—very soon now."

It was true, thought Hal, even if the invasion Bleys talked of was not likely to come quite as soon as he implied. It was also true, unfortunately, that there was an element of truth in what Bleys offered. It was possible Old Earth could absorb the enclaves Bleys suggested, without war, and the future be settled that way.

But—Hal felt an echo of the same uneasiness he had told Bleys he had felt three years before when they had been face to face in the phase-shield. The feeling nagged at Hal that if Bleys got what he asked for, somehow the road to the Creative Universe that he now thought he saw so plainly before him would be blocked as surely as it would be by Tam's death, unless he found the entrance to it before then. Should Hal reject this now—that might be the answer for everyone now alive—in a gamble on what he might be able to do for them and all generations to come?

He knew which choice he wanted.

"Maybe you're right and it would work," he said to Bleys slowly, "but I was never one for shaking hands with the Devil."

"I thought," Bleys said, "you *were* the Devil, the Chief Devil?"

"Only according to your doxology," said Hal.

"But in any case," Bleys smiled, "what'll you tell Old Earth, when the people there learn they had a chance to be free of the phase-shield and the warships of the Younger Worlds, but you turned it down?"

"That'll depend on whether you actually make such an offer officially and publicly," said Hal. He smiled back. "There's nothing official about me, outside the Final Encyclopedia. You'd need to make your proposal formally from the United Younger Worlds to the Consortium of Old

Earth governments—and give them time to consider it. In the end, you may decide not to make the proposal, after all."

"Oh?" said Bleys. He sounded genuinely intrigued. "You think so? Why?"

Hal kept his own smile.

"Wait and see," he said. "The pattern of the historic forces changes constantly. You know that as well as I do."

"I do, indeed," said Bleys softly. He hesitated for a moment. "I think you're bluffing."

"Try me and see," said Hal.

"Yes." Bleys nodded. "I'll do that."

He had looked away from Hal and at the fire, musingly for a second. Now he looked back.

"Tell me," he said to Hal, "the last time we met, why didn't you carry through? Why didn't you move to resolve what's between us two, at our last meeting? I'd expected that to be the moment of our confrontation. You'd undeniably stolen a march on me. You'd gotten all the people you valued and needed safely hidden behind that phase-shield you'd had built around Old Earth; before I could sweep them up, one by one, or group by group, from their native worlds. When I met you in the wall of the phase-shield, itself, we were at a moment in time when you had a definite advantage. Why didn't you push for a conclusion then?"

Hal remembered again how at that particular last meeting he had noticed how Bleys had become more physically powerful in appearance, how he had put on weight in the form of compact muscle. He and the Other had been about the same height since Hal had come into his growth—that had been the original height of Hal's uncles. Ian and Kensie, Bleys had always been an unusually tall man. But when Hal had first seen him, there had been none of the evidence of physical strength that was part of him now.

Now, Bleys had apparently deliberately built himself up to match Hal. It dawned on Hal that the Other man must have put in an incredible number of hours physically developing and training himself for every possible kind of hand-to-hand conflict, with or without weapons. This, because the extra strength by itself would be only a part of making himself a physical match for Hal. Therefore he had, for his own reasons, been looking forward even at that meeting in the phase-shield wall, to possible conflict on that level with Hal.

But, even as he realized this, Hal also realized that what Bleys had tried was impossible. No adult could possibly train himself to the point of physically matching a Dorsai of comparable size, age, reflexes and ability, who had been trained from the cradle upward.

Only then did Hal remember, once more, that he now was no match for such a Dorsai either. All his physical training as Hal Mayne had been some of the tutoring from only one of his tutors, as a child of Old Earth; and even that had been a long time ago. He had tried to keep himself in shape since, helped by an active life at times, such as when he had been a miner on Coby, or a member of Rukh's Resistance band on Harmony; but that didn't make him a Dorsai. Recognition and realization took place in his mind in barely the time it took him to start answering.

"You come at an interesting time to ask me that," he answered. "Maybe it isn't so surprising though. Many of the historic forces that move you parallel those that move me, and it's natural that we'd come together under coincidental conditions."

"But you didn't answer my question," said Bleys, his eyes steady on Hal.

"That's why I say you come at an interesting time," said Hal. "If I'd had to answer you then, there in the phase-shield, I wouldn't have been able to. All I knew then was that I noticed that you were ready for a showdown; and instinct told me to back off from it. I felt—you'd have to call it an uneasiness about accepting any try to settle things there and then. Now I understand why. What I'd realized unconsciously was, as I told you then, that you couldn't win. But, as I later realized, if I agreed to the confrontation, then and there, neither could I."

"I don't follow you," said Bleys.

"I mean I believe. I would've won that contest," answered Hal. "But either of us could have; and, I'll give you this, you might have won after all. We were at a point where, with one of us gone, the other would have had an advantage. Pressed home, that advantage might have given a seeming victory."

"*Seeming*, only?" Bleys' voice was pleasantly curious.

"Yes," answered Hal. "Seeming only; because we'd merely be once more repeating a cycle of time-worn history. I learned a long time ago that even having all possible power over all the worlds doesn't make you able to change human nature; and it's that that's been the point of argument between us from the beginning, whether the individual human's nature is going to be changed or not. If I'd won I'd have gained a victory; but it'd have been only a partial victory. As, if you'd won, you'd have had only a partial victory. And the problem with any partial victory for either of us was that final victory, the ultimate victory, would've been closed off from the survivor, forever, or at least until some later generation should create the confrontation once again; and in that future time be wiser in its decision. So I chose to leave things at stalemate so that I could try for the greater victory, in my own time."

As I do again now, he thought to himself. It's the same uneasiness, the same decision.

"Did you?" said Bleys. "And, do you see your way to it now?"

Hal smiled.

"If I've found the answer," he said, "it's there for everyone. Go find it for yourself."

Bleys looked at him for a long second. It was strange to see Bleys Ahrens pause like this. He must have done so only at very rare moments in his life.

"So," he said at last, "not this time, either. But I think I'll do what you say and find whatever you say you've found, for myself. And I'll meet you at the end of the road, wherever that is. Look for me there when you reach it."

His voice softened suddenly.

"Stop the little girl," he said.

But Amanda had already been in movement. Her hand closed now over Cee's just as Cee's fingers closed on the glass paperweight containing the miniature pine cone, on Amid's desk, Amanda pried it loose from Cee's grasp. Cee struggled, silently if fiercely, to hold on to it; but her strength was no match for an adult's. Amanda came away with the paperweight.

"We don't kill people," Amanda told her. "Ever."

Cee's eyes held Amanda's and the small face was unreadable.

"She's decided you're dangerous," Amanda told Bleys. "Don't ask me exactly why. Smelled it in you, possibly, and I can't really blame her. She's right."

She turned her attention on Cee again.

"But we don't kill people," she repeated to the girl. "*You* don't kill people. Leave this man to those who know how to deal with him; like Friend, here."

Bleys was frowning at Cee.

"You don't actually mean," he said to Amanda, "she's that dangerous?"

"Yes." Amanda still held Cee unwaveringly with her gaze. "Men sent here by you made her that way. Ask your four dead Occupation soldiers—if you can talk to ghosts."

"Well . . . " said Bleys thoughtfully.

He stayed for a moment where he was, facing Hal. He rose, and Hal rose across from him. They stood close as brothers, two tall men under the close, dark ceiling of Amid's office.

"Well, I've made my offer." Bleys pulled his cloak closed again around him, and its dark folds swirled and flashed for a second in the firelight. "I'll leave you with it. You might be kind enough to send someone with me to light me down the mountainside path, so I don't go in the wrong direction and fall off a cliff. From the upper side of that stone at the bottom that closes the path, he can easily roll it back into place alone. It's only opening it from below that's a hard job for one man."

He looked over at Amid.

"Don't worry," he said. "I'll keep the secret of this place of yours, here, and any of the Occupation Army that's tempted to explore in this direction will find orders disapproving such a move after the pronounced nonsuccess of the late force-leader and his equally late groupman. You can go on living up here in peace."

He turned back to Hal.

"But they're lucky they had you with them."

"I didn't kill those soldiers," Hal said.

"So you're giving me to understand," Bleys' eyebrows raised. "This child did it for you. I find that a little hard to believe."

"It's true," said Hal.

Bleys laughed.

"If you say so."

"You see," Hal said, "you're making a mistake. Here, where you're standing, is the cradle of the new breed of Exotics. Exotics who'll be nowhere near as vulnerable to you as they've been in the past."

"If they can kill soldiers, perhaps you're right," said Bleys. "But I'm not particularly worried. I don't think this place and its people have very long to survive, even without a hand being raised against them. Now, what about that guide to light me on my way?"

"You must have rolled the entrance stone aside from below," said Amid suddenly. "How could you do it, alone?"

Bleys glanced at Hal.

"How about you?" he asked. "Are you surprised, too? No, you wouldn't be, would you? You could do it yourself. You know that there're ways of concentrating your strength. Have been ever since the first caveman lifted a fallen tree he shouldn't have been able to move, off a hunting companion in a moment of frenzy he didn't think he had in him. But you might not have thought of me before now as being equal to you, physically. I am, though. I think, in fact, we're just about equal in nearly all respects; though that's something neither of us will be able to check."

"If there is, it'll show at the end," said Hal.

"Yes," said Bleys, more quietly than he had spoken until this moment, "at the end. Where's that guide?"

"I have called for Onete to get someone," said Amid. "Here she comes now."

In fact, the door was opening, and Onete came in through it, followed by Old Man, carrying a powerful fueled lamp, already lit.

"Then too," said Bleys thoughtfully, looking at the slim, white-bearded man waiting by the open door, "there might be those about whom there could be a legitimate doubt if they could roll the stone back alone, even from the top side."

Old Man's eyes twinkled back at him.

"Then, perhaps not," said Bleys, striding toward the door. "Lead on, my guide."

Old Man stood aside to let the Other pass through the door first; then went out himself, closing it behind him. Amanda came forward to the fireplace so that she was together with the seated Amid and the still standing Hal.

"You frightened me," said Amid to Hal, "when you told him that this ledge was the cradle of the new breed of Exotics, and right after he'd promised to keep our being here a secret! Do you think he was telling the truth about leaving us in peace?"

"Bleys feels himself above ever having to lie," answered Hal. "But I'm sorry you were frightened. I wasn't just being thoughtless enough to raise a doubt in his mind; I was actually confirming his original notion you were harmless."

Amid's already wrinkled brow wrinkled more deeply in a frown.

"I don't understand," he said.

"He's a fanatic," said Amanda. "You know his background, surely? You Exotics must have looked into his background. His mother was one of your people."

Amid nodded.

"It's true she was an Exotic," said Amid. "But she turned away from us. If we were a religious people, you might have said she was an apostate."

"She was brilliant, and knew it," said Amanda. "But not brilliant enough to gain control of all the Younger Worlds, the way Donal Graeme effectively did, back in his time; and fate had caused her to be born into the one Splinter Culture whose people were best equipped to resist manipulation by her."

"Yes," said Amid, with a sigh, "at any rate she left us and went to Ceta."

"Yes," said Amanda, "and it was on Ceta, later on, Bleys was born. He's never known who his father was. Actually he was from Harmony. An unhappy older man she seduced merely to see how easily she could do it. But I think she really wanted to believe she was the only one responsible for Bleys; because almost from the day he was born it was plain he had everything in the way of abilities that his mother had liked to think she had herself, but hadn't. So she started cramming him full of knowledge from the time he was old enough to talk; and he was well on his way to being what he is now at only nine years of age, when she suddenly died. Possibly he was responsible for that. He could have been. She'd left directions that if anything happened to her he was to go to his uncle on Harmony. Do you know that part of his history?"

"Not all of it," said Amid. "When we looked into Bleys' background, years later, we found out about his mother. She had no Friendly genes in either the maternal or paternal lines of her ancestry. But the man—the Friendly on Harmony he was sent to grow up with—couldn't have been Bleys' uncle! A cousin, a number of times removed, at most."

"Well, she called him an uncle and the boy was taught to

call him 'uncle.' In any case he was a farmer with a large family; and a fanatic, rather than a true faith-holder. He raised all his children to be fanatics like himself. Some of what Bleys is he caught from that man. Though I don't suppose it was more than a week or two after he got there that the nine-year-old Bleys was controlling that whole family, whether they knew it or not. He controlled them; but his 'uncle,' or all of them, infected him with their fanaticism all the same."

"It's not easy to tell the difference between a fanatic and what you call a true faith-holder—particularly when you call them so, Hal," said Amid, looking from Amanda to him. "I'd hate to think we simply use the word fanatic for anyone whose views we disagree with."

"There's almost no difference in any case," answered Hal, "between a fanatic and someone of pure faith, though what difference there is makes all the difference, once you get to know them. Basically, they differ in the fact a faith-holder puts himself below his faith and lets it guide his actions. The fanatic puts himself above it and uses it as an excuse for his actions. But for practical purposes, the two are almost identical. The fanatic will die for what he believes in as readily as a man or woman of faith. . . ."

There came back to him a memory of a man who had been a fanatic and tortured Rukh Tamani close to death; but who now served her among the most loyal of her followers and was a faith-holder. Amyth Barbage had been an officer of the Militia that harried and tried to destroy such Resistance Groups as Rukh's on both Harmony and its sister Friendly world of Association.

He and James Child-of-God, Rukh's second-in-command of the Resistance Group, would have seemed, to anyone who did not know them intimately, to have been cut from the same bolt of cloth. Both men were harsh and uncompromising both in attitude and appearance—except that Child-of-God was old enough to be Barbage's father. Both spoke an archaic, "canting" version of Basic, full of "thee's" and "thou's." Both put what they thought of as their faith before all other things. But Barbage had been a fanatic.

James Child-of-God had been a true faith-holder. He had spent his life fighting against the Militia that the Others had found so useful and put to their own purposes; and he died, alone, behind a small barricade in the rain, deliberately giving his life to slow up the Militia companies that were close on the heels of what had by then become a sick and exhausted Resistance Group, driven by the relentless pursuit of a Barbage who had unlimited troops and supplies at his disposal.

To this day, Hal could not remember lightly his final moments alone with Child-of-God, before he had left the old man to his final battle in the rain with the foe he had opposed so long. Always the memory tightened Hal's throat painfully. On the other hand, the memory of Barbage that had just come to mind was of an entirely different nature, but showed the same kind of utter dedication to a purpose.

This other memory was of a somewhat earlier time when the Group was being closely pursued through a territory of dense woods by Barbage and the Militia Companies stationed in one of the local Districts through which the Group had been fleeing; and Hal, because of his training as a boy under a Dorsai, had been the best choice to try and slip back quietly to spy on their pursuers. He had silently backtracked and come upon the pursuing companies, temporarily halted for a meeting of their officers. He had worked his way close enough to hear them, coming within earshot at a point where the superior officer of the Companies had gotten himself into a confrontation with the knife-lean, relentless-eyed Barbage, who had apparently been sent out from Militia Headquarters and made into what he was by Bleys' direct personal influence. The scene was suddenly there, now, as he thought of it, in his mind's eye . . .

". . . yes, I say it to thee," Amyth Barbage had been saying in his hard tenor voice to the Commandant of the Mili-

tia, who was a Captain, as Barbage was himself. Hal moved closer behind a small screen of slim variform willows. Barbage was on his feet. The other, junior, officers of the Militia had all been sitting with the Captain himself in a row on a fallen log, between the two men, with the other Captain seated at the far end of their line. "I have been given a commission by authority far above thee, and beyond that by the Great Teacher, Bleys Ahrens himself; and if I say to thee, go—thou wilt go!"

The other Captain had looked upward and across at Barbage with a tightly closed jaw. He was a man perhaps five years younger than Barbage, no more than midway into his thirties, but his face was square and heavy with oncoming middle age, and his neck was thick.

"I've seen your orders," *he said. His voice was not hoarse, but thick in his throat—a parade-ground voice.* "They don't say anything about pursuing over district borders."

"Thou toy man!" *said Barbage; and his voice was harsh with contempt.* "What is it to me how such as thou read orders? I know the will of those who sent me; and I order thee, that thou pursuest how and where I tell thee to pursue!"

The other captain had risen from the log, his face gone pale with anger. The sun glinted on the forward-facing oval end of the butt of the power pistol sheltered under the snapped down weather flap of the holster at his belt. Barbage wore no pistol.

"You may have orders!" *he said, even more thickly.* "But you don't outrank me and there's nothing that says I have to take that sort of language from you. So watch what you say or pick yourself a weapon. I don't care either way."

Barbage's thin upper lip curled slightly.

"Weapon? What Baal's pride is this to think that in the Lord's work thou mightest be worthy of affront? Unlike thee, I have no such playthings as weapons. Only tools which the Lord has made available to my hand as I have needed them. So, thou hast something called a weapon, then? No doubt that which I see on thy side, there. Make use of it, therefore, since thou didst not like the name I gave thee!"

The Captain flushed.

"You're unarmed," he said shortly.

"Oh, let that not stop thee," said Barbage ironically. "For the servants of the Lord, tools are ever ready to hand."

He made one long step while the other man stared at him, to end standing beside the most junior of the officers sitting on the log. He laid his hand on the snapped-down weather flap of the young officer's power pistol and flicked the flap up with his thumbnail. His hand curled around the suddenly exposed butt of the power pistol beneath. A twist of the wrist would be all that would be needed to bring the gun out of its breakaway holster and fire it; while the other Captain would have needed to reach for and uncover his own pistol first before he could fire.

From the far end of the log the Captain stared, his heavy face suddenly even more pale and mouth open foolishly.

"I meant . . ." The words stumbled on his tongue. "Not like this. A proper meeting, with seconds—"

"Alas," said Barbage, "such games are unfamiliar to me. So I will kill thee now to decide whether we continue or turn back from our pursuit, since thou hast not chosen to obey my orders—unless thou shouldst kill me first to prove thy right to do as thou wishest. That is how thou wouldst do things, with thy weapons, and thy meetings and thy seconds, is it not?"

He paused, but the other did not answer.

"Very well then," said Barbage. He drew the power pistol from the holster of the junior officer and leveled it at his equal in rank.

"In the Lord's name—" broke out the other man

hoarsely. "Have it any way you want. We'll go on then, over the border!"

"I am happy to hear thee decide so," said Barbage. He replaced the pistol in the holster from which he had withdrawn it and stepped away from the young officer who owned it. "We will continue until we make contact with the pursuit unit sent out from the next District, at which time I will join them and thou, with thy officers and men, mayest go back to thy small games in town. That should be soon. When are the troops from the next District to meet us? . . ."

"The fact that the goal he works for is wrong won't slow Bleys down," Hal said now to Amid. "He'll do what's necessary to accomplish what he wants; just as I will. It's not the goal, but his belief that's important; and that's as strong as if his faith was as right as anyone's ever was."

Amid nodded slowly.

"I see," he said.

"But the fact that he's found me here changes things for me, personally," went on Hal. "I'm afraid I'd better be getting back to Earth and the Final Encyclopedia pretty soon, now."

"Not just pretty soon," said Amanda. "Immediately. Now."

Hal turned to her.

"You've been here all this time and you're only saying it now?" he demanded.

"She's only saying it to you," Amid said. "She told me the minute she arrived, but you were down in the forest busy rescuing Artur and Cee at the time. Since you've come back, you were first, dead for sleep, then sometime early this morning you seem to have had a revelation or discovery of some kind—and none of us wanted to disturb you until you were ready to be disturbed. What had touched you may have been too important for the future of all of us to be damaged by intrusion."

Hal sighed, and nodded.

"Yes," he said. "Actually, the fault's mine. I should have asked Amanda for news, the minute I saw her, last night."

"You were in no shape—last night," said Amanda, "to ask, or hear."

He smiled a little.

"Perhaps," he said. "What happened to me at sunrise this morning might have been blocked off by whatever news you've brought that makes it necessary I go back immediately. But I don't think so. I was deaf and dumb with tiredness, though; I'll grant you that. At any rate, now that sunrise and Bleys are both past—what is it?"

"It's for your ears only," said Amanda, "all I've told Amid was that you'd have to leave right away. Actually, that's all you ought to need to know yourself, to get moving. I'll tell you as we go."

CHAPTER 34 ■

They were well down into the forest and headed away from the direction that would have taken them back to the town of Porphyry and still Amanda had not brought up what she had promised to tell him as they went, whatever it was that was "for his ears only."

"No doubt," said Hal, at length, "you had a good reason for not letting me know up there why I had to leave in a hurry; but we're well away, now, and I'd still like to hear."

"I'm sorry." She was walking along, staring at the ground ahead of them a little ways off, and he realized she was *frowning*. "The fact is, I could have let you know long before this. But I've had my head full of the problems involved."

"Bad news of some kind?" asked Hal.

"Yes, but . . ." Amanda hesitated, then her voice picked up briskly. "In a word, Tam's sent you a message."

Hal stopped. She stopped also and they turned to face each other.

"A message?" Hal repeated. "He's hardly got the strength—"

"It's one word, only," said Amanda. "The word is *'tired.'* "

Hal nodded slowly.

"I see," he said softly. He turned and began walking on again automatically in the direction they had already been headed. Amanda went with him.

"Yes," she answered. "He said it to Rukh at a moment when she was alone with him. Ajela had been called out of his quarters for a second. He knew Rukh would understand and pass on the word to me, and I'd get it to you."

Hal nodded.

"It was bound to be," he said, on a long exhalation of breath. "He held on as long as he could—for my sake. There's still nothing wrong with him physically?"

"You needn't ask that," said Amanda. "Medical science using the Final Encyclopedia could keep his body from ever breaking down. It's his mind that's had too many years. That's—"

"I know," said Hal, "there's more to living than a body that'll go on forever. He's weary of life itself. But he's been holding on . . ."

"Rukh thinks, and I'm sure she's right," said Amanda, "that he sent the message because he can't last much longer, though no doubt he's going to try until you get back to see him one more time. If he'd had the life energy for just a few more words she's sure that's what he would have said."

Hal nodded.

"Yes, he would have," he said. "How'd the word reach you?"

"Rukh sent a courier ship to orbit at a distance around this world until it could contact us. Its driver knew approximately how far off-surface Simon's ship would be orbiting, waiting for us. He found Simon, told him, and Simon signaled me. I've got a system of signals that involves things like you saw our first day here after Simon dropped us off—the white cloth I spread out on the tops of bushes where his viewer could spot it from orbit. In this case, Simon sent down a small capsule under power with the message to a spot which he knew I check regularly for word from him. I signaled back. We'll be at a point where he can pick us up in just a few minutes—he'll be tracking us right now from orbit."

"Good." Hal nodded. "And he should have us back to Earth in a couple of days, ship time."

"Or less," said Amanda. "We'll make it in as few shifts as possible—shave right down the probability line of enough error to lose us among the stars on the way there—unless you've got some reason not to."

"No."

Hal lifted his head and squared his shoulders.

"Well, at any rate, I've got something to tell Tam, when I see him." He paused, then went on, "I might still be able to give him what he wants, in time; enough fro him to let go with an easy conscience."

"You see why I didn't dare break the news to you, even in front of Amid? To too many people, on too many worlds, Tam Olyn's a symbol of hope even bigger than the conflict between you and Bleys."

"It's not a personal conflict," said Hal gently.

"I know. Forgive me," she said. "I put it badly. But there're too many people who may start to lose the one hope they've hung on to, ever since the Others took over completely on the Younger Worlds. Even there—Bleys' propaganda about you and everything else hasn't been able to shake their hope in Tam. If they think he's close to being gone, now, with nothing found, the heart could go out of a lot of them. That could have been a reason behind Bley's offer, just now. As long as Tam was still alive, they could hope for a miracle that'd set everything right."

"They can still hope for one," said Hal.

"But who's to convince them of that?" said Amanda. "Bleys has done too good a job of blackening your reputation for them to believe in your word alone; and there's no one else of comparable stature."

"There's Ajela."

"Who really thinks much, or even knows much of her, outside of Earth?" asked Amanda. "Besides, she's the second problem, not the solution—here we are."

They had reached a natural opening in the forest, something that on another world, with a different sort of groundcover from the creeping ground vines of Mara at this altitude, would have been called a meadow.

"Simon should be here inside an hour—maybe even in minutes, now," she said.

She stopped at the edge of the open area and Hal stopped with her. He studied her face in profile.

"Why did you say 'the second problem'?" he asked.

She turned to face him.

"Tam's going to die," Amanda said. "Don't you realize what that means in the case of Ajela?"

"Oh," said Hal, "of course."

"More 'of course' than I think you realize," said Amanda "With Tam's death Ajela's going to collapse; and as things stand she's the working executive head of Earth. Who's to fill in for her until she can take control again, and how can we handle things while keeping Tam's death a secret?"

"You're right," Hal answered. "I thought about that a little while I was up on the ledge."

"You've had your own search to occupy you. But now, I think maybe you should set that aside for a moment. Hal, you know everybody's done all each one of them could to leave you free to search for the answer you were the only one able to find—"

"Including you taking yourself off to risk your life daily on worlds the Others held in the palms of their hands, just to keep yourself out of my reach?"

"Not just to keep myself out of your reach," she said swiftly. "This work I do is too badly needed to be taken on as just an excuse. But at the same time, your search *is* something you have to do on your own. We all know that. If I was around, I'd be a distraction to you, whether you wanted me to be or not."

Their eyes met.

"I'm one of time's soldiers, too, Hal," she said, "and it was my duty to be elsewhere."

"And what if it's to be we never have time for ourselves?" Hal asked softly.

"You asked me that before. We will," she answered. Her eyes still held his steadily. "We will. I promise you."

An unreasonable happiness leaped up in him, but just at that moment the air quivered about them like soundless thunder, felt not heard, and they both looked up. A dot was flashing down out of the sky toward them in jumps, growing with each jump more into a visible shape, and nearer. It was Simon Graeme doing what the Dorsai did as a matter of course, but few pilots from other worlds would risk—phase-shifting down to almost the very surface of a world, so as to avoid any but the briefest sound of a ship coming through the atmosphere to a landing.

"We'll talk more—later," said Hal hastily.

"Yes, we will," she answered; as with a sudden brief explosion of displaced air and atmospheric motors, the courier ship landed in the open area less than fifty meters from where they stood.

They went forward, but the entry port sung open before they had reached it and Simon looked out. He gripped Hal's hand briefly as they came aboard, and punched the key that closed the port behind them.

"We'll have to move fast," he said. "There're more Younger World ships in orbit than I've seen here before;

and that courier from Earth coming out to contact me was noticed. Find your seats, strap in, and we'll lose ourselves outside Procyon's orbit as soon as possible . . ."

It was almost two days, after all, before they reached safely through the phase-shield and landed inside the Final Encyclopedia. Simon and Amanda had taken turns driving the ship, so that the next shift to be calculated was always being worked on even as they were making the current jump. So abrupt had been their departure that they had left with nothing but the clothes they had on—in Hal's case, some gray trousers and a light blue shirt that had been made for him at the Chantry Guild. In Amanda's case, they were her standard bush clothes for travel out of sight of the local military; boots, trousers and jacket, both of khaki twill, the shirt with a number of pockets.

Rukh, who was waiting for them in the docking area at the entrance to an access corridor as they stepped out of the parked ship, showed no interest in how they were dressed. She herself was looking unusually, almost ominously formal, in a long black skirt and high-collared white blouse, with her usual lone adornment the steel neckchain with its pendant granite disk incised with a cross, showing in the collar's short opening, in front.

"Hal!" she said.

She hugged him. There was still a remarkable strength in her thin arms. She had seemed made of monocellular cord and steel when he had first known her as a commander of her Resistance Group on Harmony. Now, she felt so light as to be almost weightless in his arms; but he thought now that there was part of that original strength, which had survived the attrition of the days and nights of torture in the Militia cell; and the glow of her faith, which never failed to seem to set her aglow from within. For a second, holding her, he thought he touched the reason she had been so easily able to accept Barbage, her former torturer, as now one of her most dedicated followers. It was not as if she had merely forgiven him. It was something greater than that. It was as if her faith allowed her to understand how he could have been what he was then, and yet suddenly become what he was now. So that there was no need for forgiveness on her side, or need to ask for it, on his.

But she was striding ahead of them now, drawing away from them in spite of the fact that his legs and Amanda's were so much longer than hers.

"Hurry!" she said. "We've got his quarters right next to the docking area, expecting you."

And indeed, it was only some thirty meters down the silent, green-carpeted hallway between the dark-paneled walls to the single door at the corridor's end; and she led them through into the rooms of Tam Olyn. The mechanical magic, which could shift areas around within its shell, at will, had brought Tam as close to their arrival point as possible.

They stepped into the familiar main room, which had been designed long since at Tam's order to look like a woodland glade on Old Earth, the trees barring sight of the walls surrounding giving the illusion of the outdoors on the world below—an illusion reinforced by the small stream wandering down the center of it, among the massively overstuffed easy chairs that were scattered around what seemed to be the grass of a tiny meadow. Two people were already there. One was Ajela. She was seated, holding one of Tam's veined hands in both of hers, as he occupied the chair opposite.

Tam sat with the utter motionlessness of extreme old age. He was dressed as if for the day's work, in a business suit of the sort he had worn all his life. If the heavy cloak, red and white on one side and with a dark inner lining, of an interplanetary journalist had been added, there would have been no difference in his dress now from the time when he had been just such a newsman, with no plan to ever set foot in the Final Encyclopedia again, after his single early visit to it. Like Hal, he had needed to leave the Encyclopedia in order to find it again. But it had been over a century now since he had been the young man who had made that single visit, at his sister's insistence, and heard the voices as Hal and Mark Torre had done.

Only they three had heard, as they passed through the centerpoint of the globe that was the Encyclopedia, but in the case of each of them, that hearing had changed their lives.

Now Tam sat waiting, holding on to life that had become a burden rather than a pleasure, trying to endure just enough longer for Hal to reach him—and now Hal was here. For the Encyclopedia's sake, he waited for Hal. For Ajela's sake, he would wait as long as he could.

It was Ajela that caught Hal's eyes now. Physically, she had not changed since he had seen her last, but what Tam's steady and obvious weakening was doing to her was made clear in her dress. Whatever the Final Encyclopedia had automatically laid out for her to wear this day, in the program she had set up in it long since to save her time in dressing, as she had come to save time whenever possible, could not have been what she was now wearing. Her choice had clearly been dictated by an unconscious desire to rouse the dying man through his male instincts, if nothing else.

She had chosen to put on a sari-like garment that wound tightly around her waist and hips. It was a hot pink, with yellow flowers imprinted over the base color. Above the sari there was a space of bare midriff, and above that a small, short-sleeved tight blouse of the same material; while on her arms were multiple slim bracelets and in her ears earrings made of multiple small chained pieces—all these ornaments of bronze—which chimed and jingled at her slightest movement.

But the sari was carelessly draped; and the sound of the bracelets and earrings were lonely in the room as she turned to look, with a shadow of desperate appeal on her face, at Hal and Amanda as they entered.

Clearly, on his part, Tam did not see them enter. Plainly he saw Ajela beside him, but equally plainly he no longer noticed what she wore. His eyes were fixed on something among the trees, or upon his own dreams, or perhaps upon nothing at all. It was not until Hal had walked up to stand almost before his chair, and knelt on both knees, so their faces should be on a level, that recognition came.

Even then, it came slowly; as if it was a great labor for Tam to rouse himself to what he saw before him. But it dawned in his eyes at last and the hint of a smile lifted the corners of his mouth. His lips parted and moved, but whatever he meant to say was not voiced loudly enough for Hal, or any of the others, to hear it.

Hal reached out and took Tam's free hand between his own two, so that he held it as Ajela was holding the other one.

"I'm here, Tam," he said softly. "I'm back; and I've found something I needed. The way's clear now. Can you hold on just a matter of hours more? It won't be long. Not long at all."

Tam's small smile saddened. Barely perceptible, but with movement enough to see, his head moved twice, a few centimeters from side to side.

"I know, Tam," said Hal. "I'm not trying to hold you here. I'll only try to work very fast, just in case you're still with us when I reach what we've been after all this time. But it's a solid promise now. The way's clear. The end is in sight. The Final Encyclopedia's at last going to be what Mark dreamed of; what you dreamed of, and I, too. Maybe it'll happen fast enough—"

He broke off as the old head before him made the same minuscule side to side movement. Tam's hand stirred slightly between his two palms; and he was puzzled for a second before he realized the other was trying to return a pressure to his touch.

Once more Tam's lips moved. But this time the ghost of a voice came from them.

"Hal . . ."

But the faint exhalation of breath died, the heavy eyelids wavered and closed. Tam was utterly motionless and the moment of his stillness stretched out and out. . . .

"Tam!" cried Ajela suddenly; and both Rukh and Amanda moved in on the chair where Tam sat. But Tam's heavy eyelids fluttered briefly and rose. For a second he focused on Ajela; and that small attempt at a smile once more turned up the corners of his lips for her.

Hal rose and moved back out of the way; as Ajela slipped forward onto her knees where he had been, threw her arms around Tam and buried her face against the ancient body.

Rukh bent over the gold-haired, kneeling figure. Hal felt a touch on his elbow and looked to see Amanda's eyes meaningfully upon his. He turned and followed her out of the door by which they had just come in. As the door closed behind them, he turned back to face her and they stood, looking at each other.

"What can I do?" said Hal. "Is there anything I can do at all for her?"

"Not directly," said Amanda. "Leave her to Rukh and me. Both of us have been through this sort of experience in our own lives. For me, it was Ian, when I was still young. For Rukh it was James Child-of-God. We can help her. You can't, except by getting on with your own work."

"Which is what I intend starting immediately," he said. "With luck, I can still achieve something before—"

He broke off. Rukh had just come through the door and joined them.

"How is she?" Hal asked.

"She's best left alone with him for now," said Rukh. "Later it'll be a matter of getting her away from him to rest for a while. Let's go to her office to talk."

With another brief use made of the Final Encyclopedia's magic, and another short walk down the corridor, they entered the office. It was, like the office of any of the others from Tam on down who worked with the Encyclopedia, merely one room of the personal living space of each within the massive structure that was the TFE. But illusion made the space chosen appear as large as was wished and hid all doors to more rooms beyond, to all but those who knew the quarters intimately.

So, as with Tam's forest glade, Ajela's working space was a reflection of her own individual identity. As his did, hers had water; but not a stream. Where Ajela worked was a round, shallow pool in which brightly colored fish lazily swam. There was indeed a desk beside the pool, but the floor space about it was furnished in lounge fashion; except that the chairs, like the desk, were floats, instead of solidly floor-standing, old-fashioned furniture.

However, the largest difference between the two personalized rooms lay in their general concept. Tam's was a slice of Old Earth. Ajela's was a nostalgic reconstruction of part of a typical Exotic countryside residence; one of those artfully constructed dwellings in which it was possible to move from indoors to outside without having realized it, so well were the two environments integrated in the design and furnishings.

The inside surface of the wall through which Hal, Amanda and Rukh now entered was simple wood paneling. But where the wall connecting to it at an angle on their right would normally be was the seeming of a vertical face of roughly cut, warm brown granite. The wall to their left seemed a trellis overgrown with vine from which hundreds of varicolored sweetpea blossoms looked inward at them. While the wall that should have been opposite the one through which they had entered appeared not to exist. Instead, they looked out on a vista of green treetops in a bowl-shaped valley lifting in the distance to bluish mountains wreathed in soft tendrils of moving white mist.

"Let's take the desk," said Rukh. She stepped ahead, leading the way, and went forward and around to seat herself behind the desk. It was a piece of office furniture that could be expanded both lengthwise and in width to make a conference table seating up to fifteen people; but at the moment it was down to its minimal size of a meter in width and two in length. Rukh sat down behind it, in a float near one end, and Amanda and Hal moved, respectively, to the end itself and the front of the desk directly opposite Rukh.

Two nearby floats, their sensory mechanisms triggered by the heat of the bodies close to them, moved forward to be used; and Hal and Amanda sat down.

Hal looked at the desk. Its present state was the one thing in the room that did not resonate of Ajela. In all the time Hal had been in the Final Encyclopedia, he had seen its surface in either one of only two states. Either it was completely bare and clean, except for a stylus next to the screen inset in the desktop where Ajela usually sat; or it was high-piled and adrift with the flotsam of hard copies of official papers, correspondence, contracts and the like.

Now, it was in neither state. It held a number of hard copies, but they were neatly stacked in orderly piles. Hal looked at these as the desk top opened before both Amanda and himself to make available to each of them a screen and stylus like that now in front of Rukh.

The neatly stacked papers were not the product of Ajela's hands. The desk showed the touch of Rukh. Hal raised his eyes to her.

"Have you taken over here for her completely, then?" he asked.

"I'm afraid so," said Rukh. "It's not official, of course. Ajela's authority comes from Tam—I should say, from you, since Tam named you Director, only you've never used the authority. She has. But aside from the fact she's got no right to pass it to someone else while you're alive, we daren't let word get out to Earth or anywhere else that she's not, effectively, at the helm. There're a handful of inner circle secretaries that know, but they keep it to themselves. Not even most of the Encyclopedia personnel realize how much she's out of the picture most of the time."

"You'd think they'd guess something like that was going on, with Tam as close to the end as he is," said Amanda.

"They do," said Rukh. "They're just loyal enough not to ask embarrassing questions. But Hal—" Her brown eyes leveled on his. "They'll feel better now you're back."

"I never did run things here," said Hal.

"No, but they know Tam looked on you to finally suc

ceed him, and in fact you were already made Director years ago, when the shield went up. They'll feel better with you actually in the Encyclopedia."

"How are you managing on your own?" Amanda asked Rukh.

The brown eyes moved to meet the turquoise ones.

"It's all decision-making," said Rukh. "The internal problems I turn over to the heads of departments. In special cases, I go to Ajela if I have to. The rest of it, particularly the problems coming up to her from Earth, are usually just a matter of common sense or mediating between two unreasonable points of view. In fact, nearly everything that comes up here for decision from the surface is something that could and should have been handled by the people down there. They did, in fact, until they woke up to the fact that we were in a war and the Encyclopedia was the one their defenders were contracted to. Not that I make any military decisions, I leave that up to the Dorsai."

"But Hal," she turned back to him. "these things aren't important. Tam is. Is there anything, anything at all, you can do for him and Ajela before he has to let go completely? In spite of what you may think by what you saw in there, he'll fight it out to the last minute. It's the way he's made. If there's the slightest chance of you discovering anything, or doing something that would make him feel he was free to go . . ."

"I have found something," said Hal, "and I'm going to try to do something. Is Jeamus Walters still with us?"

Rukh smiled.

"Does it seem that you've been gone that long, Hal?" Rukh smiled. "Right now you ought to find him in his office. Shall I call and find out?"

She picked up the stylus.

"No. Never mind. I'm going there anyway," said Hal. "I'll see you both later."

He was getting up as he spoke and was already turned toward the door.

"Call on me if you need me," said Amanda.

"On all of us, for anything," said Rukh.

"I will," said Hal, already at the door.

He went out.

Jeamus Walters was in his office, as Rukh had guessed. It was typical of the man that his work place sported no illusions whatsoever. Its bare metal walls were completely covered with shelves holding hard copies of designs and schematic drawings. His desk threatened to outdo Ajela's at its worst with an overload of hard copies. Jeamus lived for work and work was all he lived for. He had been that way, as far as Hal knew, from long before he had become Research Director of the Encyclopedia; and apparently that was the way he always would be.

Now, Hal, who had hardly seen the man in the preceding three years, during which he had been caught up entirely in his own search and work, looked at him clearly for the first time in a long while, and saw changes in him, small but unmistakable.

There was a little less hair with more gray in it, in the circlet that surrounded all but the front part of his skull like an uncompleted wreath. His square mechanic's body and blunt mechanic's hands were the same as ever; his face showed no real signs of aging, but there was a faintly dusty air about him, as if he was a mechanism that had been left unused for some time. He got to his feet with a sudden start as Hal entered after giving his name to the door annunciator.

"Hal!" he said. His hard, square palm and fingers enclosed Hal's. They made up a smaller hand than the one Hal enclosed them with, but they were hardly less strong. "How are you? Is there something we can do for you?"

"Yes," said Hal, "there is. I'm up against a time limit, Jeamus—you can guess why. I need something you can build without too much trouble—I think. But I don't want you to boggle at my plans for using it, so I won't tell you those, if you don't mind."

Jeamus frowned at him and hesitated for just a moment.

"If you say so," he said; then, his frown clearing, "everyone knows Tam expected you to take over as Director whenever you felt you were ready. It's just that I've gotten used to taking orders from Ajela—"

"And Rukh."

Jeamus glanced at the door, which was slightly open. It was close enough in the little office, so that he could reach out without getting up. He pushed it closed: and it swung back against the jamb but did not latch.

"And Rukh, of course," he said, lowering his voice, "though most, even here, don't know that. What I was going to say was that I've gotten used to taking orders from both of them; and if you say you think I might boggle at your plans, it makes me think that it's very likely either one of them would boggle, too."

"They would," said Hal. "That's why you have to do this for me without telling them anything about it."

Mentally, he added Amanda to the list of those who might not like what he wanted to do, then backed off a bit from that thought. Amanda's perception was remarkable enough that she would be the most likely of the three women to take him on faith.

Jeamus was distractedly ruffling what hair remained of him.

"This is a little uncomfortable for me," he said. "Technically, you're in control here and should be able to order anything . . . but Ajela has been in charge so long, and in control—it's hard to think of not telling her—particularly about something she might not think was a good idea. At the same time I hate to bother her right now. . . ."

He sat for a moment, frowning and ruffling his hair. Hal sat in silence, patiently waiting.

"All right," Jeamus said at last. "You've got my word. Now, what is it?"

"To begin with," said Hal, "is there a blind corridor available in the Encyclopedia? I mean a short corridor with an entrance at one end but no doors at all leading off of it?"

"Yes. There're several," said Jeamus. "They were set up originally to allow for overflow or changes in the personnel aboard. Right now they're all being used as storage areas, but we could clear one out and store whatever's in it, in some other area—we've got the available space."

"Good," said Hal. "I'll want this corridor to come to my call; no one else's—even by mistake. Can we be certain of that?"

Jeamus smiled.

"All right," said Hal, "I hadn't any real doubt, but I wanted to make sure. Would you have such a corridor cleared and call me when it's ready? Then I'll tell you what I want done."

"Why not tell me now?"

"You'll understand that, when I tell you what I want," said Hal. "All right? I'll be in my quarters. Call me when it's ready; as soon as possible, for other people's sakes beside my own."

"Tam?" asked Jeamus, a little grimly.

"Other people besides me," said Hal.

"All right," said Jeamus. "It'll be a matter of a few hours, no more."

"Good. As fast as you can. As I say, I'll be in my quarters. You can call me there."

When Hal let himself back into his own apartments, Amanda had not yet returned. This was as Hal had hoped. He seated himself on the carpeting of the carrel that was the workspace of his quarters, and summoned up with his imaging link to the Encyclopedia an image of the range of glowing red lines that was the internal map of the knowledge in that mighty body.

As he had known there would be, changes showed themselves in the lines—small changes, but undeniable ones that were the result of information constantly added, from the state of affairs on Earth, news brought by couriers from outside, and the readings of the many instruments that scanned and kept track of the wings of enemy space vessels prowling the outside of the phase-shield.

His eyes were drawn immediately to each small change, as any change is noticed in a known landscape, or the face of a loved one; and he took a few moments to incorporate all of these in his earlier mental picture of the Encyclopedia's core memory. Then he dismissed the mechanical image, and replaced it with one evolved from his own memory and imagination, comparable now with the latest and most up-to-date image the Encyclopedia itself had formed for him.

Sitting, holding it in the field of his mental vision, he could feel the complete knowledge of the Encyclopedia open to his mind, like some vast storehouse of priceless art objects, too multitudinous in number to be seen in one moment from any one single viewpoint. Then he let the rest of his mind go back, back to the chanting circle, to the first edge of the morning sun that was Procyon's bright pinpoint orb beginning to show above the far-off mountain peaks, and the single ray lancing into the dewdrop to make the explosion of light that signaled his sudden understanding of the full truth in what he and the rest had chanted . . . *the transient and the eternal are the same.*

That great and ringing verity echoed in and through him as if he was a tuned piece of metal struck by an invisible padded hammer—and it was not just as if comprehension of all the individual bits of knowledge stored in the memory of the Encyclopedia shrank until they could be contained by his one human mind; but as if the back of his thoughts, his own unlimited unconscious understanding, widened and spread to take in and possess, all at once, all that that warehouse contained.

He was not suddenly filled, as a vessel is brought to the brim with liquid—but it was as if there was nothing known here that he had not known and handled, understood and loved, in its own body and measure.

He sat as if bound, as if part of the workings of the

Encyclopedia itself, possessed of all it contained and caught up in the fact like someone mesmerized. For there had been more there than any person could hope to learn in many lifetimes; but—the transient and the eternal were the same. He had one lifetime only, but less than a moment of that could contain eternity, and in that eternity he had had time to possess himself of all that the Final Encyclopedia contained.

At last, the Encyclopedia was ready to be put to its proper purpose, the one Mark Torre had envisioned for it, without even being able to see or name that vision. He could go to Tam now, and tell him that the search was over.

But, there was still the problem of using what he had touched and come to own. All that the Encyclopedia held was no more use locked in his mind than it had been in the technological container that was the Encyclopedia itself. He would use it—then go to Tam. Surely, there was time for that.

He woke to the surroundings of his carrel to find Amanda standing and watching him. Plainly, she had caused the Encyclopedia to make fresh clothing for her. She was no longer in the bush clothes in which they had left Kultis together, but wearing a plain, fitted, knee-length dress of blue—reminiscent of the color of the wintry seas around the northern islands of the Dorsai that he remembered from his childhood as Donal. There was no way for him to tell, after that timelessness from which he had just returned, how long she had been there, waiting for him to respond to her presence.

He got swiftly to his feet; and she looked up into his eyes with a steady, almost demanding, gaze.

"Whatever it was you were doing," she said, "it worries me. Do you want to tell me?"

"To tell you it all would take—I don't know how long." Hal smiled at her to reassure her. "But I've won through— I've found what Mark Torre and Tam—and I too—have been after all these years. But there's not enough time to tell you now. I have to put it to use, before I go to Tam with the news. Will you trust me and wait a little while longer? It's your doing, you know. The key was that the transient and the eternal are the same."

"And with this," she said, "you're going to do something to make Tam happy before he dies?"

"I think so," said Hal. "Though it's only the beginnings of the full answer. But it means the rest of what we need is only waiting to be found. Let's say it'll set him free to let go, content that the end is in sight."

His voice softened, unthinkingly.

"Ajela's torn apart, isn't she?" he asked. "She can't bear to lose him, but she can't bear to let him go, either."

"Yes," said Amanda, "and she can't help that. She'll be better off once he's gone; but even if she could face that now, it wouldn't make anything easier for her. I wish you'd give me more of an answer."

"I've got to keep it a secret for myself, awhile longer," Hal said. He put his hands on her shoulders. "Can't you trust me for a little while? You and Rukh can come and see what I'm going to do as soon as anyone can. But if, with all this, it shouldn't work after all . . . I've felt so close to the full answer so many times before, I want to make sure this time. I'd rather you didn't say anything, even to Rukh, let alone Ajela, before I'm ready to have you tell them."

She stood still, under the grasp of his hands, her eyes now thoughtful.

"You're going to try something that means gambling your own life, aren't you?"

"Yes," he said.

"It's not for me to stop you. . . ." She moved away from him, and his hands loosened to let her go. They fell to his sides. She turned back and put her arms around him.

"Hold me," she said.

He enclosed her strongly in his own arms, and she held him tightly. He felt the living warmth of her body against him, and for a moment an unbearable poignancy swept through him.

"You realize," she said as they pressed together, "you can never leave me behind."

"I know that," he said. He rested his cheek against the top of her bright head, "but I can't take you with me now."

"Yes," she said, "but I'll always follow. You should know that, too. Wherever you go."

It was true. Of course, he knew. There was nothing to be said in answer. He simply held her.

A little over two hours later, when Amanda had finally left to see if she could be of any use to Rukh in Ajela's office, there was the soft chime on the air of Hal's quarters that announced someone wanted to speak to him.

"Yes?" he said, back to the surrounding atmosphere.

"The corridor's clear." It was Jeamus's voice. "The door at the far left end of the present corridor outside your rooms will let you into it."

"I'll be right there," said Hal.

He followed the directions and a moment later stepped into a short corridor with green metal walls, rather like Jeamus's own office without the shelves but stretched out in one dimension. It also smelled faintly of an odor something like mildewed paper, which Jeamus's office did not.

"We haven't done a real cleaning job on it yet," Jeamus said, "I guessed you'd be more interested in getting on with whatever you had in mind."

"You're right," said Hal, "and now I'll tell you why I wanted this space to come and open only to me; and of course, you and whoever needs to be with you to help while you're building it. What I want you to build me is something that. I think might be dangerous to someone who could just stumble across it."

"Dangerous?"

"Yes. I want you to build me a doorway—a phase-shift doorway—that's the best I can do by way of describing it. Essentially, it's to be just a single phase wall, not the complex affair you made for the phase-shield around Earth. I just want it to disperse whatever touches it, spread it out to universal position; and it should fill the corridor from ceiling to floor, wall to wall, about a third of its length from its blind end."

"Just an out-shift wall?" said Jeamus. "Where's what you're sending through going to be reconstituted?"

"It isn't, until it chooses to come back through the same wall."

"Chooses?" echoed Jeamus. "There's no choice about that. Once dispersed, unless there's a destination at which it can be reconstituted, anything you send simply stays spread out until time ends."

"That's not the point," said Hal. "Can you build it?"

"Oh, it can be built, yes," said Jeamus. "Though I think that you're talking about actually would require a double screen, one to disperse, the other to reintegrate. That means the reintegrating screen would have to be in front of the dispersing one, so that you'd need a space here around one side of it, say, to get at the outgoing screen. But what you're describing doesn't make any sense. You mean it's departure point would be effectively just a meter or so from the arrival point?"

"If there have to be two screens, yes. The closer the better," said Hal, "and, I'm sorry, but don't ask me to try to explain, now."

"Well, it can't be any other way."

"All right. Can you build it?"

"Of course we can build it." Jeamus stared up at Hal. "But I can't imagine what sort of idea you've got in mind; and the more I hear of it, the less I like doing it blind. Let me see if I've got it straight. You want to be able to put something through the screen, reducing it to universal position. Then, somehow, it's going to come back by itself; and it has to come through the screen just a step away from it—I suppose you're thinking of what you send as somehow entering the return screen from the other side—and translating back into its original form. Actually, there is no 'other side' in the ordinary sense. What makes you think something like this could happen?"

"I'm going to find out," said Hal. "The only question I

have for you is, whether you'll make it for me."

"As I say, we can build what you're asking for," Jeamus said. "But there's no way that'll guarantee you'll be able to reconstitute something already spread out through the total universe. That is, it can be built so that if whatever it is gathers itself for re-entry—and how that's going to happen baffles me—then if it does the return screen will bring it back to its original location, which is here. The same way a spacecraft, shifting, returns to its original form at the point where it wants to be. But the ship has been pre-programmed to come out at that specific spot; and the action is essentially timeless—it happens in no-time. So, in effect, if I set up a device to do what you say, the going and returning is going to be instantaneous. The second screen'll simply cancel out the action of the first, so that in effect whatever you send will only have moved a meter or so immediately—that is, if it ever comes out at all, which it won't. The point is, what you're planning to have happen is impossible."

"Not if I'm right," said Hal. "What I put through is going to stay awhile and come back when it's ready."

Jeamus shook his head.

"It can't happen," he said. "The laws of phase-shift physics just don't permit it. I don't know how much you know about them—"

"Nothing," said Hal, "and it doesn't matter because I take your word for it, completely. If you say that according to what you know it's impossible, I believe you. But that's not the point for me. Can you and will you build me what I ask for?"

"Oh, we can build it . . . " Jeamus said slowly, shaking his head. "But what good's it going to do you? I still think you don't quite understand—"

"Never mind," said Hal. "You've said you could build it. That's all I need to hear. Now, the next question. How fast can you get it done?"

Jeamus stared at him again.

"You're talking about a crash program?" he said. "Like

the building of the shield-wall around Earth?"

"Or faster," said Hal.

Jeamus breathed out sharply and almost angrily through his teeth.

"I don't understand any of this," he said. "Can you at least tell me—has it got something to do with Tam?"

"Yes." said Hal, "but it goes far beyond that."

"All right," said Jeamus. "We'll build it for you. There's nothing tricky about the technics of it. Will a master of hours suit you? A chunk more hours than it took to clear this corridor for you, of course."

"As soon as you can," said Hal. "For Tam's sake."

Jeamus looked at him.

"Tam?"

"Tam," said Hal.

Jeamus took a deep breath.

"As soon as it can be done, it'll be done," he said. "I'll call you."

Hal got up.

"I'll be in my quarters," he said. He headed back to his quarters, but was hardly back into the corridor containing his door when the transmitted voice of Rukh spoke in his ear.

"Hal, could you come to the office? Amanda's already here, and the Dorsai Commander-in-Chief."

Hal went. He found them as Rukh had said. Rukh herself was in a float behind the desk and Amanda in one of the padded armchair floats facing it. In another such over-stuffed float, placed so that his face could see and be seen by both women was Rourke di Facino, wearing a blue uniform with a single gold strip slantwise across each lapel of the jacket, and a gray scarf tied underneath, over the collar of the white shirt underneath.

Hal had not seen the little man since he had spoken to most of the Grey Captains of the Dorsai, those who by local agreement spoke for their immediate area of that world; and that had been before the Dorsai had agreed to come and take over the defense of Earth. Hal, in fact, had not kept track of who the commanding officer of all the Dorsai in the ships patrolling inside the phase-shield had been. Now, perversely, he was glad that it was Rourke the other Dorsai had elected to this post. The sharp-tongued, sharp-eyed di Facino was oddly reassuring, with his invariable certainty that there was a right way to do everything.

"Good, you came right away," said Rukh, as Hal took one of the floats. "We've just had a disturbing incident. Fifty of the Younger Worlds' warships just made a simultaneous jump through the phase-shield in formation. We lost two of our own ships and had eight crippled, knocking them out of our own space or forcing them down to surface, where they were captured."

"The damaged ships'll be back on patrol in a week," said di Facino. His light tenor voice was incisive to the point of abrasiveness. "But the two that were killed were lost with everyone aboard them. We can't afford losses."

"I assume," said Rukh, "there weren't any of the newly trained people up from Earth among them?"

Di Facino shook his head.

"All Dorsai."

"I thought," Rukh went on, "the program to train new crew had been going faster than that. I keep getting word from below that the recruitment centers are jammed."

"They are," said di Facino, "but without training, the men and women jamming them are useless. To operate a space war vessel's one thing; to fight it, something else entirely. Even our own people are rusty. It's not the way it was a hundred years ago when there was still war in space between the worlds and actual ship fighting was part of many of the contracts our people were then signing. Still, our people, at least, are drilled and have the necessary attitude. They'll do the right thing when needed. The people we get from Earth are each one of them question marks until they've actually been tested in action—and in spite of all those in the recruitment centers, only a handful are on ships so far, for final training, let alone ready to crew the new vessels they're rolling off the assembly lines down there."

"You haven't got any trained crew yet from Earth who're ready to take over regular patrol work on any of your ships?" Rukh stared at him.

"I won't say that," answered di Facino. "From a world with a population equal to that of the thirteen Younger ones, there have to be a few who have the right instincts and have had training that's very close to what we want them to learn. It's a blessing in a way, that Earth's hung on to its regional sectional national and so-forth differences all these centuries because a few of the larger land-mass groups have maintained the rudiments of a personal space force; and some of the sea-nations have underwater warships which almost duplicate a space and atmosphere-going ship of war; so a handful have come to us already semi-trained. Some of those as I say, are undergoing final training in our ships on duty just under the shield now. At any rate, it's not the matter of recruitment that brings me here. It's the question of what this last fifty-ship incursion means, in terms of what the other side has in mind. The jump into our territory was incredibly wasteful. Their ships didn't have a chance of gaining anything. Even if they'd been our equal vessel to vessel, what could they have hoped to achieve in the way of opening a path for others of their own side, or in the way of doing something to Earth?"

"Could fifty ships destroy the Final Encyclopedia?" Amanda asked Rukh.

"I'm told they couldn't," answered Rukh. "In fact, Jeamus Walters' answer to me when I asked him that was that it'd almost be easier for them to destroy Earth. He tells me that they couldn't even pull the suicidal trick of jumping a ship through the Final Encyclopedia's own protective shield, to cause a matter explosion when it reconstituted itself inside the Encyclopedia, on the obvious basis that two solid objects can't occupy the same space at the same moment. It seems there's a shunt mechanism in the Ency-

clopedia's own phase-defenses that would cause a ship trying any such thing to keep shuttling forever back and forth
between the Encyclopedia's inner and outer shield, and
never reconstituting."

"Why didn't they build that same mechanism into the
Earth shield when they were at it?" di Facino asked.

"The Earth shield is too big, apparently," said Rukh.
"According to what Jeamus told me when I asked him that
same question. There's a factor that keeps doubling, apparently, as the size of a phase-shield grows; so that only a little less than twice the size of the Encyclopedia is the
practical limit for adding the shuttle effect."

"Obviously, they'd have done it if they could have,"
said Amanda. "But suppose we concentrate on the important point, what this recent and apparently senseless attack
means. Hal, you've been sitting there ever since you came
in without saying a word, and you know Bleys Ahrens better than any of us. What's your opinion?"

"I can't be much more sure than the rest of you," said
Hal, "but my instinctive guess is, it's a message, that's all."

"A message? To Earth?" said Rukh. "What would it be
supposed to mean?"

"I think . . ." Hal hesitated. ". . . a message to me from
Bleys."

"What message?" asked the little Dorsai-in-Chief.

"That he meant what he said," Hal answered, "when he
talked about the siege mentality and a blood bath on
Earth when his forces were finally so overwhelming
they'd be able to jump through simultaneously and overwhelm any defense we had. Amanda, did you tell them
about what Bleys said when he came to the Chantry
Guild?"

"I was just about to when you got here," Amanda put
in swiftly. "Bleys came and found us where we were on
Kultis—"

"Found you?" broke in Rukh. "And you got away
safely?"

She was leaning forward tensely over the desk.

"It wasn't like that," said Hal. "He came alone to a place where we were surrounded by friends. Also, I've told you before that Bleys is as aware as I am that either his killing me, or I, him, wouldn't change things, except possibly to work against the killer. The real opponents are two forces in the human race that have developed through history to this moment. He and I just happen to be in point positions on the forces we're associated with."

"That's a somewhat simplistic way of putting it," said Amanda dryly. "You'll remember he did bring up the possibility of his killing you."

"I was in no danger," said Hal.

"About the message—" prompted di Facino. "You're saying he promised you a blood bath, if and when he finally broke through. I can see it happening, if it finally came to that. But why come to tell you, if this assault was supposed to send the same message?"

"Because he also told me he didn't like blood baths; and I know him well enough to know he's telling the truth."

"Telling the truth!" said di Facino. "He was trying to frighten you into something. A man can't be responsible for something like that and say he doesn't like doing it."

"Have you ever cut off the leg of someone, without anesthetic, and knowing—as I suppose you don't—anything about such surgery?"

"No, I haven't!" snapped di Facino. "And you're right about my not knowing anything about how to go about it."

"But you'd do your best in spite of that, if it was a case of a member of your immediate family and the only way to save that person's life was to cut, immediately wouldn't you?"

Di Facino stared at him.

"You know I'd do it," he said, "and I see what you mean. I wouldn't like it but that wouldn't stop me, if it was a matter of life and death for someone I loved. But you aren't trying to tell me Bleys is in that position in planning a blood bath for Earth?"

"Not exactly," said Hal, "but in a position very much like it. . . ."

He hesitated.

"I think I may be the only other human alive who understands some aspects of Bleys," said Hal. "You have to realize how differently he thinks from other people. Try to appreciate, for example, what his own existence has been life. He must be the loneliest human being alive. No, lonely's the wrong word. So Instead he's the most isolated of all humans; because he's never experienced anything but complete separation from everyone else and can't conceive of any state that'd be otherwise. So he suffers; but he isn't aware of suffering from this the way you and I would be, because he's never known any other state."

"He could look around and see other humans who aren't suffering that way, and learn from them that other states of being exist," said di Facino.

"Learning from them is just what he's shut himself off from," said Hal. "From the time he was old enough to notice such things, he had to see that the people around him had limited intelligence compared to his, and couldn't match him in other capabilities. Almost as soon as he knew himself, he must have felt alone in the universe, surrounded by creatures who looked and acted like him but lacked perceptions, and were easily controllable by him without their realizing it. All he had to do was put his mind to manipulating them, and they did whatever he wished. He was walked off by what he was from the rest of the race."

Hal hesitated, unsure whether he was not perhaps talking too much; then he decided to go ahead.

"There's a couple of lines in a poem by Lord Byron. He was a nineteenth century English poet; and one of his poems was called *The Prisoner of Chillon*—Chillon being a fortress prison in Switzerland; and the prisoner was in solitary confinement there. The lines come when, after at last managing to get a glimpse of the outside through the high, small window of his cell, the prisoner finds confinement has changed him. The lines go . . .

> . . . and the whole Earth would henceforth be
> A wider prison unto me . . ."

Hal looked at them. Rourke di Facino was looking back with a hint of puzzlement. Amanda and Rukh, by contrast, had expressions that were strangely sympathetic.

"So you see," wound up Hal, "while his situation was slightly different, in essence it was pretty much the same, in that Bleys learned almost from birth that all the worlds were only a *'wider prison'* for him. He could search in every face he met and not see an understanding of what he felt in himself. Fame and fortune could mean nothing to him because he knew he could have them by merely reaching out his hand for them. He had no friends. Those who thought they loved him, did so without understanding. He had been given a lifetime to spend and nothing to spend it on. So he decided to do what he didn't think anyone else could do: turn the human race down a path of future history it would never have taken if he hadn't come along. Even if the turning might mean doing some things he might not like, he'd do it. So, he went to work."

"And ran into you," said Amanda.

"I was there." Hal looked back at her.

Amanda merely watched him, steadily.

"But why the blood bath?" said di Facino. "If he finally ends up with enough ships and trained men to wipe out our defensive forces, there are certainly ways of taking Earth without that kind of action."

"There are, of course," said Hal.

"What's he trying to do, then, frighten you into promoting a surrender for him?"

"No," said Hal. "The obvious reason for the talk of a blood bath and this incident to support it is to try to push me into acting hastily. How long, would you say, Rourke, at the rate his forces outside the shield are building, until he gets to the point of having enough in ships to try that sort of mass jump through the shield and assault this world—with some hope of success?"

"I'm not Donal Graeme," said di Facino. He spoke as if the time in which Donal had been known to exist was no more than yesterday, instead of close on a hundred years. "It depends on how fast he can drive the Younger Worlds to give him ships and crews for them. Anywhere from six months to five years, absolute time."

"Let's say six months," said Hal. "If we're really only six months from such an assault and blood bath, there'd be some reason to panic. But I don't think we are. I think, as I say, he's trying to prod me to moving too quickly and making a mistake."

They all watched him. This time even di Facino said nothing.

"You see," said Hal, choosing the words of his explanation carefully, "he's not worried about being able to take over Earth. At the last minute, he can always pull a rabbit out of his hat and make the conquest in some unexpected way. He said as much three years ago when he and I met in the thickness of the phase-shield, just after the Dorsai and the Exotics had given all they had to give and the shield had gone into place to keep his ships out. He's worried about me—the fact that I also might pull a rabbit he doesn't suspect out of my hat, before he can out of his. I'm the one person he knows who might do something he can't expect. If he can panic me into moving even a little too hastily, I may fumble and not have time to produce that rabbit."

"God!" said di Facino. "What a way to try to pressure someone—with the threat to massacre perhaps billions of people."

"That threat at its closest is still six months off," said Hal. "You know, the motto of Walter Blunt, who founded the original Chantry Guild here on Old Earth, was *destruct*. What he wanted was to clear away everything and everybody but a few special people on a specialized Earth, that could then build to a special end. Note how Bleys' aim all along has echoed that. He wants to depopulate the Younger Worlds entirely and reduce the population of Old Earth to a particular group who'll mature over generations to something like himself."

"What of it?" asked di Facino bluntly.

"Just that the destruction Blunt preached never got off the ground. Instead the Chantry Guild shifted its aims toward nonviolence and an idea of philosophical evolution."

"That was then."

"Now's then, too: as the present is always made by and contains the elements of the past," said Hal. "Hold on a little longer, don't let your concern over this run away with you for six months yet."

"Meanwhile, you'll be doing what?"

"I want to have something to show you before I answer that," said Hal. "Right now, what I'm chasing has no more substance than a dream—any more than any discovery has before it's made. But I'm sure it's there; and if I'm right, it'll give us an escape hatch from this situation without any massacre and without a shooting war, long before six months are up. I'll let you know when I've some progress to report. Meanwhile, it's important that everyone on our side keep pushing ahead full speed and without any doubts."

"On faith," said di Facino.

"Exactly, on faith. There's nothing stronger." Hal glanced for a second at Rukh, then back at the small Commander-in-Chief. "Remember, the difference between our camp and his. Finally, that part of the race that believes in going forward and adventuring outward are here, around us; and those who'd turn back and hide their heads from the risk of progress are with Bleys. Everything either side does, from building ships to fighting them, is part of the thrust of that side's purpose; and it's going to be needed when the final confrontation comes."

Di Facino stared grimly at him, but sat silent for a long moment.

"We'll do our part," he said at last, "as you know we will. For the rest—you're right. It's going to take faith for us to believe that you and everyone else is doing theirs— lots of faith!"

They talked for a little while longer, but nothing more of importance was said, and the conference broke up.

CHAPTER 36 ■

Sixteen hours had passed.

Ajela, Rukh and Amanda had taken shifts staying with Tam, as he fought to live a little while longer. Hal had returned to his quarters to study the knowledge stored in the core of the Final Encyclopedia and now open to him. He had studied it awhile, then slept, then rose to seat himself again with the mental image of the core before him. His eyes saw it, but his mind was far distant, wandering the reaches of what had been stored in it over the centuries.

It was like wandering through the corridors of an endless museum. Here were the artifacts of creativity. But they were strangely lacking in some invisible element he could not put a mental finger on. Then, it came to him. Where were the souls that had created each of these things? It was strange. You could follow the creation of a piece of art or discovery down through the levels of the craft that made it actual and real. But only up to a certain point. Then you came suddenly to a gap, a quantum jump, beyond which the work became wholly the product of the individual who did it—no one else could have done it just that way—and there was no more craft bridge there to explain the uniqueness of what you saw, heard, or felt. Beyond was simply incomparable, irreplaceable individual talent made manifest, the essence of creativity itself at work, as if it were magic.

There was this gap, this vital element missing, yet. For his purposes in the Creative Universe, it must be touched, even if it could not be grasped. As one mind could never wholly grasp the intent of another mind, but could touch and understand enough of the other's intent to work with that.

For some hours now, Hal had turned his unconscious loose to search for a way to so touch what was needed; while his conscious still wandered the corridors of the Encyclopedia's storehouse, just as his conscious mind had been left to wander about, that day on the ledge—and at last the answer came to him as something he had almost forgotten.

Three years before, when he had asked Tam about how he, Hal, could learn to do what Tam did, in reading the knowledge core, he found that Tam could not describe how he did it in logical, verbal terms. He referred Hal to an old twentieth century novel, which had ended up by becoming a classic after being nearly forgotten, then rediscovered in the twenty-first century. *The Sand Pebbles*, written by an author named Richard McKenna, had for its lead character a non-commissioned officer assigned as engineer on a United States of America Navy river petrol boat in China, during a time of great upheaval.

All the other enlisted crewmen aboard had yielded to the custom of hiring unofficial Chinese understudies for their jobs. As a result, the actual work in the engine room was done by Chinese. The lead character, who loved engines and was adamant about handling his duties himself, could not bring himself to do this. He was determined to do his job with his own hands. This earned him the enmity of the Chinese workers, since his decision kept one of their own people out of a job they had come to regard as theirs.

There was a scene in the novel, Tam told Hal—and Hal later looked it up with the help of the Encyclopedia's memory—in which the lead character, pacing around the engine room while the ship was under way, suddenly found himself stopped and standing over a small trap door that gave access to the steam piping underneath the engine room floor. He had lifted the trap and found that a valve that should have been open was turned down tightly, shutting off the steam through that pipe. An act of deliberate sabotage by one of the workers.

He had opened the valve; and only much later discovered that by doing so he had earned a reputation as a magician among the Chinese workers, since apparently he had gone directly to the deliberately closed valve and opened it, although there was no way he could have known about it.

In a reminiscence by another author of the same period, the other author had told of asking McKenna directly whether, in all the noise of a steamship's engine room, someone could actually hear the difference made by shutting off one small valve. McKenna, who had worked with the engines of navy ships in just that same sort of job, had said someone could. He had noticed such changes and corrected them, himself, while on duty, in almost unthinking reaction, so used he had become to the proper sound of the engine.

As the engine sound had been to the man in the engine room, so the stored knowledge of the Encyclopedia had come to be to Hal. What he needed to do was to be able to *think* with the full knowledge stored in the Encyclopedia available to his mind from his mental image of the lines; and, now, he had found the only missing note in their silent symphony.

The individual notes of creativity, which he would need to reach out to build with, in the Creative Universe, were all around him here, then, and his ear was not yet tuned to them. So far, he had built what his own mind had already created, or a few sounds of creativity from the verse or making of others which had touched his own soul in the past. But that universe would not be truly open until it could hold and he could hear the *sounds* of others.

But that had been enough to let him create the potentiality of a split in the human race-animal, so that it might— and had—grown into two separately developing entities; one of which embodied the desire to grow and evolve, and one which tried to hold back and stay as it was.

A chime sounded suddenly on the air of his room and a voice spoke aloud in it, summoning him back to the real universe. It did not speak privately, as Rukh's voice had spoken in his ear to summon him to the conference just past. It was the voice of Jeamus.

"We're ready, Hal Mayne," Jeamus said. "You'll find the entrance to the special corridor through the door at the left end of the one presently outside your quarters."

"Coming," answered Hal to the empty air above him. He rose and went out.

When he stepped into the blind corridor, what he saw brought him to a sudden stop. The two phase-shift constructions Jeamus had promised him were there. The nearer one extending three-quarters of the way across the corridor, leaving just room to slip past it to get to the second one, which, as far as the first screen allowed him to see, blocked the farther corridor completely. But waiting for him there were not only Jeamus and a couple of men in Research dust smocks, but also Rukh and Amanda. Rukh wore her usual long, high-collared dress, black this time. But Amanda was also wearing a floor-length dress she must have ordered the Encyclopedia to fashion for her— one he had never seen her in before—of a dark sea blue. The general effect was vaguely formal, as if they had dressed themselves in authority to come here.

"I thought," said Hal to Jeamus, "I asked you not to say anything to anyone else about this?"

"I'm sorry," said Jeamus. "It turned out there was a danger we hadn't expected. In the moment of powering up these two screens, there's a danger of one or both of them trying to interface with the protective screen around the Encyclopedia itself. Once up, there'd be no danger. But in turning them on there was; and none of us could estimate what might happen. No one had ever set up a phase-window completely within another window before—"

"What about the Encyclopedia's screen inside the one enclosing Earth?" interrupted Hal.

"But they're both double screens loops, closed circuits within themselves. What you've got here isn't and can't be a closed circuit. Not it you want it to do what you asked for. So I had to turn the Encyclopedia's shield off for just a few seconds while we turned on these; and I didn't feel I could do that without warning Ajela or Rukh. Rukh wanted to know more about what was going on that made me ask for something like that."

"I suggested she ask," said Amanda. "Don't jump on anyone else. Hal. Something unusual like that had your finger prints all over it; and when we found out what it was. Rukh and I both wanted to be here. And we've got a right to be."

"I couldn't lie to Rukh Tamani when it was a direct question," said Jeamus.

"Of course not. I don't blame you, Jeamus." Hal took a deep breath. "And you're right, Amanda. You and Rukh should be here if that's what you want."

"How could we not want to, Hal?" said Rukh. Hal shook his head.

"Of course. All right. I was wrong not to tell you from the start what I wanted to do. It was just I didn't—I still don't know—if it's going to work. It could be an utter failure."

Jeamus had been looking slightly bewildered.

"I don't understand," he said. "Just what is it you're planning to put through this first screen?"

"Myself," said Hal.

Jeamus stared.

"My God!" he said. "Do you know what you're talking about doing? Committing suicide! You'll end up spread out through the universe, with no way back."

"There's that chance, of course," said Hal, "but I've got reason to think, in this case, it's not going to happen that way."

"All the same," said Jeamus, "if that's what you've had in mind all along, I'm going to pray that nothing more goes on when you step through the back screen there—that you immediately step back out, facing us, through this near one!"

"Thanks, but I hope not, myself," said Hal.

He turned to Rukh and Amanda.

"But I might be able to do what I hope to do in what amounts to no-time, like any phase-shift, so that I still come back here right away," he said. "On the other hand, it could be that time spent between the screens is the same as time spent here and it'll be awhile before I'll come back. But there's no real doubt in me I'll be back sooner or later."

Rukh came to him, put her arms around him and kissed him on the lips.

"I should have done that long ago," she said. "We'll wait for you, Hal."

He held her for a moment, feeling his heart moved once again, as it had been when he carried her out of the prison cell on Harmony four years before, by the frailness of her body, even now. Then he let her go and turned to Amanda, who also held him and kissed him.

"I love you," she said.

"And I love you," he answered. "This could be the answer, at last, what I'm going to do."

"I knew," said Amanda, and let him go.

He turned, walked away from them, around the nearer screen to the second, and stepped through it.

CHAPTER 37 ■

He was everywhere and nowhere.

His senses were no longer working. He could not feel, smell, hear or see. Instead he had an awareness of his surroundings that recognized certain patterns, some of which were in the form of objects and some of which were not; but which in any case were unimportant.

It was a place where time existed, but did not matter. A place where his now changed self had no desire to understand or act. In fact, his ability to do so was limited. He had memory, but no purpose, for he found he could not conceive of the future, and the present was forever. But he could remember, and, remembering, he recalled how he had been through something like this, once before. It had happened when he had been Donal going back in spirit to the twenty-first century, when he had worked by inhabiting the body that had belonged to the dead Paul Formain. Then, he now remembered, something had carried him through what he was presently experiencing. . . .

The memory part of him that was still working gave it back to him. Then he had expected to go beyond this to something else, to a twenty-first century Earth; and the momentum of that expectation had carried him through without realizing the concept of purpose he now lacked.

It was a remembrance of an impossibility that had yet happened. For the Creative Universe he now realized he had envisioned both then and now could not, by definition, exist until he had created it. It did not exist now; and yet he had been aware of experiencing it before, as a necessary part of going back to alter the implications of the past.

Under the limitations of this place—this Chaos—that was yet to be, his logic-limited conscious mind was not capable of understanding the contradictions. Here he could only go on faith, philosophy and courage none of which were blocked by the limits of his logical mind. With them he could accept the fact that he had been able to experience the Creative Universe once before and use it as a window to the past, because his unconscious had assumed a path back through time for his identity; and by that assumption, like the assumption that creates a poem never expressed before, had caused it to be.

His logical mind had afterwards rejected what, to it could not be, and tucked the memory out of sight in his unconscious. There it had stayed until now, because the framework of understanding he needed to develop had not yet been there to understand how it could happen. Only now, spread out between time and space, did it all, at last, make sense.

As with the making of a poem, the explanation was that here all mechanisms must be developed in the unconscious; for the conscious mind could not operate without the arbitrary concepts it had gradually imposed over centuries on the physical universe, to give that universe a shape the conscious mind could work with.

He must now, therefore, not so much *make* what he wanted in the Creative Universe, as find it within himself; in this place where conscious logic and physics did not naturally apply. He must find it, as he had found poems and other discoveries of meaning and intent, in the past.

He let go, therefore, of his now useless and almost nonexistent upper mind. In effect he passed over into the realm of dreams and daydreams; and a jumble of memories and fancies tumbled through his imaginings, like the unchained thoughts that come in moments just before sleep sets the unconscious completely free.

So, letting go, he passed into what would have been a dream, if it had not been directed by some previous, deep-held sense of purpose that had directed him back to the twenty-first century. He could feel, in this universe-that-was-not, not only that earlier passage, but all the vast information of the Final Encyclopedia. The latter worked on the former. . . .

—And, suddenly, he was where he wanted to be.

It was a dream, made real after all. Real, it was, because not only all his senses now reported on the reality of it; but his logical upper mind, that must think in the language of symbols and identities, was once more awake and capable. But it was also a dream, because he remembered how he had first dreamed it, when he had been with the Resistance Group on Harmony, under a younger and strong-bodied Rukh. He had dreamed it then, and at other times since; and now, with the knowledge from the Encyclopedia, he had made it actual. It was at the dream's opening point now, that he, with the faith, belief and courage in him, had resolved the chaos around him into actuality.

Again, he was on horseback, with others also mounted. They were traveling in a group through a lightly forested area of some landscape in the temperate zone of an Earthlike world. They rode without talking, as he had earlier dreamed they had; but now, for the first time, he had a chance to look closely about him and identify those he rode with; and there were none of them he had not known, and all of them were now dead.

Obadiah the Friendly, Malachi the Dorsai and Walter the Exotic—the three who had been his tutors and raised him as Hal Mayne, rode not far behind him. Immediately beside and about him were those of his own—of Donal's—family. Fachan Khan Graeme, his father, now dead for nearly a hundred years, rode at his right side. Beside him on his left was Mary Kenwick Graeme, his mother; and beyond her was his brother Mor, who because of him had been tortured to death by the hands of the demented William of Ceta.

Mor leaned forward in his saddle to look around their mother at him; and Hal braced himself for the look that would be in the other's eyes. But when those eyes met him the look he had expected was not there.

"Welcome back, Donny," said Mor—and he was smiling, a warm, happy smile.

With that, Hal realized that he had indeed become Donal again, in body as well as in memory.

All the other tall menfolk of the Graemes once more overtopped him, as they sat their saddles around him; and he was as he had been in his early life.

"What's the matter, Brother?" Mor said. "Did you think I wouldn't understand?"

He reached out a hand across the neck of the horse Mary Graeme rode; and, with a moment's hesitation, Hal took it and found his brother's grasp comforting and as warm as his smile.

"I didn't think it through far enough," he said. I'd never have let him do that to you, if I had, for anything.

"I know," said Mor, as their grips parted and they straightened up in their saddles, "but it brought us to this, and this is best. Isn't it?"

"Yes," said Donal-Hal, "it's a new road, at last."

He looked around. In his dream he had not had time to identify faces. Now he saw how Ian and Kensie rode on the far side of Eachan; and how beyond Mor was his other uncle, James, whose death had set him on his life's path to this moment.

He looked farther back and saw, also riding near him, the Second Amanda Morgan, eerily like the Amanda he had left behind him beyond the phase-screen. A horde of other members of the family, long since gone, rode with them, including even Cletus Grahame, his great-great-grandfather.

But, farther back, there was also James Child-of-God, Rukh's second-in-command of the Resistance Group, who had died in the rain on Harmony: and the farther he looked, the more faces he recognized. Only now they were come to the edge of the forest, to the brink of a rubbled plain that stretched away toward the horizon, with nothing visible growing upon it and only one shape breaking the horizon line where rocky surface met the gray, unbroken ceiling of the clouds overhead.

That one shape stood darkly upright, so distant that it might have been on the horizon itself; and it was a single tower, black, featureless and solid, with the shape of one of the ancient keeps of the medieval centuries of Old Earth. About it, there was a terrible sense of waiting that held them all silent; as, following his example, they all checked their horses and sat looking at the tower.

"I go on alone from here," he said to the others.

They answered nothing; but he felt their acceptance of what he had just said. He could also feel that they would wait for him, here, no matter how long it took.

He got down from his horse—as he had remembered dismounting before in his dream—and started out on foot across the endless distance of the plain, toward the tower.

In his dream it had been vitally necessary that he go alone to it; and he felt the same unexplained urgency now. At some time later, he looked back and saw those who had been with him, still sitting their horses, small under the trees, which were themselves shrunken with the distance he had put between himself and them. Then he had turned once more and continued on toward the tower, to which he seemed hardly to have progressed a step since he had left the edge of the wood.

Without warning, something he could not see touched him on the left shoulder.

He whirled about, ready to defend himself, but there was nothing there. Only the waiting forms on horseback, now farther off than ever, though when he turned back toward the tower, still it seemed that he had moved hardly a step closer to it, in spite of all the distance covered.

The pebbles and rocks that made up the surface of the plane were now larger than those onto which he had first stepped. Looking down at them, the wealth of the Encyclopedia's knowledge flowed into him and he identified them as the detritus of an old lava flow, dark igneous rock that had over centuries been exposed to extremes of temperatures; until, cracking under the succeeding expansions and contradictions of their composite materials, the solid rock had decomposed and broken into many pieces—pieces which were later covered by a sea, and tumbled one against the other until their sharp edges and corners had become rounded.

His mind encompassed all this—or did it only create it as an explanation, out of the storehouse of the Encyclopedia? In any case he found himself understanding the geological ages that had made the surface he walked on; and without knowing how it could be possible, he realized that the tower toward which he was headed had been built on what had been an island during the period of the shallow sea that had rounded off the rocks. Inconceivably, it had been built before the waters rose to cover the lava plain of cracked and broken stones. Ancient it therefore was, as ancient as the human race itself, and what was within it, drawing him to it, was as ancient.

But it was still a long way off, and he was more concerned with the discovery of its creation. For in fact, it was his dream made real. He had created it only now, but as surely as he had ever created a poem or story, out of the primeval chaos in which he had found himself. He had created his body and those of his companions and their horses. He had created the thick cloud layer overhead that hid a sun that he had chosen to be a duplicate of the star of Old Earth; illuminating this world that was itself a duplicate of Old Earth; more so then any of the terraformed planets of the Younger Worlds.

He had built it, here in the Creative Universe, that was only a Creative Universe because with the Encyclopedia's help, he had brought it finally into being. For without the ability of the Encyclopedia's knowledge available to his own creative unconsciousness, he could not have made any of this. A poem could not be written without a knowledge of what made poetry—the images, the shapes and the language. Without a knowledge of what was required to produce such works, no original painting could be painted, no cathedral built.

In the creation of the very tower toward which he now made his way, a knowledge of the forces of gravity upon its structure, and of the materials that made its walls, was needed.

Glancing back over his shoulder, he saw the tiny figures waiting behind him now seemed to stand somewhat above him, and in fact the plain between them now had dipped downward, as if he had descended onto the old sea bottom that stretched level until it rose again in the far distance to the higher land of what had been an island when the tower was young. Looking ahead once more at it now, he saw that the sea floor approaching it, which had earlier seemed level to his eyes, actually rose and fell, gradually, in swells and hollows, before it reached the former island of the tower, and that he was now gradually ascending the slope of one of the nearer rises.

Sure enough, a little farther on, when he looked back again, the plain seemed to have descended toward the horizon behind him, and the group he had left there was indistinguishable now from the edge of forest behind them.

He turned his face forward and went on—and an unexpected shadow swept briefly over him, so that he looked up, startled; even as he heard what the Encyclopedia's knowledge now within him identified as the harsh cry of a raven.

Mixed with that cry was something he could not quite be sure he heard. It was as if a sound that was soundless had still somehow managed to signal itself upon his ear. It was like the resonance of a heavy bell, struck twice. Something that somehow echoed back to the time when he had been Paul Formain. Yet it did not belong to the memory of that time, but to the future still before him.

Like a warning note, it reminded him of the possible passage of real time. He did not know whether his time spent here was merely part of a moment of no-time back in the universe beyond the phase screens, or whether a minute here might not be a day, or month, there.

He stopped suddenly. The rise in the ground he had

been ascending had steepened gradually but steadily over the last fifty meters or so, and he was suddenly much closer to the tower. He had adjusted unthinkingly from what was a walking pace to a climbing one; so that he had come to the top of the rise without warning and now he checked, looking down its short, farther, descending side.

It dipped sharply for no more than ten paces before him. At that point it broke off abruptly in an edge as sharp as any cliffs. Beyond it was nothingness, with no sight of farther surface below. He saw only a relatively short distance horizontally to what looked like another cliff edge level with this one, that was visibly the edge of the one-time island with the tower upon it.

He went forward, cautiously. For the downslope was steep and he had to lean back to brace his weight and not slide forward over the edge before him. But even when he stood on the very lip of it, he could see nothing below him; only what appeared to be an endless fall to eternity. He looked at the distance of nothingness between him and the edge of the island; it was just far enough off that he could not quite make out the nature of the rocks that made up the distant land.

He stood, baffled.

There was no reason for this space to be here, barring his way. He made an effort to visualize the gap filled in with the same sort of former sea bottom he stood upon. But nothing happened. It was as if here, alone, his creativity could not bring into being a land bridge where there was nothing. It was as if he had nothing to build with, as if what was needed to bridge the space was not in him.

For a long moment he stood, unbelieving. Then his mind began to work, and up out of the back of it came the answer that what he looked at was his own doing. He had created this gap, without ever realizing it, by his own act in going back to be Paul Formain and changing the implications of past history. He had set out to split up the Enemy that had struck at him during the old Chantry Guild's initiation ceremony, so that it became not a semi-living racial force, but a part of every human living.

It had been the only way he had known, then, of making humanity take sides, for either creativity or stasis; and so bring that hidden, inner conflict to an outer resolution.

And he had succeeded—with the Others as an unexpected and unwelcome by-product. But he had succeeded. And here was another by-product.

The road to evolution of humankind led through the Creative Universe. But to enter it himself was not enough. It must be entered by at least one other human. The tower and what it stood on must be given relevance, as he had been required to find a relevance to feel the souls behind those creations of humankind and time stored in the Final Encyclopedia.

He could not cross the gap before him, because up to this point was no more than a place he had made himself. Beyond it, on the island and in the tower, be must share this universe with whoever or whatever in the race would oppose him there; for it was there the argument would come to a head and be settled. This place he had created was only an arena for decision, by his own choice he had willed it to be so.

There was only one other person so far alive, besides himself, with the background and experience to move through the phase screen as he had and create a destination. After that one came here it would become progressively easier for those who would come after. But for now, and for that one person, the time was short. Perhaps, even now, too short.

He turned about quickly and stepped backward—with intent.

So it was he stepped not back up the stony slope away from the edge of nothingness, but out through the farther phase screen into the blind corridor of the Final Encyclopedia, where Jeamus and his crew, with Rukh and Amanda, still waited for him. . . .

"Thank the Lord!" said Jeamus.

"How long was I gone?" asked Hal.

"No time at all," said Jeamus. "Perhaps a couple of minutes, then you came out of the other screen—"

"Good," he interrupted. "Now I want this whole device moved and set up in Tam's main room, right away," he said. "How fast?"

"I—uh—" Jeamus floundered. "An hour—"

"Five minutes," said Hal.

"Five?"

"Or as close to that as you can come," said Hal. "I want to get it there while Tam's still alive. Just the minimum of what you have here to make the doorway work."

"But a minimum's all we ever had—"

Jeamus's hands fluttered, half-lifted for a moment, helplessly. Then the meaning of Hal's words seemed to penetrate. He threw up his hands; and his voice hardened. "Maybe fifteen minutes . . . or ten? Maybe even . . . five? But *Tam's quarters?*"

"Yes." As Jeamus stood uncertain, he added harshly, "I'm speaking as the Director. Move it. As fast as you humanly can. Amanda? Rukh?"

He went out of the door. The two caught up with him just beyond it.

"What is it?" said Amanda. He glanced at her as they went, for she had a right to ask. She saw deeper into him than Rukh. "Why the special hurry?"

"I was in the Creative Universe," he answered briefly. "But someone else besides me has to go there: and only Tam's qualified, because he can read the Encyclopedia's knowledge core—not as well as I, but well enough."

"There's a problem?" she asked.

"Yes. What I mentioned—and there's something else. A gap where there shouldn't be one, a gap I can't reach across. I need a bridge."

"A bridge . . ."

Still striding swiftly down the corridor he turned to look at her. There was a look on her face he knew.

"What is it?" he said.

"The cloak . . . I think," she said. Looking past him. "I don't know why, but the cloak will make a bridge."

But they were already at the entrance to Tam's quarters.

"Yes," said Rukh, as they turned to go in, after him—he realized he was back in all the size of his Hal-body, "—all thanks to God you came when you did. I have a feeling he's very close to the end . . . very close."

CHAPTER 38 ■

They went as swiftly as the Final Encyclopedia could align their blind corridor with the one leading to Tam Olyn's quarters; and Rukh led them in through the door there without waiting to ask for entrance.

Inside, things had hardly changed. Ajela was dressed now in a Japanese kimono, which Hal noted was perfectly arranged, in contrast to the disheveled sari she had worn earlier. She was sitting upright now, but still held one of Tam's hands, and Tam still gazed off at something beyond their sight; he was now holding his interstellar newsman's cloak, that he had not worn since he had returned to the Final Encyclopedia, over ninety years before. It was still set as it had been since the death of his sister's young husband, on the white and red he had worn the day of David's end.

Hal reached the side of Tam's armchair opposite Ajela in six long strides and knelt beside it, putting his hand on Tam's arm which lay strengthlessly along the top of the padded armrest.

"Tam!" he said in a low voice, but urgently. "We've

done it! I've been in the Creative Universe. Now, to make the Encyclopedia the tool for everyone, the way we always dreamed, and Mark Torre dreamed, we only need one more thing—one final effort from you. Can you make it?"

"What're you saying?" Ajela's voice rang through the forest glade that was actually a room. "You aren't going to ask anything of him now?"

Hal ignored her. Amanda and Rukh moved in to draw her aside from the chair and speak to her, in low, imperative voices.

"But he can't do anything now! He can't—"

The low-pitched but steady voices of the other two women interrupted her. Hal ignored her. All his attention was focused on Tam, his eyes staring into the faded old eyes only centimeters from his own.

"Can you do it, Tam?" Hal asked again. "I've got Jeamus and his people on the way here with the equipment to make it possible. You can go into the Creative Universe and I'll go with you. Now, in the beginning, it has to be done by someone besides me, it has to be used by more than one mind; otherwise it's just something I've created for myself. But if I can share it with you, we can go on to share it with everyone else, on all the worlds. Do you understand, Tam?"

The ancient eyes stared into his. The head moved minimally forward and back again in what could have been a nod.

"But he can't—he can't do anything!" From the sound of her voice, Ajela was crying now as she talked. "He hasn't any strength left! You can't ask anything more of him now. It's too late. He ought to be left to die in peace."

"That's what I'm offering him," Hal answered her without taking his eyes off Tam. "That's what it is, Tam. A chance for you to see the end at last; a chance to see it completed."

"I tell you he can't do anything—he couldn't if he wanted to!" Ajela protested behind Hal.

"I think he can," said Hal. "This one last thing. This final effort, Tam. Can't you?"

There was a change in Tam's face, so small as to be unreadable by anyone who did not know him like the four now with him. Again, his head moved—in a motion more clearly of agreement now.

"Good. You remember," Hal said, "how the knowledge here in the Final Encyclopedia had to be a requirement. Nothing less would do. Whoever intended to be a creator in the Creative Universe would need a memory bank at least that large."

He paused.

"Can you hear me, Tam?" he asked. "Do you understand?"

Tam gave another minuscule nod. His eyes seemed to see nothing but Hal's face.

"I thought there had to be the way in. I thought I'd find it here," Hal went on. "But for three years, these last three years, I couldn't find it here.

"Then Amanda came to suggest I take a fresh look at the problem from outside the Final Encyclopedia; and she was right. I went to a place called the Chantry Guild, on Kultis—a new Chantry Guild, Tam—and I found I'd been trying to reach the Creative Universe without giving up the rules and laws of the real universe we already know. And those rules, by definition, were the last to apply in the Creative Universe, where the first principle of creativity had to apply—that anything and everything conceivable could be made."

He paused: and this time Tam nodded without being asked.

"There were no rules," said Hal, "but there were necessities. First, it was necessary for those who entered the Creative Universe to believe in it. Next, whoever tried to enter it had to believe humans could do so. Last, it could only be entered by a mind willing to put aside the laws and rules of the real universe."

Hal paused, but only to take breath.

"That was the hardest of all, that last," he said. "From the first moment of life, instinct tells us the only laws are the laws of the place where we're born. I don't think I'd have been able to keep going if I hadn't already had my own private proof of a place somewhere with different laws. I had it with my poetry. I had it when I went back, in mind only, to the twenty-first century to alter a future not yet made; the future of the time I'd known as Donal."

He held Tam's eyes with his own and his voice held them both. "I was ready to give up when Amanda came. And you know she feels what's right. She was right this time. At the new Chantry Guild, I found it—the belief of another man who'd been as close to the Creative Universe as I'd been. He'd come up with one insight. Only one, but it was enough to point me to where I could finally understand how, just as the physical laws of our universe can be, they can also not-be . . . and that they're subject to us, not us to them!"

He paused once more. Where were Jeamus and the doorways?

"Tam, his name was Jathed: and his particular battlecry was: *'the transient and the Eternal are the same.'* At first it meant nothing to me, logically—only a contradiction in terms. And then I saw the truth of it. I broke through, finally, to that truth—and the whole Creative Universe opened out before me like a flower to the morning sun. For if the Transient and the Eternal could be the same, then all things could. All things were possible. It was only our point of view that had learned to encompass the possibility it wanted, using the knowledge the race already had, to make it real; and that knowledge was there, waiting for us, in the Final Encyclopedia!

"Jeamus and his people are going to be here in just minutes, with the equipment we need to make the trip," Hal said. He dared not take his eyes from Tam's eyes, and the strength he could see in them that the old man was trying to gather, the ancient fighting spirit of a lifetime trying to rouse for one more effort. But he could feel time slipping away from them, like the running water of the stream beside Tam's armchair.

"Amanda, Rukh—" he called, his gaze still locked with Tam's. "Isn't there some way you can call that corridor where we were? Find out how they're coming. Tell them we have to have it—now!"

He concentrated on Tam once more.

"We had the means of going there, all the time," he went on to the still face, behind which the great struggle was going on to rouse a dying spirit. "It was in phase-technology. The same thing that gave us the phase-shift and the phase-shield. But maybe even that's not necessary. Maybe it's just an excuse for the mind to go into the Creative Universe. I don't know. But we don't have time to experiment now; and I used it when I went this first time. So—"

He was talking without a pause, desperately, as if his words were the lifeline up which Tam was pulling himself to safety. There was a fear within him that if he stopped speaking, even for a moment, Tam would lose his hold, would fall back, and be lost.

"You see," he said, "you go through a phase-doorway to no set destination; which should end you spread out to infinity—"

But at last now, behind him, there was a sound of the door from the corridor banging open with unusual noise and violence; and a moment later Jeamus struggled, sweating, into his field of vision, helping one other man move the framework of one of the phase-doorways. The framework had obviously been made weightless, but they still had to contend with its mass and the awkwardness of its size and rectangular shape.

"There's a chance"— Jeamus panted, as the two of them stopped behind Tam's chair—"there may be a chance you can go—and come through the same doorway—so to save time we came—with just that. You want to try it? If so, where—where do we put it?"

"Yes!" snapped Hal. "Put it right here, in front of Tam's chair!"

He turned back to Tam, seeing them obey out of the corner of his eye.

"Now we go," he said gently to Tam. "We go together. I know you can't get up and walk through the doorway—that's what I did. But when I went back to the time of the first Chantry Guild, I only sent my mind back. Trust me. You can send your mind through that doorway the way I went then."

He looked and saw that Jeamus and the man helping him had just set up the doorway, less than a meter from Tam's feet; and other men he recognized as being from Jeamus's crew were connecting it to some kind of heavy cable that snaked out of sight to disappear among the illusion of trees to their right.

"All right," he said to Tam, and closed his hand around the wide but bony, cold hand of Tam, "come with me, now. Look through that doorway as if it was an opening on wherever you want to go to. In your mind, stand up and step through the frame to that place; and I'll go with you, by your side, holding to you as I am now."

He broke off, and stared then; for the doorway before him had suddenly become become not merely a plate of silver blankness, as it had been in the blind corridor for him. Instead it now seemed to open on a green hillside, lifting beyond the doorway for only a few meters, before it reached a crest, beyond which was only the cloudless, light blue of a spring sky. It was the sky of one of the Younger Worlds Hal had never been on; but he had seen images of it. It was a spring sky over the northern hemisphere of the small, lush world of Sainte Marie, the world on which both Jamethon and Kensie had died.

Hal rose to his feet, letting the dead weight of Tam's hand slip from his own. But—unless it was his imagination—it seemed he still felt it there; though Tam had not stirred and no one stood visibly beside Hal.

Still, he felt that Tam was beside him, that their hands were linked.

"Here we go," he said, without looking to his left, where the spirit of Tam should now be; and he stepped forward, through the phase-doorway.

At once he stood on the sloping surface of the hillside under the warmth of the different sunlight. He felt the hand withdrawn from his grasp and, turning, now saw Tam standing with him.

But it was a younger Tam; a Tam in no more than his thirties, wearing green field clothing, except for the newsman's cloak. Tam took a step forward by himself and stood, looking at the hilltop.

His face showed an expression that was a strange mixture of grimness and a hope so painfully deep it barely escaped being a fear. He had let go of Hal. Now he moved away from him. Hal stood where he was and watched.

After a moment, some little distance to their right, a head appeared above the brow of the hill, and lifted as the man bearing it approached. It was Kensie, as Hal had last seen him, riding in the place Hal had created in his different universe. Only here Kensie was wearing a Field Commander's uniform in the dark blue of the Exotic Mercenary Forces. But aside from that he was no different than ever, and the warmth of his smile directed at Tam, went like a wave before him down the slope.

Tam breathed out, a soft, deep breath; and at that same moment another man mounted over the crest of the hill to the left, wearing the black uniform of a Friendly Commandant out of the last century. He was thin and tall, but nowhere near the height of Kensie, and he also smiled. It was a grave, small smile in his narrow face, but it was there, and it, too, was directed at Tam.

Tam stared at Jamethon as he, too, came onward down the slope. But at that moment two more figures came over the hilltop, this time from directly ahead. One was a young woman, looking hardly out of her teens, with black hair and the same sharp features as Tam himself, holding hands with a man who looked no older than she did, but wore the historic battle gray of the Cassidan Field forces. His uniform was without insignia or mark of rank. These two, also, broke into smiles, coming down toward Tam, so that he suddenly ran forward toward them, the woman who had been his sister and the man who had been her husband, David Hall.

So they all came together, all five of them, halfway up the slope from Hal, in the sun; and clustered together there like a family reunited. Tam was all but hidden by the others surrounding him; but Hal, remembering Mor reaching out his hand across the crupper of his mother's horse as they had ridden together in another place of this Creative Universe, could feel what was in the man who had been Director of the Encyclopedia so long.

He turned back and stepped through where his instinct told him the phase-doorway must be, and was suddenly again in the room with the old man, beside the running stream and with the three women, all surrounded by the illusion of the trees.

Below on the Earth's surface, a cloud must have slipped before the face of the sun, for shadow fell about them as Hal stepped forth. Amanda in her long formal dress of that wintry blue that was the color of the Dorsai northern seas; Rukh, all in black, one hand at her throat holding the circle of granite on its chain, with the simple cross in its gray-white rock; and Ajela in the green, formal Japanese kimono of fleshy silk, embroidered with a design of pine branches with snow on them—these three in their colors seemed to glow somberly in the little dimming of the light like three queens at a state burial.

Hal turned just in time to see those he had left on the hillside, Tam among them, moving close together over the crest of ground and disappearing beyond. The hill vanished then; and the face of the phase-door was once more silver and blank.

Hal turned to Ajela and the others.

"Did you see?" he said. "Did you see how they met him, smiling, and took him away with them?"

"No," whispered Ajela. Slowly the other two shook their heads.

"I did . . ." The faint words were barely breathed by Tam, but they all heard. Slowly, Tam's eyelids dropped. But a new, faint smile on his lips remained. Ajela ran to him and hugged him; but it was not the desperate embrace Hal had seen her give the dying man in recent times before. It was an enfolding of warmth and joy.

Tam's eyes closed finally, and, as they watched, the tiny lift and fall of his chest stopped its movement altogether. The faint smile still remained on Tam's lips, but he had at last stopped breathing.

"*Lord*," said Rukh, "*now lettest thou thy servant depart in peace*."

And in that same moment the cloak, like a creature released changed back from the white and red it had held for so long, and shone on its basic setting, with all the colors of the rainbow on Old Earth.

Hal stared at it. Amanda had been right.

It was the bridge.